New York Times [a]
Katee Robert lea[...]
grandpa's knee. F[...]
was a RITA® Aw[...]
named it 'a comp[...]
the right amount of suspense and tension'. When not
writing sexy contemporary and romantic suspense,
she spends her time playing imaginative games with
her children, driving her husband batty with what-
if questions and planning for the inevitable zombie
apocalypse.

Dylan Rose is a writer from New York City, who is
obsessed with watching romantic comedies, taking
hot baths on cold nights and finding the perfect red
lipstick. *Take Me On* is her debut novel for Mills &
Boon Dare. Follow her adventures on Instagram
@DylanRoseRomance.

If you liked *Make Me Yours* and *Take Me On*
why not try

Forbidden to Taste by JC Harroway
On Her Terms by Cathryn Fox

Discover more at millsandboon.co.uk

MAKE ME YOURS

KATEE ROBERT

TAKE ME ON

DYLAN ROSE

MILLS & BOON

First Published in Great Britain 2019
by Mills & Boon, an imprint of HarperCollins*Publishers*
1 London Bridge Street, London, SE1 9GF

Make Me Yours © 2019 Katee Hird

Take Me On © 2019 Dylan Rose

ISBN: 978-0-263-27380-9

MIX
Paper from
responsible sources
FSC™ C007454

This book is produced from independently certified FSC™ paper
to ensure responsible forest management.
For more information visit www.harpercollins.co.uk/green.

Printed and bound in Spain
by CPI, Barcelona

MAKE ME YOURS

KATEE ROBERT

MILLS & BOON

To Lauren

CHAPTER ONE

"HAVE I MENTIONED how much I loathe weddings?" Becka Baudin grabbed two champagne glasses and handed one to her best friend, Allie.

"Only about half a dozen times—in the last hour."

She drained the glass and waited for her stomach to settle. Only then did she focus on her best friend's amusement. "It's not my fault. They give me hives. Even this one." *Especially this one.*

"Here." Allie passed over the second champagne glass, her expression sympathetic. "You know you're not losing her, right?"

"Of course I know that. I'm not a child." But she still glanced at her big sister gliding across the dance floor with her new husband. They looked like something out of a fairy tale, Lucy in a gorgeous white dress that hugged her lean form. It was overlaid with lace and gave a little sparkle with every move. Her dark hair was twisted in an intricate style that left her neck and shoulders bare except for the truly outstanding necklace Gideon had bought her.

And Gideon.

Lord, the man could wear a tux.

But it wasn't the clothes that made them the most beautiful couple in the room. It was the way they looked at each other.

She sipped her second glass of champagne. "They seem happy."

"Yes, well, that generally happens on someone's wedding day."

Becka rolled her eyes. "Yeah, yeah, I know. I'm being an asshole. It's not *this* wedding I object to— it's the rest of them." Weddings were nothing but false promises of happily-ever-after. They sold a dream most people never actually realized—more than half ended in divorce.

She gave herself a shake and eyed her glass. "I think it might be time to start with the vodka." She'd already done her duties as maid of honor, from the pictures to the people herding to the speech. Now it was just a matter of keeping her head down until it was time to see Lucy and Gideon off to the limo. *Yes, a drink is exactly what I deserve for keeping my happy mask in place.* If she didn't do something to break the tension soon, she was liable to snap at someone and make an ass of herself, and end up on some Maids of Honor Behaving Badly list. She couldn't do that to Lucy. Today was like playing through one of her personal nightmares, but Becka could do better than to act out like a spoiled child as a result. She *was* better than that. She had to be.

Becka turned to the bar and froze.

Blue eyes captured hers, rooting her feet in place even as her body tried to sway forward. Toward *him*. Square jaw, straight strong nose, sensual lips that quirked up as he gave her his own perusal. She straightened, suddenly glad that her sister hadn't followed the shitty tradition of clothing her bridesmaids in the ugliest dresses imaginable. Her purple dress set off the rich blue color she'd settled on for her hair, and it hugged what few curves she had. The stranger wore a tux even better than the groom, his broad shoulders tapering to a lean waist.

She'd never seen a more striking man in her life.

"That's Aaron Livingston." Allie's shoulder brushed hers, effectively grounding her. "He's friends with Roman and sometimes business associates with Gideon, I think. I didn't realize he'd be here."

Aaron. I like it. "I should go say hi, be hospitable...or something."

Allie snorted. "Yeah, sure. That's exactly what you're going to do." She grinned. "Have fun. I'm going to go dance with my man."

"Yeah, yeah, rub it in that you're deliriously domestically happy." The words held no sting. She *was* happy her best friend had found the love of her life in Roman Bassani. Between Allie and Lucy, it was almost enough to convert Becka to a romantic way of thinking.

Almost.

Too bad I'm well acquainted with the downsides of romance. Hard to put on rose-tinted glasses when I've been up close and personal with everything that can go wrong.

God, she was a mess. She needed to do something—fast.

There was nothing quite as distracting as a man. The one currently staring at her as if memorizing every inch of her would fit the bill nicely.

It's just a Band-Aid.

She shoved the knowledge aside and made her way to the bar, never taking her gaze off Aaron. He watched her but didn't move from his spot. Letting her approach. Letting her set the tone. Smart man.

Becka sidled up to the spot next to him and broke eye contact to order a vodka seven. This close, she could smell his cologne—something expensive that made her think of hot and dirty sex in the best way possible. *Down, girl.* If this wedding was for anyone else, she wouldn't hesitate to haul him to a convenient closet or bathroom stall to silence the ugliness inside her, but she wouldn't do that to Lucy. Her sister deserved the best on her wedding day, and damn it, Becka would make sure she had it.

At least until Lucy got into the limo.

Then all bets were off.

"Maid of honor."

God, even his voice was wonderful, low and even with just a hint of growl. She twisted to face him. "Wedding guest." He just raised his eyebrows, and she smirked. "Sorry, I thought we were throwing out labels." She held out her hand. "Becka Baudin."

"Becka being short for Rebecka?"

"Something like that." No one called her Rebecka—not even Lucy. She certainly wasn't going to hand out that name to this guy, no matter how magnetic he was or how he seemed to be so close to what she needed in that moment, it was a wonder she hadn't conjured him into existence.

But then, Becka didn't believe in magic any more than she believed in romance.

"I'm Aaron." He took her hand and pressed a kiss to her knuckles. His five o'clock shadow scraped against her skin, completely at odds with the softness of his lips. It would feel good to have him sliding his mouth along other parts of her. Better than good. Decadent and sinful and absolutely perfect.

Not yet.

She licked her lips. "I know."

"I see you've done your homework."

"More like your reputation precedes you."

"Can't complain about that if it brings a woman like you my way." He let their hands drop but didn't release her. Aaron slid his thumb over the same path

his lips had just taken, as if he had every right to seduce her with a single touch. His lips quirked into
a smile and, damn it, it made him even more handsome. "Nice wedding."

*Come on, Becka, you can do better than this. Stop
staring at him like a lust-struck idiot.* She cleared
her throat and reclaimed her hand just in time for
the bartender to deliver her drink. She turned to face
the bar fully, needing some distance, even if it was
only in her head. No matter what her plans for this
man were, she couldn't afford to lose focus until
later. *Maybe this is a mistake. Maybe you should
find someone less magnetic, less overwhelming, to
lose yourself in.* Even as she thought it, she knew
she wasn't going to. A few short minutes of conversation and Aaron Livingston had dropped a lure she
couldn't have resisted if she tried. Better to just let
things unfurl on the path they were both obviously
heading down.

*It's only one night. Tomorrow I'll go back to my
life and it will be nothing but a fond memory.*

What had he asked her? Right. The wedding. Of
course it was the wedding. That was all anyone had
been talking about for months, and they were at the
damn event right now.

She downed half her drink. "It's a wedding.
They're all flavors of the same thing." Damn it, that
sounded bitter. She took a careful breath and pasted
a happy smile on her face. "It's what Lucy wanted,

and she's happy, so I'm happy." That, at least, was the truth.

"I take it you don't subscribe to the American dream that ends with a white picket fence?"

Becka shot him a look, trying to gauge where he was going with that comment. Even if he shared her views on marriage and weddings, this was hardly the event to start bitching about how cynical they were. "We live in New York. We don't do white picket fences here as a general rule."

"True enough." Aaron's blue eyes took her in, and she couldn't shake the feeling that he saw too much. That if he looked deep enough, he'd be able to trace her aversion to the fictional happily-ever-after right back to her parents' destroyed marriage and...

Enough.

Keeping ahold of her drink, she gave him her full attention. No reason to avoid pulling the trigger on this. If by some miracle she'd misread the situation, she still had plenty of time to bounce back from any rejection he dealt and move on to someone else. "You want to get out of here?" She waved a hand at her sister still on the dance floor. "I mean, after this dog and pony show has reached its natural conclusion."

His grin widened, just a little. "I wouldn't say no to another drink somewhere quieter, where we could have a conversation."

A conversation? *Hard pass.* The conversation, the

drinks, the quiet place… It was all just frills to fancy up the fact that they wanted to bang each other's brains out. Whatever his reasons, he seemed just as onboard with this plan as she was. Except he wanted to talk. If he was anyone else, if the attraction was any more manageable… But he wasn't, and it wasn't. She knew her strengths, and while she didn't believe in love at first sight, what she had with Aaron was definitely *lust* at first sight. Better for both of them to keep things simple and define clear boundaries from the start.

Becka reached up and traced the top button of his dark gray shirt. "Is a conversation really what you're after?"

He opened his mouth and seemed to reconsider. "I'm after you."

The honesty washed over her, a fresh breeze that made the choking environment of this fucking wedding a little more bearable. *I am happy for Lucy. I am. I just can't look at her without seeing our mother, and we both know how* that *turned out. It's not the same and it won't have the same outcome, but that doesn't change anything. Not really.*

Becka managed a smile. "In that case, let's skip the drinks and you can take me back to your place for a nightcap."

If anything, his brows rose higher. "A nightcap."

"Yep." It would be good with Aaron. Exactly what she needed. The lightning nipping at her fingertips from just this small touch told her as much. They could offer each other an enjoyable night, and then she'd get back to her life with only a fond memory to balance out her mixed feelings about her friend and sister leaving her behind.

They weren't *really* leaving her. Rationally, Becka knew that. Most days, she even believed that nothing would really change even though both Lucy and Allie had gone and fallen in love.

Stop that.

Becka finished her drink and set it on the bar. "Another, please."

Aaron covered the glass with his hand. "If you want that nightcap, then you're done for the night." When she opened her mouth to protest, he shifted closer, placing his free hand over hers, his broad shoulders blocking out the rest of the room. "Trust me—you'll want to be sober for this."

His audacity made her laugh. "Yeah, no, you don't get to decide when I'm done." She was buzzed, but she wasn't anywhere near drunk. Another drink or two wouldn't make a difference.

"All the same." He removed his hand, but he didn't move away. "You're more than welcome to drink yourself stupid, but you won't be coming home with me if you do."

Sheer stubbornness almost made her tell him to fuck right off. Becka responded to commands about as well as she did to ultimatums, and Aaron had issued both in the last thirty seconds. The whole point of a night of wild abandon was the *abandon* part, and that only worked if they were equal. Letting him set the pace and lay down the boundaries was *not* part of the plan.

But then the DJ's voice laughed from the speakers. "It's about that time, ladies and gentlemen. All the single ladies on the floor to catch the bouquet!"

Desperation clawed at Becka's throat. She had to go out there and smile and be supportive, and all she wanted to do was crawl under the bar with a bottle of vodka. She glared at Aaron. "Fine. No more drinks." She turned on her heel and stalked toward the group of women gathering in the middle of the dance floor.

He'd better be as good as he thinks he is.

Aaron spent the rest of the reception watching Becka. Taking her home was likely a mistake. He might be on decent terms with her sister, but her newly acquired brother-in-law was a different story altogether. Pissing off Gideon Novak wasn't on his list of things to accomplish, especially with Aaron's business on the verge of expanding. He'd need the headhunter in the future, which was part of the reason he'd accepted the invitation to this wedding.

Becka's laugh drew his attention, the sound just as bold as the rest of her. From her blue hair to the piercing glinting against her red lipstick to her tight little body... Yeah, *bold* summed up Becka Baudin pretty damn well. She couldn't be more different from her straitlaced older sister, and even though he knew better, those differences intrigued him. She was the kind of woman who saw what she wanted and went after it, no holds barred.

Tonight, it appeared that what she wanted was *him*.

He set his empty tumbler on the bar as Becka grabbed a microphone and instructed the guests to head out front to see Lucy and Gideon off. She was the kind of woman born to stand in the spotlight. She held everyone's attention easily as she laughed and made a joke, but still managed to be firm and get everyone moving toward the door. Most of them would be coming back into the reception to keep drinking while the bride and groom went off to do what new couples did on their wedding night.

Aaron had other plans.

Becka's gaze found him across the small sea of people between them, and the barely banked heat in those blue eyes seared him to the bone. He started for the door with the rest of the guests. Despite all the jostling, he never lost sight of her in the crowd. How could he, when everything about her seemed designed to draw attention? Aaron let himself be borne along, but he managed to ensure he ended up close to her once they reached the sidewalk. As more people piled out in front of the venue, he had to step closer until he nearly bumped into her.

She glanced over her shoulder and grinned. "Hey there, handsome. You come here often?"

Before he could answer, Lucy and Gideon walked out the door, hand in hand. A cheer went up from the people around him, and the crowd surged as guests started blowing bubbles at them. The movement sent Becka teetering in her sky-high heels, and Aaron instinctively grabbed her arm and steadied her. It pressed their bodies together, her back to his front. This close, there was no way to avoid noticing the curve of her ass, or the way it lined up so fucking perfectly with his cock.

He gritted his teeth and tried to get his body's reaction under control, but Becka chose that moment to lean back against him and roll her hips, ever so slightly. In case he missed it—not likely—she shifted his hand from her arm to her stomach, tucking them tighter together. Another roll of her hips had him cursing softly. He resisted the temptation to let his hand drop lower to brush the V between her thighs. They were in the middle of a goddamn crowd, and her sister was only a few feet away.

But he wanted to.

Fuck, he wanted to.

Aaron wanted to hook his fingers beneath the hem of her dress and stroke her pussy right here. To bring her to the edge and leave her there, teasing her to see how long she could hold out from making a noise that would give them away.

Holy shit, get ahold of yourself. This isn't you. You don't lose control like this—especially with a woman who's barely more than a stranger.

A few precarious minutes later, the newlyweds were safely tucked into the limo. Before he could decide how he wanted to play this, Becka turned in his arms and laced her hands around his neck. The move pressed her more firmly against his cock, and hell if her lips didn't part and her blue eyes go hazy with need. For *him*. She leaned up until her lips brushed his ear. "You are the sexiest goddamn distraction I've ever seen."

He traced the curve of her ass and lost his battle with control. Aaron dipped his fingertips beneath the hem of her dress. "I'm not the only one." Weddings made people crazy, and he'd always thought he was immune to that particular insanity, but then, he'd never met a woman like this before. The attraction was too strong to resist, and it came on too quickly to do anything but let go and see where it took them.

Becka nipped his earlobe. "Let's get out of here."

"One thing before we go." He walked them back until his shoulders hit the brick wall, away from the people already disappearing through the door into the hotel. It took several long minutes before the sidewalk cleared of the wedding guests. All the while, he studied Becka's face, the dark fringe of her lashes, the curve of her lower lip, the way her breath caught when she met his gaze.

Aaron cupped her jaw and tilted her face up to claim her mouth. She tasted minty, a burst of freshness as intoxicating as the woman herself. Becka went soft in his arms, melting as she opened for him, her tongue eagerly meeting his, stroke for stroke. As if she'd been as impatient for this moment as he'd been.

She'd called him a distraction.

She was the distraction—one he wasn't sure he could afford.

He pressed his forehead to hers, trying to regain control. "Let's go."

"How far is your place?"

A forty-minute cab ride.

Too far.

Inside the building, a burst of laughter trailed down to them. *Perfect.* "About twenty yards."

She laughed. "That works. I don't want to wait anymore." She grabbed his hand and towed him back inside the building. They bypassed the entrance to the ballroom where the reception was being held and headed for the main desk.

Ten minutes later, they stumbled through the door to a room and slammed it behind them. Aaron guided Becka to the bed and laid her on top of it. He kissed her neck, her shoulder, the line of her heart-shaped bodice. She was fire in his arms, arching to meet his mouth, her hands busy on the front of his shirt. She shoved it down his shoulders, and he released her long enough to shrug it off. Aaron tugged her dress up over her head.

Need shot through him, rushing his movements even as part of him wanted to slow down.

To savor every moment.

He stopped short, drinking in the sight of her. She wore nothing but a silk thong in show-stopping pink. Against her pale skin, the neon color practically glowed, just as brilliant as her hair. Aaron traced the rose tattoo nestled on the inside of her left hip, noting the thorns circling the full petals of the flower, and then he smoothed his hand up her taut stomach to her high breasts. She was lean, every muscle defined in a way that spoke of serious time spent in the gym. "Strong little thing, aren't you?"

"Well, I'm a spin and TRX instructor, so that goes with the territory."

He bracketed her ribs with his hands and then cupped her breasts. "Maybe I'll take one of your classes sometime."

Becka laughed even as she twined her hands over her head, offering her body to him. "Honey, you wouldn't last ten minutes."

"Think so?" He lightly pinched her pale pink nipples, gauging her reaction. Her sharp inhale only fanned the flames within him. He needed her. Now.

"I *know* so." She grinned. "But let's be honest—

there's only one kind of exercise we're interested in right now, and it doesn't have a single thing to do with a bike. Now, stop teasing me and take off your pants."

CHAPTER TWO

BECKA COULD BARELY breathe at the look on Aaron's face as he ran his hands over her body. Learning. Reveling. *Worshipping*. It left her feeling off center, as if this was more than some horny wedding sex between two single people who'd never see each other again. She covered her uncertainty the only way she knew how—brazenly charging forward. "You're still wearing pants."

"Don't rush me." He lifted her farther onto the bed and lay next to her, his head propped on his hand. She started to protest, but Aaron cupped her pussy and she forgot whatever she'd been about to say. He stroked her over the silk of her panties, his blue eyes arrested on the spot he touched her. The slick fabric lent an erotic edge to the slide of his fingers. "Spread your legs."

She obeyed instantly. Becka normally preferred to take charge of her sexual encounters. She knew what she liked and had no reservations with demanding exactly that. Most guys found it sexy as hell and—more importantly—it ensured they both had one hell of a good time.

Aaron wasn't going to let her lead this encounter. She'd known it from the second he commanded her not to drink any more that night. And the kiss… God, that kiss had been claiming in a way she wasn't prepared to deal with.

Doesn't matter. I'm a grown-ass woman. I knew what I signed up for. I can handle it.

That didn't stop a shiver from working its way through her body as he traced her opening through her panties and moved up to circle her clit. This wasn't the rushed fucking she'd prepared herself for. He touched her as if she meant something beyond a mutually satisfying night. "Stop that."

Aaron met her gaze, his hand stilling. "Problem?" There was no anger in those blue eyes, just a kind of knowledge that said he already knew what her protesting was about and didn't give a damn.

"Don't make this into something it isn't." He didn't respond other than to slide his hand back down to cup her again. *Possessively.* She swallowed hard, fighting not to rub against him like a wanton thing. *Focus.* "I'm just here for the sex." *For the desperately needed distraction.*

He raised his eyebrows. "You're just here for the sex."

"That is literally what I just said."

"I heard you." His thumb dipped beneath the edge of her thong. "Becka, if you think this night is going to end before I've stroked, tasted and fucked you until we're both damn near comatose…" He shook his head in mock sympathy even as he kept up that teasing stroking beneath her panties, not quite where she so desperately needed him.

"I signed up for *that*." She gritted her teeth in an effort to keep still. "I didn't sign up for *this*."

"Do you want me to stop?" The arrogant tilt of his lips said he already knew the answer. She hated that he was so sure of her, hated even more that he was right.

Becka smacked his hand away from her and shoved his shoulders, well aware that he allowed her to tumble him onto his back. She was strong for her size, but he had a good six inches and fifty pounds on her. She grabbed his wrists and pinned them over his head, and he let her do it. "I don't want you to stop." She shifted, dragging her breasts against his bare chest. *God, he's breathtaking. All I want to do is rub myself all over him like some horny teenager.* She pressed down against his cock and had to bite back a whimper.

"Come here, Becka." The way he said her name was almost a purr, a soft coaxing that was no less a command than all his others tonight. "Give me your mouth."

She kissed him, telling herself she did it because

she wanted to and not because part of her quivered with need at the rough growl in his voice. He tasted like the scotch he'd been drinking at the reception, and it went straight to her head. She forgot she was supposed to be in the dominant position, to be driving this encounter, to be the one calling the shots. Instead, she released his wrists and cupped his jaw on either side, losing herself in the feel of his tongue sliding decadently against hers, his lips hard and unyielding and yet giving her everything she needed.

It was too much.

He kissed her like this meant something.

She didn't want him to be right.

She leaned back, desperate to put some distance between them, to remember the purpose for that night.

Her plans disappeared through her fingers like smoke when his lips curled into a wicked smile. "Let me taste you, Becka."

It took everything Aaron had to leash himself, to hold still as Becka considered him. The first impression he'd gotten of the wild thing on the verge of fleeing was only reinforced by the skittish look in her eyes. *She'll run at the first hint of a cage.* He filed away that information, but the truth was that he didn't want to cage her.

That isn't what tonight is about.

She worried her bottom lip even as she shifted

deliciously against him. "I can't think straight when you say my name like that."

Good. He didn't say it through sheer force of will. "This thing with us has nothing to do with thinking straight." He'd accepted the offer of a nightcap because she was beautiful and interesting, and it had been a long time since he'd let himself indulge in anything resembling a one-night stand. But this bold and slightly brittle woman intrigued him despite himself.

She sat up a little, pressing herself down against his cock. "That's a good point. A brilliant point, even. I'm overthinking things." She wrinkled her nose. "I don't usually bring this much baggage to banging. Sorry. The wedding has me all twisted up for various reasons."

"Becka—"

She charged right over him. "But that's neither here nor there." She gave a brilliant smile. "You wanted a taste."

He kept himself perfectly still as she sat up fully and stretched her arms over her head, showing off her body. And, fuck, what a body. Aaron wanted to pin her down, to lick and kiss every inch of her until she felt the same desperation coursing through his veins. *I do that, she leaves.*

Unacceptable.

Becka moved up until she straddled his face. He could *see* how wet she was against the silk of her panties, and he ran hands up her thighs, urging her to spread a little farther for him. "Perfect."

"Hey now, remember who's in the driver's seat."

He shifted his hands higher so he could hook a thumb into her panties and tug them to the side, exposing her. "Let me know if I miss the mark." He lifted his head, still holding her gaze, and flicked his tongue out to taste her.

She braced her hands on the wall over the headboard and bit her bottom lip. "More of that, please and thank you. Suck my clit, Aaron."

Fuck me.

His control snapped. He obeyed her hoarse command, sucking her clit into his mouth and rolling the sensitive bud against his tongue. Becka let loose a whimper that sent a bolt of lightning to his cock.

Getting her to make that noise again shot to the top of his list of things to do.

He lost himself in her taste, in the way her thighs went tense beneath his hands when he licked her just right. It didn't take long to find the blend of rhythm and pressure that had her rocking against his mouth, her whimpers turning into gasping cries. Higher and higher he took her, driving her ruthlessly into her first orgasm. She let loose a breathless giggle when she came, as if overtaken by sheer delight the same way she'd been overtaken by pleasure.

He fell a little bit in love with her right then and there.

"Safe to say you didn't miss the mark." Becka laughed again and slumped to the side, letting one leg sprawl across his chest as she blinked at him from beneath a curtain of blue hair. "I was right—it *is* good with you."

"Happy to live up to expectations." For the first time in so long, he wasn't thinking about his next business move or the future, beyond the moment when he got inside this woman. *Tonight. Even if it's only tonight, it's worth it for the reprieve she's offered.* Aaron rolled onto his side and smoothed back her hair. "I like the blue."

"I live to please."

He lightly pinched her nipple. "So snarky."

"Hmm, you know it." She stretched from her fingers to her toes, her body perfectly on display for one breathtaking moment before she relaxed and grinned at him. "That was a great appetizer, but I'm more than ready to move on to the main course."

He dug his wallet from his pocket and fished out the condom he'd stashed there earlier that week. Aaron always carried one with him—the better to be prepared for any given situation that arose, so to speak—but he switched it out regularly to avoid any mishaps. He took her hand and pressed it to her palm. "Do the honors."

"The honors." Becka smirked. She ripped the foil packet open. "Someone's got a high opinion of themselves." She took her time rolling the condom on, teasing him, prolonging the moment when this reached the point of no return. As if she wanted this to last as much as he did.

"That's enough." He cupped the back of her neck and towed her up so he could take her mouth. Aaron rolled them without breaking the kiss, loving the way she moved with him as if they'd done this a thousand times. She stroked her hands down his sides and gave his ass a playful squeeze as he settled between her thighs. He chuckled against her mouth. "Cheeky."

"Just call me a saucy little minx." She nipped his chin and pressed an openmouthed kiss against his neck. "I don't want to wait anymore, Aaron. I need you."

"Next time we go slow." He reached between them to position his cock at her entrance. "Ready?"

"Baby, I was born ready." She hooked a leg around his waist and arched up to meet him.

He'd expected the move, so he countered it, letting himself sink into her a single inch and no more. "Slow, minx. I don't want to hurt you."

Her laugh seemed to vibrate her whole body, and her blue eyes shone with true amusement. "That giant cock of yours is impressive, but I can take it." Becka grinned. "Do your worst."

Impossible to resist the playful challenge in every line of her body. He didn't really want to hold back any more than she seemed to want him to. Aaron slammed into her, sheathing himself to the hilt. She jolted, that delicious whimper slipping free again. He ate the sound, kissing even as he began moving. His leash had snapped without his realizing how close he was to losing control. This woman, this wildfire in his arms, she brought out something he'd fought long and hard to tame within himself.

Something savage.

He tried to pull back, tried to regain control.

As if sensing his withdrawal, Becka wrapped both legs around his waist and grabbed his hands, lacing their fingers together. She stretched her arms over her head, guiding him to pin her down. "I'm not breakable, Aaron. You don't have to be careful with me." She squeezed his hands. "I want everything."

He could no more resist her command than he'd been able to turn away from her at the bar. Aaron put his weight onto her hands and pounded into her, each thrust making her breasts bounce and drawing a cry from her lips. He watched her face the entire time, finding only a mirror to the delirious pleasure spiraling through him. Feeling more animal than man, he shifted his grip to her wrists, and her splayed fingers only drove him to fuck her harder.

"Yes, yes, *yes*!" Becka let loose another of those intoxicating giggles, her pussy clenching around him in climax hard enough to pull him over the edge with her. He thrust into her roughly, his grip on her the only thing that kept them from sliding right into the headboard, his orgasm hitting him with the force of a tidal wave.

Aaron dropped his face to the curve of her neck and pressed a careful kiss there. "Fuck, minx, nothing could have prepared me for you."

Becka shouldn't let a comment like the one Aaron just made stand, but she couldn't work up the energy to remind him yet again that this was a one-shot deal. Not with his big body pinning her to the bed, his hands still holding her down in a way that had her squirming despite coming twice in quick order. Aaron made her feel… She didn't know how to put it into words. She wasn't submissive—not really— but being at his mercy while he fucked her within an inch of her life?

Yeah, that moment was going into her hall of fame.

She stroked a cautious hand down his back and shivered as he thrust into her a little. He was still half-hard, which had her glancing at the clock and doing a quick calculation to how much time was really left in this one-night stand. *More than enough. It doesn't really end until the sun rises, right?*

Aaron kissed her neck again and then took her mouth. There was no other way to describe his mouth claiming hers, his way of controlling the kiss that made her head spin. He thrust again, and she clenched her legs tighter around him. "More. I need more. Again."

He set his teeth to her bottom lip, but just when she thought he'd give her exactly what she wanted, he cursed and retreated. "We're going to have to go back to my place for that nightcap. I have exactly one condom on me, and we just used it."

Disappointment threatened to sour her good mood, but she shoved it aside. What would it hurt to catch a cab back to his place and keep this thing going for a few more hours? He'd already more than proven he could give it to her better than ninety percent of the guys she'd hooked up with in the past. Letting a tiny technicality get in the way of more orgasms wasn't her style.

Becka reluctantly uncrossed her ankles so he could move. "I suppose you'll make it worth my while if I suffer through a cab ride."

"You know it." Her heart skipped a beat at his answering grin. His buttoned-up attitude hadn't lasted past their first kiss, but there was such mirth in that expression she couldn't stop herself from grinning in response.

Aaron pressed a quick kiss to her lips. "Let me clean up and we'll get out of here." He slid off her... and froze. "Fuck."

"What?" She scrambled back, her stomach doing a slow flip at the sight of the broken condom. *Fuck, indeed.* "Shit."

"I'm clean."

It was too much on top of everything else that

had happened that day. Becka shook her head and edged around him to get off the bed. "Thanks for the memo." She believed him, even though she had no right to take his word for anything at this point. She reached the edge of the bed and hesitated. *Think, Becka. Don't be a jackass.* "I'm clean, too. I get tested regularly." He deserved to know that, at least.

She pushed her hair back, hating that his face had immediately fallen back into the cold lines he'd worn when she first caught sight of him. *This was never going to work. Get out now before it gets even more awkward.*

"Becka—"

Becka. Not *minx*.

She shook her head. "No, it's fine. I'm on birth control. If you're clean—"

"I am."

"Then there's nothing to worry about." She grabbed her dress from the floor and tugged it on. "This has been fun, but I need to go home now."

He disappeared into the bathroom for a few seconds, and then he was back, unabashedly naked and stalking across the room to her. "We need to talk about this."

"Actually, we don't. Clean." She pointed at him. "Clean." She pointed at herself. "Birth control. End of story. This has been fun, but it's over now." Becka didn't see her panties, but she wasn't about to stick around to search for them. Instead, she grabbed her shoes and ducked under Aaron's arm.

"I'd like to see you again."

She reached the door and paused. It *had* been fun. A lot of fun, right up until that shitty ending. Becka closed her eyes, letting herself picture—just for a moment—what it would be like if she said yes. Maybe he was talking about just sex, and they'd spend a prolonged one-night stand blowing each other's minds until he got tired of her and decided to try to let her down easy, bruising her in the process. Or maybe he'd try to take her out on a date, and they'd end up fucking again, and it would end exactly the same. Even if things *did* work for a while, eventually they would explode in her face, just like every other relationship she'd been in.

Historically, men looked at her appearance and assumed one of two things.

They figured that she was some kind of manic pixie dream girl who would help them find themselves. Or, more often, they assumed that she was a kinky sex fiend who'd be down for everything and anything and not be bothered by days gone by without communication as long as the sex was on point.

Becka wasn't about to play prop to a man, and she might like sex, but she had more respect for herself than to be some guy's one A.M. booty call while he was trying to date other women. As a result, every single time she'd tried to actually *date* someone, it had gone down in flames sooner rather than later.

Like mother, like daughter.

She straightened her spine, but she couldn't look at him. If she met those gray-blue eyes, she was a goner. "It's been fun. Really fun. But let's leave this on a high note. I want to be a fond memory, something that will never get a chance to lose its shine."

His bitter laugh made her stomach drop. "Sounds like you already have the narrative set."

Better me setting the narrative than playing supporting role in someone else's. "I do." She forced her hand to turn the doorknob and open the door, because if she didn't move *right then*, she'd go back to him and let him spin whatever pretty fantasy until she actually believed it. It wasn't the truth. *She* knew that, even if he wasn't willing to admit it. "Have a nice life, Aaron."

Becka walked out the door without looking back.

CHAPTER THREE

Twelve weeks later

"THAT ABOUT SUMS it up. The new account didn't request anything fancy, but we'd be assholes if we left them exposed. Better to just go the extra mile." Aaron slid the file across the table to his business partner, Cameron O'Clery. "You want to handle this one, or should I?" Their security business focused heavily on all things tech related, and this new account was no different. Once they got the initial cybersecurity laid down, they would maintain it for as long as their retainer was paid, but it took time to figure out exactly what the client needed—and often enough, it wasn't what the client *thought* they needed.

Cameron flipped through it. "You usually don't ask me—you just dole out the clients."

Aaron tensed, but it was the truth. He tended to be the client-facing part of the company, and he picked and chose which ones he passed to Cameron because

Cameron…wasn't particularly patient with people he considered too stupid to live. Unfortunately for any prospective business-client relationships, Cameron found ninety percent of the world too stupid to live. Some clients could handle his attitude because he was the best cybersecurity expert in the city, and some couldn't. Part of Aaron's job was figuring that out. "We're partners."

"Never said we weren't." Cameron sat back and laced his fingers behind his head. He was a big fucker, his white T-shirt stretched tight against his dark skin. He narrowed brown eyes at Aaron. "You're off your game—have been for weeks. I didn't ask, but if it's going to affect the job, maybe it's time to."

"It's nothing." Just a blue-haired woman he couldn't seem to scrub from his mind. He hadn't tracked Becka down after she'd left so abruptly because she couldn't have been clearer in wanting nothing to do with him. If he was smart, he would have left what happened between them in that room behind as easily as she had.

But she haunted his dreams.

He kept waking up and reaching for her, only to find himself alone in bed. It didn't make a damn bit of sense. It had been sex—outstanding, earth-shattering sex, but sex. A single fuck shouldn't screw with his mind so effectively.

"Doesn't look like nothing to me." Cameron held

his hands up. "Not my business. Just handle your shit, Aaron. I can take this client."

He thought about the timid man who had signed the contract earlier that day and sat back. "Nah, I got it. This guy needs a softer touch."

"Shit. Take it." Cameron slid the file back to him with a disgusted look on his face. "I've got to tie up a few loose ends with the last one. She came back wanting changes despite the job being done. Nothing I can't handle, but it's a pain in the ass."

"Always is." Aaron grabbed the file and rose. "Let me know if you need an assist."

"I don't." Cameron frowned. "Though I think we might need to expand the team to include someone to handle paperwork and all that shit. It's taking too much time from the jobs themselves, and you know how I feel about paperwork."

"The same way you feel about most things." He hated it.

Cameron nodded. "I'll post a job opening. Figure they can man the phones and the main email account to field and file prospective clients. Frees you up to focus on the jobs and stop handling me."

Considering Aaron didn't know *who* they would hire who was capable of handling Cameron, he just nodded. It was a problem for another day. First, he had to arrange a secondary meeting with the new client and bring them up to date with the prospective client list sitting in his inbox. Throwing a new person into the mix without them being caught up was a recipe for disaster.

That said, it *would* be nice to delegate some of the more tedious tasks. "Sounds like a plan."

He headed out of the room. They owned the entire floor of this building, but they really only utilized their respective offices, a boardroom and a waiting room that was more neglected than anything else.

Their cybersecurity company was small, but both he and Cameron preferred it that way. With the reputation they'd spent years building, they could handpick their clients and charge top dollar for their services. But the demand seemed to be increasing lately, which meant they'd have to hire that secretary—and potentially add a cybersecurity specialist or two to their team—sooner, rather than later.

Aaron stopped in the hallway and tried to picture what the waiting room would look like with someone at the desk livening up the place. He preferred to take his meetings with clients off-site, and Cameron preferred not to take them at all. Aaron shook his head. If the secretary stayed on for more than a week, it'd be a fucking miracle.

His phone started ringing as he strode into his office. He cursed and fished it out of his pocket. An unfamiliar number scrolled across the screen. Aaron took a breath and put his professional persona on. "Aaron Livingston."

"Hey, Aaron."

Three months later, he'd still recognize Becka's voice anywhere. He walked back to his office, shut his door, and moved around his desk to sit down. "I didn't expect to hear from you." He realized how that must sound and grimaced. "But I'm glad you called."

"Yeah, well, I didn't expect to call." Her voice went thick as if she was...holding back tears? "Funny story. Remember when the condom broke? Well, apparently the pill isn't one hundred percent foolproof because, surprise, I'm pregnant."

He waited for the words to rearrange themselves into an order that made sense. They stayed stubbornly in place. "What?"

"Pregnant. With your kid." She cleared her throat. "I, ah, I wasn't going to keep it, but I chickened out at the last second, and it turns out I want this baby. I'm sorry. I swear to God I didn't know this would happen, and I don't expect anything from you. It's not your problem—it's mine. I just... I thought you should know."

A baby.

His baby.

With Becka.

He closed his eyes and tried to focus. She thought he would wash his hands of this. Aaron had questions—a whole hell of a lot of questions—but he didn't honestly believe that Becka had tricked him into getting her pregnant. She sounded upset and scared, and the fact she'd let that slip through what he surmised were impressive shields meant she was exponentially *more* freaked out. *How long have you been sitting on this knowledge, scared and alone?*

He wasn't about to let her shoulder it by herself. That child was half his, and if she was keeping it, he would be in the baby's life. End of story.

That decided, he opened his eyes, plan in place. "Where are you?"

"What? I'm at home."

"Text me the address."

She hesitated, and he could almost see her arguing with herself about having him in her house. Well, too fucking bad. Whether she liked it or not, Aaron was in her life, and he wasn't going anywhere. They had a future in common, one way or another. Finally, Becka sighed. "Okay."

"Good. I'll see you soon." He hung up and stared at his phone.

His life had just taken a hard right turn. He had no fucking idea how he was going to keep it from going off the rails entirely. *One step at a time. Talk to Becka in person. Be calm. Reassure her. Get her to see things your way.*

Shouldn't be too difficult. Right?

Becka nearly paced a hole in her floor waiting for Aaron to show up. She should have realized he was going to demand to see her face-to-face when she called, but part of her had honestly thought he'd be relieved not to be asked to do anything. Isn't that what most guys wanted in a shitty situation like this? To be absolved of all responsibility so they could go on with their lives unscathed while the woman was left to clean up the mess they'd created together?

You were projecting and you damn well know it. She caught herself wringing her hands and cursed. "I can do better than this. It's just a baby."

A baby she hadn't signed up for.

She touched her stomach gingerly. There were none of the symptoms movies had told her to expect—aside from being extra exhausted all the time—but her doctor had confirmed there was, in fact, a baby growing inside her. *A freaking baby.*

She didn't know how to be a mom. Lucy was the nurturer. The planner. The one who took care of everyone around her and was universally loved as a result. Becka had too much of their mother in her. She was too selfish, too bitchy, just too much across the board. Up until she made the call to keep the baby, she'd been sure she didn't want kids at all—better to let the sins of the past lie and not tempt fate. Lucy always told her there was no reason to think they'd end up like their parents, but Becka didn't believe her any more now than she had as a kid.

The buzzer sounded, and she jumped half out of her skin. "Shit." Aaron was here. There was no time to think of a new, better plan. There was nothing left to do but buzz him up.

Thirty seconds later, she opened the door and froze. How had she forgotten how magnetic he was? His broad shoulders took up the space of her narrow door frame, and he wore a suit that probably cost as much as a couple months of her rent. Becka belatedly realized she was blocking the entrance and stepped back, letting him into her apartment.

He looked around, and she could almost see the thoughts rolling through his head. Shabby place. Secondhand furniture. A hole in the drywall from where she'd accidentally kicked it in when she fell out of a headstand a year ago. It was clean, but she was barely there long enough to sleep between teaching classes at Allie's gym, Transcend, and her second job as a personal trainer at an upscale facility downtown. She'd never seen a reason to spiff up the place when that money could be spent in better places.

Now, she kind of wished she'd told Aaron to meet her somewhere else so he wouldn't have seen this.

He turned as she shut the door and gave her an equally thorough examination. His gaze landed on her flat stomach and then rose to her face. "You're not facing this alone."

It was tempting to throw herself at his feet and beg him to hold her until this whole thing went away. Fear ate at the edges of her mind, and there was no easy answer to combat it. Hell, there were no answers at all.

But Becka had spent all her adult life fighting to

stand on her own. She wasn't about to compromise that now for a man who was essentially a stranger. She lifted her chin. "Easy for you to say. I'm the one incubating the kid, and I'm going to be the one solely responsible for its needs."

"In this…apartment." The way he said the last word translated to *hovel*.

She glared. "There's nothing wrong with my apartment."

"You have a hole in your wall." He stalked around her kitchen. "Water damage on the floor." The living room. "The rugs are worn down to nothing." Aaron almost sounded like he was talking to himself instead of her. "If you don't have money to repair this place, you sure as fuck don't have money to give our baby everything he or she needs."

She wanted to tell him she didn't need him at all, that she'd find a way, but the hard reality was that Aaron had money and Becka didn't. She made a comfortable living for herself, but she didn't need much to get by in the grand scheme of things.

A baby changed that.

She turned away and wrapped her arms around herself. *You can compromise. Try it—just this once.* "I'm willing to negotiate some kind of…child support or something. If that's something you're comfortable with." *She* wasn't comfortable with it, but she'd suck up her pride and get over herself if it meant he could help her meet the baby's needs.

"No."

Becka turned back to find Aaron shaking his head and doing another circuit around her apartment. "What?"

"I said, no." He poked the threadbare pillow on the couch. "You can't live like this while you're pregnant. You shouldn't be living like this right now."

"Excuse me?" Anger flared through her, and she welcomed it with open arms. Easier to be angry than to be scared, easier to fight than to admit she was in over her head and didn't know what she was going to do. "There's nothing wrong with my apartment."

"The list of everything wrong with this place is longer than we have time for. Pack your bags. We're leaving."

Her jaw dropped. "You're crazy."

"No, *you're* crazy if you think I'm going to let the mother of my future child live in these conditions when I have a perfectly adequate apartment that will fit both of us and the baby without crowding." He crossed his arms over his chest and frowned. "I have a spare room, if that's what you're worried about. I don't expect you to be in my bed."

The top of her head damn near exploded. "No."

"Wrong answer."

She sputtered. "You can't just decide to move me in with you. That's not how any of this works."

Aaron stalked to the fridge and opened it. He barked out a laugh. "I suspected as much. There isn't even fucking food in your fridge." He turned and glared. "Let me lay it out for you—you have two options."

"I choose the option where you get the hell out of my life."

"That's not on the list." If anything, her anger only made him calmer, icier. He nodded at the door leading into her bedroom. "You can walk in there, pack your shit and come with me to my place. You'll settle in. It will take some adjusting, but it's doable." He shrugged. "Or I can call your sister and brother-in-law—and Roman and Allie, since they have a vested interest in your well-being—and we can all have a sit-down about your current living conditions and how you're rejecting a perfectly reasonable plan out of hand."

Checkmate.

She could actually hear the cage click into place around her. Becka didn't have a chance in hell of winning that argument with all the parties involved. Allie would be sympathetic to her plight, but Lucy would offer a secondary option of moving in with *her*. Both Gideon and Roman would go into protective older brother roles and, no matter which way they fell on the argument, Becka wouldn't come out on top. She didn't stand a chance.

She snarled. "That's blackmail."

"It's called skillful negotiation. You should try it sometime."

I will not punch my baby daddy. I will not *just chop him in his stupidly attractive throat.*

She counted to ten, but it did nothing to lower her blood pressure. There had to be a way out of this. Aaron was obviously only steamrolling her because he had an honorable streak that apparently demanded he borderline kidnap her. *Okay, maybe not that honorable.* She just needed to buy some time, to get a little distance to figure out what *she* wanted.

It was the one thing Becka couldn't pin down.

She knew she wanted the baby. The rest was terrifyingly hazy.

She gritted her teeth. "I'll consider it."

He stared at her so long, she just *knew* he was weighing his options—including throwing her over his shoulder and hauling her ass back to his place. Finally, Aaron nodded. "You have until tomorrow."

"Tomorrow?"

"At that point, I'm coming back here. Whether I come back alone or with Roman and Gideon in tow is entirely up to you." He strode to the door and paused to look over his shoulder at her. "Don't let stubbornness get in the way of what's best for the baby." He was gone before she could give in to the impulse to throw something at his head.

Becka stumbled over to her ugly green couch and sank onto it. She let her head fall to her hands and spit out every single curse she knew. It didn't make her feel better. She wasn't sure *anything* could make her feel better at this point.

"I am so freaking screwed."

CHAPTER FOUR

"OKAY, LET ME see if I have this straight—you're pregnant."

Becka didn't lift her face from the pillow. Maybe if she concentrated, her couch would swallow her whole and she wouldn't have to deal with this mess anymore. She'd called Allie in desperation, but confessing the truth had taken the last of her energy and now all she wanted was to curl up in a ball and wait for this to blow over. *Fat chance of that happening.*

Allie's footsteps echoed through the apartment. "You're pregnant," she repeated. "Okay, right. Pregnant."

"You said that already. Three times."

"Right. And it's Aaron Livingston's. And Aaron wants you to move in with him for, what, the duration of the pregnancy? Or are you supposed to live there forever?"

She groaned and pressed her face harder into the pillow. "He didn't specify."

"Because you kicked him out after yelling at him that you'd live with him over your dead body."

Becka frowned and lifted her head. Allie stood across the small living room, her hands on her hips. She looked like some kind of plus-size superhero on her day off, her blond hair windblown and her black leggings and fitted sweater comfortable and stylish. But it was the contemplative look on her face that sent alarm bells pealing through Becka's head. "You don't sound angry and self-righteous. Why don't you sound angry and self-righteous? You *should* be angry and self-righteous."

"Unpopular opinion—but Aaron Livingston isn't a total monster."

She rolled onto her back and flung her arm over her eyes. "That lack of monstrosity really commends him to be my baby daddy."

"Becka, I'm serious. He and Roman are good friends. I've hung out with him a few times." She hesitated long enough that Becka lifted her arm and shot her a look. Allie seemed to be silently arguing with herself. Finally, she said, "I think you should do it."

"What?"

"I know you, and if I offer for you to stay with me and Roman, you're going to say—"

"Hell, no." She didn't need her family and friends to swoop in and take care of her. Becka had gotten into this situation on her own—well, technically with

Aaron, but whatever—and she wasn't going to drag anyone else in alongside her. Allie and Lucy finally had things working out for them. They didn't need Becka's mistakes putting a damper on their happily-ever-afters.

Which really only left her one option.

She closed her eyes. "Damn it, I have to do it, don't I?"

"I mean, you could put on your martyr's sash and try to power through it on your own, but that's not going to accomplish anything but to save your pride—and only for a while."

She *would* need help eventually. Whether it was financially or with babysitting or… God, Becka didn't know where to start.

Easy. You start with Aaron and go from there.

"If I change my mind, he's going to have me over a barrel."

"Sounds like your kind of kink."

Becka made a face. "Very funny." The earlier encounter with Aaron had been over so quickly, she could almost tell herself she hadn't noticed how good he looked. Life was complicated enough without her still being attracted to Aaron. *Stop borrowing trouble. You have enough of it as things stand.* She sat up and pulled her knees to her chest. "I'm in over my head. I want this baby, but…there are so many strings attached. I knew there would be, but I really didn't expect him to go full-on caveman on me over this. He was seconds away from knocking me over the head and dragging me out of here by my hair."

Allie circled around the coffee table and crouched next to her. "You have options, you know. No matter how cornered you feel right now, there's always more than one path forward. We just need to sit down and figure it out."

That was the problem, though—she'd been doing *nothing* but thinking about her options going forward. Becka had always been better at acting first and worrying about the consequences later. So much inaction was not only unnatural, it stressed her the fuck out.

Allie nodded as if she'd said something. "You've already decided you're going to do things his way. That's okay. But if you change your mind at any point, that's okay, Becka. You're not trapped, no matter what it feels like right now."

Trapped.

That was a good word. Becka rubbed a hand over her face. Now that she'd actually let herself decide, there was no reason to delay. If she held off too long, she had no doubt Aaron would come charging through her door again and then she'd have to tell him to fuck off out of sheer principle and it would be a case of cutting off her nose to spite her face. That wouldn't actually help anyone.

She grabbed her phone off the coffee table and

typed out a quick text to Aaron. You win this round.
Text me your address.

The reply appeared before she had a chance to
set the phone back down. I'll pick you up in two
hours.

Becka glared. "The man is *insufferable*."

Allie leaned over to read the message. "Insufferable in kind of a sexy way, though. There's something about a guy who takes charge that's really
attractive."

"You only say that because you're deeply in love
with Roman. Seriously, do alpha males travel in
a pack, because between Roman and Gideon and
Aaron…" She shuddered. "You would have thought
they'd do the lone wolf thing."

"Lone wolves and alpha wolves are two very different things."

"Thanks, *National Geographic*." She glared
harder at her phone and stabbed out a response. I
will haul my own damn things. Give me your address. Compromise is your friend.

I can compromise. You have three hours.

"God!" She tossed her phone onto the table and
shot to her feet, nearly knocking her friend over.
She stalked to her bedroom and started throwing
clothes onto her bed. She *wasn't* moving in with him,
but she would give him the benefit of the doubt—

barely—and stay there for a little while to give the whole thing a trial.

The way things were going, it might be a very short trial.

Allie wisely decided to stand in the doorway and out of range. "What do you need from me?"

She loved her friend so freaking much for not putting any demands on her or trying to tell her how she *should* be reacting or feeling. That was Allie, though. She devoted her life to supporting women who needed it. Allie's gym, Transcend, was linked up with a local women's shelter, so the classes were women only. Becka always enjoyed getting them pumped up. It was a safe space for them to do something for themselves, and Becka was just a small part of that, but she loved it.

Allie might be understanding to the extreme, but Lucy wouldn't be. Her sister had always been her opposite, and for better or worse, Lucy would have something to say about this whole baby situation. It was the logical, collected nature of her older sibling. Becka had to tell her eventually, but she wasn't ready. Lucy would give her that look, the one that always got on her face when Becka screwed up or went too far.

When I act too much like our mother.

She couldn't stand the thought of her sister's disappointment. And there *would* be disappointment. This wasn't an oops baby between Becka and some longtime boyfriend. This was a pregnancy as the result of a one night stand with a man she barely knew.

No, she wasn't ready to tell Lucy about the baby.

She didn't know if she'd ever be ready.

Becka dumped her gym bag next to the growing pile of clothes. "I don't know what I need." She stopped. "I'm a mess, and I don't think that's going to be changing any time soon, but I promise not to be too unbearable."

"Oh honey." Allie crossed the room in a few short steps and pulled Becka into her arms. She hugged her hard. "I know this is scary and you're overwhelmed, but I don't have a single doubt about you being the best mom out there. You have the luckiest little lima bean ever."

"Lima bean."

"Well, yeah. That's about the size the baby is right now? I mean…"

"It's actually closer to a lime." She'd looked it up after the doctor confirmed the pregnancy.

"Oh wow, that's a huge difference." Allie laughed. "That's not a very cute nickname, anyways. I can come up with better."

Becka hugged her back hard. "No, I like it. Lima bean fits." She didn't have the heart to tell Allie that she wasn't sure about being even a good mom, let alone the best one. Becka didn't have much of a role model for that one, but she'd be damned before she made the same mistakes her mother did.

Except for the part where you got knocked up by a near stranger out of wedlock. So far, I'm swinging for the fences with walking in her footsteps.

Aaron half expected Becka not to be home when he arrived. He was pushing her too hard and he damn well knew it, but he couldn't seem to get control of himself. The thought of her living in that run-down little apartment by herself, where the security was lackluster at best and the walls seemed a strong breeze away from coming down around her ears… It made him crazy. He'd never really thought about kids, other than as a vaguely theoretical "someday" in the equally vague future, but now that he had an actual baby on the way, he wasn't about to stand back and let it want for anything.

That included living arrangements.

He clenched his jaw as he walked through Becka's door. The place wasn't any better than the first time he'd been there. If anything, the flaws were only more glaring. He'd missed the water stain on the wall before, where someone overhead had obviously had a leak that had come through to Becka's apartment. Or the crack in her window that wouldn't keep out the cold—or the heat.

She didn't look at him as she reached for the pile of bags at her feet and shouldered her backpack. "This is temporary, Aaron. I'm not prepared to sign my life away to be your kept woman, baby or no. If you pull another high-handed move like you did earlier, I'm out and I'm not coming back."

He clenched his jaw harder. *Do not yell at her contrary ass. Be calm. Be fucking rational.* "You mentioned compromise."

"I'm surprised you know the word."

Aaron scooped up the remaining three bags and shot her a look that dared her to argue with him taking them. "Let's go. I have a car waiting downstairs." He chose to ignore her muttering uncomplimentary things and followed her down the dim hallway to the rickety elevator. Through it all, he kept his damn mouth shut. They were both on a hair trigger, and he didn't need to be the one to set things aflame. Especially not now that they needed to sit down and have a serious discussion.

But he still couldn't stop himself from asking. "When did you know?"

"Four weeks ago." She hitched her bag higher on her shoulder and marched out of the elevator as soon as the doors opened, Aaron on her heels.

"You've known for a month and only called me yesterday."

"That is how math works."

He instinctively held the front door open for her and pointed at the black car idling at the curb. Aaron grabbed her backpack and loaded all the bags into the trunk. He joined Becka in the back seat, his irritation only growing when she pulled out her phone and started playing some puzzle game. "Why didn't you call me as soon as you knew?"

"I didn't know what I wanted to do, so there was no reason to bring you into the conversation until I made my decision."

If she wanted to keep it or not.

He stared straight ahead as his driver merged into traffic. Aaron knew he ultimately had no say in her choice, and he wouldn't have taken that from her even if the thought of her terminating the pregnancy opened a hole in his chest that he didn't know how to process. He'd known he was going to be a father for less than twelve hours. There was absolutely no logical reason for him already to be attached to the idea of this baby, let alone the baby itself. It wasn't even really a baby yet.

None of that seemed to matter.

He looked back at Becka, noting the changes he'd been too distracted to take in earlier. Even without the makeup she'd worn the night he met her, her skin damn near glowed, and her still-blue hair, though now more turquoise than actual blue, seemed glossier. His gaze skated over her black leggings and still-flat stomach to her breasts pressing against her tank top. *Those have definitely changed.*

"Stop ogling me." She spoke without looking up from her phone.

Since there was no question that ogling was *exactly* what he'd been doing, he went on the offensive.

"Have you been eating? You don't look like you've gained any weight."

Becka snorted. "Yes, Mother, I've been eating. It's normal not to gain much in the first trimester, especially since I'm so active and this is my, ah, first pregnancy."

He racked his brain for what little pregnancy knowledge he had and…came up short. Aaron's sisters were both younger than him and hadn't had children yet. His mother wasn't much of a sharer, and even if she was, she wouldn't have gone into detail with her only son when it came to her pregnancies. Besides, he'd never had a reason to ask before.

He had to brush up on his knowledge, maybe read a few books. He'd attend the doctor's appointments with Becka, of course, but Aaron didn't like to walk into any encounter without having a decent idea of how it would play out. He'd rather be armed with all the information and possibilities before the conversation even began.

He shot another look at her to make sure she wasn't paying any attention to him, and then spent several minutes ordering the top-rated pregnancy books available. Aaron hesitated, then put express shipping on the order and plugged in the address to the office. If Cameron bothered to open the box, he might give Aaron shit, but it was better than the alternative: Becka finding them and getting her back up.

Even with traffic, they made it to his penthouse in

good time. He led the way through the lobby and to the elevator. "I'll get you added to the list of people with access to the floor tomorrow. Tonight, we'll get your space set up and talk over dinner."

"I'm not really hungry."

He punched the button for his floor. "You just got done telling me that you eat."

"I *do* eat." She sounded like she was clenching her jaw as hard as he was. "I also only eat when I'm hungry, and right now I'm not hungry."

She was too skinny, surely. Aaron opened his mouth and then reconsidered. Becka might have chosen to be here with him, but it was a tenuous alliance. Even with his threat of involving her sister and friend and their respective men, there was nothing really holding Becka to him. He'd be on the birth certificate—he'd sue for paternity if he had to—but they had at least eighteen years of dealing with each other in front of them.

And he'd essentially gotten them started by blackmailing her.

Way to go, Livingston. You played this all wrong.

The doors opened into a foyer that separated his penthouse from anyone who had access. He keyed in his code and held the door for her. "This way." He slipped past her and led the way through the open living room and kitchen to the short hallway. There were three doors. Aaron pointed at the one on the right. "Bathroom." Center. "My room." Left. "Your room."

"Thanks," she bit out. Becka slid past him and walked into the room. She took it in with a cursory glance and crossed her arms over her chest. "Leave my bags. Please." The last sounded more afterthought than genuine politeness.

Aaron didn't move. "We need to talk, Becka."

"And we will." She looked everywhere but at him. "You got what you wanted, Aaron. I'm here. I know this might sound shocking, but today wore me out. I want to unpack my clothes and maybe take a bath and just decompress a little without having to plan the next six months—the next eighteen years—tonight. That okay with you?" She lifted her chin, her posture telling him she didn't give a fuck if it was okay with him.

He could keep pushing. She was off center and defensive, but maybe she needed to know he was actually all in with this shit.

Then again, Aaron didn't know Becka well enough to anticipate how she'd respond. His threat earlier was a well-placed guess based on her close relationship with both her sister and Allie—and his knowledge of Gideon and Roman. But going forward, he was in the dark in a big way. He needed more information, and he needed it fast.

Until then, there was nothing wrong with letting Becka settle into his home and make herself comfortable. He could use the time for a little reconnaissance to pave the way before the baby books arrived.

"If you change your mind about food, I can order takeout." Aaron hesitated. "Is there anything that's a hard no for you foodwise right now?"

She narrowed her eyes. "So you can keep trying to feed me?"

"No, minx, so I don't order some kind of take-out that triggers your morning sickness and makes you miserable."

Becka's eyes widened. "Oh. Well." She uncrossed her arms and shifted her feet. "No fish. I wasn't sick the first trimester, so no reason to think it will start now, but fish is a hard limit."

He kept his smile under lock and key. "No fish. Got it." He stepped around her and set her bags on the bed. "If you need anything—"

"What I need is space." She bit her bottom lip, worrying the piercing there. "But thanks. I know this wasn't exactly expected news and you're handling it a lot better than I thought you would." Becka made a face. "Stop trying to steamroll me, though."

"I make no promises." He almost reached out, almost drew her into his arms and promised that whatever came, they would face it down together…

That wasn't how this story went. The sex might have been outstanding, but the ultimate truth was that Aaron didn't know shit about Becka Baudin. He didn't know her likes and dislikes, her favorite things, her history, what kind of mother she'd be.

Six months didn't seem nearly long enough to figure it out.

One day at a time. First get the information you need, then formulate a plan of attack.

If he wanted to be in Becka's life—in the baby's life—then he needed to convince her that she wanted him there. Right now, his chances didn't look particularly promising, but Aaron had faced down impossible odds before. He would again.

After he regrouped.

But tomorrow was a new day, and he wasn't about to give her enough space to keep building the already impressive wall she had in place between them.

CHAPTER FIVE

BECKA'S ATTITUDE LASTED until she walked into the bathroom. She turned a slow circle, taking in the broody gray walls, the silvery tiles blocking out a walk-in shower, and a jetted tub big enough to fit three people. *Or a pregnant woman who's twice her normal size.*

Worry about that later.

The list of things she would worry about later continued to grow, but she'd add *that* to the list, too. Right now, her entire body hurt, as if she'd done three spin classes in a single day, and she just wanted a hot soak and to not think about anything at all. At least Aaron had backed off and given her space. Despite the nine-foot ceilings and massive square footage, the walls of this penthouse threatened to close in on her.

She wasn't trapped.

She could leave whenever she wanted.

Knowing that was the only thing that kept her from running screaming into the night. She was here by choice. It might be a manipulated choice, but it was still her choice.

Becka got the water going at the right temperature and then went snooping around the room. The cabinet under the sink had the expected cleaning tools, all damn near shining from being so clean themselves. Next were the artfully displayed soaps situated on the little corner table next to the bath. There were essential oils and bath bombs and lady-looking shower gels. Becka picked up a bath bomb and gave a sniff. It was something flowery and feminine and had no place in this supermasculine home.

She shot to her feet and marched out of the bathroom. Following the clacking of keyboard keys, she stalked into the living room and waved the bath bomb at Aaron. "When did you buy this?"

"What?"

"This." She shoved it nearly under his nose. "Were you so damn sure of yourself that you went and bought me bath products? What the hell is even wrong with you?"

His lips quirked. "I didn't buy those."

"They're in *your* bathroom." She realized what she was saying and took a hasty step back. Of course Aaron hadn't bought them. They were clearly a woman's choice, and Aaron was very much not a woman. *Oh God.* Becka pasted a smile on her face, hoping it looked realer than it felt. "I didn't realize you were

seeing someone." He hadn't been three months ago...
She was pretty sure.

No, I might not know a lot, but Aaron was single when we were together. He's not that kind of guy.

But three months was a long time in the grand scheme of things. She hadn't called him, hadn't given him any indication that she ever *would* call him. Of course he hadn't waited for her. She hadn't expected him to. It certainly wasn't disappointment souring her stomach at the thought of some mystery woman in Aaron's bed, using Aaron's ridiculous bathtub, lounging next to Aaron on his leather couch at the end of the day.

He set his laptop aside and pushed to his feet in a smooth move. It left him towering over her, and he took a step closer, bringing them nearly chest to chest. "I'm not seeing anyone, minx."

Minx.

She tried not to let the casual endearment warm her, tried to stand firm and hold on to her anger. "Then, what is this?"

He studied her, his blue-gray eyes seeing too much. "You're jealous."

"Not even a little bit." *I am totally jealous.* She took a quick step back. "There's nothing to be jealous of. I just wanted to know if I'm stepping on some woman's toes. It is such a man-stupid thing to do to invite your baby mama to live with you without talking to your girlfriend about it first."

Aaron didn't move, but he seemed closer. "Give me a little credit. Pulling something like that is a piece of shit move, and I'd never do it. Which is all a moot point because I'm not seeing anyone. I haven't since the wedding."

Since they'd had sex.

It probably had no significance. She'd be a fool to think it could possibly mean anything. *The only thing that's a moot point is this playing out in anything less than disaster. I'm having his baby. I don't know him. He doesn't know me. Moving me in with him doesn't change that.* She looked away. "That's not my business."

"Considering you're now living with me, it's at least partially your business." He paused as if debating something with himself and then shifted to bring her attention back to him. Aaron was oh so serious when he said, "I won't bring anyone back here without talking about it with you first. I don't think it's too much to ask that you give me the same courtesy."

Men. He means men.

Maybe she wasn't the only one who was jealous. Aaron hadn't questioned the baby being his, and she hadn't offered up any information. *He put himself out there, a little bit. Would it kill me to do the same?* Becka wrapped her arms around herself and stared at his left collarbone where it pressed against his plain black T-shirt. She had no business noting that he looked good in lounge pants and a shirt. Comfortable. As if in addition to doing whatever his job was—something high-powered and expensive, from the penthouse and the suits—he could also kick back with a beer and some football on the weekends.

She backed away, one careful step at a time. "I left the tub on."

"Becka."

She moved faster but paused in the entrance to the hallway. "I haven't been with anyone since then, either." She wasn't about to examine that fact too closely. In the months leading up to the wedding, she'd been too busy to bother finding someone to scratch that particular itch, and after...

"The bath shit is from my sister." He still watched her too closely. "My youngest sister, Trish, seems to think it's a crime against God for me to own that tub without some equally fancy bath products to go into it."

"She's not wrong." It was all she could handle. The strange mix of emotions curdling her stomach sent her fleeing back into the bathroom and locking the door behind her. Not because she thought Aaron would barge in, but because she didn't trust *herself*. If the sound of the water running hadn't been in the background for their entire conversation, a constant reminder that their time was limited, Becka might have done something unforgivable.

Like kiss Aaron.

She turned off the water—not a moment too

soon——and gave the bath bomb another cautious sniff. When it didn't set off any crazy pregnancy reaction, she unwrapped it and dropped it into the tub. While it fizzed and turned the water blue, Becka stripped. She took baths all the time, though the tub in her apartment was so small, she either had to have her legs halfway up the wall or sit with her entire torso freezing. She'd never once been so aware of the slide of her clothing against her skin before it fell to the floor. Impossible to ignore the fact that Aaron was *right there* on the other side of the door. In the same penthouse. Looking good enough to lick.

She gave herself a shake. *Stupid pregnancy hormones.* Everyone promised morning sickness and strange food cravings and exhaustion that never seemed to end. Becka was more tired than normal, sure, and she'd developed a fondness for peanut butter that bordered on obsession, but the main difference she'd seen was that she was turned on. All. The. Time. She'd been getting herself off twice a day for months, and half the time it barely took the edge off. She wanted, needed, and hadn't been able to take that leap.

The truth was that she hadn't wanted to.

Because the man she pictured every time she slipped her hand between her thighs to stroke her clit was *Aaron.*

The same man only a few rooms away.

"I will not be ruled by my stupid hormones. Hormones are what got me into this situation in the first place." She carefully stepped into the water and sank down until her body below her neck was submerged. A moan slipped free despite her best efforts. "Oh *God*."

Who needed sex when she had this bathtub?

Becka reached over and flipped the switch to get the jets going. She leaned back and closed her eyes. It would have to be enough. Things were complicated enough without falling back into bed with Aaron. It was one mistake she couldn't afford to make twice.

If she could just convince herself of that, everything would be fine.

Aaron waited for the water to start running before he walked to the kitchen and pulled the book from his briefcase. He and Becka had fallen into something of a pattern over the last week. An agonizing pattern, but one all the same. She left sometime around five each morning to teach one of her classes, pausing barely long enough to grab a cup of coffee and mutter a greeting to him. They both arrived back at his place around six and then shared some kind of dinner. Then she took a shower followed by a bath. In that order.

If the last seven days were anything to go by, she'd emerge from the bathroom in a little over an hour, wrapped in a towel that covered her from chest to knees and dart into her bedroom. He wouldn't see her again until morning.

It was like living with a wild animal that feared contact. Every time he got too close, or moved too purposefully toward her, she fled back into her room and shut the door. If it hadn't been for the first night, for her anger over the idea of him with someone else, he might have thought…

Aaron didn't know what he would have thought. This wasn't proceeding like he'd expected, but then he hadn't had shit for a plan to begin with.

He settled onto the couch and flipped open the baby book. It tracked pregnancy by week with the various changes to both the mother and the baby, as well as overviews of each trimester and what to expect. He was more than a little in awe, but the new knowledge wasn't enough to ignore the fact that he and Becka still hadn't actually talked.

He flipped the page to the next set of FAQs. Aaron paused, the first sentence catching his eye. *Bathing while pregnant.* He read with increasing agitation as the book outlined the recommendation of keeping bath temperatures below ninety-eight degrees, and comparing that information with Becka's pink skin and flushed cheeks every night. "Goddamn it." He shot to his feet and stalked down the hallway to the bathroom door. Aaron banged on it. "Becka! Open the door!"

Cursing sounded, and a second later, she yanked

the door open, a towel clutched at her chest. Her hair was wet, but from the half-filled tub behind her, she'd only gotten through the shower portion of her nightly routine. She glared. "What the hell do you need *right this second*?"

He held up the book and pointed to the section he'd just read. "No more hot baths."

Becka's brows slammed down. "My baths are fine."

"Yes, yes, the baths are fine. I'm talking about the scalding temperatures." He shoved the book at her and headed into the kitchen to find the thermometer Trish had insisted he needed the last time she visited New York. It was technically for meat, but it should work in a pinch. He strode back into the bathroom, finding Becka exactly where he'd left her, reading with a pinched look on her face. Aaron slid past her and stuck the thermometer into the bathwater, impatiently watching the red line climb. It hovered just over one hundred degrees, so he cranked the cold water more fully on. "It's bad for the baby—and you—if it's too hot."

"Aaron."

He waited for the thermometer to read the appropriate temperature before he sat back on his heels and turned to find Becka watching him with a strange look on her face. "What's wrong?"

"You bought a pregnancy book." She looked at

him like she'd never seen him before. "You're *reading* a pregnancy book."

"Well, yeah." He stood and dried off his hand on his shirt. "I said you aren't in this alone, and I meant it. I don't know shit about pregnancy or babies, and until we know our plan, I'm hardly going to call up my mother and ask her for information. Books are the next best thing."

Emotions flickered over her face, too fast for him to decipher. "You'd call your mother and ask her about my pregnancy."

There was something going on here. Something more than just her being surprised he was doing his homework. Aaron approached her slowly, carefully. She just watched him without moving, her hand still fisting the towel just above her breasts. He stopped just within arm's reach. "My family might kick my ass for knocking you up and letting you falter for three months without my being there, but this baby will be my parents' first grandbaby. They're going to care." He made a face. "Honestly, as soon as he or she makes an appearance, I fully expect the entire Livingston clan to descend on this penthouse."

Her lower lip quivered, just a little. "I didn't know you were close to your parents. They're still together?"

The question sounded innocent enough, but there were undertones there. Deep ones. "Thirty-seven years and counting. I'm the oldest, and I have two younger sisters. We're close, though they both live a few hours north of the city so I don't see them as much as everyone would like."

"That's nice." The words were right, but they sounded forced.

He could pick up a clue, so he didn't ask about her parents. He knew enough from Lucy to know that they weren't in the picture—and hadn't been for a while—but Aaron wasn't willing to poke until Becka wanted to tell him. He *wanted* her to want to tell him, but he didn't expect miracles. It wouldn't happen this week. Or this month.

Patience.

His gaze snagged on Becka's mouth, on the perfect curve of her bottom lip. Even after all this time, he could still taste her. *Wanted* to still taste her. He clenched his fists to keep from reaching for her. He was the one with all the power in this scenario. He wouldn't abuse it. He refused to. What were they talking about before?

Right. My family. He cleared his throat. "I think you'll like them."

"Aaron?"

"Yeah?"

"I don't want to talk about your family anymore." She let the book fall to the ground and released the towel. It hit the floor and Aaron found himself holding his breath as he traced her naked body with his gaze. He'd been wrong before—her stomach *had* changed, but it was such a gentle curve, he wouldn't have noticed if he wasn't looking for it. Her rosy nipples had darkened, and they pebbled as he watched, goose bumps raising along her skin in a wave.

He held himself chained in place. "What do you want, minx?"

"I think that's kind of freaking obvious, don't you?"

Yeah, but he wasn't willing to make a single fucking assumption right now and risk damaging this tentative thing between them. "I'm going to need you to say it."

She huffed out a breath and propped her hands on her hips. "You, jerk. I want you. Preferably naked, with your hands and mouth all over me, cumulating with me coming on your cock."

CHAPTER SIX

BECKA WOULDN'T REACH for him. She had little but her pride left at this point and, honestly, she didn't have much of *that*, either. Whether he realized it or not, Aaron threatened to hold all the cards in every single one of their interactions. She couldn't give him even more power by following her very clear invitation up with anything other than waiting.

She'd made her move.

The ball was in his court.

Thank the Lord above, he didn't make her wait long.

He walked to the bath and shut off the water and then he was there, engulfing her with his presence, wrapping his arms around her until her entire world narrowed down to him. As if he meant to shield her from anything life threw at her.

Stop that. He didn't make anything resembling a promise when it comes to me. I can't afford to get mixed up over him wanting to take care of the baby and him wanting me.

That didn't keep her from leaning into his strong chest and inhaling deeply. His faint cologne made her toes curl, and she wanted to get beneath his shirt to see if it smelled different on his skin. Things had happened so quickly the first—the only—time, she hadn't had a chance to explore him.

She wanted that chance now.

Becka reached for the hem of his shirt and tugged it up and over his head slowly. She silently marveled at the cut of his muscles. They were even more pronounced now than they had been three months ago. "Someone's been spending time in the gym."

"I had a lot of frustration to work out." He rested his hands on her hips, letting her explore his chest and stomach. She was so busy tracing the line of his pecs that she almost missed his next words. "I still do."

No way to misconstrue *that* statement.

He's talking about me.

"Oh." *Good job, Becka. Excellent witty response.* To cover up her confusion, she went onto her tiptoes and kissed him. The move pressed her breasts against his chest, and she moaned at how good it felt. Everything was more sensitive than normal, as if someone had hooked a live wire up to her and it covered every inch of her skin. "Touch me."

He grabbed the backs of her thighs and lifted so she could wrap her legs around his waist. Aaron turned around and walked them to the bathroom counter and set her carefully on the marble. He ran a hand down the center of her chest, guiding her back to prop herself onto her hands and let him look at her. Though *look* was too mild a term. The man devoured her with his eyes, staring at her like she was an oasis in the middle of a desert and he wasn't sure if she was real or a figment of his imagination. He was so damn buttoned up the rest of the time, but when he got his hands on her, a different part of Aaron came out to play. It made Becka feel just as wild and out of control to know that *she* was the cause of that switch being flipped.

She shoved down his pants just enough to free his cock. Becka stroked him, every muscle in her body shaking in anticipation. A person shouldn't be able to be addicted to a cock after a single sexual encounter, but the sight of Aaron looming with his hands braced on the counter on either side of her hips and his cock in her hand…she couldn't think of another place she'd rather be or another person she'd rather be with.

All she wanted was this moment.

This man.

Becka met his gaze as she guided his cock into her. There was no need for protection, not when that ship had most definitely sailed already, not when neither of them had been with anyone else in the meantime. And, crazy as it might be, she wanted him inside her with no barriers.

They had enough barriers in every other part of their lives to keep them apart. She didn't want one here, too.

A muscle in Aaron's jaw jumped as he sank into her inch by delicious inch, filling her completely. "You make me crazy."

"You're not the only one." She didn't even sound like herself. Her voice was too low, too breathy. Becka didn't care. Not as long as the pleasure kept spiraling through her. "I need more, Aaron."

"I've got more to give you, minx." He hooked an arm around her waist and pulled her to the edge of the counter, until she had to cling to him to keep from toppling off. He used his free hand to cup her jaw, tilting her face up so he could claim her mouth, and then he began to move.

Aaron slammed into her even as his tongue gently teased her lips open. He pounded into her while giving her the sweetest kiss of her life, and her body couldn't make the two dueling sensations match up. There was no fighting it, though, and she wasn't even sure she wanted to. Instead, she clung to him and let him have full control of everything.

He tilted her back, still kissing her slowly, luxuriously. The new angle allowed him deeper, until his cock bumped the end of her with every thrust. It was too much and not enough. Pleasure built in brutal waves, each taking her closer and closer to the edge of no return. She gasped against his mouth, begging without words for completion. He responded by grinding his pelvis against her clit, and the friction sent her hurtling into an orgasm that made her toes curl. Aaron kept moving, drawing out her pleasure until she went limp in his arms. "Damn, that was good."

His chuckle vibrated through her entire body. "We're not done yet."

She belatedly realized he was still hard inside her. Becka shivered. She wanted more. Of course she wanted more. But there was a difference between losing her mind and having a quickie in the bathroom and an entire night's worth of sex.

What was that you were saying about the ship already sailing? If you wanted to keep the lines between you firm, you shouldn't have jumped on his cock the first chance you got.

Shut up.

"Aaron…"

He leaned down to rest his forehead against hers. She closed her eyes and simply breathed in the scent of him—of them. It was easier to talk like this, to open up just a little. "I don't know what we're doing."

"I don't, either." His words brushed her lips. "But I don't want to stop."

She opened her mouth to tell him she did, but it would be a lie. There were so many reasons she should call this whole thing off, but she wanted to pretend, just for a little while, that she wasn't really alone. He made her feel so damn good, and she wasn't a decent enough person to turn away from what he was offering tonight. Becka licked her lips. "I don't... I don't want to stop, either."

Aaron shifted back and ran his hand down the center of her chest. He paused for the beat of a heart, with his hand over her slightly rounded stomach, and lifted her, her legs still wrapped around him, to walk out of the bathroom and down the short hallway to his room. The movement of his steps had his cock shifting inside her, and she squirmed in his grip. He nipped her ear, and she could have sworn he was grinning when he said, "This time, we're going slow."

How could he be so measured when she had just come out of her goddamn skin?

Becka ran her hands up his arms to grip his biceps. "I'm willing to be convinced."

"Mmm." He laid her down in the center of his stupidly large bed. "We're just getting started."

He should have been talking to Becka, not fucking her brains out, but Aaron couldn't convince himself to stop. It felt too good to be inside her again, to have her moving in sync with him as they both chased pleasure. Even if they figured nothing else out, they could figure *this* out.

She wanted control. Hell, he wanted it, too.

It wasn't on the agenda right then.

Aaron pulled out of her and moved down her body, reacquainting himself with her. He palmed her breasts, kissing her nipples gently, and then harder when she laced her fingers through his hair and moaned. She'd been responsive before, not shy about telling him what she wanted, but seemed even more so now. He grinned against her skin. "Sensitive, aren't they?"

"You have no idea." She arched her back, offering her breasts to him again. "Don't stop."

He didn't stop. He lavished her breasts with attention until she was writhing beneath him and cursing and praising his name in equal measures. Then and only then did Aaron move down her body to settle between her thighs. He was too wound up to keep teasing her, and the sight of her wet and wanting overwhelmed him. He fucked her with his tongue, stopping only when he had to hold her hips down, and then he shifted to suck her clit, working her with his lips and tongue. Her cries only spurred him on, making him as crazy as he was determined to make her.

Her breathless little laugh when she came did things to his chest that he didn't know how to deal with.

Becka tugged on his shoulders. "Come here."

He crawled up her body, but she was already turning, going up on her hands and knees. The picture she presented, the muscles lining her spine drawing his gaze down to her biteable ass… "Fuck, minx. The things you do to me." He nudged her legs wider and guided his cock into her. Becka immediately dropped her chest to the mattress, the new angle drawing a curse from his lips. She didn't just feel good. She felt like fucking heaven. He smoothed a hand up her spine and braced it against the mattress next to her head.

And then he started to move.

It had been fast and hard in the bathroom, but Aaron was determined to hold himself in check this time. He noted every catch of her breath, every moan, every time she pushed back to take him deeper. He gave her everything, focusing everything he had on coaxing another of those addicting giggles from her lips.

Lightning shot down his spine, but he fought it back, fought to hold out as long as he could. "Touch yourself. You promised to come around my cock. I want to feel it again."

She snaked a hand under her stomach. He knew the exact moment her fingers made contact with her clit. She gasped and clenched around him, and it was everything he could do not to release then and there. So good. There were so many things wrong with this situation, but *this* wasn't one of them. Every move she made was perfection, her body flowing in direct counterpoint with his, heightening his pleasure until he could barely breathe past it.

He wanted this to last forever.

He was afraid it might kill him if it did.

Aaron clenched her hips tighter and drove into her harder. She met him stroke for stroke, and then her entire body went tight and tense and that goddamn giggle slipped free. *I could spend the rest of my life pursuing that fucking sound.* He'd thought it before, but it never seemed realer than in this moment. His strokes became more frenzied, the need to imprint himself over every part of her taking him to the edge and beyond. Aaron cursed as he came, the pleasure going on and on until he slumped onto the bed next to her.

"Feel better?" Becka rolled to face him. Her hair was tangled on one side, and she had a sleepy smile on her face. The fact she was in *his* bed didn't escape him in the least. *It could be like this if we got out of each other's way long enough to give it a chance.* That was the problem, though. He didn't know if it was possible to create a lasting peace. He didn't know nearly enough about a lot of things when it came to Becka.

Belatedly, he realized she'd asked him a question. He propped his head on his hand. "What?"

Some of the sleepiness disappeared from her eyes. "Did the sex distract you from your worrying long enough to make you feel better?"

Was that all this was? No. He couldn't believe that. He *wouldn't*. Aaron reached out and tucked a strand of her brilliant blue hair behind her ear. "I could think of worse ways to relax."

"Me, too." She closed her eyes, almost seeming to lean into his touch. "God, I would kill for some pancakes right now."

"Pancakes," he repeated. He glanced at the clock. "It's after ten."

"I know. I shouldn't."

This was his chance to extend their connection past a couple of shared orgasms. He forced himself to drop his hand, to not cage her in even that tiny way. "I think I have the stuff to put together some if you're in the mood."

Becka opened her eyes. "Are you serious?"

"As a heart attack." Unable to help himself, he leaned down and pressed a quick kiss to her lips. "I wouldn't tease a pregnant woman about food."

He regretted the words as soon as they were out of his mouth.

She shut down. He could actually see her walls coming back up to keep him out, her posture becoming more guarded, her gaze resting on the sheets instead of on him, her lips pressed together as if she attempted to keep sharp words inside. This was it. She'd tell him to get the fuck away from her, and what little ground he'd gained would be lost.

But Becka finally sighed. "Pancakes really do sound good."

"Say no more." He knew better than to push her now, not after his idiotic misstep. As Aaron climbed out of bed and headed into his closet for a pair of pants, he allowed himself a kernel of hope. Even with everything stacked against them, he now had two avenues to make headway with Becka—food and sex.

He could work with that.

CHAPTER SEVEN

BECKA COULDN'T STOP looking at Aaron. He was shirt-less in the kitchen, making pancakes for her, and she'd never seen a more beautiful man. The muscles of his back flexed as he moved, and she clenched her thighs together despite the several outstanding orgasms he'd just delivered. The whole thing was so...domestic.

The only time she'd lived with anyone was room-mates back in college. They were always too noisy, too messy and too in evidence everywhere she looked.

Becka didn't mind noise—her spin classes were so loud with their pumping music that some people wore earplugs. Having the bass thrum through her body as she shouted and directed and got everyone moving for the workout of their life was her happy place.

She didn't even mind people. Not really. Being a personal trainer was a different kind of happy, work-ing with people who wanted to get healthy or accomplish some specific goal. She loved watching them put in the work and being their own personal drill sergeant and cheerleader, all wrapped into one. And the look on their face when they realized the moment their hard work had paid off and that they'd accomplished what they'd set out to do? Priceless.

But when she was done with work for the day, she wanted to come home and just…be.

Roommates normally made that impossible.

Aaron as a roommate should have made it doubly so.

She twisted on the bar stool to look over the apartment. It was a study in minimalism—a place for everything and everything in its place. There wasn't a speck of dust on the entertainment center that framed the massive TV, and the leather couch and twin chairs on either side of it didn't have any wear and tear or so much as a scrape on them. The kitchen was equally freakishly clean. If he wasn't cooking in it right this second, she would have suspected that he *didn't* cook by how clean the countertops were. The man obviously didn't believe in clutter.

Which was a relief, but at the same time, Aaron being a control freak was stamped over every inch of this place. This was a man who didn't like messes, and their situation was the very definition of a mess.

As if sensing her thoughts, he flipped the pancakes and turned to lean against the gray marble countertop. "I think it's long past time for us to talk."

She couldn't keep dodging him. It was freaking exhausting, and if Becka actually planned to reduce Aaron's position in the baby's life to sperm donor, she never should have moved in with him in the first place. She wrapped both hands around her orange juice and stared hard at the swirl in the marble that looked like Abraham Lincoln's beard. "You are going to be in the baby's life. I'm living in your penthouse. Don't you think that's enough for now?" Even without looking up, she knew his expression had turned stormy, his eyes leaning more gray than blue. She pushed her juice away. "You keep pushing me, and it's stressing me out. The learning curve on this situation is pretty rough and, this might be shocking, but I'm overwhelmed. You trying to micromanage everything from my bath temperature to…"

"Drink your orange juice."

She gave a half-hearted laugh. "Yeah, like that."

"I'm serious." His big hand appeared in her line of vision and nudged the glass back into her hand. "The calcium and vitamin D are good for you."

She closed her eyes and counted to ten. Twice.

Maybe we should just keep banging it out and stop talking, because obviously we are not *even close to being on the same page.*

"Aaron—" She stopped short at the sound of his sliding a plate to her. Becka opened her eyes to find two perfectly shaped pancakes on the plate. She might have stopped breathing completely when he set both the smooth and the chunky peanut butter next to the plate, each with their respective knives. "How did you know?"

"I'd have to be extremely dense not to notice you walking around with a spoonful of peanut butter in your mouth the few times you've graced me with your presence." He eyed the tubs of peanut butter with narrowed eyes. "They're both depleted from the last time I checked, so I wasn't sure which you'd prefer. Let me know and I'll pick up more next time I get groceries."

Heat spread up her chest and took residence in her cheeks. It shouldn't surprise her so much that he picked up on her eating habits, not when he was obviously watching her *so* closely, but the thoughtfulness of the simple gesture had her throat closing and her eyes burning. "I, ah, use both."

Conscious of his eyes on her, she spread first the chunky onto each pancake, and then took the other knife and covered it with smooth peanut butter. She carefully cut the food into tiny bites instead of rolling it up like a burrito the way she would have if she was alone. "Thank you."

"We can make this work, minx. You just have to trust me."

That was the one thing she couldn't do. She *did* trust that he wasn't a total asshole, and that he showed every evidence of probably being a good father and a decent friend. But if she let herself sink into the ease of being with him, she was in danger of forgetting exactly how devastating her inevitable heartbreak would be. Everything else might have changed, but *that* hadn't.

If anything, her reasons for not tumbling head over heels for Aaron had just multiplied. This wasn't some guy she could avoid after things fell apart.

He was the father of her future child.

She couldn't just keep shutting him out, though. He was right about that. There had to be some kind of compromise that got them through this with the least amount of strife. *That compromise probably doesn't include amazing sex and screaming his name. Way to muddy the waters.* She silenced the snide little voice inside her. There would be plenty of time for self-recrimination on her seventh run to the bathroom in the middle of the night.

She finished her pancakes and sat back. "Did you want kids? I mean, if life played out according to your perfect plan."

"What makes you think I have a perfect plan?"

Becka rolled her eyes. "I pay attention, that's what. I think you're even more type-A than Allie and Lucy—combined. That's saying something."

He made a face. "Guilty as charged. Though I only ever really had a plan for my professional life. I've known I wanted to work in cybersecurity since I was in high school, and it only took my first internship in college to solidify that I wanted to work for myself and own my own business. That goal kept me busy enough that the personal stuff was always being pushed to the back burner. And the last time I agreed to a date, my prospective date ran off with the matchmaker."

His date, her sister.

It hurt to think about, but he and Lucy might have fit. They were both ambitious and driven and more than a little pretty. Lucy and Gideon were perfectly matched, of course, but that didn't change the fact that Gideon had thought *Aaron* was a good match for Lucy when he compiled his list of bachelors. That was back when Lucy had hired the headhunter to find her a husband—a position Gideon ended up filling in the end.

Becka couldn't be more different from her sister if she'd tried. She was driven, sure, but her dreams had never been to make partner in some law firm or to own her own business. All she wanted to do was live her life to the fullest, to do what she loved and make enough money to pay her bills and travel to places she'd never been before.

Hard to travel with a baby.

She took a hasty drink of her orange juice, aware of how closely Aaron watched her. "That's nice."

"Uh-huh. To answer your question—yeah, I want kids. I always have. My sisters might have been aggravating to grow up with, but we're pretty close now, and there's something comforting about the chaos of a home filled with a family."

She wouldn't know anything about that. Becka's parents had divorced early on, and her mother had always been more concerned with *her* agenda than with her daughters. When Becka was bullied, it wasn't her mother she ran to. It was Lucy. Her sister had started filling that parental role from an early age, and she'd never quite stopped.

She still remembered the moment when she realized she was more like her mother than she'd ever be like her sister. Becka was fourteen and had been going on about some drama that she didn't even recall now, years later, and thirty minutes into her bitchfest she'd realized that Lucy was upset—had been upset through the entire conversation while Becka went on and on about her petty problem.

It turned out, Lucy hadn't gotten into the school she'd pinned her hopes and dreams on and was crushed.

And Becka hadn't even noticed.

She'd promised herself right then and there that she wouldn't walk their mother's path. She wouldn't keep being a burden on her sister the same way their mother was. She'd be independent and strong and take care of her own problems.

A promise she'd mostly kept over the years. Sure, Becka developed a wild streak in college that never quite went away, and she knew her sister worried sometimes about her resistance to the idea of settling down, but those were small sins compared to the kind they'd grown up witnessing.

At least... they *had* been small sins.

Until now.

She shook her head, suddenly aware that Aaron was looking at her like he expected some kind of answer. "I'm sorry, I missed what you just said."

"I asked you if *you* had ever wanted kids."

She pushed to her feet. "No. I never wanted kids."

Aaron watched Becka walk away with her shoulders bowed, looking like someone had just kicked her puppy. Things had been going well. Better than well. They'd been going *good*. She'd teased him a little, the sex had been outstanding and they'd managed to share a meal and half a conversation.

It's possible you need to set the bar for "well" a little higher.

He wanted to chase her down, to try to talk her into telling him what put that haunted look on her face. It was more than not wanting children. Even as the words came out of her mouth, she looked conflicted, as if it wasn't quite the full truth. She wanted kids. She wouldn't have gone forward with the pregnancy otherwise.

Which meant there was something holding her back, some reason she thought she *shouldn't* want kids.

He could call Lucy, but that meant letting her in

on the fact that Becka was pregnant, and if Becka didn't want her sister to know yet, it wasn't his place to share that information. He'd threatened to, of course, but what had been said in anger and frustration before would be a betrayal of trust now. No, that wasn't an option.

Not to mention, he wanted Becka to trust him enough to let him in and let them both get to know each other. He couldn't do that if he kept fumbling shit so thoroughly.

Aaron weighed his options against the inherent risks that went with any path forward. It was possible that if he left things alone and maintained the course, she'd come to him again.

He couldn't risk being wrong, though. The stakes were too damn high.

So he did the slightly less risky option and called his baby sister. Aaron had always been closest to Trish, partly because she never allowed him to take himself too seriously and partly because their age difference meant they were never competing quite the same way he and Mary did through their younger years.

That mattered, of course, but the reason he called her now instead of Mary was because at twenty-four she was the closest in age to Becka—and the closest in personality. Though Becka was all thorns and prickly edges and Trish was both softer and sweeter, they both harbored free spirits and avoiding being tied down. It was comfortable to be the older brother to that kind of personality. It was significantly less so to be having a child with someone like that.

The line rang several times before it clicked over. "Hey, Aaron. Is everything okay?"

He glanced at the clock and cursed himself. It was almost midnight—way too late for this to be a casual call. "Yeah, everything is okay. I just need some advice and didn't think to check if it was too late to call."

"My big brother asking me for advice? You're right, that's not remotely serious at all." She laughed softly. "I'm awake, and you have me on the phone, so stop thinking about how you're going to make some excuse and call me tomorrow."

Since he'd been about to do exactly that, he gave a rueful grin. "How are you?"

She sighed. "I'm fine. Just as fine as I was a couple weeks ago when we talked, though I'm about to start chewing through the wall if I don't get out of this house soon. I love Mom and Dad, and they're trying to be supportive and not push me, but it's driving all of us crazy."

Trish had moved back home after college until she could find a job and it…hadn't gone particularly well. He made a sympathetic noise. "Well, I have some news that will get you out of the doghouse as least favorite child."

"That sounds like trouble." She lowered her voice. "Are you sure everything is okay?"

"Yeah. I mean, it's not, but it will be." He had to believe that. He couldn't allow for any other outcome. Aaron had half a second to wonder if this call was a mistake, but he had gone too far to change his mind now. "I don't know what I'm doing, Trish. There's this woman, and we connected, but she won't give me the time of day and…" *She's going to have my child.*

She laughed. "Oh, Aaron. She's got you twisted in knots, hasn't she? You already tried to plan your way out of this and it blew up in your face."

He narrowed his eyes. "How'd you know?"

"Because you're our fearless leader. You attack every single problem the exact way—as if you're going into battle. Which is great, and useful, and the reason that you're as professionally successful as you are now." Another laugh. "But you can't date like that, Aaron. I mean, you *can*, but if you're calling me, that means she's independent and isn't going to respond well to that sort of thing."

Aaron started piling plates in the sink. "Everything I do pisses her off."

"Hmm. Have you tried *listening*?"

"She doesn't want to talk."

"Because you make it into an interrogation when you aren't paying attention. Figure out what she likes. Do that. See if you relaxing doesn't relax her a little bit." A hesitation. "Though if she's fighting you this hard, maybe it's time to write the whole thing off? Some walls aren't worth beating your head against."

"This one is." He forced a smile into his voice. "Thanks, Trish. You should come down to the city to visit soon."

"Sure thing. Just as soon as I figure out the rest of my life. Love you, big brother."

"Love you, too." He hung up the phone and went to work on the dishes. His sister's advice wasn't necessarily groundbreaking, but she had a good point. He'd approached this from the baby standpoint, because the baby was the only thing they appeared to have in common.

Well, the baby and the sex.

Aaron shook his head and scrubbed harder at the pan. If he wanted to pave the way to a future with Becka and the baby, he needed to *know* Becka.

He stopped.

Was that what he wanted? Both of them? Because that was a different scenario than simply being a father. He just had to be able to be cordial with Becka in order to do *that*, and they'd both go on with their separate lives. It was the simplest solution for a child born of a one-night stand.

And yet.

He thought about the vivid woman who'd caught his eye in the first place, the determined one who'd faced him down time and again over the future, and the bowed shoulders she'd worn tonight when she walked back to her room alone. *Complicated* did not begin to cover Becka Baudin.

There was nothing wrong with complicated, though.

Aaron finished the dishes and dried the pan, still thinking. He just needed to figure out what common ground they had and work from there. It was entirely possible that they had *nothing* in common and this was all a lost cause, but he wasn't prepared to believe that. There was *something* there. Aaron just needed to figure out what it was.

CHAPTER EIGHT

AARON WAS GONE by the time Becka crawled out of
bed the next morning. She tried to tell herself that
it was for the best, that she didn't *really* need to see
him every single morning before they both left for
their respective jobs, but the truth was that she'd gotten used to their shared silence as they drank their
daily cup of coffee in the kitchen. He never seemed
to feel like he needed to fill the silence. It was nice.

She opened the fridge and stared. Three plates sat
on the shelf at eye level, each with a yellow sticky
note attached. *Peanut butter and grape jelly. Peanut
butter and strawberry jam. Peanut butter and sliced
bananas.* Becka smiled, shook her head and grabbed
the peanut butter and banana sandwich. She turned
to the coffeemaker and found another sticky note.
Still smiling, she read his chicken-scratch handwrit-
ing. *Have dinner with me tonight. No baby talk,
promise.*

"How can I resist an offer like that?" She checked

the time and typed out a quick text promising to be home by six.

The day flew by. She had spin at nine, TRX at eleven. The first two classes were at Transcend.

After TRX, she got cleaned up and changed then headed to the elite gym where she coached. Half her clients were looking for weight loss, and the other half were hard-core training for various events. All four of her sessions that afternoon were of the extreme variety. She normally liked to switch up her schedule a little more—the intensity could wear on her after a while—but today she welcomed the requirement of extra concentration.

Anything to keep her from watching the clock and counting down the hours until dinner tonight.

She probably shouldn't have agreed to go. It wouldn't end well, and the whole point of this exercise was to create a stable foundation between her and Aaron so that the baby wouldn't suffer. Dates were *not* part of the equation.

Still, she didn't linger at the gym like she usually did after work. Becka took a cab back to Aaron's apartment and, after arguing with herself for a solid five minutes, jumped in the shower and started her beautifying process. She didn't have to pull out all the stops for dinner—it would look weird if she *did*—but that didn't mean she had to go in fitness wear and without makeup.

Compromise. Jeans. Nice shirt. Decent makeup but not over the top. Blow out your hair.

She wasn't overthinking this. She was just being reasonable.

I'm totally overthinking this.

Despite being out of practice, she was nearly ready well before the time Aaron had given her, but she ran into a problem when she pulled on her jeans.

They wouldn't button.

Becka stared down at the offending button and the gap between it. She knew she'd been putting on weight—that happened in a pregnancy—but she'd mostly stuck to leggings and workout pants, so she hadn't put too much thought into what that meant for her wardrobe. "No jeans for me, apparently." She wiggled out of them and considered her options. It was early enough in the fall that New York hadn't gotten totally frigid, so a dress would have to do— preferably something stretchy.

Except she hadn't packed any dresses, because why would she? The only thing she'd needed when she was bullied into agreeing to these living arrangements were her workout clothes and…that was it. She sat on her bed and dropped her head into her hands. *This is not something to get emotional about. They're just clothes. You can run back to your apartment and…*

But there wasn't time.

She pressed her lips together. Hard. She was overreacting, turning this into something bigger than it should be. Yes, she wanted to dress nice for whatever this date entailed, but there were workarounds that didn't involve dresses or trying to jury-rig her jeans into place. Becka took a steadying breath and went through her clothes again, more slowly this time. She finally settled on a pair of black leggings and a lightweight tunic-length sweater in her favorite color of pink. It was a little more laid-back than she would have preferred, but it would work.

She'd just pulled the sweater over her head and smoothed it down her hips when the front door opened and Aaron called out. "I'm late, I know, I'm sorry. Give me fifteen minutes and we can go." Footsteps sounded past her door, and a few seconds later his shower started.

It was all too easy to picture Aaron in the shower, tilting his head back beneath the spray, letting the water sluice down his body. Becka mentally traced the path the droplets would take. Down his chest, over his cut abs, to his cock...

Down, girl.

Exactly fifteen minutes later, Aaron walked out of his bedroom in a pair of slacks and a button-down that looked indistinguishable from what he wore to work every day. He took one look at her and frowned. "More low-key date, then."

She didn't really want to admit that she couldn't fit into her pants anymore. It wasn't that she thought

Aaron would be an asshole about it—actually, the opposite—but knowing what little she did about him, he'd do something like drag her out shopping for clothes she couldn't afford. And then insist on paying for said clothes, which was a nice gesture, but she couldn't take a wardrobe in addition to everything else he was providing and… Becka studied her thick gray wool socks. "Ah—"

"Say no more." He walked back into his room and reappeared a few minutes later in a pair of dark jeans that hugged his thighs and a cable-knit sweater. When Aaron caught her looking, he ran his hands over the deep green wool. "My mother is a knitter, so for every Christmas, we all get sweaters." He made a face. "I don't wear mine often, though. Mostly when I go home to visit during the winter months."

His mother loved her children so much, she spent hours upon hours knitting them sweaters. It took Becka two tries to speak. "That's really, really nice." She studied the fit of the sweater—perfect—and how the coloring complemented Aaron's features perfectly. "Green is your favorite color, isn't it?"

"Guilty as charged." He chuckled. "Though she tends to lean more toward grays, since they're staple pieces, according to her."

"She's right." The amount of thought and love that went into that gift blew Becka way. She knew good parents existed. Of course they did. They weren't magical unicorns that subsisted on mere myth. But she'd never had cause to come across them. Growing up, most of her friends' parents were divorced, and there was an aura of benign neglect that everyone just sort of dealt with. No harm, no foul. There were always kids in her groups of friends that *did* have the happy life everyone was told to want, with loving parents who didn't forget birthdays and showed up for every extracurricular activity and always had dinner on the table around the same time every night. It just hurt too much to spend time in those households and have her face rubbed in everything she was missing.

She'd had Lucy, though, and Becka thanked her lucky stars every single damn day for that. Who knew where she would have ended up without her strong older sister plotting their course? Their parents being flakes never seemed to affect Lucy. She just adapted and moved on, never letting their dropping the ball get in the way of her goals and aspirations. It wasn't that she didn't care, she just managed her expectations, and after a while, the disappointment and rejection lost its sting.

Becka had never quite mastered that trick.

"Minx, what's wrong? What did I say?"

She shook her head and swallowed past the burning in her throat. "It's nothing. I'm just really glad the baby will have awesome grandparents like your parents."

He narrowed his eyes but seemed to reconsider

pressing her for more information. Aaron's smile was only the slightest bit strained. "What sounds good for dinner?"

"Taco truck tacos."

Now he was really looking at her like she'd grown a second head. "You know, from what I read, pregnancy is supposed to create strange cravings but peanut butter and taco truck tacos…" He shook his head and offered his arm. "I wouldn't dream of standing between you and your desired food."

"Smart man." She gingerly placed her hand in the crook of his elbow, feeling a little ridiculous, but then they were moving and there was no more time for second-guessing. As they stepped out onto the sidewalk, Becka inhaled the crisp autumn air and sighed. "I love this city."

"Are you originally from here?" Aaron studied the street and turned them left.

"Sort of. We were born down in Pennsylvania, but Lucy and I both grew up here. Not in this part of town, obviously, but in the city." It felt good to stretch her legs, good to walk next to Aaron and talk as if the future wasn't hanging in the balance.

Pretend there isn't a pregnancy. Pretend this is a real first date that might have happened if you hadn't run scared.

It sounded good in theory, but Becka didn't make a habit of dating. Dating led to expectations and demands and compromises—usually involving her.

And that was if she even bothered to get past the lackluster text conversations and unsolicited dick pics to actually *go* on a date in the first place.

No, things were easier when everyone's boundaries were clearly defined, and she avoided anyone who might tempt her into changing her internal rules when it came to romance and love.

Until now.

There was no avoiding this.

They dodged a power-walking man on his phone, and she continued. "I know the American dream is supposed to be to raise your kid in a small town with some random field in the distance and a whole lot in the way of overalls, but I think it's bullshit. This city has a culture and life all its own, and I wouldn't be the person I am today if I hadn't spent my formative years here." It struck her that their child would be raised in the city. She pressed her hand to her stomach, staggered by the thought. "I sound preachy, don't I?"

"I'd say passionate." He smiled. "And small-town living isn't for everyone. I might have grown up in one, but I happen to agree with you when it comes to the city."

They walked for several more blocks while Becka chewed on that. She both wanted to know more about Aaron's past and didn't. *This is dumb. Being jealous that he grew up in an unbroken home is the height of stupidity.* She took a deep breath. "Tell me something no one knows about you."

"I watch poker tournaments on TV."

She shot him a look. "You're joking. That's like saying you watch NASCAR or golf."

"I know." He pressed his free hand to his chest. "It's my deepest, darkest secret. I can't get enough of that shit. Playing the odds and being able to see the entire table's hand at once is addicting. Even while I'm telling myself I should turn it off, I get sucked in and can watch for hours."

Becka could see it. His mind obviously ran analytical, and there were few games more analytical than poker. She frowned. "Why not blackjack?"

"Blackjack, you're playing the odds. Poker, you're playing the rest of the table. It's a combination of playing the odds and reading the people you're playing against that I love."

"Remind me never to play strip poker with you," she muttered.

His slow smile made her stomach flip. "Didn't I tell you? That's what we're doing after dinner."

Aaron meant the words to be a joke. He wanted to get to know Becka better, and though there were certain things playing poker with her would tell him, *strip* poker was sure to short-circuit his brain the same as every time they got naked together. But she licked her lips and flashed a grin and suddenly he was looking at the woman he met three months ago instead of the cagey one who'd been living with him for the last week.

Not wanting her to switch back—which always seemed to happen when she let herself think too hard—he tugged her closer and slipped his arm around her waist. "Okay, you convinced me. Strip poker is on the table."

She laughed. "It was never on the table, though that was an excellent try. Very nice line. You get a B minus."

"B minus!" He turned them around the corner down in the direction of a taco truck he knew of. "My delivery was spot-on."

"Mmm, yes." She leaned into him as the wind kicked up. "But you should have saved it until after dinner, once you had me back at your place and were plying me with drinks."

"Sounds underhanded."

"Only if I wasn't planning on getting naked with you already." She tilted her head back to look at him, her lashes seeming impossibly long against the blue of her eyes. "If I let you ply me with drinks, it's already a done deal."

"I'll keep that in mind." He stomped down on his body's reaction to her words and her nearness. It might be sexy as hell to press her against the nearest wall and go for a repeat of their first kiss, but that wasn't the goal. It *couldn't* be the goal. "What did you want to be when you grew up?"

"Travel agent." She made a face. "Right up until I realized most travel agents don't actually travel that much. There's nothing quite as agonizing as planning someone else's trip over and over again while stuck in a crappy office surrounded by four beige walls."

He was inclined to agree, though the travel bug had never bitten Aaron. "You were just down in the Caribbean not too long ago, right?"

She missed a step and shot him a look. "Right. I forgot. You and Roman are friends." If anything, her expression became more agonized. "Allie's going to want a double date before too long—mark my words. And once she decides on something, no one in their right mind gets in her way."

A double date didn't sound like the hell she seemed to consider it, but he chose to keep that opinion to himself. "She's good for Roman. He's been more relaxed since they started dating than I've ever seen him."

"Regular sex will do that to a man," she muttered.

"And to a woman."

She chose not to comment on that, which was just as well. They reached the taco truck and got in line behind a mother and her two kids. Because they were standing so close, Aaron could feel the tension bleeding back into Becka's body until she stood rigid against him. He studied her, trying to figure out what the issue was. The mother? The woman was in her midtwenties, and though she looked tired, she was handling herself well and both her young children were relatively well behaved. They collected their tacos and disappeared down the street, leaving Becka staring after them.

He bided his time, waiting until they'd ordered, collected their food and eaten it at one of the benches not too far from the truck. Only when she crumpled her paper napkin did he sit back and say, "What was it about her that bothered you so much?"

She gave him the courtesy of not pretending she didn't know what he meant. "I don't know if you guessed it, but my family life was hardly idyllic growing up. Lucy was the bright spot, of course. She still is. But my parents were a hot mess from day one, and they only seemed to get worse over time. My mom never would have done something as simple as that." She waved her hand in the direction the mother had gone. "That's sad, right? I'd more or less made my peace with it, but the whole impending-motherhood thing has the ghosts of my past banging on my closet door again." She shook her head. "Sorry. I'm a mess."

"No apologies necessary." He took her hand and laced his fingers with hers. "Were they…"

"Abusive? No, nothing like that." She stared at the people walking past, but she didn't take her hand from his. "They were just selfish assholes who were more wrapped up in themselves and their petty dramas than they could ever be in their children. I don't think they ever planned on staying together, but Lucy was an oops baby and the only thing to do at the time was get married. I don't think my mom ever even wanted kids, but one thing led to another and then she had two."

Not too difficult to read between the lines. Benign neglect was one thing, but it sounded as if Becka had been reminded on a near constant basis that she wasn't wanted, that perhaps her parents' lives would be so much better if she wasn't in them. He didn't tell her he was sorry, didn't offer her sympathy she might mistake for pity. "I'm glad you had Lucy."

"Me, too." She finally looked at him. "She was always there. For nearly every game, for every important event. Even after she went to college, she was never too far or too busy to be there for me. I don't deserve her."

"She loves you." For most people, it was as simple as that. They loved someone, they showed up. At least Becka had *that* influence in her life, even if the people who should have been there for her above all others…weren't. He hesitated, but finally asked, "Have you told her yet?"

She opened her mouth as if she was going to say something, but seemed to change her mind and shook her head. "I'm getting kind of cold. Mind if we go back now?"

The opportunity slipped through his fingers like
water. He couldn't force her to open up to him. The
fact she'd told him even as much as she had was a
small miracle. It was progress, which was a positive
sign. Though it might not be enough, it was a start.

Aaron could be a patient hunter when the situation called for it and the stakes were high enough.
With Becka, they'd never been higher.

CHAPTER NINE

BECKA WAS ON edge the entire trip back to the penthouse. She kept waiting for Aaron's tension to translate to more questions or pressing her for further information, but he just walked next to her with his arm around her. He respected her emotional retreat, if not a physical one.

They walked through the front door and she had to smother her first instinct, which was to flee to her bedroom and barricade herself inside. Even if they'd danced on some of her buttons during their short walk, on the whole it'd been pleasant. More than pleasant. She liked walking down New York City's streets with Aaron's arm wrapped around her waist and the warmth of his body soaking through her sweater. She liked teasing him about his intentions. God, she even liked the reserved way he'd watched her when she spoke about her parents, as if he knew exactly how hard it was for her to confess even those small details and he didn't want to do anything to spook her.

Damn it, I like him.

And because her emotions hamstrung her retreat, she said, "You promised to ply me with drinks." When he opened his mouth, no doubt to quote some statistic about pregnant women and alcohol, she cut in, "I'll take cranberry juice."

"Cranberry juice," he repeated, as if he wasn't sure he'd heard her right.

"Yep. I picked some up yesterday. It's in the back of the fridge."

"I see." He guided her to the bar stool with his hand on the small of her back. She could feel the tiny touch even through her sweater, and it was everything she could do not to arch into his hand like a cat begging for strokes. Aaron pulled out two wineglasses, retrieved the container of cranberry juice, and poured some into both. "You know I can provide whatever you need, minx. You only have to ask."

She pressed her lips together to keep from snapping back. As a result, she sounded only mildly irritated when she said, "It's cranberry juice, not a college fund. It sounded good, so I got some on the way home. Simple as that."

"Home."

She opened her mouth, reconsidered and shut it.

Aaron nodded as if she'd spoken. "I'll try to relax. I just have more than enough money, and it's silly for you to spend your limited funds when I can take care of it." He held up a hand. "That came out wrong."

Do not yell at him. He's trying to be helpful.
High-handed.
Overbearing.
But helpful.

She hissed out a breath. "Aaron, this isn't going to work if you keep reminding me of our unequal roles financially. I've been living here a week. Believe me, I know you make a whole hell of a lot more money than I do. You don't have to whip out your wallet for every little thing to prove it." He narrowed his eyes, but she kept talking, determined not to ruin their evening. "And you know you don't have to skip alcohol on my account. I'm the only one required to be depressingly sober for the next however long. No reason for both of us to suffer."

"It's hardly suffering." He nudged her glass across the counter to her.

If she squinted just right, she might be able to pretend it was wine. Not that Becka *wanted* to drink. The thought of the *scent* of wine was enough to have her wrinkling her nose in distaste. Safe to say she wasn't going to be one of those pregnant ladies who indulged in a glass or two from time to time. That said, it would have been nice to have the option. She took a drink of her cranberry juice instead. "So, about that strip poker."

Aaron choked. "I was joking."

"I know. But it sounds fun, and if we can't drink

together and make bad life choices, we might as well go ahead with the bad life choices anyway."

"You have a strange way of looking at things."

Didn't she know it? "Strange, but compelling." She pushed to her feet and padded over to the coffee table. "Come on. I know you have cards around here somewhere." Becka sank cross-legged onto the floor next to the table and set her wineglass on a coaster. Knowing Aaron, the piece was probably painfully expensive, and she wasn't going to be the one to ruin it.

The baby won't know better, though. Babies destroy shit. It's in their genetic makeup, I'm pretty sure.

She pushed the thought away. No use working so damn hard not to ruin tonight if she was going to let herself do it despite everything. She looked up just as Aaron came back into the room, cards in hand. He sat on the other side of the table and raised his brows. "You sure?"

"You say that like I'm going to lose and you're trying to give me a gracious exit."

He laughed, the deep sound doing funny things to her stomach...and lower. The twinkle in his blue eyes didn't help her control any, either. "Aw, minx, you're cute when you're in denial."

"Denial?" She sank as much fake outrage into the word as she could.

"Denial," he repeated. "You're going to be naked and coming on my mouth inside of five hands."

Her jaw dropped even as she shifted to her knees and pressed her thighs together. As if that would be enough to stop the need his words suddenly had pulsing through her body. "Pride goeth before the fall, mister."

"And sometimes the pride is just reality." He was still smiling, the heat in his eyes barely banked as he dealt out two cards to each of them. "I'm assuming Texas Hold'em works for you."

"My favorite." She studied her cards—a king and an ace—and laid them facedown on the table. "You know, if you're trying to punish me for losing, saying I'm going to be coming on your mouth is hardly the way to go about it."

He leaned forward and propped his elbows on the coffee table. "It's not about you losing."

"Actually—"

"It's about me winning." He stared at her mouth and then lifted his gaze almost reluctantly. "You naked on my couch, your thighs spread wide, and feeling you come while I suck on that pretty little clit of yours? That's winning for me, minx. No question about it."

She couldn't quite draw a full breath. "Sounds like I'm still getting the better end of the bargain."

"Maybe." He shrugged. "But you still lose at cards."

And that was something she'd never willingly do. Becka forced herself to inhale and straighten. "In

that case, when you lose—yes, I said when, not if—
then *you're* going to be naked and *you're* going to
be coming in *my* mouth." The shocked look on his
face was almost as good as actually winning would
be. She pasted an innocent expression on her face.
"Sorry, is there a problem?"

Aaron cleared his throat. "No problem." He nodded at her cards. "You ready?"

"I was born ready, baby." She laughed, her stress
falling away for the first time in months. Right now,
in this moment, nothing outside the two of them and
this game of cards mattered. She could stress about
the future and she and Aaron could go back to warily
circling each other in the morning. Tonight, she was
going to enjoy herself.

And she was going to enjoy the fuck out of Aaron,
too.

Aaron was losing. He didn't know how Becka was
pulling it off, but he was down to his boxer briefs and
cursing himself for not throwing on an extra layer of
clothing before their date. She wore her bra and her
leggings and nothing else, but she had a look in her
eye for this hand that he didn't like.

As if she knew she already had the win in the
bag.

He flipped over the final card and bit back a curse.
His two pair was good, but he didn't think it would
be good enough. Sure as shit, Becka gave him the

most wicked grin and set her cards down faceup.
"Full house."

"Fuck," he breathed.

"I plan on it." She pointed at his hips. "Off." And
then the little minx licked her lips like she could already taste his cock. She rose to her feet, her gaze
never straying from him as Aaron slid his last item
of clothing off. He sat back on the sofa and let her
look her fill, forcing himself to hold perfectly still
as she rounded the coffee table and knelt between
his thighs. Becka gripped his cock and gave him a
teasing stroke. "It's not right that a gorgeous man
like you is just as gorgeous here, too." Her tongue
darted out and flicked the underside of his cock.
"Then again, I'm not about to complain." She shot
him a look. "Keep your eyes open. I want you to
watch me."

No way in hell would he risk missing a moment
of this. Aaron gripped the couch cushions as she
slid his cock between her pretty red-painted lips and
sucked him deep. She released him slowly as if savoring his taste and then smiled. "You're right. This
is what winning feels like." Before he could digest
that statement, she took him deep into her mouth and
throat until her lips met his base. He kept perfectly
still, letting her hold the reins, and she rewarded him
for his restraint with the best fucking blow job of his
life. She teased him, sucking hard and then backing
off until it was everything he could do not to curse.

Finally, Becka raised her head. "Aaron?"

"Mm-hmm?"

"I have a tiny, itty-bitty request."

Considering the way she put it, he didn't know whether to be worried or so turned on he couldn't think straight. "Yeah?"

She ran a single finger the length of his cock. "I love teasing you, but what I really want right now is for you to stop holding back and fuck my mouth the way you're obviously dying to." Her smile had his heart skipping a beat. "I can take it. Promise."

He shouldn't say yes. Their first time might have been rough and deliriously good as a result, but things were different now.

Weren't they?

The answer was written across her face. Becka sat back on her heels and reached around to unsnap her bra. She slid it off and tossed it aside. "I won. Remember?" She wrapped her hand around his cock again. "This is mine until you come in my mouth. Unless you're going back on the bet."

"Not on your life." He pushed to his feet and shifted until he could stand in front of her. Seeing her on her knees, staring up at him with *that* expression in her eyes... He laced his fingers through her hair on either side of her face, pulling it back so he had a clear view and holding her tightly so he had control.

Her eyes slid half-shut. "That's it. That's exactly it." She licked the head of his cock, her gaze on his as she sucked him back into her mouth. It had been hot before. Now it was *scorching*. Heaven was the sight of Becka's red lips around his cock, a challenge in her blue eyes, daring him to do exactly what she'd commanded. *To fuck her mouth*.

He thrust lightly, testing her. But there was no panic on her face, just an eagerness as she took him deeper without effort. As if she loved this as much as he did.

Keeping a tight leash on himself, Aaron started to move. He held her head in place as he picked up his pace until she could only relax and take it. The moment she gave herself over to him completely, his knees threatened to buckle. Becka's surrender was temporary, and he wouldn't have it any other way, but it was a gift all the same. It was *more* a gift because of its fleeting nature.

Her eyes flicked open as if she heard his thoughts, and when they met his, it was too much. He orgasmed with her name on his tongue and, God help him, she drank down every drop of him.

Aaron carefully stepped back and urged her to her feet. "Come to bed with me."

Becka blinked. "What?"

He was rushing, and he didn't give a fuck. They weren't going to leave tonight half-finished, and he wanted her in his bed. Beneath him, over him and later…sleeping next to him.

He wanted it all.

He couldn't tell her as much right now. Even with desire smoothing the stress and worry from her expression, she would panic if he pushed too hard. *Damn it, think.* Aaron kissed her hard, stroking her tongue with his until she swayed against him. "You won, minx. You got your reward. Now come to bed and let me take my consolation prize."

She smiled against his lips. "Sounds like sketchy reasoning."

"Skillful negotiation." Before she could think of an argument around *that*, he scooped her into his arms and started for the bedroom.

Becka relaxed against him with a soft laugh. "Okay, I'll bite—what does your consolation prize entail?"

"Because you asked so nicely, I'm inclined to share." He nudged his bedroom door open and kicked it shut behind him. "I'm going to lay you down on my bed and spend some time enjoying your body. First with my hands. Then with my mouth. And finally with my cock."

This time her laugh bounced through the entire room. "Greedy."

"Mmm, well, I'm feeling generous, so if there's something you'd like to add in along the way, I think we can make it happen."

She looped her arms around his neck and grinned up at him. "Did I say greedy? I meant so, so generous." Her lightly mocking words didn't detract from the happiness lurking in her eyes.

Happiness he'd helped put there.

*This isn't forever. This is just a reprieve in the
midst of a storm.*

He didn't care. He'd take it.

Aaron laid her on the bed and nudged her back
until he could kneel between her thighs. The picture
she painted, from her wild blue hair to her smirking lips to her rocking body... It just flat out did it
for him. *She* just flat out did it for him. He traced
the rose tattoo just inside her hipbone. "Why this?"

"A reminder." She didn't say more, but she didn't
have to. He understood. Roses were gorgeous flow-
ers, but their thorns were legendary. Kind of like
Becka.

He pulled off her pants and underwear and tossed
them aside, leaving her gloriously naked before him.
"Where did you learn to play poker?" He cupped her
pussy, spearing two fingers into her. "You're good."

"Bitter you lost?" She arched her back and dug her
heels into the bed, trying to drive his fingers deeper,
but he used his free hand to pin her hips into place.
Becka fisted the sheets above her head and cursed.
"I learned to play free-roll poker in high school. It's
how I made extra money after I graduated."

He could see it. All she'd have to do was smile and
giggle a little and men would be falling over themselves to "teach" her how to play. Then she'd clean
up and walk away while they were still wondering
what the hell had happened. "Tricky."

"Tactical. Thought you'd approve."

He twisted his wrist and teased her clit with his thumb. "I do. I'm going to demand a rematch, though."

Becka writhed in his grip. She grabbed his wrists and met his gaze. "Stop teasing me and let me come, Aaron. I've been aching for it ever since I had your cock in my mouth." She smiled slowly, as if she knew exactly where his thoughts had gone—to seeing himself disappear between those bright lips. She affected a pleading look. "Please."

"Since you asked so nicely." He moved, dragging her around until he leaned against the headboard and Becka was sprawled between his legs, her head at his feet. Aaron lifted her hips so he could play with her at his leisure. The blow job had barely taken the edge off for him, and the entire night stretched out before them. A promise of as much pleasure as she could handle and more. He parted her and traced her opening with a single finger, not penetrating her. Teasing.

"Aaron."

"That's right, minx. You keep saying my name like that and I might consider giving you my cock again before the end of the night."

CHAPTER TEN

BECKA'S ENTIRE EXISTENCE narrowed down to Aaron's fingers between her thighs. He teased her, doling out pleasure in waves and then drawing her back from the edge at the last possible second. She held out for longer than she could have thought possible, but then the words came. "Please, Aaron, please let me come. I need you, just please, please, *please*."

"There it is." He growled and withdrew his hands.

She barely had the space of a breath to whimper in protest when he wedged his hands beneath her ass and lifted her to his mouth. This time, he didn't mess around. After a thorough kiss that curled her toes so hard they cramped, he sucked her clit into his mouth and worked her ruthlessly. She dug her nails into her palms as she came, his name on her lips in a cry that seemed to shake the walls.

At least, it shook the walls surrounding her heart.

Aaron didn't give her a chance to recover. He set her back on the bed and then he was inside her, stretching her, filling her. The slow slide of his cock and the delicious friction it caused brought her back to herself heartbeat by heartbeat, and she became aware of his murmuring in her ear. "Beautiful minx. You're so fucking perfect and it makes me so damn crazy I can't think past my need for you." He kissed her shoulder, her neck, her jaw and then claimed her mouth.

His need called hers to the fore, and she locked her ankles at the small of his back and laced her fingers through his hair, rising up to meet him even as she met his tongue stroke for stroke. *I can't think past my need for you, either. It scares the shit out of me, and I don't know what to do with that.* He ate the words before she had a chance to give them voice, which was just as well.

She wished she could blame the sex or orgasms for the way her inner compass had failed her so spectacularly, but neither of them were the problem.

It was all Becka.

Aaron hooked a hand beneath one of her thighs and hitched it higher, allowing him deeper. The contact tore a cry from her lips, and the building pleasure reached a crescendo she couldn't have fought off if she tried. She clung to him as his strokes became less measured and he followed her over the edge, kissing her as if his next breath lay in her lungs.

Afterward, they lay tangled together, their jagged breathing a perfect match. Becka raised a shaking hand and pushed her hair back. "If that's the consolation prize, I might consider losing at poker more often."

"Mmm." He kissed the sensitive spot behind her ear. "Stay with me tonight, minx. Let me hold you."

She should say no. Having sex was one thing, but literally sleeping together crossed even more lines. She'd fought so hard to put boundaries in place, and Aaron insisted on trampling over every one he found. This was no different. If they were going to have sex, they should at least sleep in different rooms to keep things from getting messy.

But lethargy stole through her body and she couldn't quite keep her eyes open. "Just tonight."

"Sure." He answered a little too quickly, but she didn't have the energy to call him on it. Aaron shifted away, and a few seconds later, he pulled the blanket up and over them both. He tucked her against the front of his body, and she tensed in response.

Becka didn't cuddle. It muddied those boundaries she'd clung to so hard up to this point. But with his warmth soaking into her body and his slow exhales dancing across the back of her neck, she couldn't force herself to move. As sleep teased her, Aaron pressed his hand to her stomach just below her belly button.

Right where the baby currently grew.

His touch was different there, almost reverent as he explored the slight curve of her stomach that hadn't been there three months ago. He didn't say anything to break the silence, and she couldn't speak past the burning in her throat. *This isn't real. It might feel real, but we aren't a couple expecting our first baby. We're strangers who banged once and now are trying to figure out what the hell we're doing.*

You can't afford to forget that.

It was only for tonight. Tomorrow, she could go back to keeping precious distance between them and ensure Aaron knew that he needed to stop blurring the lines when it came to her and the baby.

Tonight...

Tonight, she just wanted to pretend for a little while. To sink into the feeling of him holding her, to luxuriate in what was probably the best date of her life. After they'd gotten past the uncomfortable topics and relaxed into being with each other, she'd had *fun* with Aaron. And she hadn't had to worry about making a clean getaway because what they had together was already so damn complicated.

Becka closed her eyes and let herself relax. Aaron responded by cuddling her a little closer, and she fell asleep to the even sounds of his breath, feeling safer than she ever had before.

Aaron woke early and put together a light breakfast for Becka while he contemplated his next step. Last night had been good—better than good—but he wanted to take steps forward. To claim ground Becka had previously held back from him. Since both pregnancy and her family seemed to be off-limits, that meant he had to find a different way to connect. He flipped the pancakes, still thinking hard.

"You're spoiling me."

He didn't jump, but it was a near thing. He turned and held out his arm, and Becka slipped under it and nestled against him. She must have noticed his surprise, because she sighed. "Last night was really nice and I'm still riding the nice vibes, so let's not think about it too hard, okay?"

Considering he'd been doing exactly the opposite just now, he didn't like his chances. "You're just drunk on power after your poker win."

"And you think you're a comedian." She leaned forward and eyed the pancakes. "I shouldn't have these before my class. They'll sit heavy on my stomach."

"Wrap them up in tinfoil and add the peanut butter later. It will be cold, but still a nice protein boost after class."

Now she really was looking at him strangely. "Thanks." She stepped away from him and snagged an apple off the counter.

Aaron could actually feel her retreating, and it made him crazy. "What do you do for fun?"

"Drink." She made a face. "Okay, that sounds bad. But happy hours are one of my favorite things. Most bars Allie and I used to hang out in have trivia or bingo or some kind of game while they pour half-priced drinks. The people-watching is superb, and we've already established that I have a competitive streak."

That, they definitely had. "Would it bother you to go for trivia night if you can't drink?"

She seemed to consider that as she took a bite of apple. "I don't know. No? I mean, we'd have to pick a place with good food, but that's easy enough to manage in this city."

We.

The fact she casually looped him into the prospective plans warmed him through. It was just a word, two simple letters that Aaron used every single damn day. But from Becka's lips, it took on a new meaning, a different mentality, making them a unit. She might not be willing to admit as much, but her thinking she was on this road alone had obviously shifted in the last week.

I'm making progress. Slowly, but surely.

He kept his body language as casual as his tone. "You free tonight?"

"Tonight?" She took another bite and chewed slowly. "I could make tonight work."

"Why don't you bring an extra set of clothes and shower at the gym? I can pick you up at…five?"

"Sure…" She grabbed her phone off the counter and backed away. "That sounds nice. Let's do that. 'Bye."

Aaron watched her run from him, but there was none of the frustration he'd grown accustomed to when it came to dealing with Becka. They'd taken a big step last night, whether she wanted to admit it or not. If she needed to retreat a little in response, he'd allow it.

But she wouldn't get far if she tried to bolt for real.

He shook his head and used a spatula to move the pancakes from the pan to a square of tinfoil he'd laid out when he started cooking. A few seconds to cool, and then he carefully rolled them up and grabbed the mini jar of peanut butter he'd picked up yesterday. The jar and the tinfoil wraps went into the lunch bag he'd found in the back of his pantry. He could hear Becka getting dressed in her room, so he poured her a cup of coffee into a thermos. Ten to one, she was about to rush out of the penthouse without worrying about her coffee or her lunch, and he didn't need her going without because he'd spooked her.

He stepped into the hallway and caught her mid-sneak. Her blue eyes went wide. "I'm going to work now."

"I see that." He passed over the bag and the thermos, and her jaw dropped when she took them. Aaron used a single finger to close her mouth and pressed a quick kiss to her lips. "I'll pick you up at five."

"At five," she parroted.

He stepped back so she had a clear escape path.

Becka blinked at him one last time and nearly sprinted to the front door. It slammed behind her, and Aaron chuckled. *That went well.* The woman obviously had been taking care of herself for a very long time. From what he knew of both her and Lucy—and what she had and *hadn't* said—he suspected Becka went without to ensure her big sister didn't feel any unnecessary guilt about their parents being shitty. He respected the hell out of that, even if he wanted to go back in time and wrap her younger self up and protect her from the ugliness she'd lived through.

He couldn't fix her past. He wouldn't even know where to start.

But if he was careful, Aaron could maneuver around her thorns to take care of her in the future.

He cleaned up the kitchen, changed and headed out for work. Becka had him entirely too distracted, but work with his new client went over well enough. The client wanted an audit of their existing computer systems and a comprehensive risk-assessment report. It was a simpler job than he normally handled. Cameron much preferred the clients who wanted cybersecurity set up from the ground up, but this particular job was a referral and not one they could subcontract.

Even though it was something he could put together in his sleep, that didn't mean he could get away without giving it all of his attention. They were paying him for the best, and that was what he needed to provide.

Cameron stood in the lobby, a scowl on his face, as Aaron walked through the door. He stopped short. "What's wrong?"

"Kim Jones walked." Cameron glared at the phone as if it was the sole responsible party. "I told her that cutting corners would undermine the integrity of our work and if she wanted a cheap option, she should have gone with one of our half-assed competitors." He glared harder. "She said that's exactly what she planned to do."

"Fuck," Aaron breathed. "I had her in the bag. Why the hell would you tell her that? We'd already agreed on the package she wanted. Our job is to give it to her—not rip her a new one because we think it's the wrong choice. That's not your call to make, Cameron."

He strode past the lobby and into his office, Cameron hot on his heels. The man's agitation rolled off him in waves. "I told you I can't do this shit, Aaron. They ask me a question and I'm not going to pussy-foot around with the answer. Honesty is supposed to be an asset."

He held on to his patience through sheer force of will. "Yes, but your brand of honesty has also driven off every single person we've hired to help manage the workload. I don't have a problem being the client-facing part of the company, but I can't do both. So, if we can't find suitable admin support, we either need to hire another tech expert or we need someone who can work under me to consult with the clients. I don't care which way we go on things, but something has to give."

"We haven't found someone qualified to fill either of those roles." Cameron frowned. "I can't even find someone qualified to man the damn front desk, and that's a simple enough job."

"You don't think *anyone* is qualified." Finding someone to work with them who could handle the job—and Cameron's surliness—was an impossible task.

"I have exacting standards."

"More like…" He caught a strange expression on Cameron's face. "What?"

"What the hell is this?" Cameron stalked over and snatched the top baby book off the pile Aaron had placed on the far side of his desk when the box showed up. He flipped through it, the book looking tiny in his massive hands. "You planning on procreating?"

He hadn't planned on sharing the information like this—or at all until strictly necessary. Aaron rubbed a hand over his face. "A girl I was, ah, seeing. She's pregnant."

"It's yours?"

He gritted his teeth. "It's mine." Becka said it was, and he had no reason to doubt her. Going down that path lay madness and ensured that any relationship blossoming between them would be dead and gone.

"Huh." Cameron set the book down. "Congrats, then, I guess. Or condolences?" He narrowed his eyes. "Which way do we fall on this?"

"I don't know yet." It was nothing more than the truth. The baby was unplanned and even with the surprise and shock wearing off, he had mixed feelings. He'd never planned on having a child with someone he wasn't married to. The whole concept was old-fashioned and he should just set it aside, but it bothered him. Things with Becka weren't buttoned up—and showed no signs of *being* buttoned up any time in the foreseeable future. They were making progress, but it was slow going. "We're keeping it, and that's enough for now."

"Guess so." Cameron scrubbed a hand over his shaved head. "Look, I'm sorry about Kim Jones. I didn't know that offering my opinion would make her freak the fuck out like that. And then she was yelling and I was yelling and..." He shrugged. "I said we'll hire someone and we will. I'll set up another round of interviews this week."

He opened his mouth, but there was no point of going round and round with this shit. He'd known who Cameron was when he went into business with the man. Aaron had made his peace with being client-facing, but he hadn't expected it to chafe quite so much. If they could get a good third in here, it would smooth over a lot of their random little issues. It just had to be someone Cameron wouldn't scare off inside of a week.

But his partner had said he'd handle it, and so he had to let it go. "Appreciate it."

"Now, get to work. Sounds like you have more mouths to feed in the near future." He grinned. "Any chance it's twins?"

"Oh, fuck right off, Cameron." He shook his head and sat behind his desk. There was plenty of work to be done, and he had to get it finished in time to pick Becka up after work. No matter what bullshit arose during the day, he wasn't going to let anything endanger another date with her.

Not when he was actually starting to make progress.

CHAPTER ELEVEN

BECKA RAN BACK to her apartment on her lunch break to grab more clothes. She stood in the middle of the living room and wrinkled her nose. Living surrounded by Aaron's understated luxury made it hard to see this place as anything other than the shithole he'd labeled it. It was home, sure… Or at least it had been. It didn't feel like much right now except for a letdown. She gave herself a shake and headed into her room to grab a bag to throw some dresses into. At some point soon she'd have to face the reality of maternity clothing, but she wasn't ready to deal with it yet.

Great job, Becka. Just avoid anything and everything related to the baby until you absolutely have to face it. That sure won't blow up in your face.

Impossible to ignore the little voice when it spoke hard-core reason at her. She'd asked Aaron for time before they got down to the nitty-gritty about baby stuff, and he'd mostly respected that in the few days since. Her reprieve wouldn't last, and she could hardly blame him for that. They were about to be responsible for another *person*, and flying by the seat of her pants might have gotten her this far in life, but his regimented scheduling and research-based personality were probably better suited for parenting than hers was.

It seemed like *everyone* was better suited to be a parent than she was, and yet look how things had turned out.

As if summoned by her thoughts, her phone rang. Becka knew who it was even before her sister's name scrolled across the screen. Lucy had been calling every couple of days for the last month, and Becka could tell her excuses for not picking up were starting to wear thin.

She had to tell Lucy the truth sooner or later. Before she could talk herself out of it, she answered. "Hey, Lucy."

"Becka! I thought for sure I'd get your voicemail again."

"I know, I've been terrible. I'm sorry." Her treacherous hormones threatened to close her throat, thickening her voice.

Lucy picked up on it. Of course she did. She'd spent too long taking care of Becka not to read her easily. "What's going on? And don't tell me that it's nothing. We both know you don't disappear like this unless you're avoiding telling me something." She lowered her voice. "Is this because of Gideon? I thought you were okay with it—"

Oh no. She should have known that her sister would jump to *that* conclusion. "No. Hell no. I am legit happy for you. I promise." There was no getting out of the truth now. Becka took a deep breath. "I'm… I'm pregnant."

"*What?*" Lucy rushed on before she could respond—not that she had a response. "Becka, if this is your idea of a joke, it's not funny."

Her stomach dropped and she closed her eyes. Disbelief in her sister's tone, yes, but also disappointment. The very reaction she'd feared. "No one's joking. You're going to be an aunt in roughly six months."

"I… Wow…" Lucy cleared her throat. "Sorry, you just caught me by surprise. I didn't realize… No, but you would have told me if you were seeing someone."

Her sister didn't mean anything by it, but every word was a knife to Becka's heart. A confirmation of what she'd always known to be the truth. She was far more like her wayward mother than she'd ever been like her responsible older sister.

Lucy finally managed to get her reaction under control. "How are you doing? Are you okay?"

Even now, even when she was obviously caught off-guard and disappointed, she still managed to set it aside and worry about Becka. "I'm fine. He's a good guy." She wasn't willing to shock Lucy further by telling her the father was Aaron. "He's pushy and determined to research this thing to death and he's constantly on my ass about making me eat, but he wants to be in the baby's life."

"It sounds like you care about him."

She pushed to her feet, but there was nowhere to run with the phone against her ear. Becka bit down on her impulse to yell that it was a one night stand and she couldn't possibly care about him because she barely knew him. It wasn't the truth. Not anymore. She swallowed hard. "I don't know how I feel about anything anymore."

"Relationships aren't always like it was with them." No need for her to ask who Lucy meant. Their parents. "Gideon and I might argue sometimes, but he's my rock. It might be nice if you had someone to be your rock, too."

"Yeah. Maybe." She glanced at the faded digital clock over her oven. "Hey, Lucy, I've got to go if I'm going to make my next appointment. Talk to you later?"

"I'm here for you, Becka. No matter what. You know you can call me anytime, right? For anything."

"I know." Damn it, now she really was going to cry. "Love you."

"Love you, too."

She hung up and stared at her phone. That had gone... *Well* wasn't the right word. Even with Lucy offering unconditional support, she couldn't shake the fact that her DNA had outed once and for all, realizing both their worst fears.

That Becka was just their mother 2.0.

She headed for her first personal training appointment for the day, and then there was no more time for worrying about her worst fears coming true. Time went too fast, and it felt like seconds later that she was in the locker room and jumping in the shower. She pulled on a sheath dress in a brilliant pink and orange pattern that hid her growing baby bump and slipped into simple flats and a funky cropped jacket. Becka pulled her hair back into a deceptively simple braid and threw some mascara and lipstick on.

Feeling like herself for the first time in a long time, she hurried out of the locker room just as her phone dinged. She smiled when she saw Aaron's text. *I'm out front.*

Punctual as always.

She hefted her bag more firmly on her shoulder and strode out the doors. *It will be okay. Just because I'm off center and scared all over again doesn't mean I am going to ruin tonight.*

I refuse to ruin tonight.

Aaron had his hands in his pockets and wore a well-fitting black suit with a dove-gray button-down underneath. His smile dimmed when he caught sight of her bag. "Let me carry that."

"Honey, I can bench 150 and I have arms to rival

Michelle Obama. I got it." She caught herself and sighed. "But if you're going to turn into a human storm cloud, you can take it."

"Being chivalrous is not being a human storm cloud." He took the bag easily and offered her his free arm.

No point in arguing about the damn bag further. Truth be told, her back was bothering her a little, but she'd sew her lips shut before she admitted as much to Aaron. He'd probably load her into a cab and rush her to the hospital or something in response. "And here I thought chivalry was dead."

"A nasty rumor. Nothing more."

She fell into step beside him. "You know, you're funnier than I thought when we first met. At the wedding, it was all intensity and come-fuck-me eyes, and here you are, cracking sly jokes at the drop of a hat."

"I don't know how you remember the wedding, but you didn't leave much room for jokes." He slid his arm around her waist the same way he had on the walk to the taco truck. It pressed the entire sides of their bodies together and sparked desire through her in response. Aaron, damn him, knew it.

"I was in a bad way, and you had exactly what I needed." She hadn't meant to say it aloud, to offer up even that much information, but her earlier conversation with Lucy still had her off her game. The words saturated the air between them and there was no taking them back.

Aaron kept quiet for half a block. Finally, almost reluctantly, he said, "I imagine weddings aren't your favorite thing, let alone your sister's wedding."

"I'm happy for her." The response was so automatic, it almost felt real. He shot her a look and she cursed. "Okay, fine, I was sick to my stomach from the time she told me Gideon proposed until they got in that limo and drove away. Rationally, I know that not every marriage goes down in flames, but it's hard when my heart and brain get to battling. She was engaged to a douchebag before Gideon, and he did a number on her. I *know* Gideon would rather set himself on fire than do anything to hurt her, but that doesn't stop me from worrying. What if something happens to him? She'll never recover."

"There are no guarantees in life."

Becka rolled her eyes, even though her amusement had died a terrible death at the mention of her sister's wedding. But then, she'd been in a funk all day. "Thanks for that fortune cookie–pat answer. I know that. Of course I know that. But there are enough painful moments in life without inviting the bastard to kick you in the teeth at the first available opportunity. Even you have to admit that."

He pulled her closer without missing a step. "Life is hard. It's full of all the bad stuff, sure. But it's full of good stuff, too. The difference is that sometimes you have to take a leap of faith and grab onto the good stuff with both hands. Avoiding anything that might cause you pain down the road..." He hesitated. "That's no way to live, minx."

She wanted to believe him. She wanted to so badly, she could taste the need like on the back of her tongue. It would be the simplest thing in the world to let go, to step into Aaron and let go of all her fears.

To grab onto a possible future with them together with both hands and hold it close until it became reality.

The strength of the desire startled her. Terrified her. She opened her mouth to shut down this line of conversation, but couldn't make herself do it. "Yeah, you're probably right."

Aaron had to fight to put aside their conversation as they walked into the bar. It looked like millions of other bars across the city, from the faded wood tables to the blinking neon lights of various beer signs to the half a dozen televisions positioned strategically around the room. But the floors weren't sticky and the place smelled pleasantly of something he couldn't quite place.

Becka led the way to a table near the bar where trivia was being set up. She took a paper to fill out and sat down before he could pull out her chair. Aaron repressed a sigh and took the seat diagonal from her. He picked up the menu and flipped through it. Instead of the normal bar food he expected, it was all Asian fusion. "Huh."

"The sushi is great, and so is anything stir-fry." She spoke without looking up. "There are also wings on the last page."

Strange place. He eyed the paper she was filling out. "What's our team name?"

"Cunning Linguists."

He barked out a laugh. "Clever."

"I aim to please." She smiled at the waiter that walked up. "Can I get cranberry juice and a starter of the egg rolls?"

"Sure thing." He looked expectantly at Aaron. "And for you?"

What he really wanted was a beer, but he'd been serious about not drinking in front of her for the time being, so he ordered an iced tea. "And add the wontons to the starters." He'd seen Becka eat, and he had no illusions about getting any of those egg rolls for himself.

Becka waited for the man to leave the table before sitting back to pin Aaron with a look. "I'm surprised you didn't decide to educate me on how unhealthy egg rolls are, being fried and all."

He didn't bother to hide his grin. "I figure you might dump that glass of water over my head if I did."

"Smart man."

"I have my moments." He snagged the paper to look over the categories. "Plus, you're a personal trainer. You eat better than I do most of the time.

If you want egg rolls for a starter, you can have egg rolls."

"Wow. Thanks for permission."

Aaron growled. "Don't make this into a fight, minx."

"I'm not. You—" She snapped her mouth closed and looked a little sheepish. "I might be making it into a fight. Sorry. I'm a little on edge."

Whether it was hormones or their earlier conversation made no difference. He was smart enough not to agree with her. Instead Aaron pointed at the trivia paper. "Dungeons and Dragons is one of the categories."

"Is it?" She blinked deceptively innocent eyes at him. "Did I fail to mention this was an ultimate geek trivia night?"

"Must have slipped your mind," he muttered. He glanced over the categories again. The tech gadget one he had a chance at. He was relatively well versed in Harry Potter just by virtue of living in current times and having both internet and cable. The rest might as well have been Greek for all he had a chance of deciphering it. "You like this stuff?"

"I've been known to run a campaign or two." She caught his look and laughed. "I like playing against type. Besides, it's fun if you have a good group." Something like a shadow flickered over her face, and he didn't have to ask to know that there were times when she hadn't had a good group. Knowing what little he did of geek culture and how a portion of the population treated women, he could guess how that had fallen out. Before he could ask, Becka gave him a bright smile. "Stick with me, young padawan. I'll show you the ropes."

The woman running the game stood up and introduced herself, and then they were off to the races. Despite being the weak link for their duo in this realm, Aaron found himself drawn into Becka's enthusiasm and competitive spirit. She really *did* know a whole hell of a lot in this subset of trivia, and they ended up taking second place in the competition.

After paying for their tab, he slung an arm around her waist and they headed out. She brandished their second-place sticker. "Next time, we're going for gold. You just need to brush up on about ten years' worth of knowledge in a week."

"Consider it done."

She laughed. "You took being upstaged rather well, all things considered. Most guys would have bitched and stomped out of there when the elves questions came up."

"Just because I was outmatched doesn't mean I didn't enjoy myself." He pressed a casual kiss to the top of her head. "Besides, you're into it. I had fun."

"Me, too." She sounded almost surprised by that fact. "Aaron."

"Yeah?"

"I like you."

From the way she braced as if expecting a blow, the words had taken a lot of courage to say. He stepped out of foot traffic. Aaron turned her to face him and tipped her chin up so she couldn't hide from his gaze. "I like you, too."

She worried her bottom lip. "You're right, you know. We have to talk about the baby."

This change of tone should have spelled victory for him, but he found himself reluctant to push her. He kissed her forehead and then her lips. "We can talk when you're ready—really ready."

"What if I'm never ready?" She laughed softly. "Because at this point, I don't know what I'm doing, and even thinking about it is enough to have me borderline panicking."

"You're not alone, minx. You're not facing this by yourself. I'll be there every step of the way. Never doubt that."

She smiled against his mouth. "I don't."

He didn't believe her for a second, but Aaron let it go. He was making progress, and that was all that mattered. A week of fragile peace couldn't combat an entire lifetime of living a certain way. Becka might not trust him completely, but he'd do whatever it took to win both her trust and her willingness to be in his life.

If the last few days had done anything, they'd confirmed something for him.

He didn't just want to be in the baby's life.
He wanted to be in *Becka's*.
He wanted to be *with* Becka.

CHAPTER TWELVE

BECKA LOOKED UP as the door opened and Aaron walked in. He missed a step but recovered almost immediately. "I didn't realize you'd be home before me today."

"My last appointment canceled. He's got food poisoning." She flipped through the channels for the twelfth time in the last hour. Nothing held her attention, and she'd already circled through the kitchen to stare blankly into the fridge four times before shutting it and returning to the couch. Becka didn't do well with a lack of activity, and today was no exception. She had energy to burn off and she didn't know what to do with herself. She sat up and eyed Aaron. "You in a hurry?"

He shrugged out of his jacket and hung it in the closet just inside the door. "I have some work I brought home, but it just needs to be done sometime tonight. Why? You have something in mind?"

"I do." She bounced off the couch and came

around to press a quick kiss to his lips. "Let's take a spin class."

Aaron stopped short. "That did not go where I was expecting."

"You thought I meant sex." She laughed and started down the hall. "We can bang it out later. Riding your cock is great cardio, but I didn't have a spin class today and I'm going to drive us both crazy if I don't do something about it." She pulled out her phone and paged through the app she had that gave her all the nearby gyms' schedules. It didn't take long to find one that would fit the bill.

Becka turned, but Aaron hadn't moved from his spot by the door. She stopped short and cursed herself for being an idiot. It took effort to keep her shoulders square and the disappointment from her voice. "You don't have to go, Aaron. It's okay. I just got excited."

He gave himself a shake. "No, I want to. You surprised me is all." He crossed the distance between them in two large steps and kissed her hard enough that her back hit the wall. When he finally raised his head, both their breathing had turned harsh. Aaron smiled. "I've been curious about your particular brand of spin since Roman told me about it a while back." He paused. "I'm happy you're sharing this with me, minx."

He made it sound like a much bigger deal than it should be but...

No, that wasn't fair. It *was* a big deal. She'd made plans for both of them without stopping to think about it, and she'd been disappointed when she thought he didn't want to go. Little by little, Aaron had eased into her life until she *wanted* to share parts of herself with him. Her classes and her personal training were two things important to her that she never shared with the guys she dated. She'd never *wanted* to share them.

Since she didn't know what to say to any of it, she gave him a half smile and ducked into her room to change. Fifteen minutes later, they were on their way. The gym was a trendy little boutique workout place that offered a small selection of classes, similar to Transcend, but they were open to both men and women. Becka had never been to this branch before, but she'd attended a few classes at one of the locations closer to her apartment.

After they got checked in and put on their spin shoes, she shot Aaron a look. "Uh… I know you work out, but have you ever taken spin before?" *Probably should have asked that before springing this on him.*

"Yeah, though not for a while. I prefer lifting weights and the elliptical."

She made a face before she caught herself. "Just, ah…" She put an extra dose of brightness into her tone. "It'll be fun!"

"What did you sign me up for?"

Instead of answering, she headed into the room and chose a bike in the middle row, slightly off to the side. Aaron took the one next to her and adjusted his seat without hesitating. Maybe it wouldn't be *that* bad.

As the class started, she lost herself to the bumping beat of the music and the rhythmic pedaling. The instructor didn't have as many bike pushups in his routine as Becka did, which was just as well, but he had a few fun moves she made a mental note to incorporate at some point in the future.

The hour passed in the blink of an eye, and she belatedly remembered to check on Aaron as the slow song that signaled time to stretch came on. He was just as soaked in sweat as she was, and the look he gave her when she turned to him singed her right down to her core. Becka froze. "Uh, so that was fun."

"Fun." He didn't sound totally out of breath, but he shook his head and unlocked his shoes from his bike. "I don't think that word means what you think it means."

She burst out laughing, drawing looks from the people around them. Well, at least the class was over. Becka followed him out of the room, her gaze lingering on the way his sweaty shirt clung to this muscled back. She knew working out was an aphrodisiac, of course, but she'd never done it *with* someone before. Not like this.

Suddenly, all those couples' workout videos on the internet made sense.

She grabbed Aaron's arm and towed him around the corner and down the hall, searching the signs on the doors. There were a handful of gender-neutral bathrooms and… *There.* If this gym was anything like hers, no one actually used the showers. Even if they did, there were two. She shoved Aaron into the room, cast a quick look behind them to make sure no one was paying attention and stepped in and closed the door behind her.

He was on her the second she locked the door. Aaron grabbed her hips hard enough that she had to catch herself on the door and shoved her shorts down her legs. Half a second later, his cock was there, filling her in one rough move. Her fingers scrambled over the smooth wood of the door, trying to find purchase. "Oh God."

"This is what you wanted." He pulled out for a second, looped an arm around her waist and carried her to the sink. She braced her hands on the porcelain and met his gaze in the mirror. He smoothed a hand up her back. "This is what you wanted," Aaron repeated. This time it sounded more like a question.

"Yes." He sank into her again, and she shoved back against him, taking his cock deeper yet. "Hard. Fast. Now."

He gripped her shoulder with one hand and her hip with the other and drove into her. Hard. Fast. Exactly what she needed. His expression was like a man possessed, just as out of control as Becka felt. It had never been like this, desperation clawing through her to get closer, to have more of him touching more of her. He must have felt it, too, because Aaron withdrew and lifted her onto the sink. He yanked her shorts the rest of the way off and spread her thighs wide. "Hang on to me."

She was already moving, hooking the back of his neck and dragging him down to claim his mouth as he started fucking her again. The new angle hit that sensitive spot inside her with every stroke, winding her tighter and tighter until she came with a muffled cry. He followed her seconds later, grinding hard into her as he orgasmed.

Aaron laughed softly. "I think I can get onboard with this spin thing."

"Yeah... Me, too." She shivered as his cock twitched inside her. "But we can never come back to this gym again—ever." She wasn't shy, but they'd just crossed a line, and she wasn't going to be able to look anyone in the face as they left.

"You hungry?" He pumped slightly, drawing a gasp from her lips.

She blinked. "Is that a euphemism?"

"I know a place that makes some mean peanut butter and jelly wings." He was still moving inside her, little thrusts that had her body going molten all over again. "We could pick up takeout and go home to enjoy them properly."

Becka moaned and shoved him away. "Stop that or we're going to keep fucking in this bathroom until someone comes banging on the door."

"Doesn't sound so bad." His gaze dropped to her pussy. "You're looking needy, minx. I've got just the thing."

The man went from talking about takeout to looking like he wouldn't mind giving her enough orgasms to bring down the rage of the entire staff of this gym on them. She hopped off the sink and pulled her shorts back on. "If you wanted to keep playing with me, you shouldn't have mentioned peanut butter and jelly wings."

Aaron kissed her and cupped her pussy through the thin fabric of her shorts. He circled her clit with his thumb. "I'm going to take care of you tonight." He slipped his hand into her shorts and fingered her. "Fuck, Becka, I'd think they pumped something into the air of that room if I didn't know it was all you. You make me so goddamn crazy for you." He kissed her again. "Come for me, minx. One more time to tide me over until after dinner."

Oh God. She spread her legs to give him better access even though she knew they were running out of time before someone came knocking on the door. Maybe it was that lack of time that made this whole thing hotter. It didn't matter. All that mattered was

Aaron's growl in her ear and his fingers working her pussy. He pushed two fingers into her and went back to circling her clit with his thumb. She was already on a hair trigger from coming earlier, and when he bit her neck lightly, it threw her headlong into another orgasm. He brought her down so sweetly, kissing her as he gentled his touch and finally slipped his hand out of her shorts.

Aaron readjusted her clothing and washed his hands. He pressed a quick kiss to her lips. "Let's get you those wings."

"Yeah," Becka said, more than a little dazed. "Can't forget about the wings."

"Come here." Aaron reached out to pull Becka back beneath the spray of the dual showerheads he had set up in his bathroom. They'd made it back to his penthouse in record time—with a quick stop at the wing place on the way to pick up their food—and he'd dragged her into the shower with him nearly the second they walked through the door.

She smacked his hand and bared her teeth in what was almost a grin. "Food, Livingston. Not only did we do spin class and then walk home, but you blew my mind seven ways to Sunday in the bathroom earlier. I need calories and, before you say anything, *not* the kind of calories that come from your cock." She paused in the gap leading out of the walk-in shower and surveyed him. "Though it's a mighty fine cock and I plan to use and abuse it later."

He barked out a laugh. "Noted. Go get started on your calories. I'm right behind you."

"Better enjoy the view then." She gave a little shake of her ass and hell if he didn't enjoy the view before she wrapped a towel around herself and walked out of the bathroom.

He wasted no time finishing scrubbing down and followed suit. He found her in the living room, setting up the wings on the coffee table. Aaron ducked into the kitchen to grab them glasses of water and an extra glass of cranberry juice for her, and then he joined her on the couch.

It was only then that he noticed what she was wearing.

Becka sat cross-legged, her petite body swallowed up by one of his college T-shirts. The thing was so old, it was one of the softest he owned, and the image on the front had faded away to almost nothing. Rationally, he understood why she gravitated to the shirt, but his gut said it marked her as *his*. That she was settling in for the long haul and this was a fucking relationship, not two people who happened to live together and would have a baby together in the relatively near future.

Whether her choice in clothing said that to her was another story.

She tasted the jalapeño jelly dip and made a little

moaning sound. "Oh, damn. This was such a good call."

"Glad it's hitting the spot." To keep himself from staring at her as she ate, he grabbed the remote and flicked through the channels until he landed on something that halfway caught his interest. It was an old movie, and he instantly recognized the blonde waltzing her way across the screen.

Becka obviously did, too, because she nodded. "*Gentlemen Prefer Blondes.* Good choice."

Even if he hadn't planned on keeping it there, he would have set the remote down at her interest. "I take it you like it?"

"What's not to like? Lady friendships, a smoking-hot private investigator and some killer songs thrown in for spice." She cut one of the peanut butter wings in two and dipped it into the jelly. "It's a classic, and I used to say I was Dorothy to Allie's Lorelei." She made a face. "Minus all the gold-digging stuff. That sort of thing leads to nothing but trouble."

Aaron draped his arm over the back of the couch. "You like old movies, play D&D and are a jock in your own right." He grinned. "You like to keep people guessing."

"Maybe people." She sipped her drink. "Maybe just you. Most people try to slap a label on me the second they meet me, but they never bother to dig deeper. Their loss, I guess. *My* people get me, and they don't expect me to change so they can shove me into a neat little box." She shrugged.

He should keep his damn mouth shut, but Aaron was sick of fucking around. He wanted Becka—in his bed and in his life permanently. Even if he slow-played this thing into the ground, he couldn't sit on his hands indefinitely. It wasn't fair to either of them. "I could be one of your people if you'll let me get close enough, minx."

"I know." She sighed. "Look, this is weird for me, too. I like you. It freaks me out, which is normally the part where I ghost whatever dude I'm seeing, but that's obviously not an option in our case, because where the hell am I going to run when I have to come track you down in about six months?"

"You want this to stop because it's not doing it for you, that's one thing." He watched her closely, took in the tension in her shoulders and the way she stared pointedly at her food. *Too damn bad, Becka. This is going to get said.* "But to try to run from me because you care too much? Fuck that."

"Try?"

"You heard me. I care about your contrary ass, and you care about me right back. I'm not pushing you right now, but if you bolt, I'm going to track your ass down and have a conversation like adults."

She finally twisted to face him, blue eyes flashing. "You call this not pushing?"

"That's exactly what I call this." He clenched his

jaw and worked to modulate his tone. "We have time. You need more, then you have it. But I'm not going anywhere. I'm not your commitment-phobic dad and you're sure as fuck not your flighty-ass mom. Stop using them as an excuse to keep me from getting close to you."

"You were pretty damn close to me an hour ago."

His body flashed hot at the memory, but he wasn't about to let her distract him with sex right now. "Admit that you care about me."

She threw up her hands. "Fine, asshole. I admit it. I care about you, and that scares the shit out of me in a way I'm not prepared to deal with."

"Was that so hard?"

"Yes!" She turned back to face the TV and crossed her arms over her chest.

"It spooks me, too, minx." He pressed a soft kiss to her temple. "You're not alone. Remember that when the panic gets too bad."

"I'm trying," she whispered.

CHAPTER THIRTEEN

BECKA DIDN'T MEAN to fall asleep. But the wings filling her belly and Aaron's warm thigh under her head combined with the throw blanket he'd tucked around her as they watched the movie was too compelling to resist. Her blinks became longer and longer, and when Aaron started absently running his fingers through her hair, she was lost.

Or maybe she'd been found.

She didn't know. The only thing she was sure of was that at some point, Aaron carried her into his bedroom and tucked them both into bed. He curled his body around the back of hers, as if he could shield her from the worst the world had to offer by his sheer presence alone.

Becka wasn't thinking about comfort, though. Not with her wearing only his shirt and his cock pressed against her ass. She shifted back, rubbing against him, and was rewarded by his hand spasming on her stomach. He pulled her closer, snuggling against her, and inched the shirt up, baring her from the waist down. They moved slowly, as if he was as hesitant as she to break the strange half awake, half asleep sensation of their movements.

She reached behind her and gripped the back of his neck as he pressed an openmouthed kiss to the top of her spine. Instead of touching her where she ached for him, Aaron shifted, bringing one arm under her and cupping her breasts with both hands. He squeezed gently and then pulsed his hands, creating the smallest amount of friction between his palms and her nipples. She responded by rolling her hips harder against him.

She took one of his wrists and guided his hand between her thighs. He cupped her pussy as if assuring himself that she was wet and wanting and *his*. Aaron touched her in a way she'd never experienced before. It wasn't just a touch with him.

It was a claiming.

He idly dipped a single finger into her and spread her wetness up and over her clit. The gentle sensation only heightened her desire, but she didn't want to break the spell. Not yet. She released his neck to reach back and dip her hand into his boxer briefs to stroke his cock.

"You're supposed to be asleep," he growled against her neck.

She grinned into the darkness of the room. *He*

broke first. "I am asleep." She gave his cock another pump. "So, so asleep."

"Don't think your story checks out, minx."

"You caught me." She twisted in his arms to face him and hitched her leg over his hip. A quick move shoved his boxer briefs below his hips, and she guided his cock into her. "I'm awake."

"Now the truth comes out." He rolled onto his back, taking her with him.

Instead of breaking the heightened intensity, being face-to-face with Aaron only made the whole encounter sexier. Becka kissed him as she moved over him slowly. Leisurely. Each stroke strengthened the feeling of being in a dream where nothing could touch them. Desire took hold, and she straightened to get a better angle, chasing her own pleasure.

"Ah, ah. Not yet, minx." He lifted her off his cock and up to straddle his head.

She grabbed the headboard to hold steady. Between her thighs, his face was bathed in shadows. He could have been anyone… But, no. The thought fled as soon as it rose, chased away by the slow glide of his tongue over her pussy. This was Aaron.

It will always be Aaron.

He licked and sucked at her, using his hands on her thighs to urge her to ride his mouth. Becka let the last of her worries dissolve beneath his touch. She closed her eyes and gave herself over to the pleasure building with every deep exhale that ghosted against the most private part of her.

Her orgasm rolled over her slowly, dragging her deeper than she'd ever gone before. She shuddered and slumped against the headboard, blinking into the darkness. *Ruinous. That's what Aaron Livingston is. Fucking ruinous.* She couldn't bring herself to care.

He pulled her down to spoon again and hitched her leg over his thigh so he could guide his cock into her. He stroked her clit with each slow thrust, murmuring in her ear the entire time. "I can't get enough of you, minx. I could live for another sixty years and I'd still never get enough of you." His breath hitched against her ear. "Let me keep you, Becka. Let me keep both of you."

She opened her mouth to say... She wasn't sure what. But he ground hard against her and circled her clit once, twice, a third time, and the only thing she verbalized was a breathless shriek as she came again.

Aaron flipped her onto her stomach and lifted her hips to drive into her. He moved like a man possessed, the dreamlike feeling of their encounter up to this point fading away in the feel of his cock filling her completely as he chased his own pleasure.

As he marked her as his own.

The next month passed in a blur of peaceful contentedness. Aaron came home every day to Becka. She shared his bed and gave him precious tidbits about herself and her past as they settled into what could be their life together. But she still held back part of herself, and the closer they got, the more that denied bit made him crazy. He'd promised her time, though. He'd honor it, damn it.

She met him at the door one night, looking nervous. She wore a pair of brightly colored leggings and one of the slouchy shirts she'd become fond of since moving in with him, and she was all but wringing her hands.

Aaron dropped his briefcase and carefully shut the door. "Is everything okay? Is it the baby?"

"What?" She shook her head and gave a rueful smile. "Sorry, I shouldn't have ambushed you at the door with this. I, ah…" She stared hard at the wood floor beneath their feet. "I have a doctor's appointment tomorrow. I meant to mention it to you last week, but you kind of distracted me with ice cream and that thing you do with your tongue."

Despite her obvious nerves, he grinned. "I seem to remember you liking that thing I do with my tongue."

"I do." She twisted a lock of blue hair around her finger. "I know it's last minute and I completely understand if you can't come. It's at one at a clinic close to my apartment."

He stepped closer and framed her face with his hands, guiding her to meet his gaze. "Of course I'll be there. I have a meeting, but I can reschedule. One of the perks of being the boss." She looked so unsure that he smoothed his thumbs over her cheekbones. "Unless you don't want me to go?" Aaron wanted to be in that room with her more than anything, especially since he'd missed her appointment last month. He'd only known about it because Becka mentioned it in passing, giving him a rundown as if it hadn't occurred to her to bring him and his presence there was no big deal.

It had stung. Fuck yes, it'd stung.

But ultimately having him there was her choice. If he'd learned anything in his time with Becka, it was that he couldn't badger his way into *anything* when it came to her. She'd just dig in her heels and set her jaw in that way that would be adorable if it didn't signal the start of a knock-down, drag-out fight.

She pressed her lips together. "I'd like you to be there. It just feels like a big step."

He laughed. He couldn't help it. "I hate to be the one to break it to you, minx, but having a baby is about as big a step as two people can take. We're already there."

"Correction—we'll be there in just over five months."

He bit back a sharp response to that. Her insistence at holding off talking about anything resembling the future was the one black spot on their time together. "I'll be at the appointment. Do you want me to pick you up or meet you there?"

"Might as well meet me there." She huffed out a breath. "This is silly, right? I shouldn't be so stressed out over a doctor's appointment."

It *was* a big deal. This would be the appointment with the ultrasound, the halfway point through the pregnancy. It was also the appointment when they'd get a good idea if the baby was progressing as it should—or if there were glaring problems.

Aaron pulled her into his arms and hugged her tightly. "No matter what happens, I'm there." Maybe if he said it enough times, she'd actually start to believe him. Maybe. He didn't know what the right words were. Hell, he didn't seem to *have* right words when it came to Becka. He wasn't walking on eggshells, but he was aware that one wrong step might fracture the careful peace they'd formed around themselves.

Not for the first time, it registered that things couldn't last as they stood now.

But as he looked down into her worried expression, he couldn't bring himself to pull the trigger. Not yet. Tomorrow after the doctor's appointment would be more than soon enough. They could have tonight. The real world—the future—had waited this long. It could wait another eighteen hours or so.

Aaron smoothed back her hair. "Are you hungry?"

She gave him a half smile. "Is that a trick question?"

If the baby books he'd read had taught him anything, it was that every pregnancy was different. Becka didn't seem to be suffering many of the ill effects that often showed up, but her appetite was unrelenting. It amused him even as he worried that she wasn't getting enough. With her job, she burned a significant number of calories every day, and even with her near-constant snacking and meals, it was possible she was in deficit.

He took her hand and led her into the kitchen. "Protein, veggie, carb."

"Chicken, spinach, rice." She didn't miss a beat. "Preferably with some kind of cheese on top."

Aaron laughed and dug through his fridge to find the chicken and spinach and then pulled a bag of rice from the pantry. He loved these moments with Becka. She dictated dinner, and he put it together while she sipped what had become her customary cranberry juice and they chatted about their respective days.

This is what it could be.

This is what it should *be.*

She propped her chin in her hands and watched him. "I think I have a solution to your Cameron problem. I mean, at least in theory it's a good option."

He covered the chicken breasts in wax paper and pounded them with a meat tenderizer to flatten them. "At this point, I'm about to start praying to some ancient god for patience." They'd managed to hire a secretary...and the guy lasted exactly forty-eight hours before he quit in a huff after a snarling conversation with Cameron about their differing methods of filing.

"He's the best damn security-tech expert in the country, but he is just as good at alienating people. It was never an issue when we were a different kind of company, but our workload grew and our clients changed—and Cameron didn't." It wasn't that he expected his friend to change. Cameron was Cameron, and that was one of the things Aaron had always liked about him. But something had to give, and it had to happen fast. He hadn't talked to Becka about it yet, but he fully intended to take some time off after she had the baby so he could be there to help.

So she wouldn't be alone.

So he could spend time with his new baby.

The only way he'd be able to pull that off, though, was to find the time to hire someone to handle the client-facing aspect of the company so Cameron wouldn't drive off every client they had with his inability to tolerate corporate bullshit while he was gone. He was belatedly realizing that a secretary wouldn't cut it. He needed someone with a wider skill set.

Becka laughed. "I don't think that will be necessary. Didn't you say that your little sister was looking for a job? That she was tired of living with your very wonderful parents?"

He *had* mentioned Trish more than few times over the last month. His little sister had been badgering him to let her come visit. He'd eventually told her about Becka and the pregnancy, and Trish had been asking to come check out the future mother of his child. Aaron had barely held her off. He fully expected to turn around one day in the near future and find her at his front doorstep with her sunny smile and determination.

Aaron moved to the stove and started the rice. "Trish's degree is in sales."

"Yes, you mentioned that. Three times." She smiled. "That skill set would be really useful if you want to ease back from dealing directly with clients on the level you do right now."

She had a point.

He transferred the chicken back to the pan and started lining up the cheese and spinach to fill the chicken breasts with. "It could work. Though Trish is the sweetest person I know, she's pretty damn determined. If she set out to carve a place for herself within the company, not even Cameron's surliness would be enough to stop her." He grinned. "I might actually pay to sit in on that first meeting."

"See!" Becka spread her hands and wiggled her fingers. "I'm brilliant."

"You are." He leaned over the island and pressed a quick kiss to her lips. Gratitude and happiness welled up inside him, a bolt straight to the heart with that single casual contact. Aaron rocked back on his heels as the truth settled inside him.

I love her.

He had for a while, if he was going to be honest with himself. He stared at the chicken in front of him, keeping his jaw clenched to prevent the words from escaping. If there was one thing he was sure of, it was Becka's reaction if he dropped that truth on her. She cared for him—she wouldn't act the way she did otherwise—but her fear of retreading her parents' footsteps made her so gun-shy, one wrong word was enough to close her off from him for days.

If he dropped *this* bombshell?

He might lose her forever.

Aaron cleared his throat. *Just because I love her doesn't mean I have to tell her. Not yet.* "I'll talk to Cameron tomorrow before the doctor's appointment, and call Trish after. Though we'll have to get her set up in a place, otherwise she'll move in here and take over the spare bedroom."

"My room." She rolled her eyes at his look. "Okay, fine. I haven't slept in that room in a month, so I guess it's not technically my room for the time being."

For the time being.

She kept putting qualifiers on what they were. She couldn't seem to help herself.

He set aside his frustration just like he had every other time and focused on finishing dinner. Becka was in his life and in his bed—for now. He'd do whatever it took to keep her there and ensure she didn't let the past poison the possibility of their future together.

Unfortunately, that was easier said than done.

CHAPTER FOURTEEN

BECKA COULDN'T STOP pacing as they waited for the doctor to arrive. It had been bad enough during the last appointment, sitting by herself in the consulting room with the knowledge like a rock in her gut that everything had changed and there was no going back. That was before her body had started actually showing changes. Now her stomach had a definite curve and she could actually feel the baby move regularly.

This was real.

It was happening.

She should sit down. Should be able to handle this despite feeling like she was one sharp move away from coming out of her skin. She couldn't. Nerves kept her moving despite Aaron's increasing stillness. He'd stopped watching her several minutes ago and had taken up staring at the door as if he could summon the doctor faster through sheer willpower. Knowing Aaron, it was entirely possible.

She was fucking this up, but she couldn't stop. The future sat like a weight around her neck, threatening to take her to her knees. She might be able to forget the circumstances that had brought her and Aaron back together when they were going about their lives. Playing house. There was no forgetting in that clinic room. The truth was in every diagram on the walls and the table with its thin paper laid over it. It was in the sterile hospital smell that even places like this held. It was even in the quiet murmur she could hear from beyond the walls on either side of them and in the hall as nurses led other patients through the warren of rooms.

I'm having a baby.

I'm having a baby with Aaron.

A knock on the door brought her up short. Dr. Richardson, a short Filipina lady who'd been Becka's gynecologist since she was sixteen, poked her head in and smiled warmly. "Becka, it's good to see you again." She stepped into the room and closed the door softly behind her before turning and extending a hand to Aaron. "Dr. Richardson."

"Aaron Livingston." He gave what appeared to be a firm handshake and sat back.

The doctor motioned to the table. "Shall we?"

Becka sat on the table and suffered through having her vitals taken while Dr. Richardson asked her the normal questions. No, she had no concerns. Yes, she was taking her prenatal vitamin. Yes, she was getting enough sleep. No, no weird cravings for non-food items. Unsurprisingly, her blood pressure was significantly higher than normal.

Next, she lay back as her doctor measured her uterus and felt around. Becka stared at the ceiling, just wanting the whole thing to be over. *Until next month when I have to come in again.* She held her breath as Dr. Richardson brought out the machine to listen to the baby's heartbeat.

This was it. The moment when there was no denying how real this whole fucked-up situation was.

But as the seconds ticked by, Dr. Richardson's dark brows drew together. "Your little one is being difficult today."

"Is that normal?" Aaron hadn't moved from his chair, but his question sliced through the air and made Becka wince.

The doctor gave a reassuring smile. "The baby can be in certain positions that make finding the heartbeat challenging, but we'll do an ultrasound just in case."

In case the baby's heart isn't beating.

Becka's breath hitched in her lungs, and she couldn't seem to find the strength to exhale. She blinked blindly at the ceiling as her doctor wiped the slimy shit off her stomach and helped her sit up. Dr. Richardson squeezed her hand. "Don't panic, Becka. I'm sure everything's fine."

The world snapped back into focus, and she

wheezed out a breath. She latched onto the doctor's hand. "I need my baby to be okay."

"I know. Just give me a few minutes to see when we can slot you in for the ultrasound." She slipped out of the room, leaving Becka staring after her.

She turned to Aaron. "I need our baby to be okay," she repeated.

Instantly, he was on his feet and before her. He pulled her into his arms and hugged her tightly. "Like she said—listening to the heartbeat with that machine is an imperfect system. The ultrasound will tell us more."

But there was no guarantee that it would deliver good news.

She buried her face in Aaron's chest and listened to the beat of his heart. Too fast, a perfect match to her own. "I didn't think I wanted this baby. I mean, obviously I did because I kept it, but I didn't *really* want it. I wasn't excited. I was just dealing with it and pretending I wasn't pregnant because I don't know what I'm doing." She fisted her hands in Aaron's shirt. "I want this baby. I want *our* baby."

"I know." He smoothed a hand over her hair and down her back. Over and over again. "I know. I want our baby, too."

She didn't know how long they sat like that, her trying and failing not to cry, him whispering words that ceased to have meaning as he rubbed her back.

A knock on the door signaled Dr. Richardson's

return. Her expression was perfectly placid as she took them in. "There was a last-minute cancellation, so we can get you in right now, if that will work?"

"It does," Aaron answered for her, which was fine by her.

The doctor nodded. "This way." She led them deeper into the clinic, to a darkened room where she introduced them to the ultrasound tech. Dr. Richardson hesitated. "The nurse will bring you back to a room once you're finished and then we'll go over the results."

Because the technician wasn't allowed to tell them anything.

Becka managed a nod.

And then it began again. The cold lube stuff on her lower stomach. The wand pressing into her sensitive skin.

She couldn't bring herself to look at the static-filled screen for more than a few seconds, for fear of what she might see. Instead, she turned to Aaron. He held her hand, his gaze glued to the screen as if he had suddenly acquired the knowledge to decipher it. Hell, knowing the man, it was possible he'd found and read a book about ultrasounds along with every other aspect of pregnancy he'd researched.

The ultrasound tech clicked things on her computer and typed in other things, but she didn't say a word until she removed the wand and handed Becka a handful of tissues. The woman gave a soft smile.

"You don't have to be worried." Her smile became less tentative. "Do you want to know if you're having a boy or a girl?"

How could you ask me that if I don't know if my baby is okay?

Aaron squeezed her hand, grounding her. "It's up to you, Becka."

She swallowed hard. "I'd like to know."

The nurse's smile widened. "You have a beautiful baby girl."

Even as joy suffused her, an insidious little voice in the back of her mind murmured, *A little girl. You really* are *repeating history, aren't you?*

Aaron kept a grip on Becka's hand as much for his benefit as for hers. *A little girl. Is she okay?* The nurse led them back to the room, and they spent ten agonizing minutes waiting for the doctor to return. Becka didn't say anything, so he kept his silence. There would be plenty of time to talk once they had the verdict.

Rationally, he knew from his reading that people lost babies all the time. Miscarriages were significantly more common than Aaron could have imagined, and there were a number of factors that went into them—but the overwhelming consensus was that it was rarely the mother's fault.

Becka would blame herself, though. He saw that truth written across her face.

Dr. Richardson arrived and closed the door behind her. She gave them both a bright smile. "Good news. The baby is perfectly fine and measuring right on track for where she should be. The mischievous little one just decided to be difficult earlier." She walked over and patted Becka's knee. "You're doing wonderfully. Just keep it up and let me know if anything changes or if you have any concerns."

"Thanks, Doc." Becka's smile didn't quite banish the worried expression in her eyes.

After assuring her that they had no further questions, the appointment ended and Aaron trailed behind Becka as she strode out of the clinic. The baby might be fine, but the adrenaline still coursed through his system. So many things had raced through his mind as they waited through the ultrasound, but chief among them was the knowledge that if they lost the baby, he'd lose Becka in the process. There was nothing tying her to him. She'd only contacted him again because she was pregnant. If that hadn't happened, she would have moved on with her life and left him to do the same.

Without the baby in the picture, no doubt she'd do exactly that again.

There would be no more shared meals. No more nights spent wrapped up in each other. No more of her lively presence brightening up his home and his life.

He'd lose her—for good this time.

Aaron drove them back to his building and cupped her elbow as they took the elevator up. But as soon as he shut the front door behind him, he couldn't keep the words inside any longer. "Marry me."

Becka spun around and would have tripped if he hadn't caught her. She shook her head. "I'm sorry. I thought you just said 'marry me,' but there's no way you actually said that, because that would be *crazy*."

"As crazy as moving you in here and realizing we'd actually be good together." The brakes that had kept him quiet up to this point were long gone, and the sheer horror on her face only spurred him to keep talking. He'd only get one chance to convince her of this. Aaron clasped her shoulders. "Becka, I love you. I think if you weren't so scared, you could admit that you love me, too. And today more than proved that we both already love this baby. We're not your parents. We're not going to make those same mistakes, no matter what you think. Trust me."

"Trust you." A laugh burst from her that edged toward hysterical. "How can I trust you when you just turned around and did everything you promised you wouldn't? You *promised* to give me time."

Frustration ignited into fury. "I have given you time. I've respected your childish desire to hide under the covers and ignore what's happening instead of planning accordingly and facing it. I've sat back and watched you play pretend for six fucking weeks, Becka. That ends now."

"I see." She nodded and stepped back, out of his reach. "I wasn't the only one playing pretend, though, was I? You had this idea of what the future was supposed to look like, and you've systematically ignored any piece of evidence that doesn't line up with that plan. I'm not some perfect little wifey who's going to fall into line just because you will it to happen. I'm only me, Aaron. I've only ever been me. And you've been asking too much from the very beginning."

The floor seemed to tilt beneath his feet, but he was too angry to care. This was the truth he hadn't wanted to face, the thread running through her that he didn't have the words to combat. Even if he had, Becka possessed a singular ability to tune out anything that didn't fit with her worldview. Just like she was doing right goddamn now.

He crossed his arms over his chest and strove to keep his tone even and not yell at her. If he could just get her to *listen*, they could talk their way through this. "I'd rather shoot for the stars than be content to live in the dirt just because I'm too afraid of repeating my parents' mistake. The last month has more than proven that you're not like them—like her. Why can everyone see that but you?"

Her blue eyes flashed. "Really? I'm the one who's letting my parents' lives get in the way of reality? Because your happy home that you grew up in has given you a wicked case of rose-tinted glasses. Wake up. Life isn't like that for most people. More than half the people who get married turn around and get divorced again within seven years. *That* is a fact you can hang your hat on—not this fantasy future you've created in your head. You and I?" She motioned between them. "We would never work. Not outside this fucked-up situation, and sure as hell not in a marriage." Becka shook her head. "I should leave."

He'd fought so fucking hard to make her see, and he might as well have been yelling into a hurricane. Both actions accomplished a grand total of jack shit. She had her reality, and she fought tooth and nail to stay there. Aaron knew a thing or two about fear, but he'd always faced that emotion down until he conquered it. It was the only way forward. Her flat-out refusal to even try...

It's over.

"No need for you to leave. I will." He turned for the door but paused. "It doesn't have to be like this, Becka. All you have to do is take a leap with me and trust in us." Aaron found himself holding his breath as he waited for her answer.

But she only shook her head again, her eyes shining. "We won't fly, Aaron. The free fall might feel like it for a little while, but the landing will ruin us both."

He searched for something more to say, but in the end it wouldn't change anything. "I'll be at the next appointment."

She hesitated like she wanted to tell him to fuck

off but finally gave a short nod. "Wouldn't expect anything different."

This was it. It was really over.

Aaron turned without another word and walked out of the penthouse.

Becka barely had the energy to walk down the hallway to collapse on her bed. She buried her face in her cold pillow, hating that it wasn't the one on Aaron's bed that smelled like him, and hating herself even more for wanting that in the first place. She screamed into the offending pillow, but it didn't make her feel the least bit better.

Why would it?

Aaron had left.

Not only left—left because *she'd* freaked out on him and kept yelling until he couldn't stand to be in the same space as her. Just like her parents.

No, that wasn't fair…

But Becka didn't feel much like being fair right then. He threw that marriage proposal—if someone could even call it that—at her like it was the most logical step to take. And when she—understandably— freaked out, he cut and ran.

He *left* her.

She rolled onto her back and stared at the white ceiling. "Okay. Okay, he left. Which is a shitty way to end an argument. But this is Aaron we're talking about. Maybe he just needs to walk it off a little bit and then he'll be back here with some kind of plan and we'll figure this out in a way that doesn't involve a shotgun wedding." She took a shuddering breath. "And then I will put my issues on hold and *talk* to him instead of freaking out." Not an easy task by any means, but she could make an effort. She *would* make an effort.

She might not be ready to marry him, but she *did* care about him and she didn't want to be *without* him. Becka scrubbed a hand over her face. Trust their first real fight to be one for the record books. She rolled over to get more comfortable and stared at the clock. An hour—two, tops—and he'd be back there. She just had to smother her instinct to flee the penthouse until then. She curled her legs and hugged the second pillow on the bed.

Just a little longer...

CHAPTER FIFTEEN

TWENTY-FOUR HOURS LATER, Becka ran out of excuses. Aaron hadn't come home last night, and though she'd called in to both her jobs because she wanted to be here when he *did* come back…he didn't. She checked her phone, but her single text had gone unanswered.

He left me.

No, stop that. Maybe something happened. This is Aaron. *He wouldn't have just left. Not like that.*

She scrolled through her contacts to find the one Aaron had given her when she'd first moved in. There might be times when she needed to get ahold of him and wasn't able to, and so he wanted her to have Cameron's number. She held her breath as she pressed dial.

An unfamiliar voice answered almost immediately. "Cameron O'Clery."

"Hi, Cameron. This is Becka. I'm, ah, Aaron's… Whatever. I was wondering if you've seen him?"

Please say he's okay. I wouldn't be able to stand it if something happened to him.

"Yeah, he's in his office right now."

She stared at the wall, her breath leaving her in a whoosh. It had been bad to think that Aaron might be hurt in some hospital in the city and unable to contact her. Knowing that he was fine, that he'd *chosen* not to call her or come home...

It was worse. So much worse.

"Thank you," she said through numb lips and hung up.

Becka looked around the room that had ceased to be hers the second she'd ended up in Aaron's bed a month ago. She'd built this fiction around the idea that Aaron was different from her father—that being with him was different from every relationship her mother had ever been in. From every relationship *Becka* had been in. She'd believed him when he said they were in this together, when he claimed she wasn't alone. That declaration had only lasted as long as their honeymoon period had. The second things got rough—and they *had* gotten rough—he'd bailed.

He *left*.

She shoved to her feet and rushed to the closet. He wanted in the baby's life? Fine. She might feel like he'd ripped her heart out of her chest and thrown it into a wood chipper, but she wasn't completely delusional. He loved the baby as much as she did.

He just didn't love *her*. If he really had, he wouldn't have pulled a cheap stunt like this.

Maybe he's clearing the way for me to move out without him having to deal with me again.

She threw her clothes onto the bed and had to lean over to wait for the lurching of her stomach to pass. A lie. It had all been a lie. Becka packed as fast as she could. She had things in *his* room, but she couldn't bear the thought of crossing that threshold and being assaulted by all the good memories they'd made there.

All that mattered was getting the hell out. She could go back to her apartment. The thought brought her up short. Just because he obviously didn't want anything to do with her didn't mean he'd back down from his ridiculous condition of her not living in that apartment. He couldn't have it both ways.

Unless he calls my bluff and hauls me back here to live in the spare room and then we have to see each other on a daily basis while he holds himself apart.

No. She couldn't do it. The pain in her chest was so sharp, she could barely breathe past it *now*. Seeing him and trying to function as if she wasn't emotionally bleeding out at his feet? She'd rather actually bleed out.

Becka fumbled for her phone and dialed. Allie answered almost immediately. "Hey, girl. What's up?"

"Are you home?" Her voice cracked in the middle of the sentence.

Instantly, all happiness was gone from Allie's tone. "I can be there in fifteen. Is everything okay? Is it the baby?"

The baby. She pressed her hand to her stomach. The doctor said the baby was fine, but this level of stress had to be releasing all sorts of crazy hormones that couldn't be good. She took a slow breath and tried to calm her racing heart. "It's nothing like that. I just… Remember when you offered to let me crash at your place? Does that still stand?"

"Of course." Allie, bless her soul, didn't hesitate. "Meet you there?"

"Yeah, I'm getting in a cab in two minutes." She'd have to offer an explanation, but at least her friend was willing to wait until they were face-to-face.

It took Becka forty minutes to cab it to the new apartment Roman and Allie had bought together last year. They'd compromised on location, so it was roughly an equal distance between her gym and his office. Allie buzzed her up, and she walked into an apartment smelling of peanut butter cookies.

It was too much. She dropped her bag on the floor and the burning in her eyes got the best of her. This apartment practically reeked of love and happiness from Roman and Allie living here. It was there in the little details—the table next to the door with a key bowl and a little notepad where they wrote notes to each other; the framed picture of them just down the hall, staring at each other with such love in their eyes that it made Becka want to cry. She could have had that. She almost *did* have that.

No longer.

She wrapped her arms around herself as Allie poked her head out of the doorway leading to the kitchen. Her friend took one look at her, and her expression fell. "Oh, honey. What did he do?" She rushed to Becka and pulled her into a hug. It was a good hug.

She clung to Allie. "Why do you assume he did something and not me?"

"Because that's not guilt on your face. That's heartbreak." She rubbed soothing circles on Becka's back. "And I talked to you two days ago, and you were all giddy and very much in love."

Becka blinked. "I'm not…" But there was no point in hiding from the truth anymore. Only love could feel like a spiked arrow through her chest, digging in deeper with each heartbeat that dragged her into a future that didn't have Aaron in it. "Shit, I love him."

"I know." Allie huffed out a laugh. "Come sit down. I grabbed the cookie dough and some cranberry juice on the way here. Eat your sorrows and we'll see if I need to go key Aaron's car by the end of this conversation."

Becka gave her a look. "While that might be satisfying, that's also a little criminal."

"Worth it." Allie ushered her into a chair at the small nook table and placed a plate of cookies and a glass of cranberry juice in front of her. "Now, spill."

And she did. Every little detail of the nightmarish doctor's appointment and the ensuing marriage proposal that resulted in the fight that broke them. She broke the cookie she hadn't managed to take a bite of and set it back on the table. "He left, Allie. I overreacted maybe—probably—but he just...walked out. And didn't come back."

"Which triggered every single issue you have." Allie reached over and covered her hand with her own. "Why don't you plan on staying here at least a couple days? Roman adores you, and it'd be nice to spend some more time with you."

She was too devastated to make a swinger joke, which more than anything told her just how screwed up this situation was. She tried for a smile. "Thanks."

"If you don't want to see Aaron while you're here, you don't have to. We'll keep him away until you're ready to deal with him."

The burning in her throat got worse, but she managed to whisper. "I don't think that's going to be a problem, Allie. He made his choice. Now I just have to learn to live with it."

"Fuck that."

She jerked back. "What?"

"If you're done with him, that's fine. I know you were kind of cagey about living with him in the first place." Allie narrowed her eyes. "But if you're retreating because you're scared of getting hurt or rejected... Fuck that, Becka. Sometimes you have to be the one to take the lead and fight for what you want." She held up her hand. "Not today. Not even tomorrow. But when the smoke clears and you can think again, you need to decide what *you* want. If that's to keep going without him, then fine. If what you want is Aaron, then you need to fight for him."

"Not today," she said.

"Not today," Allie agreed. She came around the table and gave her another hug. "Roman's going to be working late, so why don't we order in and watch a movie? Something mindless and no pressure."

"That sounds good." Her voice was thick with unshed tears. "What did I do to deserve such a great best friend?"

"Takes one to know one." Allie tugged her to her feet, grabbed the plate of cookies and nudged her out of the kitchen and into the living room. "Besides, I seem to remember someone dragging me to a tropical island paradise not too long ago, and look how that turned out."

She'd met the love of her life there.

Becka managed a smile. "Someone should make that someone more cookies."

"On it!"

She settled into the couch and grabbed a throw blanket to wrap around her. While she waited for Allie, she replayed her friend's words through her head.

Fight for him.

The very thought was laughable. How could she fight a losing battle? Aaron had made his choice. Not only had he left, but he'd stayed gone and iced her out. She couldn't fight if there was no one there to fight with.

Becka swallowed hard. It was too soon to think about it. She could barely draw a breath without pain lancing her chest, and all she wanted to do was curl up with this plate of cookies under a blanket and cry for the next twelve hours. After that?

After that, she'd figure out what she was going to do.

Aaron stared at his computer screen, the letters blurring together the same way they had for the last thirty-odd hours. He couldn't focus, too distracted by replaying his fight with Becka over and over again. Her outright refusal to talk about the future and willingness to stick her head in the sand when it came to every single future subject still made him see red. But beneath the surface-level anger was a fear he didn't know how to deal with.

She didn't want him.

Or, rather, she wanted to cling to her walls and keep him at a distance more than she wanted to actually be with him.

A knock on his office door brought his head up. Aaron minimized the screen and sat back. "Yeah?"

Cameron walked in and dropped into the chair

on the other side of his desk. "Think it's about time we had a talk."

"Did we lose another client?" He couldn't even work up the energy to be pissed about it. Becka's solution for bringing his sister in to work as a junior consultant was still hanging in the wind. He had been too twisted up inside over Becka to worry about work, which was ironic, because he'd been at the office since their fight.

His partner laced his fingers behind his head and stared hard at him. "Doesn't sound like you'd care if we did."

He didn't in that moment, but he *would*. Aaron straightened in his seat and tried to focus. "I can get them back, whoever they were."

"Probably, but there's no crisis to deal with." Cameron raised a single eyebrow. "Except the one I'm looking at right now. What the fuck is going on with you and your woman? You're walking around here like a zombie, and judging from the state of the couch over there, you slept here last night."

He glanced at the couch, guilt flaring. The thought of going back to his penthouse and fighting with Becka more, of having her layer rejection upon rejection over him had been…too much. Cowardly didn't begin to cover camping out here for the night, but he wasn't ready to be done and he hadn't figured out a plan to keep it from happening. He *would* figure it out if he could just *think*. "You have a point. Get to it."

"My *point* is that you're fucking it up. I don't do relationships and even I can see that." Cameron shook his head. "She called earlier and sounded just as messed up as you do. Go home. Fix your shit. Don't come back to the office until you have it taken care of."

Aaron frowned. "What are you talking about? She didn't call here." He would have heard the phone. She *had* texted yesterday, but it was so damn confrontational, he'd set his phone aside without responding. *A plan. I just need a damn plan.*

"No, she didn't call the office. She called *me*." Cameron leaned forward and propped his elbows on his knees. "Seems she couldn't get ahold of you, which is confusing as fuck to me because you're sitting right here with two phones on your desk and yet it looks like you walked out of a fight and have been acting like an asshole ever since." He gave Aaron a disgusted look. "She wanted to make sure you were okay. Didn't say as much, but the relief and hurt practically radiated through the phone, and if leaving her hanging like that isn't some bullshit, I don't know what is."

She'd called Cameron.

Horror flooded Aaron. He hadn't responded to her text. Hadn't called. Hadn't done anything to let her know where he was or where his head was at.

For her to call Cameron, she had to have been in a bad place, worried about him, and he hadn't done a single thing to stop that. He'd let his own hurt get in the way of everything. He'd *promised* her that he would be in her corner no matter what, and the first time she got truly skittish on him, he acted like a dick and left her.

He shoved to his feet so fast, he tipped his chair over. "I'm an asshole."

"Finally." Cameron sat back. "Took you long enough to figure it out."

He rushed out of the office, barely pausing long enough to grab his phone and his keys, and then took the stairs down to the street because he didn't want to wait for the elevator. The trip to his penthouse took on a nightmarish quality. No matter how fast he moved, it wasn't fast enough.

He should have taken a walk around the block and immediately come back after the fight.

Fuck, he shouldn't have left in the first place.

It would have played on every single insecurity and fear Becka had. And then to leave her hanging...

He was well and truly an asshole.

Aaron raced through the doors of his building and took the elevator up to his floor. He burst through the door. "Becka? Becka, where are you?"

Silence greeted him.

I'm too late.

He closed the door behind him and stalked through

the penthouse. The answers he sought lay in the spare bedroom. The closet doors hung open, all her clothing gone, along with her suitcases. Even knowing it was a lost cause, Aaron walked to the bedroom they'd begun sharing together and opened the door.

It looked exactly like it had when he'd left for work two days ago. A pair of Becka's shoes had been tossed in the approximate direction of the closet. Her towel still lay in a pile on the dresser where she'd set it while she was getting dressed. There was even the slightest indent on the pillow she'd claimed as her own.

Aaron leaned against the wall and closed his eyes. It was worse seeing evidence of her here compared to the searing lack in the other room. It meant she hadn't been able to force herself through the door. He'd hurt her that much.

Fuck.

He didn't know how to make this right. There wasn't a single plan that would work—he knew, because he'd labored over countless ones while he sat in his office and didn't work. Becka was *gone*. He was to blame.

Each second ticked by, a reminder of the way he'd failed her. Aaron pushed off the wall and rushed back through the penthouse, looking for some indication of where she'd gone.

Nothing.

No note, no convenient piece of evidence that would lead him to her.

Think, damn it. You can't go running down the street bellowing her name.

Even though that was exactly what he wanted to do.

Aaron dug his phone out of his pocket and called Lucy. It barely rang once before he hung up. What was he thinking? She might have told her sister she was pregnant, but showing up there would just reinforce her incorrect belief that she was somehow failing Lucy. Becka wouldn't go to Lucy.

No, she'd go to Allie and Roman.

He started to call his friend, but Aaron paused. If there was one truth when it came to Roman, it was that the man loved Allie beyond all reasonable doubt. If Becka was there, he would stand sentry over her and Allie if it was what the women wanted. An admirable quality, but it would put them directly at odds, and Aaron couldn't risk the possibility of being kept from her.

He couldn't make this right if he couldn't see her.

What do you think you're going to do? That you'll show up and she'll be so relieved you decided to stop being a dick that she'll fall at your feet in gratitude? Not likely.

The odds were Becka would throw something at his head rather than sit still long enough to hear him apologize. He deserved it. There was no doubt about *that*.

He reached the ground floor and headed out onto

the street. He had no plan. No guarantee that she wouldn't kick him to the curb the second she saw him. Nothing.

Nothing but his love and an apology he didn't even know how to put into words.

It didn't matter.

He would make it right.

The alternative—a future with Becka moving peripherally through his life—was too heartbreaking to even consider. If he fucked this up, they'd share a child and nothing else. He'd have to stand by and watch her move on. She might avoid relationships like a plague right now, but eventually she'd come across a man determined enough to get past her barriers, who would be patient with her skittishness, and who would earn her love as a result.

Fuck. That.

Aaron wanted to be that man. Aaron *was* that man.

He just had to prove it to her.

CHAPTER SIXTEEN

BECKA COULDN'T SETTLE into the movie. It was more than her bladder crying foul every fifteen minutes or the fact that too many peanut butter cookies had upset her stomach. She kept running over Allie's words, and every repeat put her more on edge. She sat up. "I *did* fight for him."

"Hmm?" Allie turned to look at her. "What's that?"

"Aaron." She pushed to her feet and pressed a knuckle to the small of her back, where an ache had started. "I moved in with him. I went on dates with him. I shared his damn bed. I was making an effort."

"Uh-huh."

She paced back and forth, energy snapping through her limbs. "You know what I need to do?" Becka continued before her friend could respond. "I need to go down to his office and say what I need to say. He can't just ice me out and expect me to fade quietly into the night." She spun around. "I love that asshole, and people that love each other don't have a single fight and break up. That's bullshit. He can't ghost me. I'm having his freaking baby."

Allie cleared her throat. "Well, technically, he *could* ghost you." She held up her hands when Becka growled. "I mean, this is Aaron, and obviously he's not going to because he's Aaron. But just wanted to point that out."

"You're not helping." She snatched up her phone and headed for the door. "I'm going to track that jerk down and figure this out."

"Go get 'em, tiger."

Considering Becka had said almost the same thing to Allie after she and Roman had their bumpy start, she didn't growl at her friend again. "I'll call you later." She stalked to the door and threw it open.

And almost plowed right into Aaron.

He stood there, one hand raised to knock. "Becka."

She froze. "Aaron." Now that they were face-to-face, her anger drained away as if it'd never been, leaving only the hurt and heartbreak behind. She stepped back and wrapped her arms around herself. "What are you doing here?" He shifted, and she zeroed in on the plastic containers in his free hand. They looked familiar… "Are those peanut butter and jelly wings?"

He slowly lowered his hand. "I figured my best chance of getting you to sit still long enough to hear me apologize was if I provided your favorite food." He motioned to the containers. "And if it brought up some of the good memories to combat what an asshole I've been, I wouldn't complain about that, either."

It was right about then that she realized they still stood half in the hallway outside the apartment. "How did you get up here?"

Guilt flared in his blue eyes. "One of my old clients lives on the floor below. I asked him to buzz me up."

Shady. He obviously didn't want to project his arrival for fear of how she'd react, which was enough to tell her that Allie had no idea he was coming. Becka shot a glance over her shoulder, but if her friend was eavesdropping, she was being subtle about it. After a quick internal debate, she stepped back. "Why don't you come in?" Allie had set her up in their spare bedroom, so she led Aaron there.

He didn't speak as she shut the door behind him, but he did set the food on the dresser. Becka opened her mouth, but she didn't know what to say. The fear rose again, the instinctive desire to retreat behind her shell to avoid being vulnerable. Letting Aaron in had *hurt*, and if he had showed up just to reject her…

Have a little faith.

She cleared her throat. "I overreacted. You startled me with the marriage thing, and instead of talking it out like a reasonable adult, I flipped my shit and unloaded a couple decades' worth of issues on you. That wasn't fair." She pressed her lips together.

"But I still think marriage isn't the answer. Not like this—not in response to being pregnant."

Aaron sank onto the bed and looked up at her. Her pain was reflected in his eyes, and it struck her that these two days apart hadn't been any easier on him than they had been on her. He scrubbed a hand over his face. "After the doctor's appointment... After that scare..." He shook his head. "All I could think about was that if we lost the baby for some reason, I could survive it. I'd be upset and sad because I've gotten used to the idea of being a father, but I'd survive. But losing the baby meant that I'd lose you in the process. You made it more than clear that the only reason you got back in contact with me again was because you were pregnant. The thought of losing *you*..."

He'd proposed because he wanted a way to link her to him, an assurance that she wouldn't leave him.

Becka crossed the room to sit on the bed next to him. "You know, you could have just asked me if I planned on bolting if that happened." As soon as the words were out of her mouth, she winced. "Then again, I probably could have been more forthcoming with the fact that I'm in love with you."

"You're in love with me." He went so still next to her, she didn't think he drew breath.

She stared hard at the door—anything was easier than looking at him in that moment. "Yeah, well, I don't know if you noticed, but you're kind of the greatest guy I've ever met and I'd have to be crazy not to fall for you." The next part was harder to get out. "I have issues, Aaron. They aren't going to magically disappear because of the love of a good man, but I'm trying to work on them. But you can't leave like that. I sat in that penthouse for over twenty-four hours wondering if you'd left me, or if something had happened to you and… We're going to fight. I don't know a couple that *doesn't* fight—even Lucy and Gideon—and I need to know that you aren't going to hurt me like that again. I can deal with the arguing. I can't deal with you disappearing on me."

"I'm so fucking sorry." He lifted her into his lap and wrapped his arms around her. "I promise I'll never do it again."

She leaned her head against his shoulder. "Good. Because next time I'm liable to hunt your ass down and cause a scene."

"That won't be necessary." He pressed a soft kiss to her temple. "Come home, minx. I promise not to throw you over my shoulder and sprint to the nearest courthouse."

She laughed, though the sound faded almost as soon as she'd given it voice. "I don't know where we go from here. I was kind of hoping you had a plan."

"I don't." He cuddled her closer. "Turns out, plans don't save you from fucking up from time to time. I love you. You love me. We're going to have a baby together. Maybe we don't have to have every little detail ironed out right now."

God, she loved this man. But he wasn't the only one who would be making compromises. Becka looked up at him. "I'm not ready to rush into marriage or anything but…maybe let's not take it completely off the table?"

"If you're sure."

She laughed and, this time, it was downright joyous. "Oh, I'm sure. You're stuck with me, Aaron Livingston." She leaned up and kissed him. "But I'll be honest—I'm going to go balls out when I propose to you. Think those crazy prom proposals, but just downright extra."

He grinned against her mouth. "I can get onboard with this plan."

EPILOGUE

"GET READY TO PUSH."

Aaron braced himself behind Becka and tried not to wince as she clasped his fingers in a death grip. Her entire body went tense, little ripples making waves in the birthing pool they sat in. He couldn't help her. He couldn't step in and take away the pain radiating from every pore of her body as she tried to bring their daughter into the world. All he could do was hold her and let her crush his fingers and breathe the way they'd been taught in their birthing classes.

As the contraction passed, Becka slumped against him. "Ouch."

"You're doing wonderfully," Lucy said as she mopped Becka's brow. She had her dark hair tied back and a look of concentration on her face, as if she could will Becka to have an uncomplicated labor.

"You are," the midwife confirmed. "The baby's in position and engaged. A few more pushes and you'll get to hold your daughter."

Aaron smoothed back the damp hair from Becka's forehead. "I love you. You're amazing."

Becka huffed out a strained laugh. "I'm thinking murderous thoughts about *you* right now."

"You can tell me all about them if it would help." He reached between them and gently massaged the small of her back. The contractions were coming fast now, and they had less than twenty seconds before the next one by his count.

"No energy." She drew in a long breath. "Here we go."

"You've got this, Becka. Almost there." Lucy mimicked the breathing pattern they'd been taught to use.

The battle to bring their daughter into the world was exactly that—a battle. Becka bore down with a determined silence that scared the shit out of him. There was no screaming. No yelling. None of the things he'd read about and tried to emotionally prepare for so he could support her. Nothing but a focus that left him totally and completely in awe of her.

"This is it, you're doing great. Don't stop. Harder, Becka. Push harder. You can do it!" The midwife's commanding tone had Aaron biting back a snarl; Lucy held her breath in utter stillness, but Becka let loose a muted shriek and the midwife crowed in delight. "Here she is!"

He barely got a glimpse of a wrinkled pink face

before their baby let loose a scream to shake the rafters. The midwife grinned. "Healthy set of lungs."

Things moved quickly after that. Aaron could barely process that the event had finally happened—that they were parents—in the midst of all the insanity. Lucy fielding the news out to Allie and their men. Nurses coming and going. Becka being checked out and pronounced perfectly fine.

Both Aaron and Becka changed into dry clothing while their daughter was weighed and measured and underwent all manner of poking and prodding.

Finally—*finally*—the last nurse shut the door and they were alone.

He pushed out of the chair he'd been relegated to and crossed over to sink onto the edge of the bed. Becka lay with her eyes half-closed, their daughter lying against her naked chest. Aaron carefully stroked the baby's downy-soft hair. "She's here."

"She is." Becka smiled, and a tear escaped the corner of her eye. "She's perfect. More perfect than I ever dared dream."

"You both are." He pressed a soft kiss to their daughter's head and then another to Becka's lips. "What do you think? Is she a Summer or an Evangeline?" The two names they'd finally settled on after months of rigorous debate and even a fight or two.

She looked down into the baby's sleeping face. "Summer. Definitely Summer. She's been in this world a grand total of two hours and she's already brightened everyone's life she touched." Becka made a face. "Oh God, motherhood is going to turn me into one of *those* people, isn't it? I'm so happy I can't even think straight, and if I had my phone, I'd already be sending pictures to everyone in my contact list."

He chuckled. "I already texted a picture of her, along with her weight, length and time of birth, to all our friends and family." He'd restrained himself to a single picture, but he already had half a dozen in his phone. Aaron grinned. "How long do you think it will be before Roman stages an intervention?"

"Two months—tops." She smiled back. Becka reached out and covered his hand with her own. "Hey, Aaron?"

"Yes, minx?"

She nodded at the bag they'd packed and repacked three separate times in the last month, convinced that they'd forgotten something important every time. "Can you grab my purse out of there?"

Curious, he dug through the bag until he found the tiny clutch that she'd insisted on. He handed it over and watched as Becka used her free hand to dig inside it. She paused. "Okay, so in my head, this would be all soft lighting and I wouldn't be feeling like I've just been ripped in half and look like day-old roadkill, but squint a little and pretend with me." She pressed her lips together. "Aaron Livingston, you are the best man I've ever met. Better than I deserve, and I damn well know it. I can't promise that your organization and borderline compulsive need to research things won't drive me to drink sometimes, but I *do* promise that I'll love you for the rest of our lives.

"There's no one else but you for me. I want a life with you. I want to fill our home with a couple more kids. I want meandering walks to delicious food trucks and old movie marathons and the early-morning talks over breakfast and the nights spent wrapped up in each other."

She glanced at Summer and laughed. "Though I suspect we'll both be too exhausted for the next however many months to do more than sleep in that bed. But the point stands—I want a future with you. With *us*." Becka leveraged open the tiny box in her hand and turned it to face him. "Will you do me the immeasurable honor of being my husband, Aaron?"

He lifted the ring out of the box. It was a dark gray that he suspected was titanium and had a faint abstract pattern etched on the outside. "You proposed."

"Well, yeah. I did say I was going to."

He left the bed long enough to grab a nearly identical ring box from the side pocket of the bag. Aaron returned to her, smiling so hard his face hurt. "You beat me to it, minx." He opened the box and showed her the princess-cut diamond he'd had commissioned over a month ago. "The answer is yes, Becka. I'll be your husband if you'll be my wife."

She touched the ring, smiling as hard as he was. "I was thinking three kids, but that might be the left-over adrenaline making me loopy, so that is completely open to negotiation."

They both glanced down at Summer. Aaron shifted to drop a lingering kiss to Becka's mouth. "I love you. I love you so much it makes me crazy in the best way possible."

"The feeling is very much mutual." She smiled against his lips. "Do you want to hold her?"

He carefully took Summer from her and cradled their daughter in his arms. Aaron's chest hurt with how *right* it was to have this right here, right now, with this woman. "Welcome to the world, princess."

* * * * *

TAKE ME ON

DYLAN ROSE

MILLS & BOON

This book includes an extended sneak peek of
Mr Temptation by Rachael Stewart
that we think you'll love!
Enjoy the story—and the extended excerpt!

CHAPTER ONE

MacKenzie Fox sat in the back of a car, en route from the airport to her hotel, and already she was sweltering. It wasn't just the lack of A/C. The driver had rolled the windows down, letting in a gust of hot air that swept across her cheek each time the car picked up speed as they rolled down Collins Avenue. Plus, she was seriously overdressed. Attired in her go-to travel outfit—comfy black leggings, Ugg boots and a zip-up sweatshirt emblazoned with Honor Yoga, the name of the studio she owned back in Brooklyn—she knew she looked like an out-of-place New Yorker. Just a few short hours ago she was slugging through the slushy February streets, bundled up against the frigid temperatures.

Glancing out the window, she could see the heat rising off the hot bodies that filled the sidewalks. A woman in a pair of jean shorts cut so high that her perfectly rounded bottom was almost completely visible. A group of girls laughing as they crossed the street at an intersection, wearing nothing but neon string bikinis, their bodies bouncing and glistening as they walked. Jogging alongside the cab was a perfectly chiseled man running with his shirt off, with warm brown skin. She noted the beads of sweat glistening on his chest and back and imagined he tasted like salted caramel.

Whew! She had only been in Miami less than an hour and already Kenzie was feeling the heat.

Just as the car pulled up to the entrance of the legendary Fontainebleau Hotel, Kenzie snuck a glance at her appearance in the rearview mirror. She pulled her long, curly brown hair into a messy bun on the top of her head and reapplied a swipe of her signature crimson gloss to her lips. The driver, an older man with tanned, wrinkled skin and hair graying at the temples, gave her a wink.

"Enjoy Miami, *chica*."

"Thanks," Kenzie said, opening the door and slinging her only luggage—a small overnight bag—over her shoulder.

But Kenzie wasn't here to enjoy herself. It wasn't that she didn't need a longer vacation. God knows, she could use a break from the seemingly endless string of blizzards they were experiencing back home. But this trip was all about business, not pleasure. And it was business she was eager to get out of the way.

A week ago, to the day, her great-aunt Lilly had

passed away. Having never met the woman, Kenzie didn't think it necessary to fly down for the funeral. But within a day of hearing the news, a lawyer had contacted her, letting her know that she was named in Aunt Lilly's will. There were a few pieces of family jewelry, a savings bond, and most interestingly, a stake in a small rum distillery.

When the attorney mentioned there was an interested party willing to buy out her share, Kenzie was relieved. Not only did she have no interest in running a distillery, the money from the sale would likely allow her studio to stay in business, despite the astronomical rent hike her landlord had slapped her with earlier that month. Although her business was profitable, the skyrocketing city rents were in danger of putting her out of business.

Kenzie entered the palatial lobby and was heading toward the front desk when a voice stopped her in her tracks. She turned toward the bar where the laughter was coming from and her eyes landed on an olive-skinned man in dark blue jeans, a black T-shirt and a sports jacket. He was seated next to a scantily-clad, beautiful Latina. Apparently, whatever he had said was extremely amusing because the woman was laughing with her head thrown back, a long mane of hair cascading down her spine. The man, dark-haired with a strong face and piercing brown eyes, looked past his companion and momentarily locked eyes with Kenzie, sending a shiver up her back. He flashed her what was most certainly a devilish smile before turning his gaze back to the woman.

Wow. Kenzie unzipped the front of her sweatshirt, pulled out a magazine from her bag and fanned herself furiously as she waited to check in. It had been a while since she had experienced this kind of instant attraction to someone. There was something animalistic about the way he had looked at her, with those dark eyes peering out between strands of his black hair, which was just long enough to be sexy. In that brief glance, she had taken in the entirety of his perfect form. Her mouth went dry as she imagined the mysterious stranger kissing the sensitive spot on her neck that always sent the blood rushing straight to her nether regions, causing her nipples to harden and her insides to melt like butter.

"Bottle of water, miss?" asked the desk clerk.

"Yes!" Kenzie croaked, stepping up to the desk and taking the bottle, relieved at the opportunity to cool down this fire that a stranger had suddenly ignited.

"How many keys will you be needing?" asked the clerk as she typed quickly on her computer.

"Just one," Kenzie answered. *Just one* had been the answer to that question for quite a long time now. It wasn't that she wasn't interested, but with running her own business, the last thing she had time for was dating. Ever since her fiancé Cole's death a few years ago, she had thrown herself into her work—

and it had paid off. Sure, there had been interest from many guys, mostly fellow yogis who showed up at her studio or hung around the vegetarian café she frequented in her neighborhood. She was a bit ashamed to admit it but in recent months she had found herself craving something a little bit…meatier.

With the key to her room in hand, Kenzie took the elevator up to the 28th floor and found her room at the end of the hallway. Opening the doors, she sighed at the sight of the giant, king-size bed at the center of the room. Further exploration revealed a serene bathroom with a claw-foot tub, and out on the balcony, a view of the ocean. Her first idea was to strip off all her clothes, get into the plush bathrobe the hotel provided and plop herself down on the bed in front of the TV and order room service. But then she thought of Missy, one of the yoga instructors at the studio, and how disappointed she'd be if all she did in Miami was binge-watch *Queer Eye*. "You need to get out there and have some fun!" her friend had told her.

Kenzie had a flash of the handsome stranger from the bar's devilish grin and, wondering if he was still down there, opened her carry-on and pulled out a silky, magenta slip dress she had tossed in her bag as an afterthought.

Why not? she thought to herself, kicking off her boots, and pulling off her too-heavy clothing until she was standing naked in front of the giant mirror positioned directly in front of the bed. Kenzie caught a glimpse of herself and couldn't help but smile. It was true—she had a pretty rockin' body, and it was hard-earned, with many hours spent running, doing yoga, challenging herself both physically and mentally. She swiveled her hips to the side, checking out what her friends referred to as her "yoga butt," which was ample and firm. Kenzie slipped the flimsy dress over her naked breasts, thought about putting her bra back on for a moment and then decided against it. A tiny pair of black panties and heels completed the look. Letting her curls loose from the bun, they cascaded over her creamy white shoulders. Now that was more like it!

Back down in the lobby, Kenzie made a beeline for the bar but was dismayed to see that the handsome stranger was no longer there. What was she thinking, anyway, seeking out a random businessman in a hotel lobby? Okay, a totally hot businessman, who looked like his sole purpose on the planet was pleasuring women, but still. The obvious conclusion was that Kenzie Fox was desperately in need of a good fuck. All this pent-up sexual energy was bad for her prana. Sitting down on a stool, she flashed a smile at the bartender, ordered her usual—a club soda with lime—and pulled out her phone. Maybe Missy was right, it was time to try online dating.

But before she had time to search for a dating app, she felt a hand graze across her lower back. It was a strong, firm hand—clearly a man's—and the surprising touch sent a tingle up the length of her spine.

"I was hoping to see you again," said a sultry male voice with the slightest hint of a Spanish accent.

Kenzie turned to her left and laid eyes on the arresting man she had noticed earlier. Up close, he was even more handsome than she'd previously noticed, with intense, dark eyes that made it impossible for her to look away from him. His longish dark hair was thick and full, and Kenzie imagined raking her hands through it in the heat of passion.

"Do you mind if I sit down?"

Kenzie nodded affirmatively. She wasn't usually at a loss for words but somehow her ability to form them was suddenly impaired. She felt her cheeks get hot and hoped that he didn't notice she was blushing.

"My name is Antonio Navedo," he said, extending his hand to her. "I noticed you earlier, when you were checking in."

"Yes, I noticed you, too." Okay, there was no hiding it. She was seriously blushing now. "MacKenzie Fox. My friends call me Kenzie."

"Where are you traveling from, Kenzie?" he asked, taking the bar stool next to her and turning his body toward her so that their knees were almost touching.

"New York," Kenzie answered, regaining her composure. "I'm here on business," she stated matter-of-factly.

"But there has to be a little room for pleasure, no? I find that to be very important."

"Yes, you seemed to be enjoying yourself when I saw you earlier," Kenzie ventured with a hint of challenge in her voice. She watched as Antonio's face changed from amused to slightly serious. There was a flash of danger in his eyes that was incredibly sexy.

"That was my business associate," he said in a serious tone. "I often take my meetings here."

Kenzie let out an amused little laugh. *Business associate in what?* she wondered. But did it really matter? She tried her best to stop her gaze from traveling from Antonio's sensual lips down to the small V of skin exposed at his shirt collar, but her eyes went there anyway.

Just then the bartender reappeared, placing the club soda in front of Kenzie.

"What can I get for you, Antonio?" he asked. Kenzie raised an eyebrow. Was he a regular at a hotel bar? That was a definite red flag. What kind of business was he involved in anyway?

"The Atlantico Reserva, neat. Thank you, Jose. And for you?" he said, turning to Kenzie. "Something besides the water?"

"I'm good with this," Kenzie said, pursing her red lips around the straw and taking a long sip. She felt Antonio watching her mouth and suddenly felt downright pornographic. Removing the straw from her mouth, she smiled. "I don't drink."

DYLAN ROSE   11

She said it offhandedly, disguising the fact that her choice to abstain was a heavy subject. Three years earlier, Cole had been at the wheel in a drunk driving accident. When Cole didn't survive, she had stopped drinking alcohol, thinking that it could do no good in her life.

Antonio raised an eyebrow and smiled back at her. "So, what do you do to relax? When you're not 'on business'?"

Kenzie thought for a second and realized she couldn't remember a time in recent years when she wasn't totally consumed with her business. It was the most important thing in her life now, and ever since she had found out the studio was in danger of closing, she'd had trouble sleeping. Maybe some relaxation would be just the thing to set her mind straight.

Kenzie turned her body toward Antonio's so that her bare knee grazed the inside of his leg. "I own a yoga studio. So, I guess you could say my work is my relaxation. Do you practice?"

Antonio's eyes lit up and he laughed loudly. "Uh, no. I prefer other forms of physical activity."

Who was this guy? On the one hand, his smile was so warm and inviting, she felt like she already knew him. But then there was that glint in his eye, and the way he commanded the room that suggested to her that he was someone very powerful, and quite possibly, dangerous. In any case, he was oh so different from the gentle, overly-intellectual men who tried to court her back home. Antonio was such a…man!

Falling back to the hair-twirling habit that manifested itself whenever she was nervous, Kenzie twisted her hair up to the top of her head and formed a makeshift bun and exhaled deeply. Was the air-conditioning out of whack or was she just not used to all this intense heat?

Unexpectedly, Antonio reached his fingers into her glass and fished out an ice cube. Taking the slippery cube between two of his manly fingers, he reached around Kenzie and began to trace circles with it at the base of her neck.

"Better?" he asked, maintaining direct eye contact with her as droplets of water melted down her back.

"Oh yes," Kenzie whispered. Emboldened by his move, she leaned closer to him. "Maybe I could show you some yoga poses, I'm sure you could benefit from them."

Antonio leaned toward her, matching her body language. They were so close that she could breathe in his scent—a mixture of fresh cologne and sweat that nearly made her swoon, making the hairs on her arms stand up on end and sending electric signals straight down to her lady parts.

"I would like that very much," Antonio said in a low, husky voice. Kenzie glanced down at his crotch and could see that he was feeling the same shock waves, too. Part of her wanted to reach out and put her hand on that sexy bulge, right there in the bar, but propriety, and the nearby table of vacationing senior citizens, stopped her.

"Should we go to my room?" Even though she was usually confident, Kenzie surprised herself with how forward she was being. Maybe being away from home was making her feel especially free.

"Yes," Antonio responded immediately. There was an urgency to his tone that was both flattering and vulnerable.

Kenzie slid off the bar stool and tossed a bill onto the bar. As she turned and strode confidently toward the elevators, she could feel the tender area between her thighs getting wetter with every step. It had been a long time since it had happened spontaneously, and the sensation surprised her. Without needing to turn around, she could feel that Antonio was following close behind.

Pressing the up button a few more times than was necessary, Kenzie imagined stepping inside the elevator with Antonio, and thought about what he would do to her. Envisioning him pushing her up onto the side of the wall, his mouth devouring her lips and neck, she teetered on her high heels, praying for the moment when the doors would finally open.

As they did, Kenzie was dismayed to see a large family crowding the small elevator car. When they didn't exit, she stepped inside, disappointed to see that Antonio was separated from her, forced next to the opposite wall by the family's gargantuan stroller. Antonio made eye contact with her and shrugged. After what seemed like an eternity, the car stopped on Kenzie's floor, and they politely excused themselves past the vacationers, alone at last in the deserted hallway.

"It's right over here," Kenzie whispered, leading the way to her room. Part of her wanted to turn around and let Antonio take her, right there by the ice machine, but the good girl inside her told her to wait. With Antonio so close behind her, she could feel his hot breath on her neck, she keyed into the room and he followed her inside, letting the door click shut behind them.

Turning to face him, Kenzie wrapped her arms around Antonio's neck, bringing her mouth up close to his in a dizzying haze of anticipation.

"Wait," he whispered, breaking the spell and pulling back from her. "I thought you were going to show me your yoga."

Kenzie tilted her head to the side in confusion. "You want me to do yoga? Seriously?"

But Antonio didn't need to answer. She could tell by the way he was assessing her form that he was totally serious.

"Okay." She shrugged, moving away from him. If this was what he considered foreplay... "Get down on all fours."

Antonio laughed, but then he removed his shoes

and suit jacket and did what she told him to. Kenzie assessed the muscles of his back, visible through his T-shirt, and his firm ass through those tight-fitting jeans before getting down on the floor next to him.

"Follow me," she said, leading him through a cat-cow sequence. "Arch your body up—like a cat. Then open your heart forward…"

Kenzie turned to see that Antonio not only had perfect form, but he was syncing his breath with hers. She looked straight ahead, pushing out her chest and could feel Antonio's gaze wandering toward her ass, which she knew was on display with her dress riding up, exposing it to his view. When pushed back like that, it took on its roundest possible shape.

As she continued the sequence, Antonio moved in front of her. When she tilted her gaze up to meet his, she could see the unbridled desire in his eyes.

"I have to kiss you now," he said, pulling her up toward him. They were facing one another, both on their knees, and Antonio grazed the side of Kenzie's neck. His mouth was wet and hot, and the sudden contact sent a shiver running through her body. Hungrily, she moved her mouth to meet his and instantly they were locked onto each other, a swirl of tongues meeting, taking turns playfully biting each other's lips as they gasped for breath. It was so crazy that she was doing this with someone she'd just met. Kenzie couldn't remember the last time she had felt such a sense of urgency. She glided her hand down the length of Antonio's body until she found the hard bulge in the front of his pants and tentatively began to touch it.

Meanwhile, Antonio was doing some exploring of his own, his hands going down the curves of Kenzie's body, awakening something inside her that she had been ignoring for too long. With a look of confidence that made her head dizzy with desire, Antonio pulled Kenzie's dress up and over her head, and began kissing her naked breasts. Kenzie threw her head back and closed her eyes, savoring the moment and really letting herself feel every sensation.

With her nerves tingling, she looked at Antonio and pulled up his T-shirt, managing to get it over his head while taking in the view of his chiseled chest and abs. His body was perfect—sexy and fit without being overly muscular—and she allowed herself to enjoy it without restraint, planting hungry kisses on his torso. For a second, she worried that her forwardness showed just how ravenous for sex she really was, but before she could really think too much about it, Antonio had gotten behind her, putting his strong hands on her hips.

Kenzie eased back into an on-all-fours position and waited with anticipation to see what he was going to do next. Her question was answered almost immediately, as Antonio cupped her pushed-out bottom in his hands. He sighed audibly, squeezing her ripe bottom as she stared forward. Kenzie quivered as he ran a finger down the center of her still-clothed rear until it found the wet spot. Moving the soaked fabric to the side, Antonio quickly found her most sensitive spot and began making circles around it, which forced Kenzie to let out a deep sigh, almost like an "Om." This was more fun—and more intense—than any *vinyasa* she had ever experienced.

Just when she thought she was about to come, Antonio abruptly stopped his massage of her nub of oh-so-sensitive nerves. Glancing back at him, she could see the look of determination in his eyes as he unzipped his pants, releasing the erect rod that was now so close to her body. Hooking his fingers on the sides of her panties, he quickly yanked them down. Kenzie suddenly felt the nakedness of being totally exposed to him. She wiggled her hips from side to side, her way of inviting him in without saying a word. But Antonio was still admiring her, still holding back on giving her what she really wanted—the full length of him inside her. Kenzie thought that if he didn't touch her in the way she wanted soon, she was going to explode. It was a delicious form of torture, but she was done waiting.

"Please," she croaked, hating to admit that she needed anything this badly, but unsure how to stand another moment without it. Kenzie didn't have to wait any longer. In an instant, Antonio gave her exactly what she needed—the full length of his cock buried inside her, and she sighed in relief. She hadn't realized how much she had missed that feeling of fullness, and she sank down, reveling in the sensation of the firm drilling she didn't know she had needed so badly.

But before Kenzie could relax into the feeling, Antonio grabbed her now-unfurled long hair in his hand and pulled her back up to him. Kenzie moaned in pleasure at being wanted—and taken. She knew that both of them were close but didn't want things to end just yet. Not before she had shown him her most erotic posture.

"Come join me over here," Kenzie said invitingly, lying down on the bed. Taking an ankle in each hand, like she had done so many times before in her practice, she opened herself up to him. *Ananda Balasana*—it was one of her favorites. She had never before thought of it in such an erotic sense, but in the moment it seemed like the perfect introduction for Antonio to yoga, and so much more.

Antonio stood at the edge of the bed and looked hungrily at her. Sliding his lean body over hers, he plunged into her and moaned out in pleasure. Seeing her like that had obviously been too much for him to take, too difficult to hold back. Letting go of her ankles, Kenzie reached down to her pleasure center and with him still inside her made quick back-and-forth motions over her erect nub until she came, hard, her face buried in his shoulder.

Antonio rolled over onto his side, his breath ragged from the encounter. Kenzie was also gasping for breath, trying to recover from the heights of pure pleasure and also doing her best to sort out what she had just done. *It's no big deal*, she told herself. It wasn't like she was going to fall for the guy. This was clearly a one-time thing. Okay, so maybe she wouldn't turn him down for a second spin, but that was the extent of it—an itch that needed to be scratched, nothing more.

The next morning, Kenzie awakened alone, like she always did. But somehow, this morning she felt especially invigorated. She knew that it had everything to do with the sexy man who had shared her bed, if only for a few hours. But what a few hours it was! She felt simultaneously disappointed and relieved when Antonio had gotten out of bed and walked, stark naked to the bathroom to put his clothes back on. Sure, it would have felt great, sleeping the night in his arms, but that wasn't what this was. Besides, she'd done the impossible. She had broken her dry spell and there were no strings attached! It was really the perfect situation.

She wanted to text Missy, to tell her about her crazy adventure with the sexy Latino, but she knew that if she didn't shower and dress quickly she'd miss the meeting at the lawyer's office—the whole point of this spontaneous trip.

Attired in her most professional yet form-fitting pantsuit, Kenzie took an Uber to an office building downtown and, staring out the window at the rows of palm trees that they passed, replayed the events of the previous night in her head. It was so unlike her to be that spontaneous, that reckless. But she couldn't suppress the smile that now seemed to be a permanent fixture on her face. Now all she needed to do was get this deal over with and fly home with a big fat check which she'd summarily place in front of the building's landlord. Better yet, maybe it would be enough to start investigating a bigger space, in her favorite neighborhood of Red Hook.

When she reached the office building, Kenzie took the elevator to the third floor and found the suite for the law offices of Melinda James, whom she had been emailing. Kenzie was buzzed in through a set of double doors and stepping inside a large open space filled with cubicles, she looked around for someone to guide her to the correct office. Just then, Melinda, a tall woman in a floral top and skirt, rushed over to her and shook her hand.

"Thanks for coming," she said, leading Kenzie into a conference room decorated with a potted palm that seemed to be an attempt at Floridian décor. "Mr. Navedo and his associate have just arrived as well."

Navedo? That name seemed to ring a bell, but why? Kenzie got her answer as soon as she set foot in Melinda's office. There, seated at the conference table, was Antonio and Elena, the young woman she had seen him with at the bar yesterday.

"Antonio?" Kenzie blurted, unable to hide her surprise.

"You two know each other?" asked Melinda, a bemused smile playing on her lips.

"We've met before," Antonio calmly explained.

Antonio may have been calm but Kenzie's blood was boiling over. What was going on? Who was this man?

"Who doesn't know the most successful distiller in all of South Florida and the Caribbean?" Antonio's associate chimed in.

"Very true," Melinda conceded.

"Antonio, may I have a word with you—in private?" Kenzie asked, her voice shaking.

"We'll give you two a moment," Melinda said, gesturing for Antonio's lawyer to follow her out of the room. Once the door was closed, Kenzie practically pounced over the conference table.

"What's going on here?" she demanded.

"What's going on," Antonio said calmly, "is that I'm interested in a property that you've recently acquired."

"Did you know who I was...last night?" Kenzie's eyes were ablaze as she waited for an answer.

"I may have gone there to scope you out," Antonio admitted, "but it was you who seduced me."

Kenzie was speechless. Okay, so maybe it was her that did most of the seducing, but Antonio had been a willing participant. More than willing! And the fact that he hadn't revealed that he knew who she was seemed unnecessarily deceptive.

"Were you afraid that if I knew who you were I wouldn't sleep with you?" Kenzie asked, narrowing her eyes at him.

"No," Antonio answered emphatically. "I was afraid that maybe you wouldn't want to do business with me. But I couldn't stop myself." His last sentence was whispered, and the two of them both instinctively looked toward the door, where the other women were waiting.

"I'm sure we can work out a good business deal," Antonio said with a smile. "One we can both benefit from. My family has a long history of rum production. And I'm sure you have no interest in a little, run-down distillery."

"Why are you so sure about what I'm interested in?" Kenzie asked, her tone simultaneously flirtatious and challenging.

Antonio looked up and chuckled. "I just figured…"

"That because I'm a woman I don't know anything about how to run a business?"

Antonio reached out and touched Kenzie's hand. "No. Not at all."

The door handle clicked, which caused Kenzie to jump, pulling her hand out of Antonio's grasp.

"Everything okay?" Melinda asked, peeking her head back into the office.

"Everything is fine," Kenzie said, looking directly at Antonio. The practical side of her said to put her pride aside, take the check and catch the next plane back home. But something else in her was beckoning her to take a risk. So maybe she didn't know anything about the rum business, but she also hadn't known anything about opening a yoga studio when she'd started one. When was the last time she'd taken on a real challenge? Looking at Antonio, she could feel that there was unfinished business between them.

Kenzie turned to Melinda. "We were just discussing the terms of Antonio's proposal," she said, almost sweetly. "And I think we both agree that I have a lot to offer." Kenzie locked eyes with Antonio who raised an eyebrow with what looked like a combination of genuine surprise and unmitigated lust.

"Well, this is a surprise," Melinda said matter-of-factly. "Any thoughts on next steps?" she asked, looking back and forth between the two of them. Kenzie wondered if she suspected that there was something more between them than an unsigned contract. At least for Kenzie, the electricity she felt ricocheting off the walls was undeniable.

"If you don't mind, I'd like to go see my distillery now," Kenzie said, unable to prevent a small smile from forming on her lips.

CHAPTER TWO

THE EARLY-MORNING MIAMI sun blazed through the white curtains. Antonio Navedo stirred in his bed. It had been a strange night for him, full of racing thoughts and strange dreams. He usually slept straight through, but last night had been different. He found himself getting up every few hours, taking trips to the bathroom and pacing around his large, professionally-decorated bedroom. He couldn't figure out what was off. Everything about his bedroom was perfectly in place—the blue-and-gold throw pillows piled neatly on a nearby chair, the glass and pitcher of water he kept next to his bed were filled, and all of his devices were docked and charged. But something still felt off. It probably had to do with his dealings with the self-assured and beautiful New Yorker.

Antonio was used to getting his way—in business and with women. Perhaps that was why his encounter with Kenzie Fox had him so frustrated.

He had expected, no, *counted on* her accepting his business proposal at first offer. The buyout he and his lawyer had drawn up was more than generous. In fact, it was so much in her favor that it bordered on ludicrous.

It was the crack of dawn, the time Antonio usually reserved for a dip in the surf to begin his day. But this particular morning he found himself unable to unravel himself from the twisted sheets of his king-size bed. He always thought that staying in bed, even an extra few minutes, was lazy. He liked that he could start each day with vigor and enthusiasm. He was always ready to meet any challenge, but this morning he sank back into the pillows and let himself daydream.

Thoughts of Kenzie's long curly hair falling over her perfect breasts, her pert nipples pointing out to him, just begging to be sucked, sent his mind into a daze. That, and the image of her ample ass pushed out toward him back in the hotel room played on a seemingly endless loop in his head. Absentmindedly, his hand traveled down the length of his naked body to the aching hard-on that arose every time he pictured that brief but oh-so-hot encounter.

After the meeting in Melinda's office yesterday he had needed to relieve himself so badly from the feelings she aroused in him, he had excused himself to the bathroom to take care of business. The fiery look in the brunette beauty's eyes when she had yelled at him was enough to make him want to come on its own. But that, coupled with how her businesslike yet somewhat tight suit revealed the outline of her very fit but also voluptuous form meant that he had been useless for anything that didn't involve stroking his own cock for the rest of the day.

Antonio ran his hand up and down the length of his formidable manhood, feeling simultaneously annoyed and titillated by what was turning into a perma-erection ever since he had met the mysterious Ms. Fox. He knew that he could quicken his strokes, increase the pressure, play with himself a little bit rougher until he pictured Kenzie lying back on the bed and the sight of her gorgeous, well-formed body waiting for his touch that would make him come and at least momentarily relieve his constant state of arousal. Instead, Antonio growled and threw back the sheets. The Miami sun was an unforgiving alarm clock to him and he knew there was work to be done. He had to be showered and ready in an hour to meet Kenzie. Thankfully, she had agreed to wait a day to tour the ramshackle Baracoa distillery. The last thing he wanted was to head over there with his whole legal team in tow. Melinda was a shark when it came to looking out for his business interests, but he knew that if he wanted to try and persuade Kenzie to come around to his way of thinking he needed the chance to be alone with her again.

Already naked, Antonio strode into his en suite

bathroom, turned on the shower and stepped into the tiled stall. The multiple faucets hit his body from all directions, and he purposefully turned the water toward cold, hoping the spray would lower his blood pressure and cool his heated thoughts.

What did a teetotaling New York City woman want with an ancient rum distillery? Even more frustrating was the fact that he had upset Kenzie, which meant there could be a chance he would never get to feel her body underneath his. There was so much more he wanted to do with her. It was curiosity that had sent him to the hotel lobby that night. He hadn't planned on doing anything more than possibly checking out this woman who he had Googled immediately upon learning that she was coming down to Miami. Something about her reminded him of Clarissa. But he tried not to think too much about that. A constant parade of different women in and out of his bedroom had been a good enough distraction from his one serious girlfriend's departure over a year ago. His life was full, he reassured himself. And besides, who wanted to be tied down?

Shutting off the water and grabbing a towel from the rack, Antonio quickly dried himself off and dressed in a pair of expensive gray trousers and white linen shirt with the sleeves rolled up to expose his muscular forearms.

Grabbing the keys to his convertible Lamborghini, he glanced in the hallway mirror to check his appearance: a few days' worth of stubble worked, he decided, running his hands through his jet-black hair. Grabbing his favorite pair of aviators, he headed out the door, feeling mostly self-assured that he would change Kenzie's mind about his business proposal— and maybe even calm that New York attitude of hers down long enough to enjoy some of his hot and spicy Miami flavor.

"Where is he already?" Kenzie questioned the uniformed doorman standing at the entrance to her hotel. She looked at the time on her phone. It was already ten minutes past the time Antonio had agreed to pick her up and she was getting antsy. The doorman shrugged and turned his attention to the hotel's shuttle bus which was arriving with a full load of guests. Kenzie sighed and blew a curl out of her face and peered down the street, not knowing what car she was looking for but wanting to do something besides stand there like a statue. The longer she waited, the more she regretted her choice of clothing—an off-the-shoulder white cotton top with a matching skirt that showed off her breasts and tiny midriff.

It had been a mistake to agree to let Antonio give her a tour of Baracoa. He would likely try to convince her to sell him her share of the distillery. In truth, that was probably the move that made the most sense, logistically and financially. But she couldn't bear the thought of giving this arrogant man exactly what he wanted. Besides, maybe the place was a gold mine, or at least a diamond in the rough. It made good sense to at least go see what she would be giving up.

Just as Kenzie reached into her bag for her room card, her mind suddenly set on going back up to the room to change into a business suit, an azure-blue sports car roared into the semicircular driveway of the hotel, causing Kenzie and the busload full of tourists to all stop and stare.

"Buenos dias!" Antonio called to her, flashing her a sexy smile and lowering his shades to unabashedly check her out from head to toe. *Damn*, Kenzie thought. Her game plan of acting cold and indifferent to the man who had taken her to bed knowing full well that she was a potential colleague was going to be hard to keep up with. Why did he have to be so good-looking? Kenzie flashed back on the moment up in the hotel room when Antonio had pulled her hair, his hard cock inside her, and felt the same shock waves that tingled from the roots of her curls all the way down to the very core of her nether regions as if it were actually happening again.

Cars pulled in and out of the circle in front of the hotel, but Kenzie was focused only on the car in front of her. She wondered where it might take her, and if it was a ride she was really ready for. Glancing at Antonio, who was confidently leaning in her direction, she decided to take a chance.

"You're late," Kenzie stated firmly, reaching for the door handle of the insanely showy but somehow elegant car. Her hand was trembling a little and she tried to steady herself by taking a deep breath. Everything around her felt so foreign—not just the expensive vehicle, but the palm trees, the intense heat and the tourists in the colorful dresses and shorts. Back home, the streets were gray and slushy with dirty snow. Here, everything was in Technicolor and it was throwing her off.

Before she could sit down, Antonio was up and walking around to the passenger side. When he was close enough that she could feel the heat coming off his body, she inhaled sharply. It was no wonder the eyes of the other hotel guests were on them— she had to admit that together, they made a striking scene. Antonio was a foot taller than her, but somehow their looks complemented each other. At only five foot two she somehow always found herself dating the tall guys.

"Here," he said handing her the keys. "You drive."

Kenzie laughed and looked skeptically at the fast car in front of her. She wasn't much of a car person and usually when she saw guys in them on the highway she figured they were overcompensating for something. But looking at it up close, she had to admit it was pretty incredible looking. Still, she hoped Antonio wasn't serious about wanting her to drive. "You do realize the last time I drove was for my driver's ed test? I was seventeen."

Antonio gave her a puzzled look.

"I'm a New Yorker," she explained. "We take the subway." In truth, it had been years since she'd driven, and she was terrified of crashing this beautiful vehicle that probably cost more than all of her worldly possessions, combined.

"This is more fun than the subway," Antonio promised, pressing the car key into her hand.

Kenzie reluctantly walked around to the driver's side, slid her body into the leather seat and turned on the ignition. The car's powerful engine roared and she felt a quick hit of excitement.

"You can adjust the mirrors over here," Antonio explained, leaning across her to toggle the side-view mirrors switch. Kenzie involuntarily inhaled Antonio's clean and masculine scent and the pheromones hit her—hard.

"Got it," she said, and pulled out of the drop-off area fast, sending Antonio back against the passenger seat. "Buckle up," she cautioned him with a smile.

Kenzie made good time getting them to Alligator Alley, and soon the road opened up to reveal the greenery of the Everglades. It was such a contrast, going from the colorful buildings of downtown to this otherworldly swamp region. The grass was greener than anything Kenzie had seen in months in New York and the sun beat down on them as she drove a straight shot, picking up speed as she got more comfortable in the powerful ride.

"It's stunning," she commented, momentarily taking her eyes off the road to take in the lush scenery. For a second, she even thought she saw an actual alligator. She had heard that they were all over the place down here, and the thought freaked her out. New York City subway rats she could deal with—giant reptiles were something else. She appreciated nature but was definitely not looking to get up close and personal with it.

"I agree, it's beautiful," Antonio said. Instead of looking for wildlife, his gaze was firmly planted on her. His unabashed stare made her blush. She wasn't used to being looked at so intensely, especially by someone she was so attracted to. Suddenly, she had the overwhelming impulse to turn the steering wheel sharply to the right and pull off to the side of the road.

She saw herself hiking up her skirt and straddling Antonio right there in the car, not caring if anyone else would see. Her panties got wet with the idea of his manly fingers moving her undies to the side and exploring the soft folds of her most intimate area. She looked over at Antonio and guessed that he was thinking of a similar scenario, too. But instead, she floored it, eager to reach Baracoa before she found herself doing something equally as reckless as two nights before.

When they pulled off the highway, Antonio directed her through the side streets until they came to a series of buildings in an open field that looked more like ancient ruins than a working rum distillery.

"This is it," Antonio announced, stepping out of the car and gesturing toward—well, to be honest, Kenzie wasn't a hundred percent sure what she was looking at.

"Is it still operational?" she asked in a more sheepish voice than she normally used. She was definitely out of her territory here. Her domain consisted of yoga mats, *asanas*, breathing techniques and meditation. The rum business was as far from her own business as she could possibly imagine.

"It's a working distillery, yes," Antonio answered, "but on a very small scale. Here," he said gesturing toward what looked like the main building. "Let me show you around."

Kenzie's thin white outfit was already sticking to her skin as the hot sun beat down on them. "Okay," she said, following right behind Antonio, which gave her a chance to wipe some of the perspiration on her face and chest with the back of her hand. How did Antonio manage to look so cool and collected? She wondered. She definitely wasn't used to such intense heat.

Inside the main building there were a few huge metal fermentation tanks where Antonio explained that sugar cane was turned into molasses. They walked past the distillery tanks and into a huge, cool open area where the barrels were stored.

"Some of these are aged," Antonio explained, "which affects how dark the rum will be."

Antonio waved at a worker driving a utility vehicle who was transporting barrels which were presumably ready to be stacked and aged. Apart from him, Kenzie saw no other people and it seemed like there was very little activity going on.

"They've been doing things the same way here for a long time," Antonio explained. "We have a much more intricate process at our Little Havana locations. Our master blender is always coming up with new flavors, new processes."

Little Havana—Kenzie knew the name from some quick internet research she had done on Antonio after, ahem, they had gotten acquainted, so to speak. Apparently, his family was the owner of the largest rum distillery outside the Caribbean, and also had a hand in several smaller operations. Judging by a "Millionaires under 40" article she had come across in *Forbes*, this little distillery was definitely off his radar.

"We would have fully acquired this distillery a long time ago, and absorbed it into our main businesses, but the previous co-owner held on."

Aunt Lilly. Kenzie still wasn't exactly sure who she was, and why or how she had become involved in the liquor business.

"Some people like holding onto things," Kenzie whispered. Suddenly her thoughts shot back to Cole—to the last time she had seen him alive, barely breathing in a sterile hospital room. It was liquor that had destroyed their relationship, destroyed both of their lives. Kenzie suddenly felt queasy, and her breath was short.

"Excuse me, I need some air," she apologized, and darted out the double doors straight ahead of her.

When she reached the outdoors, Kenzie noticed out of her haze that she was standing in the most serene, run-down little courtyard. Pink and red azaleas bloomed out of the crevices of the rocks and the sound of birds was audible from the palm trees.

"Are you alright?" Antonio had raced after her and now had a protective arm around her waist.

"Yes," Kenzie answered, composing herself as best she could. "This is all just a little…overwhelming."

Antonio frowned, and she was touched that he seemed so seriously concerned about her well-being. Kenzie did her best to shake off any bad feelings the sight of those rum stills had stirred up and instead decided to focus on the beautiful, tranquil surroundings.

"It's like an oasis here," she commented.

"It is quite beautiful," Antonio agreed. She noticed that he still had his hand on her. The warm pressure on the small of her back radiated up her spine and made every inch of her skin feel more sensitive.

"Believe me, I would love nothing more than a beautiful partner in the operations here," Antonio said seriously, turning to face her. "But you have no use for this place." He said it so firmly that for a moment, Kenzie believed it. "Why not make a deal? Let me do what I do best. You'll walk away with a lot of money and then..." he boldly reached out and moved a curl off Kenzie's face, "then we can celebrate both of our good fortunes."

Kenzie smiled tentatively and assessed Antonio. His words were so commanding, so smooth, it was hard not to be persuaded by him. But something in his eyes betrayed this extreme confidence. She thought maybe it was a hint of vulnerability. He was looking for something, just like she was, too.

"I don't know..." said Kenzie, allowing herself to think out loud. Antonio's face was so close to hers, she could easily lean in and feel the stubble on his face, rough against her soft skin. She took a step back.

"Something tells me that this place has potential," she said, looking around.

Okay, so it was probably ill-advised, but when Kenzie got one of those feelings, she knew there was no stopping her. It was the same feeling she had when she saw the abandoned warehouse space that was now her thriving yoga studio. She had a way of seeing beyond what things were and envisioning a greater end result. Maybe there was something great to be brought out in Baracoa. She just needed to uncover it.

"I have a proposition," she said, looking at Antonio pointedly. "If I can get this distillery on its way toward turning a profit in a week's time, you give me all of your shares and I own it outright. If I fail, then it's yours to keep."

Antonio shook his head. A bemused smile played across his lips. "Kenzie… I know you are a smart businessperson." Antonio spoke slowly, and it seemed like he was trying to choose his words carefully. "But you don't know anything about running a distillery. I don't want to rob you of your inheritance."

"Don't worry about me." Kenzie reached out and touched Antonio's bare forearm in a gesture to drive her point home—and maybe as an excuse to have physical contact with him again. "I've gotten this far by trusting my gut."

Antonio grabbed Kenzie's arm and pulled her close to him. The electricity ricocheting back and forth between their bodies was undeniable.

"I've wanted to do this again since this morning," Antonio whispered, leaning his face in toward Kenzie, ready to kiss her. Oh, how she longed to feel his mouth pressed against hers again, to bite his lips and allow his tongue to penetrate not just her mouth but all of her orifices. She wanted to feel those strong shoulders again. She needed to make sure they were really as solid as she remembered from the first time she had allowed herself to touch them, to let her hands linger over the muscles just long enough to get totally turned on. Taking a deep breath, the kind she instructed her students to do to begin their yoga practice, she collected herself and held him back with her hand placed firmly against his muscular chest.

"You're used to getting everything you want, aren't you?" she asked him, her eyes gleaming with a challenge.

Antonio raised an eyebrow and met her gaze. "I know what I like, and I go after it," he said plainly. "And I really like you." He put his hand around her waist and pulled her in toward him.

Kenzie's knees weakened. She could feel his hardness pressing into the side of her hip. She couldn't deny what a boost to her ego it was that he was this turned on and all they were doing was talking. "Tell me you don't want this, too," he whispered, speaking directly into the spot on the side of her neck that was her most sensitive place. She could feel the stubble of his half-grown beard grazing up against her skin and a shiver ran through her body.

"How about I sweeten the deal?" Kenzie asked. The sensible part of her brain was telling her to keep her distance, to be cautious, but the primal side of her was allowing her to relish the long kisses Antonio was expertly administering to the side of her neck.

"I like the sound of that," Antonio murmured in between licks and bites.

"If I don't turn Baracoa around, you also get all of me."

Antonio paused his exploration and looked pointedly at Kenzie. "Hasn't that happened already... back at your hotel?" he asked, his voice heavy with lust.

Kenzie tilted her head to the side. Her resolve was shaking but she kept her voice firm. "I don't just mean my body. I mean all of me. Really."

Antonio nodded. "A relationship?"

"Let's just call it a chance to go...deeper. So, do you think you're up for it? Do you want to take me on?"

Antonio stepped back and exhaled, raking his fingers through his hair. She had been right, her words had obviously rocked him to his core. She smiled, knowing she could have this effect on him without even touching him.

"There has to be a catch," Antonio said cautiously. "If I lose? Which I won't..." he added.

Kenzie's eyes narrowed. "Then I go back to New York and you never see me again."

Ooph. It sounded harsh when she heard herself say it out loud. But truthfully, it was the only outcome Kenzie could really imagine. They would have some fun, she would of course win, and then be on her way. Like she always was.

The proposition made Antonio shake his head. "You really like torturing me, don't you?"

"Maybe just a little." Kenzie smiled. She had to admit, she was enjoying this playful banter. It had been a long time since she had actually wanted to flirt like this with someone, to delight in seeing their reaction to her. And Antonio's reactions were anything but subtle.

"Okay," he acquiesced. "But you can't leave me like this." Antonio looked at her wantonly. "I won't make it back to the city."

Kenzie observed the bulge that was currently testing the limits of Antonio's trouser zipper.

"Take off your pants," she instructed.

Antonio hesitated. "But you just said…"

"Take off your pants," Kenzie reiterated, her voice firm now.

Antonio glanced around. There was no one else in sight and the only sounds that were audible were the birds and the gentle whirring of the fermentation tanks. In one swift motion, Antonio's pants were off, and he stood before her in just his shirt, his proud erection pointing straight toward her.

"The shirt, too," she said matter-of-factly.

Kenzie relished the vision of his naked body in front of her. The other night she hadn't really had a chance to assess him, but now she took her time, committing all of the details of his form to memory. His body was muscular but not bulky, with defined pecs and abs and a treasure trail leading from his belly button straight down to one of the most formidable members she had ever laid eyes on. It was perfect really, long but not too long, with a beautiful, rounded head that was just begging to be sucked on. His balls were nice too—cleanly shaven—but it was his rock-hard thighs that really impressed Kenzie the most. She could see his strength in them with long, firm muscles that showed what a man he really was. It occurred to her that she could come so easily, just rubbing her clit up against one of Antonio's perfectly defined quads. It was the best idea that had occurred to her a long time, but it would have to wait.

"I want you to touch yourself," Kenzie instructed. She felt powerful saying it, and Antonio readily complied, spitting into the palm of his hand and keeping eye contact with her as he began to rhythmically stroke himself. She wanted so badly to run to him, to sit down on top of him and have the ride of her life, but she knew that in order to maintain the upper hand she had to delay her pleasure.

She could see that Antonio's strokes were beginning to get faster and that he was close to coming.

"Come here. Please," he practically begged, his voice filled with urgency.

Overcome with desire, Kenzie rushed to him, wrapping her arms around his neck and pulling his mouth toward hers. It was a kiss she had been imagining ever since yesterday morning. As they kissed, she reached down and grabbed a hold of his hardness and took over where he had left off, moving her hand up and down the shaft. She could feel his whole body respond to her touch. With his heart practically beating out of his chest, she quickened her strokes until he cried out in ecstasy. Stepping back, she realized that her heart was racing, too.

Antonio looked exhausted and he pulled Kenzie back toward him, wrapping his arms around her small waist.

"What about you?" he asked.

Kenzie wanted so badly to have her turn, to let Antonio bring her to the heights of pleasure, just as she had done for him.

"Let me make you feel good," he whispered.

Antonio didn't know it, but he was already doing that. For a moment, she considered lying down right there in the courtyard and allowing him to work his magic between her legs. She already knew how skillful he was with his mouth and wanted to see what else he could do with it. But the businesswoman in her got the best of her, and she reminded herself to be cautious.

Besides, there was something fun about knowing that she had taken him over the edge, but that she didn't need the same in return. She kind of liked having the upper hand.

"I'm ready to go back to the city now," Kenzie said, matter-of-factly. "There's a lot of work to be done."

CHAPTER THREE

AT THE HOTEL, Kenzie spent the rest of the afternoon looking over the papers from Aunt Lilly's estate. She thought about how incredible it was that a relation of hers was a business owner and regretted the fact that she never got to know her. Regrets over the deceased was a feeling Kenzie was all too familiar with. Since Cole had been taken from her, she really tried to do everything to the best of her ability and to live without worrying about what other people thought. But there was always that aching in her heart—no matter what she did and how wonderful it was, a little voice would chime in to ask what it would have been like if Cole were still alive. What would they be doing? It was a question that colored all of her experiences.

Except for the past two days. Kenzie had somehow allowed herself to really live in the now with Antonio—to fully feel all the sensations he had awakened in her. But one thing was certain—this wasn't love, and never could be. That was a feeling she reserved for the one person she thought would have been her husband. It was a role no other man could ever fill. Sex was one thing, but her heart belonged to Cole.

After Kenzie finally put away the paperwork, she changed into the string bikini she had stuffed in her carry-on and went down to take a dip in the hotel pool. The water was cool but felt wonderful after even a few seconds of being outside in the heat, and she swam a few laps before allowing herself to float in the shallow end for a few minutes.

Afterward, she sat in a chaise lounge, watching a young family play in the water. In the hot tub, she observed a young couple, probably on their honeymoon. They were both tan and fit and the man was busy picking the woman up and pretending that he was going to dunk her under as she held up a hand to protect the large, sleek bun on the top of her head. Kenzie smiled wistfully. Part of her wished for both of those scenarios but part of her was beginning to think that wasn't the way it was meant to be.

After a while, she dried off and came back to her room to lounge around in a fluffy white bathrobe. The swim had made her feel exhilarated and a little looser. She thought back on the oh-so-hot encounter with Antonio at the distillery. She couldn't stop a smile from crossing her lips when she remembered how shocked he was when she had cut their encounter short. She also got a little thrill thinking about the business venture she was about to embark upon.

The yoga business could be unpredictable, but it was a realm she knew well, and most of the time she felt sure of herself. Part of her liked feeling like she knew nothing—that there were still things left to be learned, new territories left to explore.

She knew that if she put her mind to it, she could do anything. But she was also smart enough to know she couldn't do it without help.

"You agreed to do what?" Missy asked incredulously when she told her about the bet—minus the sexy stuff, of course.

Missy was holding things down at the yoga studio in Kenzie's absence and she was also Kenzie's biggest cheerleader in all of her business ventures.

"I know," Kenzie sighed, plopping down in the center of her king-size hotel bed and staring out the window at her ocean view. The sun was setting, and the sky had taken on a pinkish hue. "But I really think this is doable," she told her friend. "Don't forget, I started Honor Yoga in a month with a thousand-dollar savings bond."

"You are a magician," Missy agreed. "But turning a business you know nothing about around in one week's time? Sorry but I don't see how we can do it."

Kenzie twirled a curl around the click pen she was holding. "What about a rum mixer?" she offered.

"Like, a big party?" Missy asked.

"Kind of, but something that would really put Baracoa on the map." Kenzie was envisioning the courtyard where she and Antonio had been transformed with little gold lights and music into a fabulous pop-up venue.

"Oh, I get it." Missy was getting onto Kenzie's wavelength. "Publicity first, then build from there."

"Exactly," Kenzie said, punctuating her idea with a click of the pen. "We stir up some major interest, get written up in the media, and then suddenly we have a hot commodity on our hands."

"I like it," Missy said.

"But we need something—or someone to help make this newsworthy."

"Hey," Missy said, the enthusiasm in her voice building. "Isn't Catalina Cortez from Miami?"

Kenzie's mind started to whir. Of course! Catalina could help them. She was one of Kenzie's celebrity clients—an up-and-coming pop singer who had been coming to the studio for her 6:00 a.m. class since before she had a record deal. She was not only beautiful but also extremely talented and had over a million Instagram followers who watched her every move. One post or Tweet from Catalina alone could cause a product she liked to sell out in minutes.

If she could get Catalina to appear at the mixer it would all be a done deal.

"Perfect," Kenzie said, not needing to explain herself further to Missy. Her right-hand woman always understood what was needed, and never failed in helping her to execute her vision.

"I'm going to reach out to her today," Missy said. "Now go enjoy some of that Miami sun. I'm expecting you to come back with a full-on tan!"

Kenzie rolled her eyes. "Not with my fair skin," she countered. "You know me, 100 SPF."

"Any hot prospects down there, by the way?" Missy asked with a hint of innuendo in her voice. She was in her early twenties, super fit and extremely hot with short blond hair in a pixie cut that accentuated her strong features. She was constantly going out and dating (and sleeping with) a different new and exciting person pretty much each week. Kenzie was pretty sure Missy saw her as an old lady when it came to her social life.

"Nope," Kenzie said curtly. She was a bad liar and knew Missy would see right through her, but she didn't feel like explaining her spontaneous sexual adventures of the last forty-eight hours. For one thing, she knew Missy would get overexcited and start grilling her for details. The truth was, she didn't yet know what to make of Antonio. Was this just his usual form of entertainment, seducing potential business partners, or…something else?

Whatever it was, she was happy to keep it under wraps, at least for now.

"I'll check in with you again tomorrow after the distillery tour," she promised. "Good luck with Catalina."

"You got it, babe," Missy said as her sign-off.

Kenzie debated going out but quickly decided it was a room service kind of night. After phoning her order in, she changed into her yoga clothes—a pair of light blue and lavender floral leggings with matching bra top—and moved some of the furniture around in the room to clear a space where she could do a few quick vinyasas.

Reaching her arms up to the sky and then diving down, she exhaled out all of the stress and tension of the past few days and set an intention to keep the focus on taking care of herself. It was sometimes easy to forget to do that with everything she had going on. Gliding up into an upward dog position, she caught herself thinking about Antonio and quickly returned her thoughts to her practice. It was going to be hard work, taking down the cocky millionaire who thought he could do no wrong. And although she tried to keep her gaze fixed as she swept her arms up into warrior 2, she couldn't help but break out into a gleeful smile. This was going to be fun, for sure, she thought.

After enjoying her room service in bed with the TV on, Kenzie drew a bath, and when she was finally relaxed, returned to bed and switched out the lights. She had a big day ahead of her tomorrow. She was going to need her energy.

Just as she was about to close her eyes, she saw the blink of a text message notification. Unable to resist the urge to check it, she picked up her phone and saw Antonio's name on the screen. They had exchanged numbers in the lawyer's office, but still, the fact that he was texting was unexpected.

Any chance you're still awake? it read.

Kenzie racked her brain for an appropriately sexy response, but after a while decided that maybe it was more intriguing to not respond at all. Antonio, she thought, licking her lips and hitching up her white cotton nightgown. She half wished she was back home so she could just reach into her bedside drawer and pull out the tiny silver bullet vibrator that always did the trick, buzzing her clit into an almost-instant state of orgasm. Since she hadn't packed it in her carry-on, her fingers would have to suffice. She began to rub circles around her clitoris, feeling herself getting wetter with each stroke. She thought about Antonio coming for her, almost on cue, and being so completely under her spell. The thought of Antonio grunting in ecstasy like that caused Kenzie to quicken her circles, but she held back from touching her clitoris directly just yet. She knew that when she did, she would explode in orgasm, and she wanted to delay it as much as possible, to savor the memory of the day's activities. Reaching up with her other hand, she touched her breasts, and thought about their encounter earlier at Baracoa. The thought of doing something so dirty, where others could have possibly seen them, was too much for Kenzie to handle. Breaking her own rule of waiting, she switched to a rough back-and-forth motion directly over her clit. This instantly took her over the edge, and she moaned out loud with pleasure, her other hand pinching her nipples as she came.

Lying back on the pillows of her bed, she took some deep, deliberate breaths and steadied herself until her heart rate returned to normal. It was the one bedtime activity that usually worked better for her than hot milk. And it had worked—with her eyelids heavy, Kenzie rolled over, pulling the covers up over her until she was in a little cocoon, and drifted off to sleep.

"Here are the reports you requested, Mr. Navedo."

It was early morning and Antonio was standing on the second floor of the Little Havana distillery, surveying the operations from his vantage point. Everything was running smoothly, as usual. He looked over at the woman standing next to him, proffering a file folder, but couldn't for the life of him remember what reports he had requested, or who she was for that matter. Clearly, she was one of the many administrative assistants he employed. And by the way she was smiling and waiting for his response, he was certain he had not slept with her.

"Thank you," he said taking the folder from the gorgeous brunette whose round ass, squeezed into a form-fitting pencil skirt he would have fixated on a week ago. But ever since meeting Kenzie, all of his sexual energy was aimed at one target. The small yet sassy New Yorker had really gotten into his head.

With no further response or directions, the secretary sauntered away, leaving Antonio to gaze down on what he considered the crown jewel of his family's liquor empire. Little Havana was taking over the rum market worldwide, growing at a rate that production had to race to keep up with. It was a good problem to have, and a challenge that he was sure he could meet.

And even though the floor looked immaculate—everything was business as usual—Antonio felt a little wistful. What good was all of the success and money if there was no one to share it with? he wondered. He thought back on his days with Clarissa, the good times before she had left, suddenly hell-bent on pushing him into some awful suburban existence with a minivan and 2.5 kids. Things between them had been so perfect. He still wondered why she had to go and wreck everything. He had loved her—this much he was certain of, even though when he thought back on their time together, he realized it wasn't something he had expressed directly to her. Why hadn't he said the words? He wasn't sure. But she had to have known, hadn't she? They had built a house together from the ground up, a whole life, really. Sometimes he thought maybe things would have been different if he had told her, had really fought for them to stay together. Or maybe they just wanted different things. Now it was too late.

But no matter. Even though Antonio still felt sad about their breakup, the thoughts were usually fleeting. He had so much to contend with at work, there was literally no time to wallow. Glancing at his watch he noticed it was time for the first tour of the day to begin.

Antonio usually eschewed the tour groups. He had no interest in tourists with little understanding of rum's history or complex flavors who were just looking for something to wash down with a gallon of orange juice and pineapple. The rums he was most proud of were meant for sipping—not cocktail umbrellas. Just as he was about to turn around and return to his office, he noticed the group being led into the open lobby and fixed his gaze on a woman with a giant sunhat. He didn't recognize her, but there was something about the way she walked that struck him as familiar.

Antonio made his way down the winding staircase to the first floor and stood a few feet behind the tour group. He could see that the woman was taking notes on what the tour guide was explaining. At the moment she fell behind from the rest of the group, engrossed in her notepad, he grabbed the woman around the waist and guided her into one of the neighboring tasting rooms.

"What the hell?" the woman yelled.

Antonio looked under the brim of the woman's wide-brimmed hat and locked eyes with Kenzie. He had been sure of it from the moment she had walked in. Well, almost sure.

"What are you doing, taking a tour of my distillery?" Antonio demanded.

Kenzie sputtered before forming her reply. "I'm just doing some research!" she confessed. "I wanted to see how a real distillery is run," she said more quietly.

Antonio smirked and took in her adorable form. She was wearing a floral dress that showed off her legs and curves. He wondered if she had any underwear on, or if he could simply slide his hand up her thigh and once again touch the sweet entrance to her body that got wet so easily under his expert touch.

"You could have just asked me. I'm happy to show you," he said.

"I know," Kenzie said. "I just like doing things on my own terms."

"I noticed that," Antonio said with an unabashed smile. Without hesitation, he took her hand in his. "This way," he said, leading her out the door and across the lobby, in the opposite direction of the tour.

Antonio led Kenzie into the warehouse, and he smiled when she stopped to marvel at the endless racks which held barrel upon barrel of rum, all in specific positions depending on how long they would be aged.

He took in the sight before him. She looked so luscious in the short floral dress, it was as if her whole body was in bloom. He could almost taste the sweetness of her round breasts, which were fully on display, he hoped just for his viewing pleasure.

"So…" she said, looking at him coyly. "What are you going to teach me?"

Without speaking a word, Antonio approached her, and in one swift motion, lifted her up and sat her down facing him on one of the barrels. Immediately, he went to work opening the buttons that ran down the front of her dress to reveal first a lacy black bra, and lower down, a pair of matching panties. Kissing the inside of her thighs, he felt her rake her fingers through his hair, which instantly caused his hard-on, which had been growing in size since he laid eyes on her in the tour group, to spring to full attention.

But he had to hold on. He felt some internal duty to reciprocate the amazing time she had given him in the courtyard at Baracoa. Okay, so it was more than just duty. Truth be told, he was starving for a taste of her.

"I have to have you," he whispered into the side of her neck. Kenzie turned her head so that she was facing him and kissed him hungrily. For once, Antonio forgot all about work and who was watching and focused solely on the incredible shock waves that Kenzie's touch was sending throughout his body. The way she pulled him in toward her as they kissed, like she needed to be as close to him as possible, was such a turn-on. He winced a little and tried hard not to make a sound as her nails dug into his back as they continued to kiss.

It was too much to take, this slow, sensual kissing. Although it was enjoyable, he needed more, and right away.

Pulling her panties down to reveal her naked sex, he took in the sight of her for a moment before pressing his mouth down hard on her clit, sucking it until she squirmed from his unrelenting suction.

Intent on making her come, Antonio grabbed Kenzie's round ass cheeks in his hands and pulled her sex toward his mouth. She was moaning loudly now and wiggling from side to side as he continued to give her the pressure she needed to reach her peak.

"You're making me come," she cried, which nearly made Antonio ruin the front of his trousers. *Take it easy,* he told himself. There was no way he could embarrass himself by ejaculating too quickly in front of a woman like Kenzie. He had to wait, no matter how difficult it was. He held on with the promise of good things to come. *Soon.* He reassured himself, trying to take the focus off the familiar ache in his cock, the urgent need for release. *Soon.*

Kenzie let out a primal moan as she rode the wave of her orgasm. Now, instead of fighting the pleasure Antonio was administering, she grabbed him by the roots of his hair and pulled his face onto her, which only made him even harder, knowing how bad she wanted—and quite possibly needed—this.

Taking a deep breath, Kenzie looked down at Antonio with serious eyes.

"I want you to fuck me," she said plainly.

He could have exploded right then and there. Hearing a woman ask for exactly what she wanted was damn sexy. Somehow, he managed to tame his urge long enough to get his pants unbuttoned. With his cock mere inches from the entrance to her sweet, soft home, they suddenly both froze in silence, hearing the approach of footsteps and garbled voices.

Diving down to the floor and hiding behind a row of barrels, Antonio could see the legs of the tour group guests filing into the warehouse. His breath still ragged, he prayed that the tour guide would keep everyone exactly where they were standing. As the owner and face of the brand, there was no logical way he could explain his naked presence in the warehouse in the middle of the day. At least they hadn't caught the two of them in flagrante.

Antonio peered out from between the barrels, listening to the tour guide's lengthy explanation when he felt Kenzie's hand on his cock. The sudden interruption had wilted it slightly, but with a few long strokes she quickly brought him back to full attention.

"Shh!" Antonio hissed, simultaneously wishing she would stop and needing her to continue. His leadership position was more than a job—it was his whole life. She was facing him now, crawling onto his lap, her dress still on her shoulders but her bra clasp open in front, revealing her large, luscious breasts to him. Her hair was wild and her eyes drunk with lust. Oh god, she looked sexy.

Antonio tried to think of a way to stop her, to at least hold off until the group had moved on to the next room, but before he could speak Kenzie was straddling his lap. She had removed her panties and in one slow, sensual motion, lowered herself down onto the full length of his erection.

His mouth found hers as she bounced on top of him and he kissed her long and hard, doing his best to stay quiet. Antonio tried to hold on for as long as possible, but her steady rhythm, up and down, combined with the sensation of her hard nipples grazing his chest caused his explosion to come on with full force. Kenzie buried her head in Antonio's shoulder as he involuntarily grunted, causing the tour group to go silent.

The tour guide glanced in their direction before he quickly ushered the group out of the warehouse. Good man, he thought to himself, spent from the anxiety over being discovered and the relentless ride Kenzie had taken on him.

Antonio could have fallen asleep on the floor right there, but somehow, Kenzie was already standing and doing up the buttons of her dress.

"That was extremely enlightening," she said,

grabbing her panties off the floor and stepping back into them.

"Glad to be of service," he answered, enjoying the opportunity to look at her. Her temperament was fiery, just like Clarissa's, and she was just a touch crazy, and strong-willed, and astonishingly beautiful. But would she hurt him, just like his ex had done? It seemed so right, having her here at Little Havana, but he knew better than to let someone in, especially so soon.

"I still think you're crazy, taking on this challenge with Baracoa," he added. Kenzie's contented expression morphed into one of exasperation.

"Well, thanks for your vote of confidence," she said curtly.

What was he doing? Part of him wanted to grab her and hold her and confess his feelings, tell her that the stupid bet about the distillery didn't matter, that he would give her anything to just stay.

"You're out of your league with this, Kenzie. I just think you're a smart enough businesswoman to recognize that."

"I'll be sure to take that under consideration," Kenzie said. As she turned around and headed away from him, all Antonio could hear was the sound of her high heels clicking on the stone floor as she made her exit.

Antonio did his best to regain his composure. As he got up off the floor a startling thought occurred to him. It wasn't just the fact that Kenzie was beautiful, or unafraid to put him in his place that appealed to him. It was that on some level, he knew that she was his partner, his match. Apart, they could be successful, sure, but together, he was quite sure that there was nothing they couldn't accomplish. And all that was in addition to how attracted he was to her, physically. The sight of her small, perfectly formed figure aroused something primal in him that he could not deny. Would he ever be man enough to tell her all of this? He didn't know. So he did the one thing he felt sure about and picked himself up and went back to work.

CHAPTER FOUR

BY THE END of the day Kenzie was seriously in need of a shoulder to lean on but being far from home she decided to settle for the hotel lobby bar. It was almost nighttime and Kenzie kept replaying the events of the day—the tour of the distillery, the mind-blowing sex with Antonio and then, his strange plea for her to give up on her venture. Was it that he didn't trust her to run the business? Or maybe he just didn't trust himself. Kenzie knew a lot of men like that from her years working in offices—the ones who always put her ideas down because they actually had none of their own, or otherwise they just weren't very smart to begin with. Striking out on her own to start a business had been one of her best moves to date. So why was Antonio so dead set against her trying to revive a distillery that a few weeks ago, he most likely never even thought about?

And then there was the fact that she was probably jumping headfirst into something she wasn't really ready for. Okay, so it had been three years. But the truth was, she wasn't over Cole, and she probably never would be. Still, Antonio was the first man who she actually thought might live up to the high standards Cole had set. She loved his self-assuredness, and how hardworking he was. They were things that reminded her of Cole, sure, but when she thought about it, they also reminded her a little of herself. Was it possible that beyond being great in bed together, there could be something more there? Kenzie wouldn't allow herself to dwell on this for long. Even if this was nothing more than sex, it still wasn't fair for her to only give half of herself when inside she was still so tied up in the past.

Kenzie sat down on a bar stool and sighed deeply, which got the attention of Jose, who was busy changing one of the beer taps. She hadn't registered it the first time she had seen him behind the bar, but now that she took a moment to take in his looks, she could see that he was quite handsome. He had gorgeous, olive-toned skin, high cheekbones and a slightly receding hairline that probably made him look a tad older than he actually was. When he glanced in her direction, she noticed his arched eyebrows that gave him a sly, devilish look, like he had a juicy secret to tell.

"Hey!" he exclaimed when he saw her. "Club soda and lime, right?" he said, pointing to her knowingly.

Kenzie nodded affirmatively.

"Hard day?" Jose asked, placing a coaster in front of her.

"A hard few years," Kenzie said, surprising herself with her candor. She didn't usually like to open up to people, not even her best friends knew about how much she still thought about Cole, how she could barely sleep at night, the recurring nightmare of his accident playing a loop in her unconscious mind. Her brother had suggested therapy, but she was never the type to want to sit in a room and talk about her feelings. It was her yoga practice that saved her during that first terrible year without him.

"It can't be all bad, can it?" Jose asked, placing the club soda in front of her.

"It isn't all bad," Kenzie replied, thoughtfully swirling the cocktail stirrer. "But that's kind of the scary part. When something makes me happy, it kind of feels like I don't deserve it. And then that makes me sad. I know, crazy, right?"

"Not crazy," Jose said, looking at her sympathetically. "Just human." Jose watched as Kenzie took a big sip of her club soda. "You a friend of Bill's?"

"Huh?" Kenzie replied, before quickly remembering that was AA speak for finding out whether someone else was in the program. "Oh, no," she said quickly. "I'm not an alcoholic." Hearing her words, she started to blush. "That came out wrong."

"It's okay," Jose said, pulling a chip out of his pocket. "Two years for me," he said, showing her the token.

"That is amazing. But isn't it hard for you—working here?"

Jose shrugged. "Eh, I'm used to it. And I figure I'm going to be around alcohol. If I can come to work, do this job and stay sober, then I know I'm okay."

Kenzie nodded understandingly.

"So, what's with all the water then? You trying to stay hydrated?"

Kenzie laughed. "No. Well, yes, but it's for a different reason. My fiancé—he died. In a drunk driving accident. He was at the wheel. With a blood alcohol level of 0.20%."

"I'm sorry," Jose said. "I get it. I was almost there, too. But you have to know that there was nothing you could have done. People have to be ready to change—for themselves."

"I know." Kenzie nodded, brushing a tear off her cheek. She didn't talk about Cole much but when she did, the tears came easily, the memories too fresh.

"But the important thing is that you don't live your life punishing yourself. You're allowed to enjoy life," Jose said seriously.

"I know." Kenzie nodded. "And I'm sure I'd be fine to drink, it's just that I haven't done it in so long. I'd probably be wasted from one glass of wine."

"Well it's your decision," Jose said, patting her hand protectively. "And I'm here to make you a stiff one if you change your mind." He smiled.

Kenzie smiled back and just as Jose walked away to help another customer, her phone buzzed with an incoming call. It was Missy, calling from the studio's main line.

"Hey, Missy," Kenzie answered, glad to see her friend and coworker's smiling face flash across the screen.

"Hey, babe," Missy said, her voice not in its usual upbeat timbre. "I've got some bad news."

"Are you okay?" Kenzie asked, putting a hand over her other ear to block out any of the bar noise.

"I'm fine, but a pipe burst in the studio. I have a plumber here, and it's going to cost you. I'm sorry. I didn't know what else to do."

"You did the right thing," Kenzie said quickly. Her tone of voice was unfazed, but her mind was racing. She knew that contacting the landlord with a problem or request was useless. She needed the money to get her studio into a better place. And yet here she was, gambling with one business to start another.

"What are you thinking?" Missy asked. Sometimes she was too perceptive.

"Ah, I'm just worried that I've put too much on the line with this distillery plan," Kenzie said, finally admitting her fears. "Maybe I should have just taken the money and run."

"No!" Missy's protest was emphatic. "You said yourself that you saw something there. You have a knack for these things."

It was the truth—Kenzie did have an uncanny ability to see past the surface, and home in on a business's full potential.

"I just wish I knew more about the business," Kenzie lamented.

"Why don't you ask Aunt Lilly?" Missy suggested.

"Um, that would be difficult at this point," Kenzie countered.

"I don't mean directly, duh. I mean, find her friends. Find out what she was doing in the liquor business. Maybe it'll shed some light on why she held onto it, or what it once was."

It was a sound proposal. But how could she begin to figure out who to speak with? All she had on Aunt Lilly was a Florida address and a cell phone number that was already out of service.

"I'm going to go see where she lived," Kenzie decided, letting Missy in on her plan. "Maybe there will be some kind of clue."

"Are you planning to go with Antonio?" Missy asked coyly.

"How do you know his name?" Kenzie asked, almost shouting. She had purposefully not mentioned too many details about the man who was trying to buy her out—and bed her every time they were together.

"I have a computer, I know how to Google," Missy said, laughing. "He's only the biggest rum distiller in all of Florida. And judging from Google images, he has a pretty nice ass, too."

"There are pictures of his ass out there?" Kenzie blurted.

"Ha!" Missy said triumphantly. "I knew you were getting it on with someone. You sounded so mellow the last time we spoke."

Kenzie threw a bill on the bar, which accounted for her drink and a sizeable tip for Jose, and walked to a secluded couch in the lobby where she could speak more privately to her friend.

"Okay," she acquiesced. "We've been doing it."

Missy snorted. "And…?"

Kenzie lowered her voice and looked around furtively. Of course, Antonio was not there in the lobby, but she didn't want to risk being overheard. "It. Was. Incredible."

"Yes!" Missy exclaimed in happiness. "Give me details!"

"I will not!" Kenzie replied, though secretly she was dying to tell someone about the sexy Latino who so expertly knew how to make her come with the flick of his tongue or the friction of his strong, callused fingers. She knew Missy would understand the excitement she felt every time she saw the outline of his cock in his trousers, knowing that his arousal was for her, that she excited him to the point where he couldn't contain himself.

"He's very sexy," Kenzie said slowly.

"Uh-huh," said Missy, hanging on her every word.

"And very...skilled, if you know what I mean."

"Oh, I do," said Missy.

"Missy," she said, lowering her voice and looking from side to side. "He went down on me—in his distillery, in the middle of the day."

"Oh my god."

"Yeah. No little silver bullet required with this guy. Though I'm sure he wouldn't mind if I used one."

"Wow. Well, you have fun down there and don't worry, I think we've got this flood under control."

"Flood?"

"More like a mini flood," Missy assured her. "A few drips. Ruined a few of the mats, but it's all replaceable."

"Namaste," said Kenzie.

"Namaste, lady," Missy laughed, ending the call.

Early the next morning, Kenzie was in a rental car, heading to the Sunset Lakes Retirement Community where apparently, her aunt had resided. On the drive over, she thought about calling Antonio. She was so unhappy with the way things had been left the other day. Was he really so hell-bent on protecting this small distillery, or was his sudden guardedness about something else entirely?

Kenzie was driving with the top down (she had splurged on a convertible, totally susceptible to the rental car salesman's pitch to upgrade) and the feeling of the wind through her hair was amazing. She hadn't gotten this much Vitamin D in ages, and she had to admit it felt great.

The security at Sunset Lakes was extremely rigid, and it took a full five minutes of explaining to the man at the entrance the reason for her visit. *As if someone would want to sneak in here!* she thought to herself when the guard finally let her through.

In the main clubhouse, seniors were abuzz with activity, playing cards, eating lunch, some of them were even in exercise attire, and heading to a Zumba class. Kenzie fixed her gaze on an elderly couple, holding hands and walking, albeit slowly, across the lobby. She wondered to herself if she would ever find a love like that again, someone who would hold her wrinkly hand and fetch her prune juice on request. Given her current circumstances, it seemed highly unlikely.

"Hello, can I help you, miss?" A smiling blonde in a pastel pink skirt suit was approaching, and Kenzie could see the name Beatrice emblazoned on her gold name tag.

"Yes," Kenzie said, shifting her weight to the side and cramming both hands in the back pockets of her jean shorts. "My aunt Lilly used to live here, and I was wondering if…"

Before Kenzie could finish her thought, Beatrice

clamped a hand down on her shoulder in excitement. "Oh! You must be Lillian's daughter!"

"No," Kenzie said, backing away in a manner she hoped was polite. "I'm her niece. I didn't know her, really."

Beatrice, obviously disappointed by Kenzie's lack of familial connection turned her mouth into a little frown. "How can I help you?"

"I was wondering if I could speak to any of her friends. Did she have friends here?" Kenzie questioned.

"Oh yes!" Beatrice exclaimed. "She was one of our most popular residents—" Beatrice covered her mouth and whispered in Kenzie's direction "—due in no small part to her little 'sips' she liked to share. We had to tell housekeeping never to touch her bathtub. Lilly always had something new brewing for us."

It made sense now. Aunt Lilly was a lush! But what was she doing—making bathtub gin in a senior living apartment when she owned a stake in a still?

"Did she ever mention anything about owning a distillery?" Kenzie asked cautiously.

"I don't know anything about that," Beatrice said, shaking her head. "But if anyone would, it would be Trudy," she said gesturing toward an elegant woman sitting by herself watching the *TODAY* show. "They were best friends."

"Thank you," Kenzie said, nodding at Beatrice and making her way over to the elderly woman.

"Hi..." Kenzie started, but Trudy held up a thin hand to silence her.

"Shh!" she hissed. "They're doing 'Who Knew?' It's my favorite."

"Sorry," Kenzie said softly. She stood there and waited patiently until the segment was over.

"What can I do for you?" Trudy asked, turning her attention to Kenzie. She had white-blond hair that was cut in an attractive bob and crystal-blue eyes that seemed to cut right through you. Unlike many of the other residents who were sporting activewear, Trudy was gracefully attired in a delicate blouse and capri pants.

"I think you were friends with my aunt...my aunt Lilly."

Trudy's face went pale and her eyes seemed to glaze over.

"You must miss her," Kenzie said sympathetically. "I'm so very sorry for your loss."

"Our loss, correct?" Trudy said skeptically. "I guess you're here about Baracoa," Trudy said with a hint of resignation in her voice.

"So, you knew about it?"

"Knew about it?" Trudy said incredulously. Kenzie noticed the color rising in the paper-thin skin of her cheeks. "I was the master blender there for fifty-three years!" She paused long enough to take in Kenzie's shocked expression. "That's right. Your aunt was the business person, I was the creative."

"And you stopped working there?"

"I had to. My daughter-in-law says my hands are shaky. But it's boring just sitting around here, especially now that she's gone."

Kenzie had a brain wave. "Why don't you come back?"

Trudy snorted.

"I'm serious."

"Doesn't the Navedo family still own a stake?"

The hairs on Kenzie's arms flickered awake at the sound of Antonio's name being spoken.

"Yes, but I, I mean we, have a chance to get it back from them."

Trudy gestured for Kenzie to sit down next to her, and she complied. "The history is complicated," Trudy began. Suddenly, she was looking a bit more animated than when Kenzie first walked in. "Your aunt was a secretary at Baracoa and the owner was in love with her. He left the distillery to her when he died. She and I were a great team. But then things got more difficult. We were hemorrhaging money. It was what she had to do to keep Baracoa afloat."

Now it made sense. Aunt Lilly had only sold shares to Antonio's family because she was forced to.

"All the more reason we should get it back then," Kenzie said pointedly. Trudy nodded in agreement as Kenzie's cell phone began to buzz. "Will you excuse me?" Stepping away, Kenzie contemplated her cell phone screen—it was Antonio. Did she want to speak with him?

"Hello?"

"Kenzie, there's a problem. You need to come to Baracoa right away," Antonio said with more urgency in his voice than she had ever heard.

"I'll be right there," she said instantly.

Kenzie apologized to Trudy for needing to run but left her cell phone number and emphasized that she hoped she would reach out. She wished she could stay and talk more, and even regretted not ever having gotten to know Aunt Lilly. But then she remembered the way Antonio sounded on the phone and knew it was time to jet.

When Kenzie arrived at Baracoa, Antonio was standing in the courtyard. There was destruction all around, from building rubble to spilled spirits.

"What happened?" Kenzie asked, trying to take in the scene and make sense of it.

"A wall collapse," Antonio said, shaking his head. "Nine thousand barrels of aged rum came crashing down. Gone," he said, emphasizing their sudden disappearance by gesturing with his hands.

From where she was standing, Kenzie could see that gallons of rum had been wasted. There was golden brown liquid spilling out from everywhere and a small team of workers were doing their best to clean it all up.

"What?" Antonio said, his nostrils flaring. God, even when he was angry he still looked sexy. "You're not accusing me of doing this to sabotage you, are you?"

"I didn't say that," Kenzie quickly interjected. Wow. She honestly hadn't thought of that angle. Maybe the yoga business just wasn't as cutthroat as the liquor one was.

"I'm sorry," Antonio apologized, rubbing the fur-rowed spot between his eyebrows. "Truly, I blame myself. I knew there were structural problems with the distillery, but I ignored it for too long."

Kenzie reached out and touched his arm gently. "You have a lot going on. You can't always be on top of everything."

Antonio snorted. "But I'm supposed to. It's my responsibility."

Kenzie wished Antonio wouldn't be so hard on himself. She knew what that was like, trying to do everything yourself and always coming up short. Putting her feelings for him aside, she thought about her inheritance.

"Is there anything left?" she asked, hoping for good news.

Antonio stepped over some wreckage and gestured into the barrel room. "Some."

In a gesture of solidarity, or maybe just as a peace offering, Kenzie slid her small hand into Antonio's.

"It's truly a tragedy," she sighed, unable to pro-

DYLAN ROSE 75

cess what this would mean for the distillery going forward. She looked around at the broken barrels and imagined the rich history of the place—all the people that had worked there, the struggles they had been through. She also couldn't help but wonder if it would still be possible to recreate the amazing time she and Antonio had together, hiding behind the barrels at Little Havana.

Antonio squeezed her hand tight. "I'm afraid this might be it for Baracoa," he said gently, putting his arm around her and pulling her in close. Kenzie melted into Antonio's side, breathing in the scent of his sweat and cologne. The fire that he had lit inside her was still burning strong. Then she said something to him that surprised her, that she had never planned to say.

"I think we need to go get a drink."

Antonio wasn't sure why he was standing in a tapas bar with Kenzie when what he really wanted was to be back in her hotel room, recreating the hot-as-hell chemistry they'd had on their first night together. He never imagined that yoga could be so enticing—or that a woman's body could be so limber. The way she had opened herself up to him was totally unlike anything he had experienced before. Looking at her now, in those tight denim shorts, standing up on her tiptoes to get the bartender's attention, he couldn't help but mentally undress her. He pictured that firm, yet round ass right where he wanted it—directly in his face, his mouth savoring those soft, ample cheeks, his tongue seeking out her forbidden opening. He knew without a doubt that he wanted to lick it, to probe it.

"Want anything?"

Antonio snapped out of his reverie and saw that Kenzie was facing him.

"A beer," he said.

"Two beers," he heard her tell the bartender.

"Wait," Antonio said, grabbing her by the arm. "You're drinking?"

Kenzie cocked her head to the side. "Yeah. Why not?"

Antonio wasn't sure of the reasons Kenzie abstained from alcohol, but he knew that the decision to take a drink had to be a heavy one for her. He hoped it didn't have anything to do with the fact that the disaster at Baracoa would surely put her inheritance in jeopardy. He felt a nagging sense of guilt that he had somehow encouraged Kenzie into this predicament of potentially losing both of her businesses. The last thing he wanted to do was to make life more difficult for her.

"You sure?" he yelled to Kenzie over the thumping bar music.

Kenzie thought for a moment and then nodded. "I'm sure."

"Well then," he said, putting aside his worries and

leading her to a bar stool that had just opened up, "let's do this the right way, then." Antonio leaned across and ordered them both dark, aged rums, the kind meant for savoring and sipping. Kenzie swirled the contents of her glass around, the ice cube bouncing off the sides of the glass as she contemplated it. Antonio watched as she brought the drink to her lips, and slowly imbibed a sip of what he considered to be a rare, intoxicating blend.

"Ooh," she said turning to him. "That's strong."

"What flavors do you taste?" he asked, probing to see if her palate was on point.

"Mmm... I taste caramel," she said, trying another sip. "It's warm against the back of my throat."

"Yes," Antonio encouraged her. That wasn't the only thing he wanted against the back of her throat, he thought dirtily. Kenzie was facing him, and he slid his hand up the inside of her thigh.

"It reminds me of maple syrup, a little," she said, now sounding surer of herself. "I like it."

Antonio leaned in and placed his mouth over hers, tasting the toffee-flavored liquor on her lips. He explored her mouth with a slow swirl of his tongue. Her lips were parted, and she was open to him. Somehow it was almost more intimate than fucking, and there they were, doing it in full view of all of the other bar patrons.

When she put her hands on his shoulders and

pulled him in toward her his cock twitched in his pants. It needed to find a home.

"Let's go back to my place," he whispered in her ear.

Kenzie looked up at him with lust-drunken eyes. "I have a better idea."

Before he knew it, she was down off her stool and leading him by the hand through the crowd and toward the restrooms. Kenzie tried several doors that were all locked until she found a single stall bathroom that was free and pulled Antonio in with her and locked the door behind them.

Inside the bathroom, the lights were out, and a candle flickered on the toilet tank, giving the small bathroom a warm glow. The marble sink was modern and the exposed brick walls had been painted to give the interior a rustic look. But Antonio wasn't focused on the fixtures or the decor. His eyes were fixed on Kenzie's face. He scrutinized her features, trying to figure out this enigma of a woman. Her lips parted slightly like she was going to speak, but then she didn't, and he knew the only thing was to go to her, to kiss her. When their mouths met, he felt a strange sense of relaxation. It was a lot to process, what happened at the distillery, but here, entwined with Kenzie, his mouth on hers, suddenly nothing was complicated.

He moved his hands down the length of Kenzie's amazing figure, exploring her body like he was touching her for the first time again. He wanted to memorize every curve of her body. Kenzie pulled back from their make-out session and smiled playfully at Antonio, raking her fingers through his hair. For a second, he worried that perhaps the liquor was impairing her judgement. After all, she wasn't used to drinking. Or maybe it was the Miami sun? She had definitely unwound over the past few days. Antonio wondered if he could take some of the credit for that.

"I need you inside me," she said in a husky voice. It was the only invitation he needed. Antonio pushed Kenzie up against the wall and began kissing her neck while shoving a hand down the front of her jean shorts. Pushing her undies aside with haste, he plunged two fingers inside her and she moaned with pleasure, her body arching back toward him.

"You're so wet," he whispered in her ear between long kisses on her neck. He had observantly noticed that there was a spot on the side of her neck that, whenever he kissed it, made her practically purr with pleasure. He loved knowing that he was learning her secret, erotic spots. He looked forward to finding more of them.

Kenzie kissed him back hungrily, biting his bottom lip. "I need you to fuck me. Now," she instructed him. Antonio's adrenaline went into the red zone at the suggestion. It shocked him that she could arouse real emotion in him one second, and pure lust the very next.

Not one to disappoint a woman, especially one who knew so very well what she wanted, Antonio spun Kenzie around. She was facing the wall now, her palms pressed into it to steady herself. In one swift motion, he pulled down her shorts and underwear and taking out his cock, plunged it deep inside her.

The little yelp of pleasure she emitted when he first entered her nearly caused him to lose it, but this was too good of a time to not enjoy. Antonio wanted to go fast, to give his audacious new friend the drilling she so rightly deserved. But he knew instinctively that it would be better to go slow, to prolong the pleasure he had to make her—and himself—suffer a little.

With one, two, then three slow plunges, Antonio took his time, letting her feel every inch of him. He could tell she wanted more by the way she wriggled her hips and pushed back into him, but instead of giving in, he grabbed her hip with one hand and reached his other hand around to find the small nub of sensitive nerves at the top of her entrance. Teasing her clit, he continued the slow in-and-out rhythm he'd begun. Kenzie's cheek was pressed into the wall and he could see the look of ecstasy on her face, and soon she was biting down on her bottom lip.

If she was trying to prolong her orgasm, it wasn't working. After a few more slow dips, Antonio began to flick her clit faster, knowing that he had found the perfect combination of cock and clitoral stimulation to take her to the edge—and then tumbling over it.

"Please don't stop," Kenzie whined, and Antonio had no intention of doing such a cruel thing. The walls of her pussy tightened around his cock as she leaned into his touch, allowing the powerful spasms of orgasm to overtake her.

Just as she began to catch her breath again, Antonio pulled out. He thought about changing positions, about maybe sitting down on the toilet and pulling her onto his lap, but his balls were too heavy, his hard-on too pressured for anything else. Tapping the head of his cock a few times against the softness of her ass was all it took for him to release what seemed like a larger-than-usual orgasm. As he watched the thick, white semen coat the center of her ass and then trickle down the insides of her thighs he took a mental picture of the moment, knowing it would be fodder for another day when he needed it, when Kenzie was gone.

"That was amazing," Kenzie said, turning around and kissing him.

Antonio wondered what this all meant to Kenzie. Was he her Miami fling or…he hesitated to even let himself think it…something more? On the one hand, their encounters were so primal, so raw, he could understand if it was just about the sex. But then there was the way she kissed him—not just the urgency with which she pressed her mouth to his, or how she grasped his shoulders, pulling him as close as possible. It was the way she unflinchingly met his gaze that told him that just maybe, there was a true connection. At least he hoped there was.

Antonio heard a knock on the bathroom door and quickly pulled up his pants, adjusting himself and trying his best to hold this wave of feelings, both physical and emotional, at bay.

Kenzie looked slightly unsteady as she teetered toward the toilet and sat down. Antonio averted his eyes and straightened his shirt.

"It certainly was," he said in agreement.

CHAPTER FIVE

WHEN KENZIE AWAKENED the next morning, it took her a few beats to put together where she was. The crisp, white sheets that were softer than anything she'd felt on her body since maybe ever, the floor-to-ceiling windows that the Miami morning sun was pouring through, the artwork hanging on the walls that looked like it was done by an actual artist and not a friend at a paint n' sip night. Yep, this had to be Antonio's house.

Kenzie sat up, resting her back on the mountain of pillows behind her. She was alone but could hear the faint sounds of activity coming from somewhere in the house. Closing her eyes, she replayed the events of the previous night as best she could—she remembered the disaster at Baracoa and then drinks—maybe a few, or just one strong one? She wasn't sure. What she did remember was the hot sex scene she and Antonio created in the bar bathroom. It was like something from out of a movie, and she couldn't help but smile thinking about what a wild woman Miami was turning her into.

But quickly enough, the memories of the disaster at the distillery came flooding back. Kenzie wondered if Antonio had gone back over there. Kenzie stretched her arms up over her head, and leaned from side to side, trying to work out the kinks in her shoulders. She inhaled deeply, trying to calm her racing thoughts. The smell of freshly ground espresso filled her nostrils, causing her weary eyes to flicker open, as if suddenly caffeinated.

Just then, Antonio appeared in the doorway. He was already dressed in a T-shirt and joggers, and his usual five o'clock shadow was now dangerously at the point of becoming a full beard.

"Good morning," he said, smiling at her. Suddenly aware that she was naked, Kenzie pulled the comforter up to her neck and smiled back—a ridiculous gesture of modesty since Antonio had seen every inch of her body last night. He'd seen so much, in fact, that he could probably describe every inch of her body better than she could. Not that a situation would ever necessitate someone describing her lady parts in detail. Never mind. She was spiraling.

"How are you feeling?" Antonio asked, a sincere look of concern crossing his face.

Kenzie took a moment to actually assess herself and produce an answer. "I'm fine," she said firmly. "Absolutely fine."

"You got pretty wild last night," Antonio commented.

"The drinking?"

Antonio chuckled. "You had one glass of rum. No, I'm talking about what happened in the bathroom." She noticed that anytime he talked about something intimate, he lowered the timbre of his voice. It was so damn sensual, she felt herself getting wet all over again just hearing him speak to her like that.

"So, I wasn't drunk?" Kenzie asked nervously.

"No, you were just...happy."

Happy. Now that was a word no one had used to describe her state of being in quite some time.

"Should we go back over to Baracoa?" Kenzie asked hesitatingly. She knew they needed to, but part of her just wanted to deny reality and spend the day lounging in bed together.

"We should," Antonio answered matter-of-factly. "But first—breakfast. There's food waiting downstairs, I'll give you a moment." Antonio exited the room, closing the door behind him, but not before giving her a sexy stare that made her feel how naked she was between his sheets. Although she was starving, what she really wanted was Antonio back in the bed with her again. She wanted to know what it was like to wake up with his strong arms wrapped around her. How embarrassing that she was totally zonked. Who goes to a hot guy's house, gets naked in bed with him and actually sleeps?

Willing her legs over the side of the bed, Kenzie's feet hit the plush carpet and walking around the room as if she were on a lingerie scavenger hunt, she found her clothing from the day before. Just as she was about to dress, she noticed a plush, white robe laid out on the chair next to the bed. A guest robe! Now that was pure luxury. Slipping her arms into the lush sleeves, she cinched the belt around her tiny waist, twisted her curls up into a makeshift bun and headed downstairs for breakfast.

Downstairs in the kitchen, Antonio was at the helm of the chef's stove. He was wearing an apron, which was rakishly sexy, and had something going on three of the burners. Kenzie took a seat at the place he'd set for her at the counter and wrapped her hands around the mug containing a café latte with a fancy leaf pattern in the foam.

"Wow, this is incredible," she said.

Antonio slid an over-easy egg onto a piece of avocado toast and garnished it with fruit.

"It's what I do," he said, presenting the dish to her with an almost bashful look. "There's nothing more sensual than cooking for someone you—" she could have been mistaken but she thought she heard his voice catch "—someone you care about," he finished his sentence.

Kenzie was moved by the sentiment, but suddenly there was an awkward vibe in the air, so she opted to make a joke of it. "Well, if this is a hangover, I'm down with that," Kenzie commented, smiling and digging into her breakfast.

"I don't think you were drunk," Antonio said, sitting down across from her with his own plate of food, "you barely finished one drink."

"I'm probably just hyper about having had one," Kenzie confessed. "It's been a while."

"You don't have to tell me, but did something happen that made you want to stay sober?"

Sober. The word itself was so…sobering. So much the antithesis of how she behaved in all the other areas of her life—Kenzie fancied herself as an adventurer, a risk-taker.

"Someone that I cared very much about got into trouble with drinking," she said, stirring swirls in her latte with a spoon. "He was an alcoholic." She'd never used the word to describe Cole, not out loud, before this moment. But in her heart, she was sure of it.

"Your boyfriend," Antonio concluded.

"Fiancé," she corrected him. Ugh, she knew it was a downer to go down this path. But if she was going to get to know Antonio better, if they were going to work together, to be lovers…he had to know. It was too big a part of herself to try and hide.

"I'm sorry," he whispered softly, coming around to the other side of the counter and holding her, his strong arms enveloping her small body.

Kenzie melted into his embrace. With her robe slightly open, she could feel his T-shirt on her chest, her nipples responding to the gentle friction.

"Hey, how come we didn't do anything in your bed last night?" she asked.

"We did—we slept! You were pretty tired by the time we got back here. I must have kept you up past your bedtime."

"I wasn't tired!" she said, playfully punching him.

Antonio's eyes lit up. "Lightweight," he jabbed at her, lifting her up off the stool and throwing her over his shoulder like it was nothing.

Kenzie squealed in delight as he set her ass on the counter and tugged the robe off her shoulders, casting it to the floor. The change of mood was exactly what she wanted. The few times she had mentioned her situation to potential suitors, the mood had gone all gloomy, and most of those guys had left her to wallow. Antonio was different. He seemed to be guided by a desire to look for what was positive, to find the light.

"Mmm," Kenzie moaned as Antonio's mouth found its way to her nether region. "Your breakfast is getting cold."

Antonio looked up at her with his penetrating stare. "This is much more filling."

Kenzie's fingers found their way through Antonio's jet-black mane as he kissed the lips of her pussy, which was still sore from the most excellent banging he'd given it the night before. For a second, she thought she ought to be the one pleasuring him, but every time she tried to change positions, he steadied her in front of his face. Clearly, he was a man intent on doing his job.

And boy, did he know how to do it well. Kenzie had had her fair share of men, and most of them were a complete disaster when it came to going down on her—it was usually a slobbery, ill-conceived undertaking, with either too little or too much enthusiasm and zero precision.

Antonio wasn't like that at all. His soft lips and scratchy beard were the perfect combination to provide pure pleasure. He knew how to read her body language, when something felt good, when he hit exactly the right spot with his finger or tongue, he kept going, and didn't let up until she couldn't see straight.

That was exactly what was happening at the moment—in fact, Kenzie was totally lost in the moment of pleasure, her head thrown back, her long curls unfurled, and her back arching so that her breasts were pushed out and on display.

Her orgasm hit her with such force, she was surprised by the sounds she was emitting. A moment later, she was catching her breath again.

"Okay, okay," she said, gently pushing Antonio's face out of the V between her legs, which was now slick with saliva and her own wetness.

Antonio ignored her directions and kept up the pressure he had been applying with his mouth, now bringing his skillful fingers into play, first plunging one, then two fingers inside her. This had never happened before, but Kenzie let go and came again, this time more violently, squeezing her pussy against his fingers, needing that target upon which to send all of her sexual energy.

"Good girl," he encouraged as she moaned. Antonio looked up at her with hopeful eyes. "Can you come for me again?"

Kenzie met his gaze and nodded. Throwing her head back, she allowed him to stroke her, using just his fingers this time, once again into the throes of euphoria.

She was panting now, sweatier than she ever got after a hard morning run. "How did you do that?"

Antonio smiled, using his hand to wipe some of her juices off the side of his mouth but didn't say anything.

"There must be something I can do to make you happy," she said, hopping down from the counter and leaning her naked body into his chest. He was still fully dressed, though she could feel his hard-on pressing into her leg now.

"There is something, actually," he said, pulling his cock out over the elastic waistband of his gray pants and beginning to stroke it.

Kenzie went to kneel down in front of him, but Antonio quickly stopped her.

"Not that," he said quickly. She must have seemed taken aback, because he quickly explained himself.

"Not that I don't like that. I *love* that. But I had something else in mind."

"Tell me," she insisted, feeling disappointed that she couldn't reciprocate the pleasure he had given her, that she wouldn't get to feel the girth of his beautiful cock filling her mouth.

"Come for me. One more time."

Kenzie looked at Antonio like he was crazy. She'd never had a multiple orgasm before this morning. She wasn't even sure she could do it again.

"Really? That's what you want?"

"I like watching you," he said, moving closer to her and stroking his cock a little faster. "I really like seeing you come, too."

Kenzie sat down on one of the stools, spread her legs open to Antonio's gaze and, moving a finger down the length of her body and placing it directly over her clit just like she did when she was alone, she started the side-to-side motion over her button that always brought that shivering feeling to her whole body within seconds.

She was so spent, she didn't know if it would work this time, but she knew she had to try.

"Is this what you do when you're by yourself?" Antonio asked lustily, pumping his hand up and down his rod faster and faster.

"Mmm," Kenzie replied. Even though her clit was swollen, just the thought of Antonio watching her was enough to bring on that spine-tingling feeling.

"Oh!" she cried out, showing Antonio what he wanted to see.

Fortunately, he was right there with her, and just as she peaked, he did too, grunting in unison with her cries of pleasure.

Kenzie watched as Antonio sighed deeply, recovering from his release. He looked so manly, and at the same time so vulnerable. He was sweating now, too, and still looking at her with that same lusty stare.

Who was this man and how did he know how to take her to these previously uncharted levels of ecstasy? It was almost like he knew even more than she did what she was capable of. It was a feeling that was appealing but also a little disconcerting. She was trying really hard not to question it too much, to let herself enjoy it. For too long she had overanalyzed everything—with Antonio, she wanted to let herself just be in the moment and feel whatever it was she was feeling.

"Was that good?" he asked, running a hand down the side of her cheek.

"Oh yeah," she said, throwing her arms around his neck and kissing him. She didn't want to leave any doubt in his mind that she found what they were doing together highly enjoyable.

After they showered and dressed, Antonio insisted they drive over to Baracoa to assess the damage. Kenzie wanted to make a quick stop at the Fontainebleau to change clothes, so Antonio waited in the car outside of the lobby. Bellmen were wheeling luggage carts around and a few guests sat on benches, waiting for valet service to bring their cars around. The top on the convertible was down, and it already felt overbearingly hot, even in the shade. Antonio decided he would make his offer to Kenzie one more time. He didn't like the idea of her losing her inheritance because of this freak accident. Baracoa was small change to him, but he guessed that the money would have a real impact on Kenzie's business at home in New York. Still, he had to tread carefully. Kenzie clearly wasn't the type who would accept help. She'd see his generosity as charity unless he phrased it the right way.

Before he had any time to plan out what he was going to say, Kenzie emerged from the lobby, looking fresh and more beautiful than he'd ever seen her. She was wearing a long, flowing dress with a blue-and-white print, and her hair was down. Antonio's eyes were immediately drawn to the gorgeous curves of her shoulders, which were exposed, and when she slid into the passenger seat he got a glimpse of her back, which was also visible in the halter dress.

"Can you put some of this on me?" she asked, handing him a tube of sunscreen and turning so that her back was facing him.

Antonio complied, squeezing a glob of sunscreen into his hand and slowly rubbing it from her shoulder blades all the way down to the small of her back. Even though they had just been together, he was already thinking about undressing her again. When it came to Kenzie's perfect body, he just couldn't get enough.

"Thanks," Kenzie said, turning around and taking the lotion back from him. "Gotta have my SPF!"

"You have gotten a little color since I first met you," he commented. It was true—her fair skin was now dotted with a few tiny freckles and her shoulders were a bit sun-kissed.

"My body isn't used to sunlight," she joked.

On the drive over to Baracoa they were mostly silent, but it was a good silence, a comfortable one, Antonio thought. Kenzie was just so easy to be around, he didn't feel the need to initiate polite chit-chat. As he navigated the roads, he occasionally glanced over at her and smiled. The sight of her hair, blowing wild in the wind, was amazing. Then a thought occurred to him: If she accepted his offer of a buyout, today would probably be the last time they spent together. After all, what reason would she have for staying? She had a business to run in New York, which she was probably neglecting. He was surprised to find that he was experiencing that same sinking feeling he'd gotten when Clarissa first left. He'd only known Kenzie a few days. Was he really so attached, or was it the crazy sex blurring his judgement?

Just as he was starting to despair, Antonio felt the

sudden touch of a hand on his thigh. Kenzie smiled at him and he revved the engine, taking the final turns toward the distillery with extra speed.

Parking the car right in front of the main building, he and Kenzie went inside to assess the damage. A cleanup crew was sweeping up the floor of the warehouse, trying to control the epic mess of rubble and liquor. Antonio shook his head in dismay at the disaster he was sure he could have somehow prevented.

"That's Mateo, he's a cousin," Antonio said, pointing out a man in his early twenties talking on a cell phone. He looked like a younger version of himself, albeit with slicked-back hair and trendy clothes. Truth be told, Antonio had dressed that way when he was young, too. "We made him manager, but he's rarely here," he explained to Kenzie. "My aunt has been an integral part of the business forever and she's tried to find him work but nothing sticks. I'd love to get rid of him, but I can't." Antonio turned away from Kenzie and raised his voice. "Mateo!" he shouted, trying to get the young guy's attention.

Mateo looked up at Antonio and Antonio nodded, telegraphing to the kid that this was serious business. After a moment he hung up his call and approached Antonio and Kenzie.

"Cousin," he said, opening his arms for an embrace. Antonio hesitantly hugged him, recoiling slightly from Mateo's overuse of cologne.

"What's the plan here?" Antonio asked, crossing his arms in front of his chest.

"We've got cleanup guys working around the clock," Mateo said, looking nervously from side to side.

"And what's being done to make sure the barrels that are left are in stable condition? Have you checked the temperature control?"

Mateo just stood there, apparently dumbfounded. His inability to answer was enough reason for Antonio to dismiss him.

"I'll do it," Antonio said gruffly, walking away. Kenzie followed him outside.

"Not the answer you were hoping for?" she said, taking a hold of his arm.

"If he even took the slightest interest in our business, I'd go easier on him. He's going to run this place into the ground. As if it isn't there already."

"It looks like the damage isn't catastrophic," Kenzie said, trying to push a glimmer of enthusiasm into her voice.

Antonio took her hands in his. "I know you don't want to hear this, but you need to take the money and get out of here. This place is nothing more than a money pit." Okay, so maybe the soft approach was out the window, but Antonio was never one for sugarcoating things anyway. "Please," he implored her, almost begging. "I don't want to see you lose your business over this."

Kenzie's face got tight and her eyebrows furrowed.

"Why are you always trying to rescue me, like I'm some damsel in distress?" she blurted.

"I'm not!" Antonio spat back, his temper getting the better of him. "I'm trying to stop you from doing something foolish."

Kenzie turned on her heel and went out into the courtyard. Antonio took a deep breath and let out a long exhale before following behind her.

"I want to show you something," he said, taking Kenzie by surprise by grabbing her hand and leading her out past the courtyard and into a field adjacent to the building. It was quiet, and still—the place he always returned to when he needed to think or make big decisions.

"Wow," Kenzie said, looking around wide-eyed at the tall stalks that surrounded them. Antonio found that he was happily surprised by Kenzie's awestruck reaction to his happy place.

"Is it sugar cane?" she asked.

"Exactly. This is the lifeblood of my family. We came here from Cuba and started small. This distillery, Baracoa, was how my great-grandfather got his start. That's why it hurts for me to see it neglected like this."

"I didn't know it was so personal for you," Kenzie said, reaching out to touch his arm. Her eyes were filled with compassion, which moved him, though instinct told him not to show it.

Antonio shrugged. "It's just a business. It's the people that matter. I just don't like to see things wasted, or needlessly destroyed." He thought about the liquid gold wasted on the floor and shook his head in dismay.

"Maybe that's why I'm here," said Kenzie, her voice taking on a brighter tone. "Maybe I can help get this place back up and running the way it should be."

"Kenzie," he said gently, in a way he hoped wasn't condescending. "I appreciate that. I do. But you don't know the first thing about rum production."

"No, but I do."

Kenzie and Antonio turned to see a small elderly woman standing at the edge of the field. How long had she been standing there watching them?

"Excuse me…who are…" Antonio began to question her, but Kenzie interrupted.

"Trudy!" Kenzie said, running over to the old lady and supporting her with an outstretched arm. The woman looked dainty, but also sturdy. She was wearing a simple T-shirt and jeans with the legs rolled up. He could tell that when she was younger, she had definitely been a head-turner.

"How did you get here?" Kenzie asked. Antonio saw that her face had lit up upon seeing this woman. Her expression showed a mixture of concern and excitement.

"I took a taxi!" Trudy said, as if it was the most obvious thing to do in the world.

"Does the senior center know you're gone?"

Trudy brushed Kenzie's concern off with a wave of her hand. "It's a retirement community, not jail. They'll be fine."

Antonio didn't understand what connection Kenzie had with this woman, but he could tell that it was important.

"It looks like you and your husband have your work cut out for you!" Trudy said, giving Antonio a once-over. "It's a disaster in there."

"Oh, he's not my…" Before Kenzie could correct her, Trudy was approaching Antonio.

"Your manager doesn't know the first thing about distillation! He couldn't tell a light rum from a dark!" Trudy was suddenly fired up and Antonio worried that the woman might give herself a heart attack, right there on the premises.

Antonio instinctively bowed his head. "I know," he acknowledged. "He's family," he said, shrugging. Antonio looked back and forth between the two women. "I'm sorry. How do you two know each other?"

"Trudy used to work here, with my aunt Lilly," Kenzie explained. Right. Lilly was the whole reason Kenzie had come down here in the first place.

"I was the master blender," Trudy said proudly. "Yes, a woman!"

Antonio held up his hands in innocence. He had no doubt that Trudy would at least be more capable than his cousin.

"I'll let Mateo know that his services are no longer needed," said Antonio. "Do you agree, Kenzie?"

Kenzie looked astounded by what was about to transpire, but before she could voice an opinion Trudy interjected.

"That cute boy inside on the cell phone? Keep him around," said Trudy. "I could use an assistant. Now let's get going. I have to start by checking the barrels we didn't lose." Trudy wriggled loose of Kenzie and started heading into the facility at a quick clip.

Antonio watched for a moment as Trudy set off ahead of them. He shook his head, knowing in his gut that he was probably helpless to stop this strong-willed woman from doing whatever she thought was necessary. The gentleman in him wouldn't begin to know how to say no to her. Actually, it was the same way with Kenzie. It certainly seemed like the more he tried to convince her otherwise, the more strong-willed she became in her quest to turn the distillery around according to her own plans.

"I guess I now have two women who know more than I do," Antonio said with resignation.

"I guess you do!" said Kenzie, linking her arm through his and following Trudy inside.

CHAPTER SIX

THE NEXT MORNING was Saturday and Kenzie rose early, did yoga, grabbed breakfast on the go, and hit the streets of Miami with renewed spirit. She only had three more days until the rum mixer and the PR company she worked with back in New York on her yoga studio was helping to get the word out down south. She had Trudy working at the distillery, and Catalina Cortez was already down in Florida, visiting family, so setting up her pop-up concert had been easy. Now all she needed was some spice to add to the mix.

Walking around the streets downtown and seeing the food trucks setting up for the lunch crowds, she thought about Antonio and how he would be losing a family legacy when she won their little bet. She momentarily thought of calling him and offering to be partners, but he had made it clear—and not without a condescending tone—that she knew nothing of his business. No, she told herself, she needed to stop apologizing and just continue working hard, to the best of her abilities.

But what about Antonio? Of course, he wouldn't be hurting for work—he had so many other, more lucrative properties—but the thought of never seeing him again after this week dampened her mood in a way she hadn't expected. What was the solution? Her home was in New York. And although it was fun to play at being a beach bunny, she wasn't really the South Florida type. Antonio seemed so tied to the culture here, to his family, he was basically synonymous with the city.

Why weren't there guys like him back in New York, she lamented to herself as she stopped at one of the food trucks that looked interesting. She tried to focus on the menu but kept flashing back on the image of Antonio pleasuring her in his kitchen. Back home, dating was so gamey—a long back and forth via text that usually led nowhere, or if it did, the guy would play hot and cold, making her feel crazy, as if she had done something wrong, when in reality, he was probably just keeping his options open. Antonio wasn't like that. She loved how straightforward he was—a real man who knew what he wanted and went for it.

She remembered a guy she had briefly dated in New York, shortly after Cole's death at the urging of her friends to "get out there" and "get your mind off things." She never forgot how he'd told her he was going to invite her to a Jack White concert but decided not to because it would have meant he hadn't waited the appropriate three days before calling her again. Antonio would never subscribe to something as lame as a "three-day rule," she was sure of it. In fact, she didn't think he had any regard for rules whatsoever, and that was fucking sexy.

"Anything look good?"

Kenzie blinked and transported herself out of her reverie to lock eyes with a handsome young purveyor of Latin food. He was leaning over the window of his food truck and unabashedly drinking in the sight of her. He had to be early twenties, Kenzie thought, and smiled to herself. It was still nice when guys thought she was that young. Or maybe they didn't but in any case, it was still flattering.

"Just looking," Kenzie said with a smile, and started to walk to the next truck.

"The Latin burger is amazing," the young guy called out, trying his best to lure her back. "Free soda with purchase!"

Kenzie laughed and continued walking, albeit with a little more pep in her step. Maybe she could get into the lifestyle down here. It was definitely more chill than New York, and that wasn't a bad thing. Over the past few days her practice had felt much more open. Or maybe it was that she'd been getting properly fucked all week that had made the difference.

"Kenzie, what are you doing down here?" asked a male voice that she recognized immediately. It was a voice whose very timbre could start her nether regions humming with pleasure.

"Antonio?"

When Kenzie turned around she saw him—dressed in a suit, looking more professional than she'd ever seen. A tall woman with long dark hair in an expensive suit herself was standing by his side.

"You remember Elena, my associate," Antonio said quickly, reintroducing the women.

"Of course." Kenzie smiled. "I was just investigating some food truck options—for the rum mixer," she explained.

"You have to try the Latin burger," said Elena. "It's the best," she chimed with what Kenzie thought was a little wink.

"What are you doing in this neighborhood?" Kenzie asked, genuinely curious.

"Our offices are on the next corner," Antonio said, pointing south. "I wish we could join you for lunch, but we have to get back for another meeting," he said sounding truly disappointed.

"Oh, I'm just perusing," Kenzie said. It was so weird, seeing him with Elena. With their attire and designer sunglasses and not to mention more compatible heights, they just seemed to go together—like a match. And what were they doing, attending meetings on a Saturday?

"Nice seeing you again," Elena said formally. The

two of them headed off and Antonio looked back at Kenzie briefly as if to apologize in some way.

Kenzie stood there in the middle of the sidewalk for some time, just watching them go, until they turned the corner and she had to gather her thoughts. *Deep breath,* she told herself. *This is nothing. You're spiraling.* She tended to do that, especially since Cole. When things were going well it meant that the other shoe was about to drop.

He likes you. He's never lied to you, she reminded herself, trying to reframe the negativity into positive thoughts. *Except that he came to the hotel to scope you out and had sex with you, knowing full well who you were,* a little voice reminded her.

Could she trust him? Kenzie didn't know. But she was sure of one thing: If he and Elena were heading up to the office for a midday tryst, she was going to ruin it.

Rushing back to the burger truck, Kenzie pulled out her wallet.

"You changed your mind!" the young guy said, perking up. "What can I get you?"

"I'll take one of everything," Kenzie said, handing him a wad of bills.

"You looked really hungry when I first saw you," the guy said teasingly. "I'll get this out for you in a jiff."

Ten long minutes later, Kenzie was retracing the steps she'd seen Antonio and Elena take, which led her to a glass high-rise, incongruous with the Miami architecture. Inside the cool and cavernous lobby, she noticed a directory and found the suite for Navedo Enterprises, which occupied the entire 10th floor. Giant greasy burger bag in hand, she rode the elevator up and when it stopped on the 10th floor, she hesitated before opening the glass double doors that led to reception.

Okay, so maybe this was slightly in the realm of crazy girlfriend behavior. And okay, she wasn't even Antonio's girlfriend. But for the first time in a long time, she knew exactly what she wanted. Kenzie felt her pulse racing as she pushed upon the doors to the office. She knew the risk she was taking, that a forward gesture like this could scare Antonio off. It broke all the rules to pursue a man—countless books, and even some of her girlfriends told her she had to wait for him to come to her. But with her emotions running high, she threw caution to the wind. It was time to go after what she wanted.

"May I help you?" asked the receptionist in between answering calls on her headset. "Excuse me," she said to Kenzie before she could speak. "Navedo Enterprises, how can I direct your call?"

"I'm here to see Antonio Navedo," Kenzie declared firmly, once she had the receptionist's full attention.

"Your name?"

"MacKenzie Fox."

Kenzie waited awkwardly until the receptionist came out from behind her desk and walked her down a long, carpeted hallway to what she presumed was the corner office. When she opened the door, revealing the large room with modern furniture including a few chairs and a conference table Antonio stood up from behind the desk.

"This is a surprise."

Kenzie surveyed Antonio's expression, trying to find a clue as to what he was thinking. If anything, he looked nonplussed by her sudden appearance in his office. Kenzie's cheeks burned with embarrassment. Suddenly she was sure she had made a big mistake. Antonio wasn't having sex with Elena on the conference table. He was alone, working.

"I hope it's okay that I came by," Kenzie said tentatively.

"What's this?" Antonio questioned, and indicated the bag she was holding. Kenzie just stood there for a second, having totally forgotten her ploy for showing up.

"It's burgers! I brought you lunch." *Please like burgers*, she thought to herself.

Antonio walked past Kenzie and shut the door to his office. "I was just getting hungry," Antonio said, going to her and taking the bag out of her hands. "Latin burger?"

Kenzie shrugged.

Antonio reached into the bag and pulled out a

burger, taking a huge bite. "Mmm," he said. "Try some," he said, holding out the food to her.

It wasn't Kenzie's usual fare, but she decided to give it a go. Taking Antonio's hand and moving the burger to her mouth, she bit in. It was messy and oh-so good indeed.

"I like watching you enjoy your food," Antonio commented as she swallowed. He leaned over and started to plant kisses on the secret spot on her neck.

"Are you sure you didn't have other lunch plans?" Kenzie asked tentatively, "With Elena?"

Antonio pulled back momentarily and laughed. "Elena?" he said incredulously. "Is that what this lunch delivery is about?"

"No," Kenzie said firmly, reaching for the zipper of his trousers. "I had something I wanted in mind for lunch." She tugged the band of his underwear down until she could see the tip of his cock. "Something firmer. More filling."

Antonio pulled away but kept his eyes locked on Kenzie as he went to the door and turned the latch to lock it.

"Tell me more about this," he said, dropping his pants down to reveal his package.

"Why don't I show you instead?" she countered, dropping to her knees in front of him and beginning to lick her way from the base of his shaft all the way up to the sensitive head. Antonio's eyes rolled back, and he sighed as she used one hand to stroke him while alternating between long licks of his length and giving attention to his balls. They were so full, so amazing and felt wonderful in her mouth.

Antonio was getting more into it now, and raking his hands into her hair he made noises that seemed to not take into consideration that they were in an office—his office.

Kenzie continued sucking, feeling powerful as she watched this big strong man melt like butter under her control.

"What are you doing to me?" he asked as she looked up at him, her mouth encircled around his member, her hands caressing his balls. She could tell how much he enjoyed it when she didn't forget about them.

Antonio was no longer able to hold back and grabbing Kenzie's head in his hands, he took over, fucking her mouth the same way he had fucked her pussy—deliberately and intensely. Soon she felt his balls seize up and a hot liquid rush into her mouth and she swallowed it gratefully.

"Thank you," he gasped, steadying himself on the edge of his desk.

"No, thank you," she said, standing up and still tasting the sweet and salty come that lingered in her mouth.

When Antonio had pulled up his trousers, he pulled Kenzie in for a kiss. It was so erotic, them sharing the taste of their passion together. Kenzie closed her eyes. As Antonio's tongue gently probed inside her mouth, she relaxed into the warm feeling that was radiating from the top of her head down to her toes. Time seemed to stand still as they continued to kiss, until finally Antonio broke away.

"Come away for the weekend with me," he whispered.

Kenzie laughed at the thought of it. Antonio was so serious, and the way he said it sounded like something out of a movie. Besides, she already felt like she was on vacation here in Miami.

"Where? How?" she asked, knowing that Antonio would probably have a plausible answer.

"My estate in the Virgin Islands. We'll take my private plane and be back tomorrow."

"But don't we both have a lot of work to do?"

Antonio shushed her by holding a finger to her lips. "Don't talk about work. All I've been doing is working."

That, she could relate to.

"Okay," Kenzie relented. "As long as we're back tomorrow. Let's go."

Exactly one hour later, Kenzie was seated inside Antonio's personal plane, a hastily packed overnight bag stowed above her containing only the essentials—a great dress, a bikini, and a black lace body suit with cut-outs that she'd grabbed from Victoria's Secret on the way over without bothering to try it on.

"Is this your first time?" Antonio asked, raising his eyebrows at her. He was seated across from her, with a small table in between them.

"You know that it isn't," Kenzie said, taking off her sandal and playfully kicking him in the thigh. God, his thighs were strong. It felt like kicking a wall or solid steel. Did that come from working out, she wondered, or just from being Antonio.

"Your first time in a private aircraft," he clarified, grabbing hold of her foot and beginning to massage it.

"Of course not! I take them all the time," Kenzie said sarcastically. If he thought it was culture shock for her, being down in Miami, she could just imagine how he would cope with her life in New York City. In fact, she was fairly certain she'd pay good money just to see him navigate the MTA during rush hour.

"Well, I want you to enjoy yourself," Antonio said, pushing the pad of his thumb into the center of the sole of her foot, which somehow released the tension all over her body and sent a signal straight to her nether regions.

"Mmm," Kenzie sighed, sinking deeper into her leather seat and bringing her other foot to rest in the V of Antonio's legs.

"If we had more time I'd ask you to join the mile-high club," he said in a put-on lascivious tone.

"What makes you think I'm not already a member?" she said coyly.

Antonio pulled Kenzie onto his lap and she let out a surprised little yelp. He kissed her gently, which was a nice contrast to the roughness of his stubble. Just as things were starting to get heated between them, an announcement came over the loudspeaker.

"This is your captain speaking, I'll need everyone to return to their seats as we prepare for landing."

Kenzie blushed, wondering if they had been caught, returned to her seat and dutifully fastened her seat belt.

"Are you ready for this?" Antonio asked, lifting up the edge of the window shade. Beyond it, Kenzie could see an island. There were areas of green dotted with colorful houses. As they descended, she could make out the perfect white sandy beaches and the shimmering aquamarine water. She had the feeling that this was the start of something big—not just a travel adventure, but maybe the first step toward discovering more about Antonio and more about herself. Maybe, in a way it was like a mini-vacation.

Kenzie couldn't remember the last time she had traveled somewhere purely for pleasure. Her trip down to Florida had really been for business. So maybe a weekend in paradise would do her good. She thought about putting all of her day-to-day obligations aside, and how nice that would be. She imagined the two of them on a beach together, relaxing in the sand and walking hand-in-hand along the shore, the warm water lapping at their bare feet. She even thought about what it would be like to have sex on the beach, lying in the sand with the waves crashing around them. Okay, maybe that would be a little too sandy, but she was sure Antonio's place would be more than adequate for some R & R.

Kenzie had never cared much about whether the people she dated had money or not, but she had to admit, this whole being whisked away to an island thing was not too bad. She turned and looked at Antonio. He was still looking out the window at the emerging scenery and had a look of boyish excitement in his eyes.

"So ready," she said, with a smile.

When they reached the entrance of Antonio's residence on the island, the sun was beginning to set. It was a gorgeous bungalow, directly on the beach, and the master bedroom opened out onto a swimming pool, which was illuminated by little gold lights.

"It's paradise," Kenzie said, sitting down on the canopy bed and looking out past the pool to the ocean. She thought she saw lights flickering and wondered if it was a passing ship.

"You hungry?" Antonio asked.

"Yes," she said, "but is there anything open around here?" She didn't remember passing any restaurants or stores on the short drive over.

"I know a good place," he said, taking her by the hand and leading her out toward the pool.

"Wait! I don't have shoes on!" she protested.

"You don't need them at this place," he said, pulling her away from the room and out into the star-filled night.

They walked past the swimming pool and directly onto the beach. The sand was soft and cool and felt wonderful between her toes. Directly in front of them there was a table set up, surrounded by lit tiki torches. Antonio led her to her seat and pulled out her chair for her.

"You arranged all this for me?" she asked.

"Yes. For us," he said, lifting an already-filled champagne flute up. Kenzie picked hers up. "Here's to escaping together."

"And to finding a bit of serenity," she added, clinking her glass to his.

For the next hour, a professional waitstaff served them a four-course meal filled with local fruit, fish and warm bread. When a serving of chocolate lava cake was placed in front of her Kenzie had to protest.

"I don't think I can eat another thing. Seriously, this was the most amazing meal," she said.

"It's amazing to be here with you. It's so easy to be around you," Antonio said with a bit too much sincerity for Kenzie's taste. For a second, she had the nervous suspicion that he was expressing real feelings for her. She wasn't sure what to do with that, if there was room for her to receive real love again.

Hell yes. She could do that. Friendship, sure. But her capacity for love had been closed off since the day of the accident and she wasn't sure it could ever return.

"This house, did you build it just for you?" she asked.

Antonio winced slightly, and she knew she'd hit a nerve.

"No," he said plainly. "This place was a project of love—with someone who was in my life for a long time. I hope that doesn't make you uncomfortable."

"Who was she?" Kenzie asked.

Antonio's eyes went to a faraway place, like he was remembering. "Her name was Clarissa. She was beautiful. Funny. A great businessperson. You reminded me of her when we first met," he confessed.

"So, what happened? Why didn't you stay together?"

"Our lives went in different directions…she wanted children."

"And you don't?" Kenzie knew it was a weighty question. It was one that she got sometimes too, from friends, nosy relatives, even the odd stranger. Her answer had always been, "When the time is right." But with Cole gone, suddenly that response had little meaning.

"I don't know," Antonio said, folding his hands in front of him and looking down. "Or maybe sometimes it takes someone being gone to make you realize what you want, but then it's too late."

Kenzie understood that feeling all too well. She reached out and placed her hands over Antonio's.

"It isn't easy, is it?" She smiled at him, tilting her head to the side and perhaps seeing him in a different light.

It was completely dark out now, save for the few flickering lights that surrounded their table and as an ocean breeze rippled through the table linens, Kenzie felt an involuntary shiver run up her spine.

Antonio walked around to her side of the table and in one easy swoop, he scooped her up into his arms. With her arms around his neck and his warm hands on her body, she let him carry her all the way to the giant bed in the middle of their room.

But when he laid her down on top of the sheets, she got the weird feeling that something between them had shifted. Oh no, she thought to herself. All the signs were there—him opening up about his past relationships, the romantic dinner on the beach, just the way he was now looking at her—if she wasn't mistaken, he was trying to do "lovemaking."

And wasn't it extra intense that she was probably lying in the bed that his former girlfriend had probably picked out? That they had made love on hundreds, no maybe thousands of times?

Kenzie popped up suddenly, breaking the cosmic connection Antonio was no doubt trying to induce with his gaze.

"Excuse me, I need to use the bathroom."

"Is everything alright?" Antonio called after her.

"Just fine!" she yelled, shutting the door behind her and sitting down on the toilet. She looked ahead of her and found that the view from where she was sitting was a perfect-picture window of the ocean. Damn, even Antonio's toilets were romantic.

Kenzie scolded herself for hiding out in the bathroom, for trying to escape from confronting feelings. All she needed to do was to be herself. That was enough—it had to be.

"Sorry about that," she said, reentering the bedroom where Antonio was now splayed out on the bed fully nude. It was a vision that would normally elicit a sigh from her lips and a sudden slickness on the ones further down. But tonight, things felt so much more loaded. She was starting to get the feeling that it was a big step for Antonio to have brought her here. Antonio looked at her expectantly. She wasn't sure how to begin, so she decided just to level with him.

"Can I be honest with you?" Kenzie asked, sitting down tentatively on the edge of the bed. Admittedly, it was an awkward question to ask a man whose entire package was on display. "I'm a little weirded out by how fast this is moving."

Antonio seemed unfussed by her confession.

"Okay," he said.

"I just think," Kenzie could hear the tone of her voice getting higher, "I think that we are two very different people." In her mind, it wasn't a blow-off.

In fact, she hadn't felt the desire to at least try and be truly present with someone, to truly be open, since Cole. But she was feeling that with Antonio. She just wasn't sure if she was ready for what Antonio wanted. He had built this house with someone he loved—she could hardly imagine being able to take that step with someone at this point in her life.

"I like that about us, that we're different," he said. "The same is boring. Different, it makes a spark."

"I agree. But we have to be realistic. After this week, we may not see each other again and…"

"Kenzie." Antonio stopped her by placing a finger over her lips, which felt like they had been running a mile a minute. She tended to go on and on when she was nervous. "Are you saying you don't want to make love with me?"

"See, that's it! Exactly." She hadn't wanted to say it, but Antonio had put it in a nutshell. "I think the two of us, we're more the hot, fast and dirty kind of couple."

"Fuck buddies."

"Yes!" Kenzie said, throwing up her hands. So he did understand.

"Well, what if I want more?"

The question was so straightforward, but Kenzie wasn't sure how to answer it. It hung in the air as she sat there in silence, letting the enormity of what he was suggesting sink in. Did Antonio really want to be with her?

"What if I told you that I could do more than just make you come? That I could make you feel an incredible…connection. If you let me." Antonio leaned over and took Kenzie's hand. He ran his finger down the middle of her palm. She wondered if he could see something there that she couldn't—a real future.

His words were so alluring, his body so hot, it was hard to not just fall back onto the bed and agree to everything he was suggesting, to let him devour her. But a voice inside her told her to proceed with caution.

"I'm not ready," she said plainly. "But… I can tell you that during the time we spend together, I'm all yours. I'm here. I'm not thinking about anyone else, and there's no place I'd rather be." She squeezed his hand, hoping to drive home the point.

"Okay," Antonio said, considering her response. "So, you'll continue to let me fuck you…?"

"Oh yes," she answered quickly, sliding in next to him on the bed. Now he was speaking her language.

"But—" Antonio held her back momentarily "—consider this," he said, sitting up. "If you lose our bet, about the distillery, I not only get to keep your share, I get you—all of you," he said, giving her a knowing look.

Kenzie laughed but paused before answering. It seemed like a given that she was going to pull off the mixer and have the distillery all to herself by the end of the evening on Tuesday. The chances of her having to allow Antonio to make sweet, emotional, gaze-into-each-other's-eyes love to her seemed nil.

"Sure," she said confidently. "But if you lose..." She wracked her brain for the most humiliating thing she could think of. "I get you, tied to a bed, with permission to do exactly what I want to you."

"I'd let you do that to me right now." Antonio laughed, pulling her on top of him.

"Fair point," she acknowledged, allowing him to inch the zipper of her dress down far enough so that he could remove it. "But for now..." she said, sitting up on him and allowing her dress to fall off her shoulders, exposing her naked breasts. "Will you fuck me? Can you do that for me?" Her eyes were wide, her pupils dilated, and she was starting to feel that now-familiar wetness starting down below. This was the feeling she had come to associate with Antonio. Why ruin it by getting all serious? Maybe things were perfect just the way they were—light and fun.

Antonio answered her plea without so much as a word, flipping her onto her stomach and pulling her dress the rest of the way off. Her undies were the next to go. They were the only thing keeping her from leaking her love juices onto the expensive sheets. With her body undressed, Antonio kissed his way from the nape of her neck all the way down her spine until he reached her buttocks, where he lingered, kissing both of her ass cheeks lovingly before circling his tongue around the entrance of her forbidden opening.

Kenzie sighed with pleasure. No man had ever done this to her before. It was so erotic and instantly caused her to arch her pussy up toward him. She felt so open, so ready. She needed him inside her. Gripping the bars of the headboard, Kenzie inched her way up the bed and, getting on all fours, steadied herself for Antonio's big entrance.

He didn't disappoint. After a few more well-placed kisses and caresses on her seat he plunged the full length of himself into her waiting, well-lubricated pussy, causing her to yelp out in surprise, before she relaxed back into the feeling of being fucked by this skillful man.

Just as she felt he was close to coming, she released one of her hands from the headboard, and reached back far enough so that she could grab his balls. It was enough to start him moaning in ecstasy and a second later, she felt the warmth of his come coating the outside of the area he had just been inside.

Antonio and Kenzie both lay back on the pillows, spent from the effort. This time, she couldn't wait for him to work his magic. Her clit was primed and ready and the feeling of his semen on her fingers as she worked them side-to-side across her most sensitive spot made her whole body arch up in orgasm. Having learned what she was capable of under Antonio's expert guidance, she decided not to stop once the tingly feeling subsided. Instead of pulling back she swiped more of his come from her lips and worked it, faster now, into that reliable little bud of nerves. Soon she was coming again, her pussy trembling with good feelings that shot from her feet all the way up to the roots of the hair on her head.

"You're beautiful to watch," Antonio commented when she finally lay back to relax next to him.

"So are you," she said, allowing herself the almost-tender act of burrowing her face into his chest and breathing in the scent of his manly perspiration.

CHAPTER SEVEN

ANTONIO WAS AWAKE EARLY. He sat on the edge of the bed and stretched, half hoping the movement would rouse Kenzie from her slumber. No such luck. Maybe it was the ocean air, or all of their extra-curricular activities from the previous night, but she was out cold. He took a moment to just take in the sight of her—her long, curly hair splayed out all wild on the pillow, her perfect peachy skin and lips that were rose-colored, even when she had on no makeup. She was beautiful, there was no denying it. He tried to put his finger on why she had such a strong effect on him. It wasn't just her looks, though that was a big part of the attraction. It had something to do with the way she conducted herself. She was a sharp business-person, no doubt, but could also be reckless and un-restrained when the moment called for it. Maybe he just enjoyed being around her and that was enough.

Antonio found a pair of sneakers he kept stashed in the master bedroom closet and sat down on the bed again—hard. This time it worked.

"Mmm, what time is it?" Kenzie grumbled, her eyes still closed. She stretched out an arm and her hand landed on Antonio's thigh. "Come back to bed," she moaned dreamily.

Antonio would have loved nothing more than to while away the morning in bed with her, but he had nervous energy that he needed to put somewhere. For the past few years, running had been his hobby. It was the perfect activity for nearly every situation. He ran when he needed to amp up for a meeting, or wind down for the weekend. It helped him stave off feelings of loneliness, and horniness, which had both become something of an issue especially during those first few months of being single again.

He wasn't proud of the many conquests in the days following Clarissa leaving him. At first it was fun. He knew he could walk into any club in Miami and leave within the hour with the best-looking woman there. Rumor had it that sleeping with him had become a sort of status symbol for some women. He knew he wasn't a celebrity, but he was certainly well-known as a successful bachelor under forty and it was true, he had his looks. But after a while the rotating cast of characters in and out of his bedroom all started to feel eerily similar. One morning, after waking up next to two women whose names he realized he didn't know—and never even asked—he vowed to stop playing around and put the focus back on his family's business.

It worked. Navedo Enterprises was now more successful than ever. There had even been offers to purchase the company by a very major brand, but Antonio wanted to keep things close to home. And when he stopped sleeping with random strangers, he found that his outlook was actually a little brighter, too. It amazed his friends to see him turn down women left and right. He would actually go into clubs and women would be sending him drinks. He'd always decline, politely of course, and tried his best to abstain from those encounters that were a lot like sugary sodas—tasty in the moment, but ultimately empty of anything truly fulfilling.

And now that there was someone else, someone who he could actually imagine really being with, he felt like he needed to run a marathon to cope with his feelings. Did Kenzie feel the same or was she rejecting him? Maybe he was just a boy toy for a week's vacation, a distraction from her real life in New York…

As he headed out the door, he caught a glimpse of his phone. The allure of its glow was almost too difficult to resist at times. He knew that he needed a technology break, especially when he was here in paradise, but the thought of missing out on business, of not being available when he was needed made it difficult. So instead of just heading out for his run, he decided to stop momentarily to check email. There was one from the office, Elena updating him with

the particulars on demolishing Baracoa, just one of
the options he was exploring for when Kenzie inevi-
tably realized that it was impossible to revive the old
still. That was another thing runs were good for—
making important business decisions. Leaving his
phone on the nightstand, he softly clicked the door
shut behind him and headed out to the familiar trail
that never failed to calm his mind.

Antonio started up the path behind his house at a
steady jog, not wanting to expend all of his energy
too early. He looked around at the grounds and marveled at the beauty. What was the point of having
such a beautiful place like this, he thought, if there
was no one he could share it with? As he rounded
the corner, passing a few small houses on a side road
belonging to local neighbors he had become friendly
with over the years, he found that he was starting to
sweat. His breath was usually not this short so early
in a run, but his legs had kinks in them and his gait
seemed off. He jogged up the road to where he knew
there was a water fountain and stopped to catch his
breath. Standing there panting, it suddenly occurred
to him: He never took "no" for an answer in business, so why should he accept the same from Kenzie? Enough with these silly games, he decided. It
was a stark realization but one he could not deny:
he was in love with her, and he had to make her his.

With his energy renewed, Antonio pulled off
his sweat-soaked T-shirt and rolled it up into a long

snake before tucking it into the waistband of his shorts. He took off at a quick clip, sprinting back in the direction from which he had come. He didn't want to waste another minute playing around. He needed Kenzie, needed to feel her body underneath his and taste her kisses, now. He thought about how it felt when she planted them down the length of his body, until she reached the one part of him that she had total control over and that made him run even faster.

Rounding the corner back up to the house, he felt his erection begin to swell. It was a base feeling but there was no denying it. He needed to put it in her, to connect with her. Fuck, he would impregnate her right there on the spot if that was what she wanted.

When he entered the bedroom, there was a strange vibe in the room. He noticed that the bed was made, and that Kenzie's numerous belongings were no longer strewn around all the furniture in the room. She must be taking a shower, he reassured himself. But when Kenzie emerged from the bathroom a moment later, she was fully dressed and holding her suitcase.

"I'm leaving," she said with finality and started heading toward the door.

Antonio's head was spinning, trying to figure out what had happened.

"Stop," he implored, holding her back and then releasing her. "Tell me what's going on."

His pulse and his mind were both racing. He

watched Kenzie's eyes as they moved from him over to the nightstand where he had left his phone. Where Elena's message about Baracoa was still pulled up.

"You've been going through my phone?" he asked, unable to hide the accusatory tone that would naturally go along with such a question.

"I glanced at it. I thought it was mine," Kenzie said loudly. "You're planning to knock down the distillery?" The way she said it, it was as though she took it as a personal affront.

"Kenzie," Antonio sighed. This was not how he had wanted things to go. "I can explain."

"I thought the place meant something to you, to your family." Her voice cracked when she said it. She seemed genuinely hurt, which pained Antonio to see.

"I'm a businessperson first," he heard himself saying, though what he really wanted to do was put his ego aside, to apologize and not fight with her. He wished he had just stayed in bed with her when she had asked.

"I understand completely," Kenzie said, her tone icy. "I'm taking the next flight back to Miami."

"The next flight is not until Monday morning and it would cost you upward of a thousand dollars to book. But if you're really ready to leave I can tell my plane to take us back within the hour."

"Fine," Kenzie said, sitting down on the other side of the room, the distance between them too obvious, too painful. "I'm ready to go."

Antonio searched for the words to make the situation right, to show her that he cared, but they didn't come. So instead, he picked up the phone and made the arrangements for their departure.

When Kenzie arrived back in Miami she said a quick goodbye to Antonio before hopping in a car and heading over to Baracoa to see how things were going. On the drive over, she tried to forget the expression in his eyes when she had left. He looked so vulnerable, so hurt. Part of her had wanted to just kiss him and forget the whole thing, but the truth was she didn't know if she could trust him. She felt so mixed up over the events of the last day. On the one hand, she truly cared for Antonio. But something inside her told her that this wasn't real. It was just a fling. And despite the romantic dinner and telling her his deepest, most personal secrets, she knew that at the end of the day, he had no faith in her. Maybe he just didn't understand how much she had to lose if things went wrong. She didn't have a famous family backing her every step of the way—just a few good friends and a work ethic that didn't allow her to quit something she had started.

Through these years being on her own, she had learned that she needed to look out for herself first. She couldn't worry about Antonio's feelings right now. She was hurting, too but there was so much at stake—the yoga business back in Brooklyn, the distillery and the workers that relied on it for their jobs. And she had also made a very public show of the fact that she was going to be putting on the world's biggest rum mixer party in just two short days from now. She had a celebrity coming to perform! She had to stop thinking about her love life and pull herself together.

"I've finally been able to restore a little order around here," Trudy said when Kenzie found her busy at work, nosing some of the barrels. Kenzie was at least glad to see things seemed to be going well there. She asked Trudy for an update. "We have a nice rotation of barrels, and I'm working on a new blend." Trudy seriously looked twenty years younger than the last time they had seen each other. It just went to show what focusing on work you care about can do for a person, Kenzie thought to herself as Trudy went on to enthusiastically explain how she was creating a chemistry profile for each of the rums she was planning to blend.

"It's a mixture of science and art," she told Kenzie, offering her a taste of her latest experiment. The warm alcohol burned the back of Kenzie's throat. It was unlike any rum she had ever tasted. True, she was no expert, but she knew what she liked and what she didn't like, and this stuff was good.

"I'm so glad I found you, Trudy," Kenzie said, smiling. Sometimes creating a great business was mostly just about surrounding yourself with the right people.

"I never would have gotten into this if it wasn't for your aunt," Trudy said, sitting down to rest on a barrel. "She was the true visionary for this place, back in the day."

"You said she was involved with the owner of the distillery back then. Do you remember his name?"

"Oh yes!" Trudy said instantly. "We all knew Pablo."

"Pablo... Navedo?" Kenzie asked tentatively. Trudy nodded affirmatively.

Of course! Why hadn't she put it together before? The man in love with her aunt was Antonio's grandfather.

"So, you knew him well?"

"We all had a lot of fun times together, Kenzie. I even dated one of his cousins. It didn't work out. But your aunt and Pablo, they were a real love story."

"Why weren't they ever married?" Kenzie asked.

"Well, Pablo had a wife. She was from a family who also was in the liquor business. They slept in separate bedrooms, but he would never divorce her. So eventually, Lilly, your aunt, she left. I think she felt like she had no choice."

Kenzie nodded solemnly. So, dating back then was basically the same as it was now, except without smartphones.

"I want to show you something," Trudy said, wav-

ing Kenzie to follow along after her. She went up the
winding staircase that led to a second floor. Kenzie
followed her into a room she'd never been in that
looked like it had once served as an office. Trudy
opened the desk drawer and pulled out a black-and-
white picture. Kenzie gasped and jumped slightly
back when she saw it.

"I know," Trudy said, watching Kenzie's reaction.

"She looks just like me," Kenzie said softly.

"And Antonio is the spitting image of his grandfather," Trudy said, nodding.

In the photo, a tall, dark and handsome man who
indeed did look just like Antonio except that he was
clean-shaven, stood in what looked like the courtyard
of Baracoa. He had his arm around a petite woman
with soft curls framing her face. Aunt Lilly.

"They look happy," Kenzie said, studying the picture.

"They were," Trudy said. "When Pablo died suddenly, your aunt was devastated. She couldn't attend
the funeral because of his family. Her only connection to him was this place, and the piece of it that
he left her. The Navedo family pulled away from
Baracoa after his death, so we ran the place until
we just couldn't."

Kenzie wiped a tear from her cheek with the back
of her hand. Just thinking about the situation made
her feel so connected to this relative she'd never even
met. What if she suddenly lost Antonio? He wasn't

even hers to begin with, but the thought of it was too much to bear.

"You and he are good together." Trudy smiled knowingly at Kenzie, waiting for a reaction.

Kenzie looked up at Trudy with a surprised expression.

"Oh, come on!" Trudy said, slapping Kenzie on the arm. "I know how these things work. I was young once, too."

"Yeah, but some things just aren't meant to be," Kenzie said thoughtfully, staring back down at the black-and-white picture. "Wrong time and place. Wrong life."

"Unless you decide it's right." Trudy gave her a sad smile and placed a comforting hand on Kenzie's shoulder. "Well I've got to get back to work. Thanks for giving an old bird like me a chance. Makes me think I never should have walked away to begin with."

"Trudy, you are truly amazing," Kenzie said, hugging her. She only hoped someday she could be that much of a visionary and a risk-taker when she was that age.

Kenzie walked outside into the humid Florida air and pulled out her phone to order a car. Looking down, she noticed her phone blinking with a message from Missy. Reading the transcript of the voice mail, her heart sank.

Hey lady, I have some bad news, it read.

Catalina isn't going to be able to make it tomorrow. She's laid up at home with a broken leg. I'm
so sorry...

Kenzie clicked her phone until the screen went
dark and looked back at the distillery. Without their
star attraction would people even show up to the rum
mixer? Or worse, what if they all came and then left,
disappointed? Then she would have actually done
more harm to Baracoa than if she'd never gotten involved in the first place.

Clicking her phone awake and back to the messenger screen, she fired off a text to Missy.

I think I'm going to cancel the event

Kenzie took a deep breath and waited. Seconds
later, she saw the typing bubbles flash across the
screen and she waited for her friend's reply.

Don't. Even without her you still have something
special there. You said so!

Kenzie started to type something else, but then
she clicked out of messenger and quickly ordered a
car. She had to get back to the hotel and figure out
her next steps.

By the time she arrived back at the Fontainebleau
it was getting dark. Heading up to her room, she

quickly showered and changed into her short floral dress and decided to take a walk. Sometimes that was the best thing when she needed to make a tough decision. She thought about calling Antonio and telling him the situation, but she wasn't even sure whose side he was on. Did he want her to fail? She honestly didn't know what to think.

Kenzie walked and walked, observing all of the people out and about. They all seemed to be young, tan and impossibly fit. The area had a youthful vibe and the sidewalks were buzzing with activity. Down the street she could hear a strong Latin beat and wondered where it was coming from. Deciding to explore a little further, she crossed to the other side of the street and saw the entrance to a busy-looking dance club. The exterior didn't reveal anything—there wasn't even a sign, but Kenzie could tell that this was the place to be. The flashing lights inside tossed shadows onto the street and the pavement under her feet seemed to vibrate with the sounds she could feel coming from the club. The burly bouncer gave her a once-over and a smile.

"You coming in?" he asked.

Kenzie hesitated and then pulled out her wallet. "Yeah," she said, surprising herself and handing over her ID. The bouncer read her New York driver's license carefully. He looked back and forth from her to the picture of her at the DMV suspiciously. Did he think it was a fake? She knew she looked young, but not that young!

"Go ahead," he finally said, handing her back her ID and unlatching a red velvet rope so that she could pass through into the club.

Making her way down a pink, glowing hallway in the direction of the music, she tried to remember the last time she had gone dancing. It was definitely years ago, maybe with her college friends, girls she hadn't seen in forever. The thought of it having been that long was too sad—she loved dancing, and those friends, but she hadn't made time for either in recent years, even the ones who had made the effort to check in on her after Cole had died. Life had just gotten too overwhelming. Something about that had to change, she decided on the spot.

When Kenzie finally made it to the entrance of the main room, she had to turn her body sideways in order to slither her way past the crush of hot, half-naked bodies pulsing to the beat in order to find a small square of space for herself on the dance floor. But as soon as she started to move her body it all came back to her—how much fun it was to lose yourself in the anonymity of the club, how amazing it felt to let the pulsing rhythm carry you. Dancing was something she used to do all the time, even as a teenager. If she wasn't a yoga instructor, she probably would have become a dance instructor. Why had she left it behind, she wondered, as the DJ worked the crowd into a sweaty, synchronized frenzy. She made a mental note to tell Missy that they were going out dancing just as soon as she was back in New York. Maybe she would make it a company field trip!

Suddenly a voice interrupted Kenzie's thoughts, breaking her out of her trancelike state.

"Hi."

Kenzie turned around to see a handsome man, probably in his late twenties, dancing next to her. He was actually adorable, in a cute college guy kind of way.

"I like how you move," he yelled over the music when he caught Kenzie's attention.

"Thanks," Kenzie yelled back in what she hoped was a friendly tone. She giggled to herself and gave herself a mental high-five over the fact that someone was hitting on her in the club.

"I've never seen you here before. I'm Jack."

"I'm here on vacation. I mean, business." Kenzie looked down at her feet. She didn't know why this guy was making her nervous. Maybe she wasn't old enough to be his mom, but she definitely could have been his babysitter. *Just say your name!* she instructed herself! "I'm Kenzie," she yelled.

For a few beats, they danced in each other's vicinity and Kenzie occasionally stole looks at Jack. If it were a normal night, back in New York City, she would have been excited to dance with him. But now all she could think about was Antonio. It was strange to think that a week ago, she didn't know him and now he had become so central to her thoughts.

Then the song they were dancing to faded and the DJ changed the groove to a heavier beat. Jack looked up at Kenzie and moved closer to her, so close that they were now dancing together, their bodies almost touching.

The air was thick, and it was getting a little hard to breathe. Kenzie tried to gulp a breath in, but it wasn't easy. There were people everywhere and zero personal space. Was this how people danced in Miami? Was she that out of the club scene? Or was Jack just being really bold? She was flattered but also didn't want to lead him on.

Jack smiled sexily as he kept up with the rhythm and put his hands on Kenzie's hips, so that the two of them were rocking side-to-side in time with one another. Kenzie thought about excusing herself to the bar, but then she figured, it was just dancing, just a little bit of harmless fun. Besides, she and Antonio weren't committed. It was okay to be a little flirtatious. And maybe a little part of her felt like it was revenge—she guessed that if Antonio saw her dancing with another man it would make him furious. She was ashamed to admit that was the reaction she wanted, after feeling so betrayed by him on their short trip.

"Wanna get a drink?" Jack asked when the song ended.

"Yeah," Kenzie said breathlessly. "I definitely need water." She went to follow her new friend to the glowing bar area when a hand, firmly placed on the top of her arm, stopped her in her tracks. Kenzie gasped when she spun around to see Antonio standing next to her. He had changed clothes and was now in a T-shirt that showed off his gorgeous chest, and jeans that fit his lean body oh-so well. Every woman in the club was noticing him, but it appeared that his focus was solely on Kenzie.

"Can we go somewhere and talk?" he asked, his eyes looking serious.

"I was just about to…"

"Please," he insisted, holding onto Kenzie's arm and not letting go.

Kenzie looked over at Jack, who was already jockeying his way up to the front of the bar, and then back at Antonio.

"Okay, let's go," she said, taking him by the hand and leading him outside.

Antonio stood outside the club next to Kenzie, shifting his weight from foot to foot, and wondering which one of them was going to speak first. He didn't know what had drawn Kenzie to the Paradiso, but he knew why he had gone there on the heels of their big argument. The club was like a second home to him. The bouncers and bartenders knew him by name, and he always got the prime table with bottle service every time he was there. It had been a while since he'd frequented the place, having given up on the expensive booze and easy women. He didn't want to have a meaningless encounter with a stranger. That wouldn't replace his feelings for Kenzie. But in the moment, he thought maybe it was the only thing that could make him feel better.

"You looked like you were having fun out there," he said, and was immediately angry at himself that he had allowed his tone to betray just how hurt he had been over their falling-out.

"What's that supposed to mean?" Kenzie asked. She crossed her arms over her chest.

"I know that guy," Antonio said, wishing he would just stop talking, but his pride was getting the best of him. "He takes a different woman home from here every night of the week."

"Are we talking about him—or you?" Kenzie asked.

"That's not me anymore," Antonio said quietly.

"So, is this place your regular?" Kenzie asked, turning to him.

There was something softer about her tone. She didn't seem mad anymore. But the distance between them was still there.

"It used to be," Antonio said. "This isn't what I want anymore, though…"

Before he could finish explaining himself, Kenzie wrapped her arms around his neck.

"Should we go make up?" she asked with a mischievous glint in her eyes.

Antonio exhaled and smiled for the first time since he'd gotten to the club. He was relieved that it seemed Kenzie believed him, that he had no intention of sabotaging her. It was hard, mixing work and relationships. Maybe it had been ill-advised for him to get intimate with someone so closely involved with his business. But it was too late now. He really cared about Kenzie and the thought of giving her up was unimaginable. "I'll get the car."

Five minutes later, the valet handed Antonio his keys and winked at him as Kenzie slid into the passenger seat. At that moment, he felt like the world's luckiest man, leaving the club with the only woman he really wanted to be with.

As they headed toward the Fontainebleau, Antonio tried to keep his eyes on the road but kept finding himself stealing glances at Kenzie. Seeing her dance like that with another man had made him so jealous. He simultaneously wanted to throttle the guy for putting his hands on her and was also massively turned on seeing her wanted like that by someone else. Of course other men wanted her—she was amazing. But he was the one taking her back to her hotel, he reminded himself.

Antonio grumbled and stepped on the gas harder. If Kenzie had made a spectacle of herself in the club to torture him it was working. There was no way she could have known he was watching, which made it even more difficult to comprehend. He wondered if he hadn't stepped in what she would have done. Part of him worried that she would have gone home with another man, but a bigger part of him knew that she wouldn't. Kenzie was wild, but she was also discriminating. And he knew it was a big step for her to have opened up to him as much as she had over the past few days. That wasn't something to take lightly.

"We're here," he announced, pulling into one of the parking spaces on the side of the hotel.

Kenzie and Antonio crossed the parking lot and entered the hotel together. On the elevator ride up neither of them spoke a word, and Antonio wondered what she was thinking. They walked down the hallway to her room and when she opened the door, memories of their first night together flooded back into Antonio's mind.

"I remember this place," he whispered, moving closer to Kenzie. She looked up at him and didn't say anything, but he could see in her eyes that she was remembering it, too.

Without saying another word, Antonio slowly started to undress her. He watched Kenzie's reaction as he undid the buttons of her dress. Oh yeah, this is what make-up sex feels like, he remembered. The distance between them caused everything to feel suddenly new again. Every touch was filled with meaning. When both of her breasts were exposed,

Antonio kissed each of them carefully, licking her nipples like they were drenched in honey.

Antonio was simultaneously turned on and still feeling a little jealous. Or maybe he was turned on because of his jealousy, he wasn't sure. He flicked his tongue at Kenzie's perfect pink buds, his hand sliding down into her panties and making her gasp. With his nostrils flaring and his cock straining at the zipper of his trousers, he pushed Kenzie down onto the bed and made his way into the V of her legs.

"Yes!" Kenzie shouted as Antonio's mouth went to work on her pussy. Not ready to let her come just yet, he moved up the bed and alternated between sensually kissing her mouth and playfully sucking on her nipples.

Kenzie sighed as Antonio paid close attention to the most sensitive parts of her body. Finally, he reached his hand down to tease her clit again. He brought her almost to her peak before weaning her down and then back up again. Part of him wanted to torture her the way he had been tortured seeing her at the club. But a bigger part of him knew how much she was enjoying this—and that was the biggest turn-on.

Finally, Kenzie erupted in one long earth-shattering orgasm that Antonio was sure had woken up the neighbors.

After her breathing normalized, Kenzie sat up in

bed, her hair looking disheveled and her face looking relaxed and happy. "That was great. I guess you'd better go now," she said teasingly.

"Excuse me?" Antonio said, pulling her back down and into the nook created by his strong arms. "Were you going to go with that guy? At the club?" Antonio asked sheepishly. He felt embarrassed for even asking.

"What, that child?" Kenzie asked incredulously. She picked up a pillow and hit Antonio with it. The two of them started to laugh.

"So, are we done fighting now?" he asked as Kenzie collapsed into his arms again.

Kenzie looked at Antonio thoughtfully and traced his lower lip with her finger. "All done." Kenzie propped herself up on one arm and looked at Antonio suggestively. "So. What do you want from me?"

He knew the question was sexual, but for him it was now about so much more. He just didn't know if she felt the same. "I want exactly what you won't give to me," he said pointedly.

Kenzie turned to him and her expression told him that she still didn't understand.

"I want everything," he said, looking directly in her eyes.

CHAPTER EIGHT

EARLY MONDAY MORNING, Kenzie and Antonio walked hand-in-hand through the sugar cane fields next to Baracoa. He had spent the night at her hotel, and they were out early, since Kenzie was determined to see if the rum mixer could still be pulled off, despite losing her guest of honor, Catalina Cortez.

Kenzie was still thinking about what Antonio had said in bed the night before, about him wanting everything. She assumed that meant her body, her mind, and yes, her heart. Part of her felt like she wanted to lay down her armor, to just be with Antonio, free of worry and guilt. But the awful feeling that she didn't deserve that kept rushing back to her. Ever since she was a little girl, she had believed in one true love—that the person you gave your heart to was yours, forever. That's what she had in mind when Cole had proposed. So if she could feel the same way about Antonio, didn't that contradict everything she had ever believed?

She thought about Aunt Lilly, and wondered if

she once had the same problems Kenzie was dealing with. Maybe if she were alive she would know what to do, and give Kenzie the advice she so desperately needed right now.

"Can you believe that my aunt and your grandfather dated?" Kenzie remarked as they strode toward the distillery.

"I don't know if it was dating, exactly," said Antonio with a sly smile.

"Well, it seemed like they were in love," Kenzie said, looking around at the beautiful surroundings and trying to imagine her aunt Lilly here. She didn't even know her when she was alive, but somehow, after this crazy week, she felt a strong connection to her.

"I think you're going to pull this off and put me to shame," said Antonio when they reached the distillery entrance, taking both her hands in his. Kenzie loved the way he made her feel so small, so taken care of. It was not an easy thing for such a powerful woman to admit!

"Really? I'm not so sure." Kenzie kicked up some of the gravel with the toe of her sandal.

"I think…" he said, pulling her close to his chest and turning her chin up to face him, "you are capable of anything you set your mind to."

Just as they were about to kiss, Trudy came running outside, or her version of a run which was more like a little gallop. She was holding an official-look-ing paper in her hand.

"Look at this," she said, holding the page out to Kenzie.

Kenzie read the paper, her brow furrowing as her eyes scanned the page.

"It says that we were supposed to register with the FDA and that we've failed to have an inspec-tion." She looked up at Trudy and Antonio. "We're being shut down."

"Who would do something like this?" Trudy asked. "Why are we suddenly on their radar?"

Kenzie shook her head but then instinctively, her eyes landed on Antonio. Was it possible? Would he sabotage the distillery to keep her from owning it, to keep it in his own family?

"I see you looking at me, Kenzie, but I am not re-sponsible for this," Antonio said, his voice rising. He held up a hand in a gesture of innocence.

"She's right. Who would have reported this?" Kenzie asked, throwing her arms up in frustration and re-reading the letter.

"You have to believe me," Antonio said, starting to pace. "Wait," he said, stopping and pulling out his phone. "I have an idea what this might be about."

Kenzie and Trudy waited while he scrolled through his device and watched him as he fired off a text message.

"I'm sorry, Trudy. I think this is it for me," Kenzie said with resignation in her voice. "I'm done."

"Hold on," Antonio said holding up one finger. "I have an idea who's behind this."

Kenzie and Trudy both looked at him, their eyes intense with anticipation.

"My associate Elena was under the impression that I wanted the rum mixer to fail. Of course, that isn't the case…"

"So, she's behind this? She reported us?" Kenzie said, exasperated.

"She didn't understand what was at stake, Kenzie. She took steps without my consent. For that I'm truly sorry."

"Well, it looks like you've won," Kenzie said, the pain in her voice palpable. "Please, just drive me back to my hotel."

On the drive back, Kenzie stared out the window and didn't say a word to Antonio. It was enough now, whatever crazy game they had been playing, it was over. And to think that she had gone from being a teetotaler to actually learning about and enjoying spirits. A big part of her was disappointed that this was the end of her adventure at the distillery. Amazingly, she had come to really appreciate rum and all of its complexities. Now all she wanted was to get back to her yoga studio. It was her comfort zone, and she had the sneaking suspicion that maybe she had traveled too far out of it, had taken a risk on something that wasn't hers, even though the image of Aunt Lilly was so strong in her mind.

And even though she had to admit that she cared about Baracoa, she knew that her involvement came at a cost. She'd been seriously neglecting Honor Yoga while she was down here. After all, it was her business, and these days she was relying on Missy more than ever. It was time to return to life as she knew it.

Okay, well, maybe she didn't want things to be exactly the way they had been before this trip. She had to admit, even through the loss and frustration, that the last week had been the happiest she'd been in a long time. And the thought of going back to the gray streets of the city, of bundling up in her long black parka, suddenly was not all that appealing.

But what did she have to stay for here? Clearly, she had been trying to get a foothold in a family business that had roots so deep in the community, they could shut businesses down with a phone call. There was no use trying anymore. It was time to go home.

"Thanks for the ride," she said to Antonio, giving him a sad little smile and shutting the door. It looked like Antonio was going to say something, but she wasn't about to give him another chance. It had been a mistake, trying to mix business and pleasure. She was certain that he would find someone else, probably before the wheels on her plane left the tarmac in Miami.

Back in her room, Kenzie was intent on doing

something to make herself feel better. She changed out of her dress and into some yoga clothes and called Missy in New York, knowing that if anyone could help, it was her.

"Missy, I need you to book me on the next flight back to New York," Kenzie said, sitting up cross-legged on her freshly made bed. Her suitcase was open, and she was simultaneously answering emails on her laptop. She needed to bring her focus back to the yoga business. Maybe they could raise the funds to stay in their current space, if she could get enough support from her loyal clients. If not, she wasn't sure what she would do next.

"I have you on a flight back tomorrow afternoon," Missy said, reading off the confirmation number.

"Nothing sooner?" Kenzie questioned her friend. Now that she was done with Baracoa, and Antonio, she wanted to get out of Miami and away from all of the chaos as quickly as possible. No sense hanging around a place where she wasn't wanted or needed.

"Sorry, everything's booked solid," said Missy. "I'll see you tomorrow. And Kenzie, try to take it easy, okay? You did your best."

"Thanks Missy," Kenzie replied sincerely. At least she had a strong support network in her corner back home. Here, she wasn't sure who was rooting for her, or who was really on her side.

Hanging up the phone, Kenzie made a space for herself on the floor and did a few sun salutations.

She put the focus back on her breath, and tried to push the image of Antonio's sad, confused face out of her head.

He's not your friend, she told herself, trying to bring her thoughts back to her practice.

But try as she did, part of her couldn't stop imagining the two of them holding hands in the sugar cane fields, kissing on the beach in the Virgin Islands and the first time they made eye contact in the lobby bar—it was the moment she was shaken out of the coma she'd been living in. There was no denying that he had awakened parts of her that she didn't want to let go back to sleep.

Putting her practice aside, Kenzie lay down on the bed and shut her laptop. Her pulse was racing, thinking of Antonio, and she didn't want to lose that feeling. Sliding her hand down the length of her body, she touched the area between her legs that was covered by her yoga pants and felt it getting warm. Moving her hand back and forth, the pleasurable feelings started to increase, but at the same time, hot tears inexplicably began to stream down her cheeks. Trying to push the sadness aside, she imagined Antonio's hand there, bringing her to the peak of ecstasy, in that expert way that only he knew how. Sliding her hand underneath her waistband and moving it lower down until it found the soft, sensitive area that he'd gotten to know so intimately over the past week, she closed her eyes and imagined the way he kissed her neck, his scratchy beard grazing her sensitive skin, his hot mouth enveloping her, and she quickened the pace and pressure she was applying to her clit. The thought of never feeling Antonio's rough beard against her skin again overwhelmed her with emotion. Even though Cole could never be replaced, she was now certain that Antonio couldn't be either. He was his own man, his own special person to her, even if logically, it made no sense.

Moving her other hand up to her breasts, she undid the front clasp of her sports bra, releasing her now-erect nipples and using her other hand to pinch them—hard—just the way Antonio did when he was priming her for a good fucking. She wanted so desperately to feel something other than regret.

Kenzie's hands were working quickly now, and her breath was ragged, her body trying to keep pace with her frenzied thoughts. Antonio pushing her up against the wall in the bathroom, Antonio sliding her ass on the counter in his kitchen to devour her, Antonio pulling her hair back as he fucked her, just minutes after meeting her for the first time. It was a highlight reel of their "greatest hits" and boy, were they terrific. Too bad this was where the story had to end for them.

"Antonio!" Kenzie called out as she came. The utterance surprised her, but she couldn't stop it any more than she could tell her body not to seize up in pleasure. She came hard and fast against her own hand, and then rolled over onto her side, exhausted both mentally and physically.

Was she making a mistake, leaving so quickly? she wondered.

I need a drink, she thought to herself. Putting herself together, she left her room and took the elevator down to the lobby, hoping her friend Jose would be working at the bar.

Sure enough, Jose was stationed in his usual spot and greeted Kenzie enthusiastically when he saw her.

"Hey!" said Jose. "Long time no see!"

"Yeah, I've been busy," she said, sitting down on a bar stool and wondering how much she actually wanted to share with Jose. He had become her de facto therapist on this trip. He certainly was a good listener, and not a bad advice-giver either.

"Don't work too hard," Jose advised with a wink. "So, what can I get you? Club soda with lime or... something stronger?"

Kenzie considered the question. Drinking again had felt pretty natural, which surprised her after having abstained for so long. She knew that for her it was something she could have in her life from time to time. Not everyone was able to take it or leave it.

"Something strong, but not too strong," she said. "What do you recommend?"

"I have the perfect thing," he said, reaching under the bar for a hurricane glass. Filling it with ice, he freely poured three different types of rum into the glass, and then some orange juice, followed by a small amount of another liquor Kenzie had never seen before. When he added a bit of maraschino cherry juice, the whole drink took on a colorful look, almost like a burnt sunset.

"It's beautiful," Kenzie complimented him.

"Try it," he encouraged.

Kenzie raised the glass and tentatively took a sip. She was still a bit of a drinking virgin, so she knew she had to go easy.

"Mmm, Jose, this is incredible," she said.

"Thanks." He smiled. "A new creation. I'll make it for you and Antonio the next time you're in together."

Kenzie's face must have sunk as much as her heart at the statement because Jose immediately backpedaled.

"Or I'm just happy to serve it to you anytime!"

"Actually, I'm leaving tomorrow," Kenzie said. She was surprised by how sad it made her to say it out loud. Somehow it made it all the more real. She was really giving up, saying goodbye to Antonio. She was really leaving.

"Oh no!" Jose's face fell. "But don't you have the rum mixer tomorrow night? I mean, all of Miami is planning on going."

"Actually, we've hit a snag and it looks like we'll have to cancel." Kenzie hated how phony it sounded, but what was she going to say? The situation with the distillery and with Antonio was too heavy, too complicated. And it looked like Jose had other customers.

"Bummer," Jose said. A good-looking couple who appeared to be on a first date sat down at the bar a couple of stools down. "I was really looking forward to it," he said with a smile, before moving down the bar to take the couple's drink order.

Kenzie swirled her drink around thoughtfully, took another sip and then set it down on the bar. It would probably be her last drink for a while. Her adventure in Miami was over. It was time for her to go home. But first there was one more place she needed to visit.

CHAPTER NINE

KENZIE ALWAYS HATED going to the cemetery. Not that it was something most people enjoyed, but the eerie stillness and the open graves, just waiting to be filled, freaked her out. The last time she had been to one was for her grandmother's funeral when she was fifteen. She remembered everyone wearing dark clothing and how she had huddled in between her parents, waiting for the ceremony to be over.

When Cole died, she and his family had agreed that his body would be cremated. She knew it was what he would have wanted. Kenzie was relieved to not have to witness her love's body being lowered into the ground. She couldn't bear to think of him in a grave during the winter, when the ground was cold and covered with freezing snow. Instead, she had scattered his ashes in the place the two of them had loved best. The Palisades was the place they used to go on the weekends together, to hike and just be together in nature. It was so beautiful—almost like the Grand Canyon, with steep cliffs that overlooked the glimmering Hudson River.

On a rainy June morning, Kenzie had climbed the Giant Stairs by herself, just like she and Cole had done together so many times before. Once she reached the top, she offered a little prayer and said her final goodbyes to the man she was supposed to be walking down the aisle with just a few months later. That day, she released him to the wind, but somehow the moment had not been as cathartic as she had hoped. The pain was still with her, and she carried it around everywhere she went, like an overloaded backpack. She never returned to their special place after that day.

Even though it was late afternoon, the Florida sun was still blisteringly hot, and Kenzie shielded herself with her hat and sunglasses. After receiving a map from the office, she walked along the path, following the markings until she found where Aunt Lilly was buried.

The grave was unassuming, and still unmarked with a headstone. Kenzie placed a stone on the spot where Lilly lay, and then sat down on the ground to take things in, and to think. Naturally, she assumed a cross-legged position and formed her hands into prayer mode. It seemed reverential and like the right thing to do.

"Lilly, I'm sorry we're meeting like this for the first time," Kenzie said out loud. She was alone but also didn't really care if anyone overheard her words. They were words that needed to be spoken.

"I'm sorry for not getting to know you. You seem like a pretty amazing person. Or were," she said, bowing her chin to her chest solemnly. "I wish you were here to tell me what to do. I screwed up something you worked hard on and I want to apologize."

Kenzie's eyes welled up with tears. "I tend to screw things up. In life. In love," she continued. "I guess you knew what it was like to lose someone you loved."

Kenzie closed her eyes and tried to picture Aunt Lilly like she looked in the picture Trudy had shown her. But instead of seeing the woman's face, Kenzie had a vivid picture of Cole in mind. It was the clearest she had been able to see him since the night of the accident.

I miss you, she said, this time speaking only in her mind. She saw herself and Cole, three years ago, lying on the couch together, their limbs intertwined as they channel surfed the TV. It was the last time they had spent together. It wasn't monumental or dramatic, it was just them, the way they usually were— easy and comfortable.

Drive safe, Kenzie had said before she kissed him goodbye. Cole smiled at her and went to his car. She saw his blue eyes staring at her. It was the last time she ever saw him.

That was usually what happened when Kenzie

dreamt of Cole, but this time, he kept looking at her. In her mind's eye, he was speaking to her.

Kenzie, he said, his voice so deep and familiar. *I want you to be happy.*

Kenzie opened her eyes and saw that a small tan-and-yellow bird was sitting on the spot near where she had placed the stone. She watched it for a moment and then stood, brushing the dirt off of her shorts.

"Time to go now," she whispered, wiping her face with the back of her hand.

Kenzie took a car back to the city and after getting something to eat, spent an hour just walking around in the heat until she saw a small sign with the word *yoga* printed on it. Looking at the unassuming building, she opened the door and climbed a steep stairway to the third floor where she found a small community practice.

"Welcome," said the woman seated at the desk. She was surrounded by Indian art, knickknacks and volumes of books on yoga that cluttered every visible inch of space. A small cat was asleep in the corner and a few members were talking and warming up.

"I'm not a member," said Kenzie, feeling out of place.

"Come in and join us anyway," said the receptionist. "It's free yoga. All are welcome."

Kenzie found a mat and smiled at a few of the

other yogis who were looking in her direction. Just as she went to place her phone on silent, it started to buzz with a series of incoming text messages. They were all from Antonio.

I'm sorry about today
I need to speak to you
Where are you?

Kenzie hesitated and then turned to the receptionist. "What's the address here?"

"736 6th Street," she said.

Kenzie typed it into her phone and after hesitating for a moment, she clicked send.

It was a spur-of-the-moment decision and she didn't actually expect Antonio to come. As the class filed into the main room, Kenzie followed, taking a place toward the back of the class.

The room was cozy, with candles burning and Enya playing on a boom box. The class was filled with all sorts of people—cute young women in expensive yoga outfits, senior citizens, middle-aged moms and dads, even a few teenagers. Kenzie placed her mat down and sat on it, waiting for class to begin. She loved to take other instructors' classes from time to time. It was always an eye-opening experience and she found it was a way to pick up techniques, learn new adjustments and just gain a new perspective. She needed that now, but most of all she needed to feel a sense of community, to not feel so desperately alone.

"Let's begin in a cross-legged position," said the instructor, who turned out to be the same woman who was sitting at the receptionist's desk. She was in her forties with a long golden braid that went all the way down her back and past her waist. She had a happy, peaceful expression and the class seemed captivated by her as she took her seat in front of the class.

"For those of you who are joining us for the first time today, my name is Astrid," she said, looking in Kenzie's direction. "Welcome. Let's begin with some breathing techniques."

The classes that Kenzie taught were very physical in nature, so she relished the opportunity to focus on slowing down and remembering her breath. She closed her eyes and let Astrid lead her in a simple pattern—in through the nose and out through the mouth.

Just as she inhaled, she sensed that another student had joined the class, but decided to keep her eyes closed so she could remain focused.

"Welcome, welcome," Astrid said, interrupting the instruction with a soft whisper. "Find a seat. You're fine."

Kenzie sensed someone sitting down next to her and as she breathed in, the familiar smell of masculine sweat and aftershave filled her nostrils. Unable to stay focused any longer, she blinked her eyes open and saw Antonio seated next to her.

"What are you…?"

"Shh…" Antonio whispered, bringing his index finger in front of his lips. He gave Kenzie a half smile and then closed his eyes. Following Astrid's instructions, he lifted his arms up as he inhaled.

Kenzie was the only person in the room besides Astrid with her eyes open, and she looked around, dumbfounded that Antonio had arrived so quickly, that he had actually come. She had so much she wanted to tell him, about her visit to the cemetery, about hearing Cole speak to her. But this was not the time or the place. So as difficult as it was, Kenzie closed her eyes, too, and tried her best to concentrate on the class.

She thought to herself that it was pretty cool that Antonio could so readily go out of his comfort zone to be with her. She knew yoga was not his thing, but here he was, doing sun salutations along with a group of strangers for the sole purpose of being near her. She peeked out of the corner of her eye to see that he was wearing an undershirt with dress pants, his suit jacket lay neatly by the side of his mat, and she couldn't help but crack a smile.

"Bend at the knees, flat back and open heart," Astrid instructed. Kenzie and Antonio went through the flow at the same pace, their bodies moving in unison. "Now, rise up, and inhale," said Astrid, holding her hands up high and wide like she was greeting the sun. Kenzie and Antonio matched her movements and without looking over at him, Kenzie could feel how much they were in sync. Was she making a mistake leaving this man behind?

When the class was over, Kenzie and Antonio filed outside onto the street.

"I can't believe you actually came," Kenzie said.

"I thought it was going to be a bar." Antonio smiled. "Or at least a coffee shop. Can we go get some?" Antonio looked at Kenzie expectantly. She shifted her weight from foot to foot, trying to buy time to make up her mind.

"Yeah. Sure."

Antonio led the way to Las Olas, his favorite place in Miami Beach for strong coffee and Cuban sandwiches. As they walked, he thought about reaching out and trying to hold Kenzie's hand, but he could tell that the vibe was still strange between them. He wanted to explain to her that he wasn't the one responsible for reporting the distillery—in fact he would never fathom doing such a thing. He could understand why Kenzie would be skeptical, but he still wished she would have trusted him a little more.

Inside the café, they took a table near the window and Antonio ordered for both of them. Reaching out across the table, he took Kenzie's delicate hands in his and looked directly into her eyes.

"What do I have to do to get you to stay?" he

asked. He knew he was making himself vulnerable, but he didn't care. Kenzie was worth taking the risk over.

Antonio watched as Kenzie moved her hands away from his and played with a straw wrapper. She shifted her gaze from him and looked out the window. The sun was beginning to set, and it was finally cooling off.

"Antonio, I've loved the time we've spent together," she said gently in a tone that he knew was setting up for a "but." There was always a "but" when a woman started to speak in that manner.

"But," she said, predictably, "we're from two different worlds. This can never work."

"Why not?" Antonio questioned. "I think the fact that you and I are so different is what makes us great together."

Kenzie looked like she was going to respond, but just then the waitress delivered the coffee and sandwiches to their table. When she walked away, the two of them sat in silence for a moment until Kenzie finally spoke.

"I can tell you have so much love to give. I know you'll find the right person who's worthy of it." He could see that her eyes were welling up with tears, that she was fighting an internal battle he couldn't begin to understand.

"I don't want the right person. I want you," he said, banging a fist on the table. Something about

Kenzie made him lose control of his temper. It wasn't a side of him that he liked to show, but with her it was impossible to fake being calm.

The sandwiches sat between them, uneaten. They were so close, but yet so far away from each other, Antonio thought. He looked at Kenzie and waited for some sign that she felt the same as he did but her expression was impenetrable. Standing up, he tossed a bill on the table, and made his way out onto the street.

CHAPTER TEN

TUESDAY MORNING ARRIVED, and Kenzie was all packed and ready to go. She had checked out of her hotel room and was waiting in the circle in front of the main entrance for the valet to get her a cab to the airport. Even though her flight wasn't until the late afternoon she figured she would get there early, have a leisurely lunch and catch up on some work. Just then, a bright blue Lamborghini pulled to a screeching halt right in front of her. The window rolled down and Antonio lowered his sunglasses and flashed her that devilish smile that made her heart do flip-flops in her chest.

"I was worried I wouldn't see you again," Antonio said, staring at her as a small frown played across his face.

"I'm headed home," Kenzie said, matter-of-factly. She didn't know how to be polite, or pretend things were okay when the truth was, she was heartbroken. She understood why he had walked out on her in the café. He had poured his heart out to her and she'd given him no response. But what he didn't realize was that she was saving him from heartache, from waking up a month or two from now with the realization that he was with someone who was incapable of loving or being loved. She was ignoring him out of love. He didn't realize it yet, but she had actually done him a favor.

"Get in, there's something I want to show you," he said, unlocking the doors.

"Antonio," Kenzie said wistfully. "I can't go to another sugar cane field with you..."

"That's not where I'm taking you," he said, getting out of the car and coming around to where she was standing. "Trust me. Just get in."

Kenzie reluctantly got into the passenger seat. Antonio threw her bag in the trunk, hopped back in the car and they sped off, to where Kenzie had no idea.

"So, you were just going to leave town without telling me?" Antonio asked as they drove.

"I didn't think it mattered," Kenzie said softly.

"Of course it matters. Kenzie, I spoke to Elena. I told her she was out of line to act on my behalf."

"It doesn't matter anymore," Kenzie said abruptly. "I don't want it anymore. The distillery is yours. I don't want anything in return." Her voice caught when she said that last part. And even though her words were harsh, inside she was falling apart. She was doing what she had to do to protect herself from getting hurt even more—to protect Antonio, too. But a small voice in her head kept telling her she was being a coward, running away when things were getting serious. She knew that real relationships weren't all rainbows and unicorns, but she was also pretty sure that if she stayed, she'd be setting herself up for a never-ending pattern of ups and downs. Being with Antonio could feel like the highest of highs—but when she felt uncertain about him, it was the lowest of lows. She could just hear Missy's voice chastising her, *Girl, you've got some serious abandonment issues.* Okay, so maybe she did, but not without good reason.

"Kenzie, Baracoa doesn't mean anything to me if you're not going to be a part of it."

Kenzie turned to look at him, her eyes welling up with tears. Before he could say any more, a police officer appeared, blaring a siren and redirecting traffic onto the side street.

"Must be an accident up ahead," Antonio said as he turned off the main road. "Come on," he said, pulling into the first parking spot he saw. "We can walk to where we're going."

Antonio and Kenzie walked hand-in-hand down the smoldering Miami streets. They walked past office buildings and restaurants, getting sweatier with each step and holding onto each other. Kenzie gripped his hand a little tighter when the thought occurred to her that this might be the last time she ever saw this complicated, dynamic man.

"Almost there," Antonio said, reciprocating her squeeze. "I promise, this will be worth it when you see it."

They rounded the corner and Antonio stopped in front of an empty storefront. It was a large, corner space with floor-to-ceiling windows and was totally gutted inside. Antonio opened the door and held it for Kenzie.

"Shall we go in?" he asked.

"Are you sure we're allowed?" Kenzie asked.

"Don't worry, I know the owner," Antonio said with a wink.

Was it possible that he owned the place? Kenzie wondered. Then she remembered—when it came to Antonio, anything was possible.

Kenzie watched her step and headed inside, still not sure what the purpose of their visit was.

They stepped into a giant main room, which looked like maybe it had been used as a dance studio at one point. It was bright and sunny, on a quiet street. Kenzie could tell immediately that it had a good vibe.

"What is this place?" Kenzie asked, curious to learn why Antonio had walked her twenty minutes in the heat to see an empty storefront.

"This," Antonio said with a flourish that was maybe a little over-the-top for such a bare-bones place, "is the potential home of Honor Yoga Miami."

Kenzie was speechless. She didn't know if it was the most brazen, overstepping thing anyone had ever done, or the sweetest.

"Antonio, I told you, I'm going back to New York."

"I know," he said, placing his hands on her shoulders. "But there could be reasons to come back."

He looked at her knowingly and she smiled.

"I really appreciate you thinking of me," she began.

"Don't dismiss the idea before you give it some thought," he urged. "I think about you all the time. You're all I think about," he said, looking directly in her eyes. "And I think that you feel the same way about me."

"Maybe I do," Kenzie realized as she said it out loud. "But we're from two different worlds. And I really do need to get back to my business at home, before I lose it."

Antonio's hands dropped to his sides.

"I understand," he said, looking more dejected then she had ever seen him. "Can I ask you for one favor before you go?"

"Of course," she said.

"Can I..." Antonio moved in closer, putting his hand on the back of Kenzie's head. He didn't need to ask the question out loud. Her eyes were already saying yes. When their lips met, Antonio kissed her more passionately than ever, and she felt the electricity running through her body, from the top of her head right down to her toes. It was intoxicating, better than any cocktail and much more effective.

After a moment, they moved apart, breaking the spell.

"Now can I ask you a favor?" said Kenzie.

"You can ask me for anything," Antonio retorted.

"Can you take me back to Baracoa? There's someone there I need to see."

When Kenzie and Antonio pulled up in front of Baracoa, Kenzie was surprised to see the amount of activity going on. She had told her PR person to cancel the event shortly after her drink at the bar the previous night. Maybe she hadn't gotten the message? If crowds of people started showing up it was going to be a disaster.

"Why are they setting up?" she asked, turning to Antonio as they entered the courtyard. There were tables and chairs, and a man was stringing small gold lights all around the circumference.

"Kenzie!" Trudy said, throwing her arms around her confused friend. "I didn't know if I was going to see you!"

"I'm on my way to the airport but I wanted to say goodbye," Kenzie explained gently.

"You can't leave now," Trudy said insistently. "We're just getting set up."

"Trudy." Kenzie said her name gently, taking her hand. "If we are shut down by the FDA there's no way we can hold a rum mixer. I hope you didn't continue with the planning…"

"Didn't he tell you?" Trudy looked from Antonio to Kenzie and back again. "Tell her!"

Antonio cleared his voice. "I may have found a work-around. If we are a retail food establishment, we're not subject to the inspection."

"But what food are we retailing?" Kenzie asked.

Just then, a brightly painted truck came roaring up to the entrance of Baracoa. Kenzie recognized the burger logo on the side. "Is that the Latin burger guy?"

"Hello, thanks for coming," Antonio said, waving the familiar-looking driver, who smiled at Kenzie when he saw her, through to the courtyard. Kenzie turned to see that following closely behind there was a row of about five other trucks, each selling different delicacies. Antonio waved each one of them into the courtyard.

"This is amazing," Kenzie marveled. "You did all this?" she asked Antonio, still not believing that they had gone ahead with the plan.

"We both did." Antonio put his arm around Trudy. "Thank you for all the years of service here, Trudy. You really are an artist."

"It's my pleasure," Trudy said, beaming. "This is a special place," Trudy added with a twinkle in her eyes.

"But what about the entertainment?" Kenzie asked. "You know Catalina has a broken leg and she can't be here tonight."

"Forget Catalina," Trudy said, waving her off. "Why don't you teach a yoga class? That's what you do, right?"

"It is," Kenzie said skeptically. "But really? Booze and yoga?"

"Why not?" asked Antonio. "I think people would love it."

"Okay," Kenzie agreed, feeling a smile form across her face. She would have to make it up as she went along, but she was becoming an expert in that. "Let's do this!" she said to her friends.

Later that night as the sun began to set, cars started arriving at Baracoa and the courtyard took on a magical glow. Music played as Miami's young up-and-comers filed in, all curious about whether rum was the "next big thing" as the flyers and email blasts from Kenzie's press people had touted.

Kenzie stood by herself a little bit away from the action and took it all in. It was amazing that it had all come together. And not without a little, or rather a lot, of help from some new friends.

She watched as a woman in a colorful shift dress took a sip of a tropical cocktail she was holding.

"What is this?" she asked the bartender, making yummy noises and taking another sip.

"It's a combination of three of the rums distilled here on the premises," explained Jose, who was helping out as bartender. He was dressed in a madras shirt and fedora that went perfectly with the décor. "A light rum, a golden rum and a dark rum. I call it the 'Baracoa,'" he said, turning to where Kenzie was standing and smiling in her direction.

Kenzie had nervous energy in her stomach, but she was happy, too. She couldn't believe so many people had shown up, and that people she had met so recently had all stepped up to make her vision become a reality.

Suddenly, the music faded and Trudy, now dressed in a long floral maxi dress with her hair in a silvery bun, took a microphone in hand.

"And now please grab a yoga mat and join us for the main event!" she said enthusiastically. "I'd like to introduce, world class, certified yoga instructor and part owner of Baracoa distillery, MacKenzie Fox!"

Kenzie straightened out her special yoga outfit, a gold and black sports bra with matching leggings, and stepped in front of the crowd.

"I want to thank you all for being here tonight," she said, her voice shaking. "This means so much

to me. I'd like you to set an intention for your practice now." When she said this, she looked over at the
gateway to the courtyard and saw Antonio standing
there by himself. He was wearing a linen suit, looking more handsome than she'd ever seen, and watching her as if he were mesmerized. "Deep breath in,"
Kenzie instructed, raising her hands to the sky in
prayer mode as the crowd followed along.

She led the guests through a thirty-minute session, and at the end of it, everyone applauded.

"Okay, now go drink some rum!" she instructed
to everyone's cheers and laughter.

As she walked back into the distillery to grab
some water, she felt a strong hand wrap around her
bare midriff. Antonio.

"You were fantastic," he whispered, smiling at
her and his eyes beaming with pride.

"Thank you," she said shyly. "Trudy was right.
That was fun. Wanna get a drink?"

"I thought you'd never ask." Antonio winked.

Standing in the courtyard, both sipping on Jose's
incredible concoction, Antonio leaned in to speak
so that only Kenzie could hear him.

"See that man over there?" he said, gesturing sub-
tly to a young guy in a suit and sneakers. "He's with
a major liquor brand. He made us a crazy offer to
buy you out. I think you should take it."

"What?" Kenzie said, unable to keep her voice
down. "But this is your family place!"

"It's yours now," Antonio said smiling. "You earned it fair and square."

"No," Kenzie protested. Even though she had accomplished what she said she would, taking the distillery away from Antonio didn't feel right. He had rum in his blood. And the truth was, she really cared about him.

"Unless you're involved in Baracoa, I don't want any part of it," Kenzie said with finality.

"Well, should we sell it to him?" Kenzie and Antonio looked at the young man.

"He'd probably just turn it into some soulless, corporate commodity," Kenzie said.

"You're right," agreed Antonio. "It's too bad you have to go back to New York. If you stayed, we could run this place together...and do other things."

"Well, what if I told you I could maybe see myself down here sometimes?" she said, with a little hint of flirtation in her voice.

"I would definitely be open to that," Antonio said, putting down his drink on a nearby table and wrapping his arms around Kenzie's small waist.

"So..." she said, tilting her head and looking up at him with a smile. "Partners?"

Antonio grinned back at her. "Yes. Partners," he agreed.

She held out her hand to shake on it, and he pulled her in close.

"I probably shouldn't bring this up, but there was

another part to this bet," he said, moving his hands
down her back until they reached the curve of her
ass.

"That's right," Kenzie said, as if she were remembering for the first time. "And it looks like I
won."

Antonio considered it, and then pushed a curl out
of Kenzie's eyes. "Then I guess that means that I
lose," he said, looking at her with a smoldering gaze
serious enough to melt any woman's heart, or at least
remove her panties.

"Follow me," she said, leading him back inside,
past the crowds of guests and into the distillery warehouse.

Inside, she shut the door behind them and once
again, they were alone with rows upon rows of those
lovely, full rum barrels.

"So, does this mean you get to do anything you
want with me? Those were the terms of the bet, correct?" Antonio held up his hands. "I'm game. Go
ahead. Do your worst."

Kenzie moved closer to Antonio and sat down on
a barrel in front of him.

"What if I told you that even though I won the
bet, you won, too?"

Antonio thought about this for a second and then
breathed out a heavy sigh. Without breaking eye contact, he moved close to Kenzie, grabbed her head in
his hands and kissed her, slowly, sensually, until she

could feel it in her toes. It was a feeling she could get used to and for the first time she didn't feel wistful or guilty—just happy.

"Are you saying this is real?" he whispered as she unbuttoned his shirt and pulled it down over his bare, muscular shoulders.

"I'm saying you have me. All of me," Kenzie said breathlessly, kissing her way down his chest and stopping at his waistband long enough to unfasten the clasp and zip and unleash the manhood she had gotten to know and love so well. There it was—so big and throbbing. She knew from that moment that she never wanted to be away from it—or Antonio again.

"Then let's do this right," he said. Antonio peeled off Kenzie's yoga pants and sports bra and when she was completely naked, leaned her back over the barrel. Sliding his own naked body on top of hers, and looking deeply into her eyes, he plunged his eager cock into the only place it wanted to be.

"What are we doing?" he asked as he pumped in and out of her, his pace fast and joyous. "Tell me."

"Lovemaking!" Kenzie answered playfully, grabbing a hold of Antonio's firm ass with both her hands and pulling him into her even deeper.

Antonio took a hold of Kenzie by the hair, which forced her to look directly in his eyes. Her playful smile transformed into a sensual look.

"Making love," she said softly. "We're making

love." Her eyes and her tone were serious now. "And it's the best thing in the whole world."

The two of them smiled and somehow, managed to finish at the same time without even getting caught.

CHAPTER ELEVEN

WHEN KENZIE'S PLANE landed at MIA she waited impatiently for the captain to turn off the seat belt sign. The moment it switched off she slung her carry-on over her shoulder and made a beeline for the exit. In fact, part of the reason she had booked first class, apart from the obvious perks, was to be closer to the door so she could get to her intended destination sooner.

"Hola," Kenzie greeted her usual driver when he picked her up at arrivals. Dressed in a bright fuchsia skirt and top, she no longer looked like an out-of-place New Yorker when she hit Miami Beach. The first time someone had actually asked her for directions to the design district, she was secretly elated. Imagine that, her being mistaken for a local.

And sometimes it did feel like she lived here, she visited so much. In the past six months, this was her third trip down to Honor Yoga Miami, and she had spent countless hours on the phone with her backers, all locals that she had connected with through the distillery.

As her driver rolled down the freeway, she thought about making a quick stop at Baracoa to see Trudy and the gang, but she knew in her heart it would have to wait until her next visit. Her itinerary for the forty-eight-hour trip was already jam-packed, and the first appointment was with a private client. Then there was a lunch with investors, and later, a wellness conference where she was the keynote speaker.

As she rolled down the window Kenzie closed her eyes and breathed in the salty sweet air that she had been missing. She knew she'd always be a New Yorker at heart, but Miami was like a second home now, one where she could be a little lighter, a little freer and yes, sometimes a bit wilder.

"Here you go, *chica*."

Kenzie opened her eyes to see that they were stopped on the corner of her very own studio. It was amazing, the transformation that had taken place to realize her vision of an open, airy yoga space that somehow reflected both New York and Miami. There were elements that were calming, like the free-flowing pane of water visible through the street entrance, and some that were electric, like the neon sign that spelled out You Do You, a subtle hint at her very own mantra, in and out of the bedroom!

When she walked through the doors like she owned the place, Kenzie couldn't help but giggle to herself—because she did own it. And her new location in Red Hook back in Brooklyn, too. She'd even had offers to franchise—but that was a meeting for another day.

"Welcome back, Ms. Fox," chirped the young receptionist, outfitted in an Honor Yoga signature T-shirt and leggings.

"Please, Jillian, call me Kenzie."

"Your private client is already here," she stated, looking the slightest bit perturbed.

"Oh! I thought I was early," Kenzie said, checking the time on her phone.

"You are," Jillian said as she went to answer the ringing telephone. "Excuse me."

Kenzie had counted on having at least thirty minutes to unwind from the flight and change into yoga clothes. She thought about slipping into the back office but figured she'd first better go check in with her appointment. Those who booked one-on-ones with her were the most exclusive of her clients. On her last trip she'd worked with Jennifer Lopez, Jason Derulo and two of the Kardashians.

"I'm just going to peek in and say hi," she called to Jillian.

Opening the door to the studio, she announced herself with her usual greeting.

"Good afternoon, welcome to Honor Yoga!"

Her student was already seated on the mat. His shoulders were exposed in a white Honor Yoga tank top and his strong legs were straining to stay in a cross-legged position. Between them was the most enticing-looking bulge.

"Good afternoon indeed," Antonio said, looking up at his instructor. "What do you have in store for me this afternoon, teacher?" he asked, his eyes flickering with desire.

Kenzie walked over to him and lowering herself down to the mat, sat down in his lap, facing him.

"Well, this is very unconventional," Antonio said, running the tips of his fingers over the hem of Kenzie's flirty skirt.

"Try to quiet your mind, yogi," Kenzie said, placing her hands on the sides of Antonio's head. There it was, the face she had missed every night for weeks. There was only one thing to do and that was to kiss him, softly, luxuriously and intimately. She smiled at him and whispered in his ear.

"I want you to begin by taking a deep breath in."

The two of them inhaled and exhaled in unison.

"Now, let's get started."

* * * * *

Read on for a sneak peek at
Mr. Temptation
by Rachael Stewart

*Available wherever DARE books
and ebooks are sold.*

CHAPTER ONE

'FUCKERS.'

Daniel raked his fingers through his hair and rose to sit at the edge of the bed, his body hunching over his mobile and its glaring news feed.

It was entirely expected, everything he'd envisaged the night before, so why was he so riled?

He'd asked for it. And the press had delivered. In fact, more than delivered—the article had to be the most scathing yet.

But where was the usual sense of fun, the thrill of living up to his name, of pissing on his mum's glory?

'Honey, whatever it is, let it go and come back to bed.'

The voice purred at him from behind, a set of nails down his bare back designed to add to the appeal, and yet he wasn't taking the bait. Not even a nibble. Both his cock and mind uninterested.

'You should go.' He twisted to take in the naked

rear of the woman who was last night's fix. What was it? The third—fourth time they'd slept together.

She was beautiful, everything you'd expect an elite model of her calibre to be. But he was bored, the spark already dying out; it had to be a record. He felt a pang of guilt and buried it. She wouldn't care, not really; he was careful who he chose to fill his bed. And she'd got what she came for. He always lived up to his rep.

'What time is it?' She rolled onto her back, stretching out and pulling the crisp white sheet down her front, her bared rose-tipped breasts pert and alert. His cock gave a twinge, a little interest after all…

But not enough.

It was gone eight. He was due at his sister's in less than an hour and the press were already gathering outside. The sooner they broke out, the better.

'Time you went,' he said, rising to his feet. 'I'm hitting the shower.'

'I'll come with.'

She moved to follow and he faced her off, unconcerned that the semi he was sporting gave a very different response to his, '*Nej*—don't.'

She gave a sultry pout and fell back onto her haunches. 'Party pooper.'

'Don't tell me you haven't got a rammed schedule for today.'

She rolled her eyes with a resigned sigh. 'Thanks for the reminder.'

She turned to reach across the bed and take up her mobile from the side table, her focus now on the screen while her pert little ass beckoned him.

Shower. Now.

Making himself turn away, he headed to the bathroom. He could get his fix later, find someone new perhaps. Hell, he could have his pick…maybe that was the problem…

'Annie, dahling,' he heard her coo down the phone, 'can you sort me an escape from The Shard? Seems we've caused a bit of a stir with the paparazzi…'

He set the jets of water running and drowned out the remainder of her conversation. He'd just finished with his hair when her naked body curved around the door frame.

'Sure I can't change your mind?'

Ah, fuck it, another ten minutes isn't going to hurt…

'Zara, Shit-Bag is on line one—he's after a number for a contact, apparently.'

EJ, her PA and right hand, leant back over her office chair, her head appearing through the open doorway to Zara's private office. Not even her black-rimmed glasses were big enough to conceal her raised auburn brow and sparking blue gaze. She was as pissed at taking the call as Zara was to receive it.

'Tell him I have an appointment. I'll call him back.' It wasn't a lie, she did, and she needed to get moving if she wasn't going to be late. She had the whole day mapped out touring London with her latest client, Julia Larsson, showing her abodes that matched the property brief they'd mapped out together to a T.

'Righto,' EJ said, dropping back into her own space. Although it wasn't really as if the rest of her team had any designated space as such. Not yet.

Other than her office, the walls were only partially in place, the refit as per her design spec was halfway through completion and they were all living with a rather open workspace in the interim. Not that it really mattered. Zara only had a handful of employees currently, but it paid to have space for her expansion plans and, more importantly, it paid to have the right kind of space to entertain the right kind of clients.

The kind of space she'd had up until five months ago when Shit-Bag had left her no choice but to walk out of her former company. Six months of trying to work together following their break-up having taken their toll.

'Err, Zara, he says it's urgent.'

EJ walked her chair back into view and gave her an apologetic grimace, making a derogatory hand signal against the receiver at the same time. The latter succeeded in pulling out a smirk. How very different from the way EJ had reacted to him in the early days. How very different from every woman when first being caught in his charismatic web. She'd been no exception. Falling for his clean and slick appearance, a voice that rumbled with teasing provocation no matter what was being said and a body fit for a boxing ring.

Yeah, you fell for it, all right, but no more—you're older and wiser for it now.

'It's okay,' she assured her, 'let him through.'

Her tummy twisted, but her smile at EJ was solid. She wasn't going to upset her with her own discomfort. And she most definitely wasn't going to let *him* hear how much he could still hurt her.

She lifted the phone receiver and accepted the call. 'Charles, what is it?'

'Zara, be a good girl and send me Tristan Black's phone number, will you?'

His brash condescension had her teeth clenching, her anger flaring. *Did I really find that cockney arrogance sexy once?*

'I'm rather busy right now,' she said neutrally, using the anger to her advantage. Anger she could work with, it was so much easier to control than pain. 'I'll see if I can find it later and send it on.'

'Come on, Zara, darling, it's urgent and you know full well you have his number.' If she didn't know him better she'd think she caught the hint of panic, as though he could sense she was about to cut the call. Which she was. But panic? What could be so important that he needed to reach Tristan this second? 'Look, our blasted systems have gone down and I don't seem to have it on my mobile.'

'Perhaps that's because he was *my* client.' She couldn't help the barbed comment. But hell, he'd refused to let her take anyone, enforcing the restrictive contract clauses to the letter. She'd been lucky to set her new business up at all. Even luckier to take EJ with her.

It didn't matter that he was the reason she'd had to leave in the first place. That she'd been the one who had worked twenty-four-seven to make it the success it had become. The success it still was, only now it was his baby, he was the one reaping all the benefit.

'Very true,' he said smoothly, his composure back so swiftly she'd probably imagined the crack—it was too much to hope for after all. 'But, you know, my client now, of course.'

She clenched her fist around the phone, his smarmy tone and gibe making her want to hurl. The sooner she could have him off the line, the better. 'I'll dig it out and send it on, good—'

'Wait, there's something else…'

She halted midway through hanging up, the skin at the back of her neck prickling as her memory bank came alive. She knew that tone, knew it meant some big revelation or other. Wasn't it just how he'd sounded when he'd finally been forced to admit all his extra-curricular activities?

'What is it?' She asked the question even though

every instinct told her she didn't want to know. The awkward cough he gave only confirming it. 'Charles, spit it out, I don't have all day.'

'I'm getting married.'

The air caught in her lungs, ice seeping through her veins. Of all the things she could have imagined it being, it certainly wasn't that.

The great bachelor, Charles Eddison, finally getting hitched. Five years and he'd failed to make an honest woman of her. She'd loved him with all of her being and yet it hadn't been enough. And now, one year after their break-up, someone had managed to do it, someone had been special enough...

It just hadn't been me.

'Easy, liten *syster*,' Daniel said into his mobile as he pressed the button for the lift to her floor. 'I'm here now.'

'Less of the little,' she snapped, her irritation making her London accent revert to her Swedish lilt and making him grin. 'Or I'll start calling you Danny.'

He gave a mock shudder. 'Quit the strop, then.'

Someone swept up behind him, a scent wrapping around him, vanilla twisted up in something so enticing he was damned if he could place it, and his eyes swerved of their own accord.

'Strop! You were supposed to be here half an...'

His sister's voice trailed away into the distance,

his sight landing on the woman whose interesting scent had nothing on the visual. He felt his mouth quirk, his interest instant. She was beautiful, in an unusual, edgy kind of way. So not his type, a definite 'no' on paper, but when presented with the physical, she was all kinds of yes…

She faced the lift, waiting just as he was, one purple stiletto tapping impatiently, her body encased in a fitted black trouser suit, a leather-clad portfolio hooked under one arm, all quite usual but—

'Are you listening to me, *Dann-eee*?'

'Sure, I'll be right up,' he said distractedly, cutting the call and pocketing the device.

It was her hair that fascinated him: cropped to her ears, the reddish-brown mass was parted high to one side, windswept almost. And then there was her make-up, neutral save for the liner around her eyes and the bold lip colour—*was that purple?*

His gaze narrowed over it and she must have sensed his attention, her eyes flickering in his direction. 'You know, it's rude to stare.'

Her voice was husky, a crisp edge that rasped along his spine and sealed her appeal. He was hooked.

Her eyes were back on the doors, her lack of interest obvious. He should've taken it as a sign, but since when had he backed off from anything he fancied? In truth, her lack of interest only added to the appeal.

'Rude?' he said, raising his brow. 'I've been called

many things before—arrogant, reckless, even an asshole—but rude, not had that one yet.'

Her mouth twitched but she didn't turn to look at him, the ping of the lift arriving serving as a temporary interruption.

The doors opened and he gestured for her to precede him. 'See, I'm not *entirely* rude.'

She looked to him then, her silver-grey eyes sparkling and those bold-coloured lips lifting into a smile that momentarily gutted him. *Jesus*, she was hot. The bow-like shape stretching and still the lower lip was full—swollen, even—almost as though it had just been thoroughly devoured.

Maybe she'd had to reapply that colour after it had been rubbed clean away. *Oh, to be the cause of that little misdemeanour.*

'Thank you.'

It took a second to realise she had spoken, to realise he was staring all over again, and then sanity returned. 'You're welcome—which floor?'

He pressed the number for his sister and her thick black lashes lowered to trace his move. 'The same.'

He nodded and came to stand beside her. The lift closed and together they stood, the silence heavy and loaded—*at least to him.*

Did she know who he was? Anyone with one eye on the media knew who he was: the sexy, Swedish billionaire who stuck one finger up to his celebrity roots and made it in the real world—the business world; the playboy who liked his women plentiful and hot, and always without strings.

That was pretty much how the article had summed him up that morning before really crucifying him.

Hell, maybe she knew exactly who he was and what he was like, hence her lack of interest.

If that was the case, she definitely wasn't his type.

Not at all.

Liar...

Okay, so maybe it was time to break with tradition.

Did he have *to be heading to the same floor?*

She'd had enough of arrogant arseholes for one day and here she was stuck in a lift with a self-professed one. She couldn't deny he'd amused her with his honesty and self-deprecating introduction though.

But he was trouble.

He wasn't like Charles. He wasn't smooth and perfect, clean-shaven and pristine.

No, this man was all about the stubble and the bed-head hair; a sun-kissed surfer plucked from the ocean, jazzed up and dumped in the city. The jeans and sweatshirt hugging his imposing frame looked laid-back but they screamed designer from top to toe. And the way he had her pulse tripping over itself, he was just as dangerous. On every level.

'Now you know so much about me,' he suddenly said, his accent thick and exciting her far more than was fair, 'how about you let me take you for a drink?'

She almost swallowed her tongue, the portfolio digging into her side as she turned rigid. 'I'm busy.'

'Not right this second,' he said, his amber eyes twinkling with amusement and holding her own. 'But at a mutually agreeable time, of course?'

Of course. She mentally rolled her eyes. *Would he just get the hint?*

Her resolve was good, but she wasn't immune. She could feel the temptation well enough and the sooner she got free of it, the better. She dragged her eyes away, forcing them on the intricate pattern twisting through the gold lift door ahead. 'I don't think that's a good idea.'

'Care to tell me why?'

Because I'm not a fool. 'I know you.'

The lift announced the arrival of their floor and he spoke over it. 'You do?'

'Obviously not you exactly,' she said, relief sweeping through her as the lift doors opened and she stepped out.

Purposeful, she turned left towards Julia's and hoped he would take the hint or a different direction at least. He didn't.

'Obviously,' he reaffirmed, falling into step behind her. 'I'd remember if I'd met you before.'

Her tummy gave an annoying flutter and she squashed it. She was going to have to be more specific. Brutal even…

'What I mean is, I know your type.'

'My type?'

'Hell, yeah, great in the sack, perfect bedroom material…' she sent him a scathing look '…but beyond that…well, we don't go there, do we?'

His step faltered, 'Wow, hung, drawn *and* quartered.'

She could hear his surprise, feel his unease, and victory surged warm in her veins. Her harsh assessment had hit its mark, hopefully enough to send him running.

And if that didn't, the hint of her being the relationship kind should do it.

'You have quite the opinion of men.'

She gave a derisive laugh and turned a bend, the sanctity of Julia's hotel room now only a few strides away.

'So, you're either an anti-male lesbian—' it was her turn to falter mid-step '—or you've been burned before. Which is it to be?'

A lesbian…

She laughed with reignited vigour. It wasn't the first time she'd been mistaken as such. Ever since she'd opted for the cropped hairstyle—one of her many post-break-up actions—she'd been hit on by women and men alike, hoping she swung their way.

But she wasn't about to tell him anything close to the truth.

'Typical arrogant male—just because I'm not interested in you *per se*, I have to be a lesbian.' She'd arrived at Julia's door and to emphasise her point, she faced it and rapped against it. 'Now, if you don't mind, I have work to do.'

He wasn't moving away. If anything, he was settling in right alongside her—*what the fuck?*

She didn't have time to ask what he was playing at; the door swung open to reveal her rather disgruntled-looking client—*shit*. 'I'm so sorry I'm late, Ms Larsson.'

The woman visibly cringed. 'Drop the Ms, makes me feel ancient, it's Julia…and so you should be,' she said, shrugging a tan leather jacket over a white T and looking from Zara to her unwanted companion. 'The pair of you.'

Pair of us?

Zara looked to him and he gave her a bemused shrug. 'Seems you can't get away from me that easily.'

'Oh, good God, Daniel, don't tell me you've hit on my estate agent already?' The woman's eyes flashed furiously, their colour strikingly similar to *his*.

Come to think of it, so was the golden hue to her shoulder-length hair…

'I wouldn't call it hitting on, exactly,' he said, with another one of those annoyingly casual shrugs. 'We were actually just discussing sexual tendencies.'

'You've got to be kidding me!' Julia looked at her, cheeks flushing, eyes bright. 'Seems I owe you an apology too.'

'You do?' Zara's voice sounded faint, her brain rapidly piecing the situation together.

'This *animal*,' Julia said, gesturing to him in mock disdain, 'is my brother—well, half-brother, to be exact. But seriously, Daniel, *vad fan*?'

'Brother?' she repeated, her eyes sweeping to the man himself, the realisation that she wasn't going to evade him any time soon setting off a troubling dance in her chest.

'In my defence,' he said, a curious frown creasing his brow, 'she brought it out in me.'

'That's your excuse?' Julia said incredulously, delivering a playful shove that barely moved him, his eyes remaining fixed on Zara's every bit as curious, and heated and very, very interested. 'If I didn't value your opinion so much, I'd tell you to just do one and leave us to it.'

'Seems that makes two of you today,' he said, his penetrating gaze reaching inside Zara's mind and triggering a replay of all that she had said with embarrassing clarity. 'It's a bloody good job my ego is big enough to take it.'

'No one's ego can be as big as yours, *storebror*,' Julia said. 'It's just lucky your heart is also as big.'

'And don't you forget it,' he said, looking to his sister with open affection now, freeing Zara at last,

to breathe, to think, to get with it… 'So, are we going
to take this show on the road? Or are we going to
stand here and do more *Daniel-bashing*?'

Julia gave a giggle and, God help her, Zara smiled,
the move easy. Too easy.

'For the record,' he added, 'my preference is definitely for the former.'

And then she laughed. Really laughed.

Charming. Good-looking. Dangerous.

No. No. *No*.

CHAPTER TWO

DANIEL WAS GRINDING his teeth. His arms folded across his front. His body rigid as he leant back against the door that housed what Zara had referred to as an *ample* bathroom for *this size* of apartment, in *this desirable* an area.

He'd say this: desirable or not, you could certainly save time going for your morning constitution while brushing your teeth over the sink. And the shower-over-the-bath—you had to be some kind of contortionist to use it. Why was he the only one seeing these issues?

At least this third property was an improvement on the previous two. It had natural daylight for starters, and no pounding pub or store adjoining.

He watched them cooing over the open-plan living space now—*the strategically placed sofa that permitted the perfect view of the park across the road and the minute television that was as big as it could ever be in the space available*—and bit into his tongue.

He wasn't sure what was more painful: The fact he'd been forced to take the estate agency's car—albeit a classic chauffeur-driven number, but when his state-of-the-art limo was at the ready, seriously, what sense did that make? Absolutely none. Or the fact that his opinion, when he chose to voice one, was counting for nothing, despite what his sister had said to the contrary earlier.

Or was it the fact that any fleeting look or touch from Ms Agent herself and his body stirred.

Yet she'd made it ever so clear, it wasn't happening, not in a million years.

He was now at the point where he was convincing himself his attractive little sister *was* far more the agent's cup of tea. Or indeed, her choice of cocktail, the drink suiting her fire so much better. The attention she was lavishing over Julia, totally OTT in his opinion, and yet his sister was lapping it up.

'So, come on, what do you think?' came Julia's on-the-spot question.

They both turned to him expectantly, his sister's skin annoyingly aglow and happy—*she liked it... really liked it*. Ah, *skit*.

He cleared his throat and pushed away from the door, heading to stand between them, careful to keep his eye on the window and the view beyond. 'It's... nice.'

He had *tried* to sound enthused, but the reality

was his comment stank, its tone utterly tepid. Funny enough, just how he was feeling.

'Nice?' she pressed.

'The view is good; the location is convenient and—' he shrugged '—nice.'

'What about the actual apartment?'

He turned and let his gaze sweep the living area, the dining table for two and the kitchenette; he didn't even want to think on the bathroom.

She could do better.

Her sleaze of an ex-husband should be picking up the brunt of the cost and if not him, she should be letting Daniel help. But he'd had this argument a thousand times over and she wasn't having any of it.

'You need to stop frowning so much,' she piped up. 'Gives you wrinkles, you know.'

'You're clearly not impressed,' Zara remarked and guilt nagged at him. It wasn't down to her ability, or lack thereof, to sell the place; she was doing her job plenty well enough.

'It's not your fault,' he assured her. 'My sister is being stubborn, and, rather than accept other people's money to afford the kind of place she has grown up with, she is determined to do this alone.'

Julia rolled her eyes, her arms folding across her chest as she pinned him with that pig-headed stare he was accustomed to. 'Don't start that again. Dad's trust fund is already helping me out enough. I'm not taking your charity too.'

'If not mine, then you should bloody well take Edward's money. The guy deserves to be coughing up for all he did.'

'Do you honestly think I want any ties to that man?' she said fiercely. 'It's bad enough that he did the rounds with my so-called friends. The sooner the divorce is final and I can cut all ties, the better.'

He could sense Zara backing away, could feel the personal nature of their conversation putting her on edge. 'Okay, okay,' he said, reining it back in. 'I'm sorry to have mentioned him. I just want what's best for you, and this isn't it.'

'Why?'

'It's impractical.'

'Why?'

'*Kristus*, Julia, you're a tall woman—care to explain how you're going to use *that bathroom*?' He threw his hand in its godforsaken direction and she frowned, his point failing to register. 'Allow me to demonstrate...'

He strode for the bathroom and pulled open the door. Doing his damnedest to ignore the sickly pink decor and vanity ware. He waited for them to appear before climbing into the bathtub, contorting his body to fit between the glass shower screen and the sloping wall.

He straightened as far as he could, his head slightly bowed as the shower head met with his shoulder—'S*ee?*'

They saw, all right. Their eyes glittered, their lips quivered and then they had the audacity to erupt in almighty belly laughs—*for fuck's sake.*

He dropped his gaze, dislodging himself from the enclosure with as much dignity as he could muster. 'You think it's so easy? You try it.'

'I'd rather not,' Julia blurted, her hand over her mouth as her eyes still danced.

'Okay.' He looked to Zara pointedly, ignoring how her amused gaze lit him up inside. *If she thought the apartment was so good, she could bloody well demonstrate.* 'Why don't *you* do the honours?'

His demand appeared to sober her up, her eyes flicking between the pair of them and her professionalism winning out as she said, 'Sure, could you just hold this?'

She thrust the portfolio into his chest and stepped inside the room. He realised the error of his suggestion immediately. He should have first left the confined space before goading her to enter, to get up close.

Head out of your pants, head out of your pants, head out of your pants.

'It's like this,' she said, eyes flashing defiantly, their bodies chest to chest—she could tell him anything now and he'd fall for it, but, to his surprise, she raised her hand and pulled at the shower screen, the damn thing moving towards him as she stepped away.

'Just back up a little,' she ordered.

Back up? He was pressed into the edge of the toilet as it was. He spread his legs, the position oddly vulnerable and erotically acquiescing. He watched, fascinated, as the access opened up, creating space to permit her entry, all graceful and easy as she climbed inside.

But, ha, the shower head still looked ridiculous as it brushed the tip of her head.

'And you can remove this for more height, like so,' she said, reading his mind and slipping it out of its rest. 'Which also makes it great for cleaning the bath.'

She gave a sweep of the area but in truth all he could think about now was her wet and naked and all soaped-up—not even the sickly pink backdrop could dampen the heat spreading below his waist.

'Perfectly demonstrated, thank you, Zara.' His sister gave him a smug grin. 'See, big bro, that's how it's done.'

'You're welcome,' came Zara's response, his eye swiftly returning to her and the imaginings he shouldn't be having. She slotted the shower head back in place and slipped him a sidelong glance through the glass screen. Her fingers froze over the contraption, her eyes widening ever so slightly, her pupils following suit—did she know where his head was at?

And then the moment was gone, a shutter falling

over her expression as she gave a small cough, her eyes snapping away.

'Right, well, I think we're done with this one,' she said, unceremoniously shoving the shower screen in his face and almost sending him to his ass on the pink porcelain.

'Shall we move on?' she said, already heading out.

'Yup.' Julia nodded, smirking right at him.

He screwed his face up in a childish gesture—*whatever*.

'If you both go on down,' Zara said, expertly ignoring their little exchange—*thank fuck!* The pair of them were doing his ego and renowned charm no favours at all.

'I'll join you shortly,' she continued. 'I just have to take care of an errand for the owner.'

'Great,' Julia said, moving for the front door. 'I have a quick call to make so I'll meet you downstairs.'

'I'll catch you up,' he called after her, pushing the glass door back into place and wondering why the hell he hadn't thought of that.

Perhaps because you've never had to endure one before?

He shook his head, brushing the entire incident off as he followed in Zara's direction.

'Can I have a quick word?' he asked, entering the kitchenette hot on her tail. His intention had been to talk budget with Julia out of earshot but as Zara turned in the small space, hemmed in as they were by the cupboards and the breakfast bar, all thoughts of conversation evaporated.

'Yes,' she said, her eyes wary as they lifted to his, her hands coming to rest on the countertop either side of her as she backed up against it. 'But first you need to stop looking at me like that.'

'Like what?' He knew the answer well enough, but how would she describe it, what she saw in him? She was good with words—she'd demonstrated it repeatedly throughout the day, when eloquently describing the features of each potential abode. And in truth, he could listen to her talk and talk and talk. Perhaps that was why he was so keen to criticise: he wasn't ready for her job to come to an end; he wasn't ready for her to complete a sale for his sister and vacate his life.

He watched her eyelids flutter, her tongue flicking out to moisten that bottom lip he was so fascinated with. *Was she nervous?*

'You know what.' Her eyes dropped to his mouth, their depths revealing in their helpless nature, and his lips curled upwards. So she wasn't as unaffected by him as she'd have him believe.

Power surged, his ego with it. 'What if I said I can't help it?'

Her eyes snapped back to his. 'Then make yourself help it because this—' she wagged a finger between them '—isn't happening.'

'No?' He stepped forward and her eyes widened, her lips parting on a ragged breath.

'No.' She gave a small shake of her head, the move sending a lock across her forehead and he itched to push it back. 'I don't date clients.'

'Technically,' he said, his voice gruff even to his own ears, 'I'm not a client.'

'You're as good as.'

'I disagree.'

'Whether you disagree or not, I don't care,' she rushed out. 'I'm not falling into this trap.'

His brow knitted together; she'd flummoxed him now. 'Trap?'

She paled, her words seeming to surprise even her, and then she visibly recovered, her chin rising, to say, 'The kind of trap where I let this get in the way of my business.'

He studied her face, her sincerity. 'You sound like you're speaking from experience.' He didn't like the idea one bit. *Oh, the irony.* 'I take it you've not always been so averse to dating clients?'

She hesitated, her teeth worrying over her lower lip and teasing at his concentration. Was she going to evade giving him an answer? Or should he just kiss her and be done with the whole conversation? He was veering towards the latter when she spoke.

'Not my clients, no, my ex-business partner… we…we were together.'

'You dated Charles Eddison?'

She exhaled sharply. 'We more than dated, we lived together for five years.'

Five years, Kristus!

He felt sick at the very idea.

And then she squinted up at him, her eyes suddenly curious. 'How did you know it was him? Do you know him?'

'Not personally,' he admitted, not liking the way her admission griped with his gut and keen to get back to more enjoyable conversation. But five years, *Jesus.* 'I know enough of him, considering we looked at using his services initially.'

'You looked at using him?' She frowned. 'Julia didn't mention it.'

'Why would she? She met him and took an instant dislike.' Had he met the guy too, he was sure he would have felt the same, even more so now. 'Someone on his team recommended you.'

'They did?' Her frown grew. 'I had no idea.'

'Well, now you do, can we move on?'

She didn't acknowledge him; instead her eyes became distant, their sadness unmistakable. As was her vulnerability. No doubt Charles had done this to her. Left her like this.

'When our relationship ended so did our business partnership, hence why I'm working from the ground up all over again.' She dragged in a breath and straightened, her focus coming back as her confidence fell into place. 'And hence why *this* just isn't happening.'

He faltered, his brain telling him to agree, to move past the pull that was driving him to distraction.

She's so not your type. She's a bag of emotion. She's not safe in your hands.

Instead he found himself saying, 'You're over-thinking it. As much as Julia loves me, she's already bought into your skills as an estate agent, as have I, for that matter. Nothing between us will sway her to go elsewhere.'

You idiot, why pursue her? She doesn't fit with your no-strings rule. This woman goes in for attachment. Worse still, she's been burned by it already and still suffering.

But then, if that's the case, maybe she's ready for the no-strings alternative.

Maybe she's ready to become your type.

'You have my word,' he pressed gently.

You bastard.

She lifted her eyes at his soft declaration and imme-diately regretted it.

He hovered just above her, his wolf-like gaze burning into her own, the rush of warmth it inspired sending her toes curling inside her Louboutins. His confidence in her ability to fulfil her job beating back the negative words Charles had thrown at her

on her way out of the door all those months ago—
'You'll never make it on your own.'

Ha, well, they chose me, not you...at the recom-
mendation of someone on your team, no less.

It felt good to know she still held favour there
after walking out.

As for Daniel's word, she held his eye; was he for
real? 'Your word?'

He made an affirmative noise deep in his throat,
almost enticing a reciprocal one from her as it
strummed at the heat swelling down low.

'I'm willing to bet you're just as caught up in this
attraction as me,' he said huskily. 'And if that's the
case, you'll realise this is about a bit of fun; no harm,
no foul, no jeopardised business arrangement.'

'You reckon?' She sounded breathless, out of control.

No, no, don't let this happen.

He nodded and raised his hand, her breath catching as she anticipated his touch, wanting and dread-
ing it all the same, knowing that when it came she
would lose herself in it, in him.

'I'm not very good at...*fun.*' She threw his de-
scription back at him, desperately clinging to what
she knew to be true even as the heat of his hand
brushed beneath her jaw, his touch so light it was
barely there. And she wanted it there. Wanted every
one of those fingers pressed into her skin as he
kissed her.

'Fun?' he questioned softly, his hand following the contours of her neck as her head lolled back into his palm of its own mutinous accord.

'Not this sort of fun.' She trembled; fear, excitement, all manner of urges melting away the need to break free.

'You're going to have to clarify, because I'm talking about sex, nothing more, nothing less.'

Sex. Even hearing him say it had her tummy contracting over the ferocity of her need as her confession burst from her lips. 'And so am I.'

His brow became a fierce V, his eyes sparking with something akin to surprise, disbelief, something more…but then it hooded over as he asked, 'You're afraid of keeping it casual?'

She shook her head. *If only that were her problem.*

'I'm not very good at *it*.' She stressed the *it*, praying it would be clear enough, even as her contracted tummy now squirmed in shame.

Why admit that? Why admit something buried so deep inside?

Because it wasn't so deep.

Hadn't Charles brought it all to the surface when he'd called her that morning?

Hadn't the revelation of Julia's relationship troubles kicked up her own storm?

His expression softened, a strange sense of relief shining through. 'I don't believe that.'

'It's the truth,' she breathed, her chin lifting defiantly.

She needed to convince him, to get him to back away. She hadn't been able to let anyone near her since Charles. Her revamped image was all part of her great big *back-the-hell-off-I'm-not-interested* persona. She didn't want anyone to get close enough to risk Charles's words being reaffirmed by anybody else—*'You're cold...so frigid in the sack...it's such hard work.'*

Daniel wasn't getting the message though, his intent searing her as his head lowered, his mouth brushing against hers to say, 'Why don't you let me be the judge of that?'

'I'm not...' Her words trailed away, his lips coaxing her to silence, to oblige, to move beneath the hypnotic pressure of his. She lowered her lashes, a small noise quivering at the back of her throat.

Did that really come from me?

She tightened her grip over the counter edge, trying desperately to regain control. 'We shouldn't do this.'

He closed what little gap remained, his hardness pressing up against her belly and replacing all sane thought with sensation, the pang between her legs instant and desperate. She clenched her thighs tight, nursing it, wanting it to grow and not wanting it to all the same.

His tongue flicked out to tease her mouth apart,

his free hand joining the other to hook around her neck and hold her in place. 'Then tell me to stop.'

He took her lower lip in his teeth and tugged, the effect ripping a moan from her and sending streaks of heat straight to her neglected clit—*Christ. S*he wanted him. Badly.

'I didn't think so,' he murmured against her, his tongue seeking entry as her own dared to taste him. He was so musky and male, gentle yet demanding. He teased around her mouth, testing every curve, stoking the fire inside.

And then he growled, the sound fierce as his tempo changed, his desperation breaking through his control and she ignited with it. Like a switch being flicked on, she came alive to match him, move for move, her own mouth hungry for more. Her hands seeking out the crazy flop of blond, and loving that he let her. That he didn't care. Not like Charles. Charles would have told her to watch it, be careful...

He broke his mouth away, pinning his forehead against her own, his ragged breath sweeping down her front, down the channel of her V-cut blouse. 'I think you're very good at this.'

'Is that so?' Wow, was that really her? So heated, so flirtatious?

She looked to him from beneath her lashes, every nerve-ending alert as it craved the hardness ever-swelling against her.

Yes, this was her. And this man wasn't Charles, he was as lost to the moment as she... *Or was he?*

Doubt sparked. What was she doing? She had no interest in opening herself up again. Especially with a man she didn't know. Couldn't trust.

His mouth closed over hers once more, ravenous and urgent, his hand dropping to lift her against him. She moulded into him, her neck arching under the pressure of his continued kiss, her muddied thoughts warring with the passion racing through her veins. It felt so good to feel this rush again.

Again? Who are you kidding? No one has made you feel this crazy, this hungry, this desired.

And she could trust him enough to give in to this—*couldn't she?*

He had heart enough; he wore it on his sleeve for Julia, his sister—*her client. Shit!*

She stilled beneath him, her eyes flying open.

You're meant to be working, not getting cosy with your client's brother!

She pushed him away, ignoring his widened gaze and the hard expanse of muscle that flexed beneath her touch. What the hell was he playing at, pretending to have something to discuss, only to seduce her? 'That was a dirty trick.'

'What was?'

She forced her breathing to steady, shifting her eyes away from the seductive fire in his. 'Coming in here, under the pretence of a conversation, only to make a move.'

She stepped around him and headed to the sink, amazed that she could make her jelly-like body do her bidding. She took up a plastic jug from the drainer and turned on the tap, throwing her focus into what she was supposed to be doing.

'I wasn't pretending anything,' he said, his voice still so near in the closed-in space. 'I wanted to speak to you without my sister listening in.'

'Really?' She raised a sardonic brow at him over her shoulder and regretted even looking. He was ruffled, the evidence of her touch in the state of his hair, his puffed-up lips, the heat to his cheeks. He was too hot before, now he just taunted her with what she knew to be real. What she knew she could have if she chose it.

He grinned. 'Yes, *really.* It was your provocation that made me forget it.'

'My provocation?' Water overflowed the jug in her hand but she couldn't care.

'Yes, *you.*' He reached out and cupped her chin, scanning her face with that same curious look he'd been sporting half the morning. 'There's just something about you, and I can't seem to control my reaction to it.'

She couldn't speak. Wasn't it how she felt too? Hadn't he broken through the layers she'd effectively held in place for months, all in the space of a look, a touch…?

But hell, it was hardly surprising when she'd been celibate for so long.

'Need a hand with that?' he said, reaching around her to twist the tap off and his proximity made her heart skitter anew.

'Thank you,' she said, backing away enough to escape the kitchen, jug in hand, the spark of an idea creeping up on her that she just knew she should quash before it took hold. It wasn't wise, it wasn't rational…but still, it was there…

Would one night do it?

One night—*with him*?

She walked around the flat, watering the plants that adorned it, all the while feeling his eyes on her, penetrating her, lighting her up from top to toe. He'd resumed the position he'd been in earlier, his brooding silhouette resting up against the bathroom door. And just as he had then, he clouded her judgement, her mind struggling to function under the effect of his gaze.

Would one night release her from this? Clear her mind and rid her body of this insane need so that normal service could resume?

'I think you've given that one enough.'

'What?' She frowned and followed his line of sight to the spider plant she was tending to, seeing the water pooling at the pot rim, a trickle commencing down the side. She cursed, her cheeks warming as she righted the jug. Seemed she couldn't even cope with the simple task of watering plants in his presence—*unbelievable*.

'Can you pass me some kitchen towel?' she snapped and then cringed, realising she was projecting her frustration onto him and making herself add a guilt-ridden, 'Please?'

She wished she hadn't softened her request when she saw how his eyes danced, how amused he was at her fluster, knowing it was because he understood the cause.

'Sure.' He pushed away from the door and headed into the kitchen area.

She forced her eyes away. She couldn't carry on like this. For however long it took to find his sister a home, she needed to get this under control. Christ, she needed his sister to spread a good word. Not tell every Tom, Dick and Harry that she was an airhead... Or, worse, that she couldn't stop lusting after her brother long enough to concentrate.

'Here,' he said, coming up alongside her and offering out the paper towel.

'Thank you.'

She didn't quite meet his eye as she took it and bent forward to clean up the mess.

Now was the time, she realised; if she wanted to put the idea to him, she needed to do it now. 'One date.'

He stilled in the periphery of her vision. 'A date?'

'Yes,' she said, ignoring the bemusement in his tone.

Hell, you'd be bemused if someone had just burst out with those two words.

Straightening up and smoothing her wrist over her hair to right it while avoiding the damp kitchen towel clutched in her hand, she nodded. 'Let's go on one date together.'

'You *want* to do that?'

Yes... No... Yes.

The words whirled through her mind as their gazes locked and she lost herself in his warm, amber depths, a wedge forming in her throat.

Are you crazy? Do you really know what you're letting yourself in for?

She headed for the kitchen, praying he hadn't spied her hesitation. She prided herself on knowing her own mind, for heaven's sake—why was he making that so hard?

'Yes, I do,' she said, placing the jug back on the drainer, grateful that her voice gave away none of her internal wrangling and feeling her resolve swell.

You've put the idea out there, you can bloody well follow it through.

Turning to look at him, she leisurely travelled his entirety, taking in his sheer beauty, his continued silence and bemusement, and her tummy gave the smallest little flutter. Was he going to turn her down?

Hell, no.

'Unless, of course…' she said the words softly, teasingly, her legs moving of their own volition to close the distance between them '…you don't want to?'

He didn't budge, his body seemingly fixed in place as he watched her approach, a telltale pulse ticing in his jaw as he no doubt worked to gauge her intent.

He didn't have to wait long, not in this confined space.

Once she was within touching distance she reached out, her fingers hooking over his belt buckle with daring provocation. The move bold and quite unlike her. Yet it felt completely natural, instinctive with him, as did the words that slipped from her lips. 'Unless, of course, you don't fancy a bit of fun together?'

CHAPTER THREE

A DATE?

She wasn't simply asking for a date.

She was asking for a whole lot more.

So why wasn't he straight on it? Why was okay suddenly so hard to say?

He narrowed his gaze, searching her face, looking at those steely grey eyes, all smoky with suggestion, her head tilted to one side.

Had he imagined her earlier vulnerability? Had she been playing him with that unexpected confession? But to what end? It was hardly the greatest come-on—*Hey, I'm shit in bed*—but then, perhaps that had been her game, to put him off. Only it had failed. Their chemistry was off the charts and she screamed of a woman in need of some fun. He suspected she'd not indulged since Charles had done away with her.

She toyed with his buckle, her eyes locked with his. 'One date.'

And then he watched her lashes lower, her eyes travelling down his chest as her free hand came up to rest over his thundering heart, the heat of her palm permeating through his sweatshirt and rendering him speechless, utterly captivated. What would she do next?

'One...' she lifted her gaze, her eyes almost black as the pupils drowned out the grey, her enunciation bold as she leaned closer '...night.'

A night—for fuck's sake, grow a pair: you want her, she's offering.

But he didn't do emotion.

Not in his bed.

Not now.

Not ever.

And she blazed with emotion.

And didn't that make her appeal all the more? Make her different. Make her special. Make her interesting.

She lifted onto tiptoes, her lips coming up to caress against his own as she said, 'Let me know when you've made up your mind.'

And then she turned and headed for the door so quickly he was left in a shroud of her vanilla scent, and so confidently he was left seriously doubting the emotion he'd read in her earlier.

This woman—*vulnerable*?

He looked to the teasing sway of her hips snug beneath the trouser suit, the sureness of that walk on those steep stilettos, the entire motion purposefully provocative on her part, and he realised he had to have been an idiot. There was no way.

Ja, he'd been played, all right, and he didn't care what her intent had been, only what effect her luscious body was having on him right that second.

'You're on,' he said, striding after her, his hand reaching on impulse to settle in the small of her back and making his palm tingle with the possessive contact. His eyes narrowed on the touch—*how strange*.

'It'll be the perfect opportunity for us to discuss what I need to without Julia in earshot,' he said, drawing back his senses, telling himself the reason he'd given her made the perfect excuse to keep such a get-together platonic. If that was what he needed to do, what he had to do, to protect himself, to protect her.

'So, it wasn't just a ruse, you do have something you want to discuss?' she asked, her surprise evident and making him grin.

'I never lie,' he assured her, 'no matter how much I want something…or someone.'

'Glad to hear it.' She returned his smile as she pulled open the front door and gestured for him to precede her out. 'Are you free this evening?'

'This evening?' He let his hand fall away from her back, ignoring how it itched to return as he stepped into the hallway and turned to watch her follow suit. 'So soon?'

'Why—you busy?'

'No.'

'Complaining?' she pushed, her smile becoming one of teasing as she closed the door and turned the key in the lock.

'Hell, no.' He wasn't. Not really. But her earlier behaviour had left its mark, still bothering him in the aftermath of their kiss, devoid of her lips so close to his. But did he really want that worry to get in the way of the night they could potentially share?

Fuck, no, he wasn't an idiot. And he wasn't sentimental.

One night, and then he could go back to his usual careful selection.

'Good.' She flipped open her portfolio and extracted a card, passing it to him, her eyes confident, almost hard as she said, 'My office, eight p.m.'

Definitely played. She's as sure as you are turned on—so why is that wavering doubt still clinging on?

'I'm easy on what we do from there.'

He raised his brow, unable to help himself, his thoughts going down a far more pleasing route. 'Easy?'

She sent him a smile that made him want to pin her to the wall, his unease obliterated by the rising desire, and then she turned and headed for the stairwell, leaving him to follow close behind, his mind alight with the varying degrees to which she could be deemed easy...

* * *

By the time eight p.m. rolled around, Zara was fizzing over with nerves and pent-up need.

Spending the afternoon fulfilling the requirements of her job, knowing full well what the evening held, had been a real challenge. And she'd been flat out, right up until that second, the pressures of her start-up venture not waning. But now it was time for fun.

She looked to the clock, reaffirming what she already knew, having glanced at it several times over. It had just gone eight and there was no sign of him as yet.

Had he changed his mind?

Was she about to get a call loaded with excuses? A text even?

Shit.

Disappointment sank deep in her belly, the familiar taste of rejection sitting bitter in her throat.

'What did you expect?' she muttered under her breath just as movement in the outer office caught her eye.

Daniel!

'How did you…?' She stepped out of her office, trying to calm her pulse now tripping out and dancing over the disappointment.

'Security let me up.'

'They're paid to vet visitors.'

'You can't blame them,' he drawled. 'Not when they're faced with someone as charming as me.'

'Charming?' she scoffed, her hand hooking over EJ's chair back, the move casual but in reality serving to hold her up, her knees already turning weak over the sight of him.

He'd changed, she hadn't—*crap*. She drank him in, even as her own feeling of inadequacy swelled. He wore a white shirt open at the collar, accentuating the golden hue to his skin, a dark suit that fitted his frame oh-so-beautifully and all she wanted was to strip it all away. A year of sexual abstinence and it was coming back to hound her unforgivably.

He paused two strides away, his eyes raking over her, their effect as tangible as his fingers, and she felt her nipples prickle against her blouse, her jacket still slung over her office chair offering no concealing protection as he rested there. Her braless state clearly evident. But she had no need of bras, not when she was so small, so 'boy-like', according to darling Charles.

'Happy to see me?'

The heat to his voice, to his gaze, made it clear he wasn't bothered by her teeny assets and had her hunger swelling thick and fast in return, any inadequacy on her part promptly and joyously forgotten.

How could he do that so easily? Make her forget the insecurities that plagued her?

She tried to respond but her throat had closed

tight, leaving only the ability to nod, and as she did she wet her lips. His eyes rose in tune with the move, something incoherent escaping under his breath, and then he strode forward, reaching out to crush her to him as his mouth claimed hers, ravenous and brutal, and everything she wanted.

'The feeling's mutual,' he rasped against her lips before devouring her whole, his tongue fencing with her own, his hands shifting to fork through her hair, his body walking her back until she hit the wall.

He tore his mouth away, his fingers smoothing around one side of her neck as his mouth attacked the other, a crazy mix of swirling pressure, nips and sucks that had her going out of her mind. Her head pressing into the hardness of the wall as she arched for him, her breasts desperate and aching as they thrust upwards.

'This afternoon was torture,' he grumbled against her skin, his hot breath tormenting the dampness he'd created. 'Had I known you'd been braless it would've been even more so.'

His fingers dropped with his words to stroke over one pleading peak and the electricity that ripped through her made her cry out, her body arching further.

'*Fuck, yes.*'

He repeated the move and she positively writhed. She couldn't remember a touch so potent, so thrilling. Her breasts ached with maddening intent, desperate to be bare, desperate to have him pinch, flick, suckle, anything and everything. Charles hadn't done this to her, driven her to the edge of reason. They were in the office, for fuck's sake, not a private room, not a bedroom.

He leant back, his gaze burning down into her. '*Kristus*, baby, I could take you right here, right now, to hell with dinner.'

She couldn't respond, she just wanted him back, crushing away every thought, every sense with the all-consuming lust curling its way through her, knowing the crescendo would be worth every debauched second.

She drove her hands through his hair, pulling him back to her hungry mouth, telling him with her move that the only dinner she craved was him. But then the sound of gossipy chatter in the outer corridor invaded her senses, a semblance of clarity with it— *the cleaners*.

She swallowed a curse and edged along the wall, taking him with her.

'My office,' she managed to get out, shoving the door further ajar and stumbling through it. She hit the lights off as he spun her back against the wall, kicking the door closed.

'The lock,' she blurted, reaching for it and twisting it in place. Her hands returning to him, twice as hungry, twice as confident. She slipped them beneath his jacket, uncaring of its obvious expense as she shoved it from his shoulders. He let it fall to the floor as she pulled at his shirt, tugging it out of his trousers while his hands reached for her blouse, doing the same.

As the cool air swept over her exposed torso, she froze, a second's hesitation as Charles came back to haunt her anew, the evening light illuminating her boyish body in all its glory. It was one thing to find her clothed and sexy, but would he feel the same when he saw...

Her blouse swept over her head and she dared to look up at him. All hesitation evaporated as lustful heat bore down into her, etched in every taut line of his face, the thin amber rim of his dilated gaze burning fierce.

'I want to worship every last bit of you.' His palms now gentle as they cupped each small mound, her sensitised peaks nesting at their heart, his thumbs caressingly soft. 'You are beautiful.'

Sounds from the outer office had his gaze flicking to the doorway, beyond which the cleaners were going about their job.

'You think you can keep quiet while I drive you crazy?'

The undulating ache in her lower belly swelled with glee, her head nodding, her eyelids fluttering as she struggled to breathe.

'Good girl.'

She clenched her tummy tight as he dipped his

head to nuzzle into her neck, picking up on her pulse point and toying with it. 'I'm going to make you wish you could cry out.'

She pressed her palms into the wall either side of her, not knowing where to put them, wanting to rake them all over his body, through his hair, but feeling immobilised, caught in a web of his creation.

He rolled each nub with his thumb, making her pant as they swelled obediently. 'You're going to come so hard.'

She whimpered. She knew it. She could feel its promise already building.

The rolling caress became a tweak and she bucked, a cry she couldn't suppress erupting as she realised she could come from this attention alone. She was that desperate, that deprived, that wanton…

'You'll need to do better than that.'

Better?

She tried to focus through the haze and he looked to the door pointedly—*Christ*, there was no way she could do this quietly.

'You need me to help,' he said softly.

How? She frowned.

He raised one hand, his fingers brushing over her lips, her plump and swollen flesh moving helplessly beneath his touch and relishing every teasing bit of it.

'Use me,' he said. 'I'll make you forget Charles ever existed.'

Forget fucking Charles, God, yes!

An exciting tremor rippled through her as she nodded against the wall and manoeuvred her head to nip into his palm, getting him where she wanted him. And then his head dropped, his mouth sucking in one desperate peak before releasing it from his teeth, and she cried into his hand, her nails scraping into the wall as she clawed at it.

'So responsive,' he muttered against her, his teeth grazing her swollen flesh as he spoke. 'So addictive.'

His free hand joined in the attentions, his touch wild with his own mounting need.

'More,' she pleaded softly.

He gave a muffled growl in response, dropping to his knees, his tongue gliding over her navel as he dropped both hands to her trouser fastening. He popped it undone, the zipper following suit, the fabric dropping to the floor, cold air hot on its tail, and then came his hands brushing up her bare legs, their palms hot, fingers caressing. He locked his teeth around the small bow at the centre of her thong's waistband, plucking at it, the elastic stinging her skin as her eyes dropped to his.

'*Fuck...*' she whimpered.

He was too hot, too seductive; her head was dizzy on it, intoxicated even.

He slid his fingers beneath the waistband and she bit her lip in anticipation, watching as he pulled it down, pushing it to join her trousers at her ankles. She was about to step out of them all when his head dropped, his tongue sweeping inside her seam and making her cry out. She clamped her jaw shut, her knees buckling, and he gave a deep chuckle.

'Seems you can't keep quiet.'

She looked down at him, his head cocked back, his chin resting teasingly above her strip of hair and her need took over, driving out the order, 'Rather than criticise me, put your mouth to better use.'

His eyes flashed and she rammed her fingers through his hair drawing him against her, absorbing his appreciative growl in the cluster of chaos between her legs. She was losing it in every way possible, her knees turning to jelly as she opened herself up to him, and rode his tongue, his teeth, every bit of friction he could give her.

She grabbed at his shirt, felt his muscles rippling wildly as he worked her. She reached for his hand, tugging it back to where she needed it, across her mouth. He pressed her head back into the wall with it, his hold tight, her breaths rasping over his fingers as she struggled to take in enough air to fuel the crazy spiralling tension.

She clawed at the wall again, her legs buckling further, and he used his shoulders to hold her steady and open, hungrily devouring her, sucking up her wetness, flicking wildly over her clit and layering it up with the bite of his teeth.

The tension grew with punishing force and just as the handle to her office door shifted, she exploded, her entire body convulsing with an orgasm like no other. She bucked over him, her head falling forward, her muscles rippling wildly, and he held her to him, his head moving to press against her belly as he kept her upright through the waves.

In her post-orgasm daze, she could hear the voices on the other side… 'If it's locked leave it'… 'Thought I heard something though'… 'Not for us to worry about.'

The footsteps retreated, and she felt shyness creeping in.

What the hell have you just let happen? In your office, of all places?

And then he leant back on his haunches and met her eye, pinning her with the unrestrained heat of his need, and she knew exactly what she'd let happen and why because, even in her sated state, her body was already on the up, her pulse kick-starting over its impulsive desire to please him. To strip him as bare as she and enjoy every last bit.

For a split second he sensed that same vulnerability, that same inkling that she wasn't the feisty, controlled diva her exterior made her out to be. And then it was gone, her fingers pushing him back so that he had to splay his palms out, pressing them into the floor to stop himself back-planting completely.

'My turn,' she said, slipping one heeled foot out of her pooled clothing and then the other.

Leaving her shoes on, she stalked towards him. All statuesque, confident and sexy as fuck. His blood rang in his ears, surging to the head of his dick.

'Easy, tiger,' he warned, not that it was aimed at her, but to his raging erection that was fit to explode any second.

'Lose the shirt.' She jutted her chin towards him, her silver-grey eyes as wild as her hair, her lips lifting in a one-sided smile.

He'd never witnessed anything so sexy. Never been more turned on. He did as she asked, undoing each button while his eyes raked over her, devouring every last inch. The way her breasts were still pert, her breathing still hitched, the apex of her thighs still slick, her entire body begging him for more.

Slipping the shirt from his arms, he heard the faint catch in her breath, saw her drag her lower lip inside and keep it there, her eyes lost somewhere between his pecks and his groin.

She nudged his thigh with one heeled foot. 'The rest.'

His hands moved to his trouser fastenings of their own accord. He was torn between the pull of her mouth and the pull of her pussy—both wet, both slick, and everything his straining cock needed.

Fuck, you can't lose it like some out-of-control teen!

He'd never had to worry about performing before. Why the hell was he having to now? He needed to get himself under control. He needed the situation under *his* control.

Retracting his legs from beneath her, he stood and shoved off the remainder of his clothing.

'I didn't say stand.'

It was a complaint that carried no force, her eyes now fixed below the waist, her mouth parted and hungry.

'Needs must, angel.' He bent for his jacket and retrieved his wallet, flipping it open. 'I'll make it up to you.'

He extracted a condom and tossed the rest aside, trying to stop his eyes feasting on her but doing so all the same. She was exquisite and he was imprinting every curve into his mind for later perusal. 'Turn around,' he said automatically. He wanted the whole of her.

She met his gaze, eyes wavering, and then she did as he asked, turning away slowly. He tore the packet open and sheathed himself, his eyes drinking her in. The crazy state of her cropped hair. The delicate frame to her shoulders as they undulated softly with her breathing. Her milk-like skin so pale and alluring. Right down to her narrow waist, softly flaring hips and that delicious bare ass, so pert and inviting. His cock leapt and he took a ragged breath, trying to rein it back.

Get in control.

He closed the gap between them and felt her jump a little as his cock nudged against her back.

'You are exquisite,' he whispered alongside her ear, his hands stroking at her arms by her sides. She shivered, her skin prickling beneath his touch.

'I want to fuck you over your desk,' he murmured, his head dropping to the curve of her neck as he stroked down her belly, feeling it draw tight beneath his caress, her anticipation palpable as his destination became clear.

'I want to fuck you there,' he continued, his fingers finding her nest of curls and dipping inside, teasing the silky wetness apart, 'so that every day you're in here, you can remember it.'

He found her beaded clit and she bucked wildly on a moan, her head arching into his shoulder, and he clamped his jaw shut as his cock pulsed wildly into her back. *Kristus*, he'd never known someone so responsive, so genuinely lost.

Her hands flung back to grip at his thighs, her pelvis tilting into his touch.

He stroked her, lapping up every little whimper, every escape of air. He gazed down her front, between her small, tantalising tits to where he worked her, and let his free hand trail along her collarbone, his touch barely there as it teased a path to one taut peak. He brushed across it and her head writhed against him, her whimpers increasing. He did the same to the other and her nails bit into his skin.

She was close, her rocking becoming jagged, full of tension. Grabbing her by the hips, he swung her before the desk. Disregarding the orderly array of paperwork, writing implements and whatever else as he palmed her back. He stroked from the base of her spine up, encouraging her to bend forward with his exploration. By the time his fingers caught in her hair, she'd stretched herself over the desk, her body the perfect addition to the orderly state, her milky skin contrasting with the glass top, her breath creating steam like patterns across it.

Beads of perspiration broke across his back; his jaw ached with the effort to stave off the heat surging through him.

Steady, steady...

He bent his knees and cupped her hips, teasing her ass higher into the air. Taking hold of his cock, he brushed it down the valley of her smooth, round mounds.

God, how you'd like to claim her there too.

'Please, Daniel, now.'

Her ass nudged upwards with her words, his swollen head slipping just inside her entrance, too inviting to take pause, and he thrust inside her, hard and deep. Through the whirring in his ears he heard her cry out and her body clenched around him, tight and hot. He stilled, wanting her to adjust, to be comfortable, but she wasn't having it. She wriggled over him, her hands reaching beyond her head to grip at the desk edge.

'Steady,' he ground out—to himself, to her, to them both.

He wanted to savour it, to enjoy every mounting second. But she felt so good, so wet, so inviting. Her sounds wanton and as desperate as he.

He slid one hand between her legs, seeking her out once more, loving how it made her still, her building tension palpable in every taut muscle. He rocked into her, his thighs slapping against her own, his own pleasure-filled tension working its way through every limb and taking over, ramping up his tempo.

He tightened his grip in her hair, pulling her head back, making her arch to him. He wanted his hands everywhere: on her clit, her pretty little tits, everywhere.

He caught movement ahead, saw their faint outline reflected in the window before him—*so fucking carnal*. He would take that image everywhere with him. She panted her impending climax; he watched it take hold of her body in the glass before him and it tipped him over the edge. He exploded into her, the force winding him, the cries of her orgasm breaking their way into his consciousness and compounding his own.

He dragged her up against his chest, holding her tight, the waves racking their bodies as they rode them together. He held her like that until the very last aftershock rippled through them and he could trust his voice to work. 'You are so fucking hot, you know that?'

She gave a sound that was more of a scoff than a giggle.

She had no idea. None at all. How was that possible?

She turned her head into his chest, nudging at his chin with a soft sigh. 'You're not so bad yourself.'

'Not so bad?' He squeezed his arms around her in mock offence and she rewarded him with a melodic giggle, one that rippled through his very core. 'We're not heading for more Daniel-bashing, are we?'

She gave a proper laugh. 'I wouldn't dare without your sister to hand.'

'Well, thank fuck she isn't.' He bowed his head, resting his chin upon her shoulder and wanting nothing more than to go round two, three, maybe even four as soon as he was able. 'What say we stay here and order takeout?'

'Hmm.' She stretched out against him, finding her feet, and he felt his cock protest as it slipped free. 'Sounds good.'

He hadn't realised he'd been holding his breath until it escaped with her reply, and now he grinned, pressing a kiss to her shoulder before straightening to release her. 'I take it I have to brave the outer realm to get cleaned up.'

She turned her head to give him a sheepish look. 'Afraid so.'

'Fair enough, you sort the takeaway and I'll try not to expose myself to the cleaners.'

'You're on.' She chuckled. 'Chinese, Indian, Thai…'

He deliberately chose her line from earlier that day. 'I'm easy.'

'I know.' Her eyes sparked into his and his cock bucked with it. Round two couldn't come soon enough.

'So long as I have you for dessert.'

She turned into him, her fingers tracing a path over his chest and setting off goosebumps in their wake. 'Oh, I think that can be arranged.'

A tremor rippled through his body, it was already gearing up, and then came a flash of sanity.

Don't forget your other purpose.

He almost wanted to forget. Didn't want any part of reality eating into their time together, but he still had a duty to perform and the sooner he did…

He looked down into her heavy-lidded gaze, its pull drawing him in, and forced himself to stay in check. 'I also need to have that talk with you about Julia too.'

She tensed, her fingers dropping away along with her eyes, desire giving way to professionalism, and totally at odds with her naked and entirely distracting form.

'Of course,' she said softly, her body easing back, and he wrapped his arms around her, pulling her up against him again. He wasn't about to lose her over it.

'It won't take long,' he assured her, his head bowing to caress her lips with his own as he added, 'then we can get back to more pleasurable pursuits.'

Her contented sigh filled his ears and warmed his blood, his lips curving up even as he kissed her— *much better.*

Want to know what unravels in
Mr. Temptation?
Rachael Stewart's racy romance
is available wherever
DARE books and ebooks are sold

Mr. Temptation
Copyright © 2019 by Rachael Stewart

LET'S TALK
Romance

For exclusive extracts, competitions
and special offers, find us online:

 facebook.com/millsandboon

@MillsandBoon

@MillsandBoonUK

Get in touch on 01413 063232

For all the latest titles coming soon, visit
millsandboon.co.uk/nextmonth